NIGHT ON FIRE

Also by Diana Deverell

12 Drummers Drumming

NIGHT ON FIRE

DIANA DEVERELL

AVON BOOKS  NEW YORK

AVON BOOKS, INC.
1350 Avenue of the Americas
New York, New York 10019

Copyright © 1999 by Diana Deverell
Interior design by Kellan Peck
ISBN: 0-380-97611-0

Library of Congress Cataloging in Publication Data:

Deverell, Diana.
    Night on fire / Diana Deverell.—1st ed.
        p.   cm.
    I. Title.
PS3554.E92734N54   1999   99–14874
813'.54—dc21   CIP

First Avon Books Printing: July 1999

AVON TRADEMARK REG. U.S. PAT. OFF. AND IN OTHER COUNTRIES, MARCA REGISTRADA, HECHO EN U.S.A.

Printed in the U.S.A.

FIRST EDITION

QPM   10   9   8   7   6   5   4   3   2   1

www.avonbooks.com

FOR SUZANNE STICKELS DEVERELL

ACKNOWLEDGMENTS

A special thanks to Esther and Peder Aksel Pedersen who faithfully forwarded all newspaper accounts of *rockerkrig* and graciously refreshed my memories of Danish celebratory feasting. Thanks also to Finn Pedersen who hosted me on Helsingborggade. My greatest debt is, as always, to Mogens Pedersen who married me into his wonderful family. I love you all.

I am indebted to the Warsaw Attaché Reunion whose members will recognize their contributions throughout. Writers whose knowledge far exceeds my own have unknowingly contributed to this novel through their work. Highly recommended are Yves Lavigne's accounts of the Hells Angels, Chip Barber's guide to Dartmouth and Kingswear, and Lauren Kessler's *Full Court Press: A Season in the Life of a Winning Basketball Team and the Women Who Made It Happen*. Any factual errors in this book are mine alone.

I appreciate the information, inspiration, and support I got from the following individuals and organizations: The Alley Kats Bowling League, Ambassadors John R. Davis Jr., Ralph Frank, and Deane R. Hinton, the Reverend John Pierce, Paul K. Vestal Jr., and Richard W. Wingard, CPA.

The New Writers of the Purple Page coached me through this one. Thanks to Benjamin Chambers, Nancy Carol Moody, Amedee Smith, and Lynn Daniels Anderson for their fine writing and priceless friendship. And thanks also to Jennifer Sawyer Fisher, my skillful editor at Avon Books. The last word belongs to Nancy Yost, the best literary agent in the world and maybe the universe.

1

I WAS RACING TOWARD DISASTER.

The night before, a chartered MD-11 Trijet had blown up after takeoff from Bangor International, killing all four hundred and eight people on board. I was the State Department's representative on a federal terrorism task force and I had to be on the 6:00 P.M. Global Airlines flight from Copenhagen to New York. I dodged around less hasty travelers, a blond woman in no-name running shoes loping past Kastrup Airport's duty-free shops.

Brilliant strips of neon in primary colors slid by me. I saw masses of Nordic furs, Swedish vodka, Georg Jensen pipes. Passed travelers lugging heavy bags from the liquor store. Spotted a plainclothes cop dressed too warmly for a Danish June, scrutinizing the passersby.

Up ahead the readerboard listed the status of departing flights. Beyond, harshly lit corridors branched off toward the gates.

A six-foot monument blocked my path. The cop, immovable as stone. I stopped abruptly, breathing hard. I moved to one side. So did he.

He was slightly stooped, topcoat hanging open in front, showing the regulation white shirt and tie, concealing the reason for his underarm bulge.

I flashed my passport, black with the gold embossed eagle beneath the logo. DIPLOMATIC, UNITED STATES OF AMERICA. "U.S. State Department," I said. "Urgent and official business."

"My business is also official." The cop's eyes were charcoal, pouched in sooty-colored flesh that gave his face a melancholy cast. "Also urgent," he added somberly. "You are Kathryn Collins?"

The worried gaze, the regretful tone. A messenger of death. My alarm was instant.

"Stefan Krajewski?" I asked. "Has something happened to Stefan?"

His forehead wrinkled. "I don't know that name," he began slowly, "but—"

I interrupted. "My father?"

His features smoothed out. "I have no news of your family."

Not my lover. Not my father. I shifted my weight from right foot to left, ready to sidestep him again. "I don't have time—"

He pushed his card toward me. "This is official business of the Danish police."

Reluctantly, I took the card and read. POLITIASSISTENT NIELS-JØRGEN JESPERSEN. And under that in French, LIAISON, CORPS DIPLOMATIQUE. The policeman assigned to interview members of the diplomatic corps when they ran afoul of Danish law.

A mistake then, stopping me. The digital clock on the departures board read five-fifty. "I can't miss this flight. You'll have to talk to someone at the embassy."

"I have spoken with your security officer."

"Bella Hinton? Didn't she tell you? I don't have time for this."

"I must ask you to come with me," he said unhappily.

"You know an American airliner exploded last night in Maine?"

His nod was mournful. "And you will be taking part in that investigation."

Not a question. So Bella had told him why I was leaving Denmark. I said, "I have to be in Bangor tomorrow morning."

"That will not be possible." A pair of uniformed policemen appeared beneath the fluorescent lights behind him, coming our way. I felt the short hairs rise on the back of my neck. He'd brought backup. Was he anticipating violent resistance?

"You think I'm a criminal?" Disbelief made my voice rise. "You aren't going to arrest a diplomat—"

"I would not do that." Jespersen's hand was on my elbow, his grip firm. He motioned to his two cohorts, cookie-cutter Vikings with collar-length blond hair swept back from their pale faces, boxy jackets accenting the breadth of their shoulders. They stepped behind me. Other travelers cut to the right and left of our compact quartet. I caught a few curious glances, but nobody tried to intervene. Jespersen added, "Bella assured us you'd be eager to cooperate."

He was letting me know he'd checked my status. I wasn't an accredited member of the U.S. mission, my special assignment to Denmark short-term only. Not protected by diplomatic immunity. He could arrest me if he felt like it.

The digital readout on the departures board jumped ahead another minute from five-fifty-four to five-fifty-five. I'd never make my flight. Except they'd have to hold up the plane while they extracted the suitcase of a passenger who failed to board. I had one, maybe two minutes to talk my way out of this.

I said, "I've been ordered home by the president." Technically, it was the attorney general who'd called in the special interagency task force on terrorism, but Jespersen wouldn't know that.

The task force had six members and our qualifications didn't overlap. To achieve good results, we had to work together from the beginning of the investigation. Each of us had accepted the one fundamental rule of membership: When we were called, we'd drop everything else and be on-site from Day One. I hiked the strap of my carry-on bag higher on my shoulder and tried to free my elbow.

Jespersen's grip tightened. "I'm sure your president will forgive a few hours' delay," he said. "And don't worry about your luggage. The airline company will send your suitcase to the American embassy."

I searched my mind frantically for a compelling argument that would break Jespersen's hold. I couldn't think of one. "Very considerate," I said in a voice flat with resignation. I let him start me moving toward the concourse, the other two cops sauntering behind us. Twenty feet along one hallway he took us through a door marked PRIVATE, down a set of metal stairs and outside to the area between the arrivals lounge and the police substation.

A breeze off the Øresund added the briny smell of the sea to the airport's overlay of exhaust fumes. Jespersen propelled me toward an iron-gray BMW. Its color matched the skin around his eyes. He pulled open the front passenger door. "We'll take my car."

"Take your car where?" I slid onto the leather.

He pushed my door shut. The two uniforms had disappeared into the airport cop shop. Maybe they'd decided I was harmless. Or more likely other cops were at our destination.

"What is it you need me for?" I asked as soon as Jespersen got behind the wheel.

He maneuvered us out of the parking space and headed for the highway leading into Copenhagen. He kept his eyes on the traffic and said, "*Kriminalinspektør* Blixenstjerne would like to ask you some questions."

A police inspector had questions for me? "About what?"

"A case he's working on."

The case had to be a homicide. The aura of death hung over Jespersen's every movement. Anxiety knotted my stomach. Who had died?

Before I could ask, Jespersen said, "You arrived in Copenhagen June first. And sixteen days later you're leaving?"

He'd blocked my question by asking his own. An interrogation was underway. I shifted in my seat to watch him. "I was supposed to stay three months. But that got changed this afternoon."

He glanced toward me. "You got a new assignment?"

"I told you," I said. "Ordered home because of the airliner explosion."

"And how were you given this order?"

"I got a phone call from the States around 3:00 A.M. I called a couple of people in the U.S. At five I went into the embassy to use the secure phone. Around eight their time—two o'clock here—I was reassigned."

"From 5:00 A.M. until 2:00 P.M. you were at the American embassy?"

He was making me recap my movements for the last twelve hours. I chose my words with care. "Until three. I went back to my flat to pack. Returned to the embassy around four-thirty. Picked up the paperwork and tickets, headed to Kastrup."

We were on Amager Boulevard. A leafy canopy blocked the sun. The shade blurred the rushing traffic, darkening the colorful compacts to the same dull sheen, turning us all to ashy-brown lemmings racing toward the harbor.

Jespersen said, "You moved quite swiftly?"

"As fast as possible," I said. My hand tightened on the armrest. I'd had to lobby hard to win appointment to the sole State Department opening on the task force. I was qualified—no one disputed that. But last December, I'd side-stepped an FBI interrogation and taken part in a quasi-official European investigation of an airliner bombing in Scotland. The secretary of state had approved my participation after-the-fact and I'd gotten a meritorious salary increase for my "display of initiative." But my detractors in the FBI still grumbled about that refusal to follow the bureau's lead. To win them over, I'd promised that I'd adhere scrupulously to the task force operating procedures.

The MD-11 had gone down in Maine on Tuesday night. Now it was Wednesday afternoon and I'd missed the last direct flight to the U.S. today from Copenhagen. I couldn't wait until tomorrow for the next one. A tardy arrival in Bangor would cost me. I'd have to return to Kastrup this evening and fly to another airport with a late-night transatlantic flight. There had to be someplace in Europe where I could make connections that would get me to the U.S. by morning.

I mentally urged Jespersen to hurry up.

He took the Long Bridge over the harbor and continued straight on Hans Christian Andersen Boulevard. Tourists clustered outside the entrance to Tivoli. I sat up straighter. Jespersen hadn't turned toward police headquarters. "Where is this Blixenstjerne?" I asked.

"I'm taking you to him." He didn't slow as we passed the American embassy's concrete-and-glass cube on Dag Hammarskjölds Allé. No point in inviting another nonresponse to my questions. And definitely time to exercise my all-American right to remain silent. Muscles tightened inside my chest. We were driving north onto Østerbrogade, the same route I'd followed back and forth to work for the past two weeks. Jespersen was taking me home.

Helsingborggade, the street where I lived, was blocked off with barricades and yellow tape. Late afternoon sunlight glimmered on a white ambulance, the trademark falcon outlined in stark red, talons extended as though dropping toward its prey. Clustered on the pavement around it were late-model cars in solid colors. I counted three Volvo station wagons in shades of green, so uniformly anonymous that they had to be official vehicles.

Jespersen bumped up onto the sidewalk and stopped twenty feet from the apartment complex where the embassy rented a furnished flat for me. Beside my building's front entrance lounged a uniformed cop, murmuring into the microphone on his shoulder.

"What happened?" I asked.

Jespersen said, "Get out of the car, please."

I had my seat belt undone and my door open. By the time I was standing on the sidewalk, another man had joined us. He was shorter than Jespersen, with clear blue eyes in a pink face, wearing an apple-green shirt with a plaid tie. He smoothed the tie before he said, "Ernst Blixenstjerne."

I waved a hand toward the ambulance. "What's going on?"

Blixenstjerne turned an inquiring face toward his colleague.

Jespersen shook his head. *"Ingenting."* Not a thing.

He'd told me nothing, as he'd clearly been instructed. Blixenstjerne wanted to surprise me. The tightness in my chest connected with the knot in my stomach, my whole torso tensing.

Blixenstjerne's voice was dispassionate. "When were you last inside your flat?"

"She left at four-thirty," Jespersen said helpfully.

"We'd like you to take a look at it." Blixenstjerne motioned for me to follow him into the building. In the lobby, I smelled ground pork cooked at a high temperature. Someone in the building had made *frikadeller* for dinner. I felt an instant of longing for a simple, predictable existence.

To the right of the entrance, the door to my ground floor flat stood open. I stepped into the foyer and took a breath, bracing myself for things I'd seen on television—smashed furniture, chalk outlines, blood stains. I looked through the archway into the living room and had to exhale fast to keep from throwing up.

2 A BODY SPRAWLED FACE-DOWN ACROSS THE KEYBOARD OF MY LAND-
lord's Steinway grand. The man's denim-covered backside balanced
on the edge of the ebony stool, his spine curved forward. Blood
welled from the back of his skull.

I turned to Blixenstjerne and tried to speak. I sucked in air, tried
again. "Who is he?"

"We have the same question," Blixenstjerne said.

"I don't know," I said. "He wasn't here . . ." I inhaled. "Nobody
was here when I left."

"Tell me if anything else has been altered," Blixenstjerne said.

I turned again. My gaze skittered along the wall and across the
glassed-in end of the living room, landing on the leather-and-
chrome recliner I'd used for two weeks. The back hunched forward
over the seat. The base of the telephone extended precariously past
the edge of the teak end table, pushed aside last night while I tried
to talk and take notes at the same time. Beside the phone was the
stained envelope where I'd set my coffee cup. Everything was as
I'd left it, but tarnished now by the emotional residue of violence.
My skin itched, as if I'd been contaminated, too. I shook my head.
"Nothing's missing."

Blixenstjerne said, "I must ask you to look more closely at the
victim. Perhaps you have seen him before."

I made myself step into the living room. The man had been
bludgeoned from the rear, an impressive blow that jammed his
forehead onto the keyboard. In the red pooling beneath the pedals
were white specks—bits of bone, shattered ivory or broken teeth, I
couldn't tell.

The scent of fresh blood was strong. Beneath it, I smelled stale beer and engine grease, the odors clinging to the dead man a yard from me.

Blixenstjerne was breathing audibly through his mouth. I looked away from the body, trying to get myself under control. On the floor in the corner I spotted a miniature Ionic column, lying on its side. Not more than four feet long, it belonged in the foyer where my landlord might have used it to display a potted plant. The fluted stand was solid plaster and weighed about twenty pounds.

My gaze crept from that heavy object back to the man who'd been struck. The hairs on his bare arms were the same dark blond shade as my own. On his head, the strands had reddened to strawberry, the soggy pony tail partly covering the logo arching across the back of his denim vest so that it read BAN IDOS. Below was a cartoonish armed man in sombrero and serape and centered beneath him DENMARK.

I'd seen the insignia before in a local newspaper photograph of men with motorcycles. My memory supplied the missing letter. The victim was a member of the Bandidos biker gang. He wasn't someone I knew. Yet sadness washed over me. I inhaled again, then I gagged. Spun around and pushed past Blixenstjerne into the hallway. I dealt with death regularly, lots of death. But not often with dead people. I wasn't prepared for the bone-melting pity I felt for the man whose life had ended where I lived.

I stumbled outdoors breathing hard and leaned against the building's exterior wall. It was in shade, but the bricks still radiated heat. My palm against them, I realized how cold my fingertips had gotten. I stared at my feet. The cement around them was smooth, as though someone had dusted away every particle of dirt.

A hand lightly touched my shoulder. I turned to face Jespersen. "We will have more questions," he said. "Please wait."

I nodded, too rattled to speak. The image of the man's battered skull floated through my mind and I shuddered. From the moment Jespersen accosted me at Kastrup, I'd known bad news was coming. Immediately, I'd feared for Stefan. That was a habit I hadn't yet broken. But I was trying.

I'd dreaded hearing bad news about Stefan Krajewski for as long as I'd known him. We'd met more than a dozen years ago when I was assigned to the American embassy in Warsaw. Stefan was posing as a Polish intelligence agent while secretly working undercover for the Danes. He was running a covert operation against a group of terrorists based in Warsaw and we ended up working together. We also fell in love—passionately, inextricably, and very inconveniently.

Because the Warsaw operation provoked one terrorist group into making death threats against me, I'd spent the last half of 1986 and part of 1987 on emergency leave in a safe house in Denmark under the protection of the Danish ministry of defense. The threats against me remained serious and when I returned to work, Diplomatic Security ruled that I could safely serve only in the U.S. and Canada. My enemies were persistent and the department was cautious. The security restriction remained in effect for more than a decade. I wasn't approved for overseas assignment again until early this year.

Meanwhile, Stefan's contract with the Danish Defense Intelligence Service kept him in Europe. I'd never wanted a long-distance relationship with a man. But I wanted Stefan and I put up with all the limitations. Eventually, he'd outlive his usefulness as a covert operator. He'd have to give up field work. He made jokes about that. When his cover was completely blown, he'd marry me to get a U.S. visa and find an intelligence-related desk job in the D.C. area. We'd share six-packs after work, eat breakfast together every morning, wallow in fleshly pleasure during the hours between. Marriage, as I imagined it.

The airliner bombing last December had drawn me back to Europe and into an operation that involved Stefan. The mission ended well but Stefan injured his leg permanently and Danish intelligence canceled his contract. I returned to Washington and started looking for a larger condo. I thought Stefan would join me by Valentine's Day. But he didn't arrive until March and he stayed only a week. Long enough to tell me he was going to Poland. He had something he needed to do in Warsaw. From the careful way he'd said that— and declined to say more—I knew that nothing was going to change for us.

I was mad. Hurt. Jealous. I hated those feelings. In those seven days together, I said to him all the hateful things I now regretted. About spies, tarnished by the false lives they led, hoarding their unwhisperable secrets, so closemouthed that sham becomes reality. I got angrier, he grew more tight-lipped.

I couldn't go on the way we were, waiting for him to make a life with me. Before that ever happened, I'd get a terse note advising that S. Krajewski's life had ended and the message wouldn't specify where he'd died. I wouldn't wait for that. I was done, I told him.

When he looked at me, the sadness in his eyes was terrible.

He left anyway.

He gave me instructions on how to communicate with him, as if he hoped I'd change my mind. I didn't use them. Not right away.

I'd made the correct decision last March. But my heart hadn't yet caught up with my head. When Jespersen stopped me, my first fear was for Stefan.

My second was for my seventy-six-year-old father, slowly dying from Alzheimer's back in the States.

Like someone whose car has been hit by a truck, I'd made sure my loved ones were all right. Foolishly, I'd thought because neither Stefan nor my father was involved, I could look at whatever was inside my flat and I'd feel no pain.

Wrong. I ached all over, a whiplash victim with no visible wounds. Again, I saw him, head resting on the keyboard. What was this rough-looking man doing in my apartment? And why had he uncovered the piano keys?

I braced my back against the bricks and watched Jespersen approach Blixenstjerne. Beyond them I saw sunlight flash on auburn hair. I recognized Bella Hinton. She greeted Jespersen with a handshake before she spoke rapidly to Blixenstjerne. I felt a surge of relief. Like me, Bella was a U.S. citizen and a State Department employee. We'd served together in Warsaw where she'd been the embassy's regional security officer, the RSO. By the time my work with Stefan climaxed in the spring of 1986, I trusted only two Americans in the embassy. Bella was one of them and, all these years later, she was still my closest friend. But more important, now she was the RSO at our embassy in Copenhagen and she worked closely with the Danish police. She knew me and she knew the two cops. She could get me out of this mess and on my way to Maine.

Bella shook hands with Blixenstjerne, then started purposefully toward me. She stood out among the black and white uniforms, her tunic a riotous bloom of tropical flowers over turquoise leggings and matching designer clogs. When we'd met in Poland, Bella camouflaged herself in earth-toned outfits to blend in with her mostly male colleagues in the Bureau of Diplomatic Security. In the years since, she'd stuck with the case-hardened work-style their macho culture demanded, but she'd obviously tired of their dress code.

When she reached me she leaned in close to study my face. Her hair was slicked back into a club at the base of her neck, the individual strands pasted down with gel. At each side of her green eyes was a fretwork of tiny lines, wrinkled with concern. "You all right?" she asked.

"Nearly." I pushed upright, no longer touching the wall. "I'll feel even better if you drive me straight back to Kastrup."

"Not likely you're leaving Denmark tonight," she said. "Man killed in your flat."

I must have been there minutes before the murder. Then on my way out of the country like the guiltiest of killers. It would take a while to eliminate me from the list of suspects. "You have to convince them to let me leave tomorrow," I said. "You know I don't have connections to any outlaw bikers."

"Outlaw bikers?" Bella's expression showed only casual interest, but her tone was off, tinged with something like panic.

"Victim's wearing a Bandidos vest." I kept my eyes on her. "Blixenstjerne forget to mention that?"

She didn't meet my gaze as she smoothed the hair back from her temples with the flats of her palms. "Interesting," was all she said.

Then Blixenstjerne was back, Jespersen beside him, notepad in hand.

"Do you recognize the dead man?" Blixenstjerne asked.

I shook my head. "I don't know who he is."

Jespersen jotted something down on his pad. The ink was smudged at the margins of his paper as though his fingertips were damp. He asked, "When you left the flat, did you see anyone unusual in the vicinity?"

I tried to recall the scene. When the taxi driver pushed my buzzer, I was closing my suitcase. I'd jammed it shut, grabbed my carry-on, and hurried out the door. It latched behind me. I remembered the taxi, a silvery blue Mercedes driven by a woman ten years older and twenty pounds lighter than me. I kept a tight grip on my suitcase handle, grunted as I hoisted it into the trunk. Embarrassed by the noise, I'd glanced around. I saw only an elderly gentleman in a cloth cap, strolling toward the corner market. "Nobody unusual," I said.

Blixenstjerne started in again, and for the next five minutes I repeated in several different forms the same information I'd given to Jespersen in the car. I didn't tap my foot or look at my watch, but my answers got briefer and I clipped off the ends of my words.

Finally, Blixenstjerne said, "We'll need your fingerprints."

"I'll cooperate in any way I can," I said. "But I'd appreciate it if we could finish up my part of this tonight."

"I'm not sure that will be possible." Blixenstjerne plucked the notepad from Jespersen's hands and frowned at it. "You spell your Christian name with a—?"

"Kathryn with a *K*. Excuse me," I began, wanting to acknowledge his rank, the groveling that cops always seem to expect. I realized I didn't know the correct way to address a *Kriminalinspektør*. I settled for "Sir." I added, "I need to leave as soon as possible for the U.S. I'm on the task force investigating the airliner explosion in Maine."

"Ah, yes. I understand mass murder is your specialty."

Touchy. "Not mass murder," I said. "Acts of terrorism."

He pursed his lips, two pink worms on the ruddy face. "We have little demand for your expertise in Denmark. But you may rest assured that we take each of our very few homicides quite seriously."

Hurriedly I said, "I don't know the man. I didn't kill him. I don't know who did. I don't see how I can add anything useful."

"Yes, well, we'll have to be the judge of that, won't we?" He looked back at his notes. "You go by the nickname 'Casey'?"

He was going to dot every *i*, cross every *t*. I spat out my answer. "Casey, yes."

He turned to Jespersen. "Take her to headquarters and get those prints."

The double doors on the front of the building burst open with a squeal of hinges. An attendant with greasy hair and sweat circles under his arms held the front of the gurney. The wheels at his end unlatched and clanked against the sidewalk, as he paused at the bottom of the stairs. The second attendant was female, her biceps hardening under snow-white skin. Her wheels came down, too, and she waited while her partner wiped his forehead with his bare arm.

The gurney was a yard from me, at knee level. The body was covered by a sheet, strapped at shoulders and hips. The male attendant took the helm again, pulling the sheet to one side. I saw a blood-smeared cheek, thick strands of a handlebar mustache.

Bella growled low in her throat, as if she'd choked back a scream. Then she coughed loudly to cover the lapse.

The gurney clattered away.

Jespersen had his hand on my elbow, trying to move me toward his BMW.

Why wasn't my security officer doing more to help me? "Bella," I said to her, "please explain to these gentlemen. My presence here isn't necessary. I've got to get to Bangor. Four hundred and eight people were on that flight. It's critical—"

Blixenstjerne cut me off. "The victim has the capital letters *K* and *C* inked on the palm of his left hand."

As I heard his words, I saw those letters, paired that so-familiar way. But I could not imagine those letters stark against that dead flesh. I swallowed hard.

Bella's eyes jittered from the cops to me and back again, like a nocturnal animal surprised by a bright light.

In the Warsaw embassy, I'd seen Bella deal with both a suicide and a vehicular homicide. I'd watched her clamp down on her emotions and bury her horror under professionalism. She wasn't acting detached now. What made this dead body so upsetting?

I said, "Bella—"

"Go ahead," she told me in a strangled voice. "You stay with me and Woody tonight. We'll talk."

"Miss Collins." Blixenstjerne slapped the notepad shut and handed it to his colleague. "The body was in your flat. With your initials—possibly your nickname—on his hand. Can you think of any reason for that?"

The man was looking for me. Start with the simplest explanation that fits the facts. First rule of investigation. This cop and I were using the same text. I said slowly, "I don't know why anyone from the Bandidos would want to contact me."

"We'll have to learn why," Blixenstjerne said. "Until we do, your hundreds of bodies will have to wait on our one."

3 THE SCRAMBLER PHONE CLICKED AND SPUTTERED IN MY EAR, STRUG-gling to make the secure transatlantic connection. I held the instrument tightly and stared at the bare wall, the top floor of the embassy building silent as the grave at nine o'clock on a balmy night in June. It was midafternoon in D.C. and I was trying to reach my boss in the State Department's counterterrorism office. I had to explain why I was still in Denmark.

I'd spent the early evening at the cop shop. A few minutes being printed. A couple of hours giving my statement, over and over. Jespersen followed all diplomatic protocols. Blixenstjerne was systematic. I was a fly caught on sticky paper. Not a move I could make that wouldn't bind me tighter.

The phone crackled. "Renton Funke," my boss answered.

"It's Casey," I said. I told him what had happened. I added, "The detective ordered me not to leave the country."

"Great." The disgust in his voice was audible.

I tried to stop his I-told-you-so. "I know you warned me off this assignment—"

He interrupted. "Nothing good ever comes from dancing with the spooks. You should have stayed in D.C., like I told you."

"You said it was my choice, as I recall."

He snorted. "I figured you had better sense. I didn't expect you to rush off to Europe because Gerry Davis asked for you."

"I had good reasons," I said.

"Oh, right. Going to Denmark was the quickest way to expand your knowledge of the black market in Stinger missiles." The sarcasm sharpened his voice. "If you'd listened to me, you'd be in Bangor setting up at the crash site."

"I'll get to Maine," I said. "But not tomorrow. Give me the task force's local phone number and I'll explain to Baldwin." Sam Baldwin from the FBI's domestic counter-terrorism unit had been appointed to head the task force.

Renton made a noise into the phone, a guttural rasping that hurt my ear. I could see him, fingers of his left hand yanking at his tie, loosening the collar. "Baldwin won't cut you any slack. Ever since you talked to him, he's been ranting about 'the State Department prima donna.'"

"He must've had an attitude about me before we talked." Sam Baldwin and I had met for the first time a week after my appointment was confirmed—and a day after Stefan left for Poland. I wanted to talk about the exciting work the task force would do. I hoped it would fill the gaping hole that had opened in my life. But I saw at once that Baldwin's plodding, methodical plans for us were wrong. Unfortunately, I'd been too emotionally raw to keep quiet.

I said to Renton, "All I did was remind him the task force was set up to try fresh approaches, stimulate creative problem-solving."

"And he loved hearing you tell him how to run his show." Renton made his exasperated noise again. "The man has let everyone know that he works only with *team* players."

I was silent for a few seconds, absorbing the implications. "Think he'll use this delay to get me kicked off?"

"And the reason for it." He paused, and when he spoke again anger raised the pitch of his voice. "What the hell have you gotten yourself into?"

"Same question the cops asked. I can't answer it. I don't know how that body ended up in my flat." *Body*. The word brought back the image, the head smashed onto the keyboard. I was still bothered by the memory of the open piano. Had the Bandido left something inside the instrument—some clue to his death? Again, I felt that odd hollowness behind my breastbone. I pressed the heel of my hand against my chest as if I could fill the emptiness.

Renton said, "Does this homicide connect to what you're working on?"

"Link's too obscure for me to see. I mean, a murdered Danish biker and a bunch of missing Stingers?"

Renton's voice grew caustic. "Don't rule it out. I can hear the CIA fucking things up even at this distance."

I didn't want him to repeat all the reasons why I should have refused to help Gerry Davis. Quickly, I said, "Give me that number in Maine—"

"No." His voice was gruff. "I'll handle Baldwin."

"I appreciate—" I began.

Renton was still talking. "I convinced the under secretary to back you for the task force position. She went out on a limb for me. Passed over three senior people, pressured somebody in the AG's front office—all because I argued that the task force needed your particular expertise. You can't fart around, Casey. You have to be on-site."

"I'm working on it."

"Not good enough. You have to get out of Copenhagen in the next twenty-four hours. If Baldwin kicks you off the task force, the FBI will block us from sending in a substitute. They'll argue this is a case of domestic terrorism, no role for us. They'd love to exclude the State Department. If that happens, the under secretary won't be pleased. She'll make me regret I ever put you up for the job."

The phone was slippery in my palm. "I'll talk to Gerry—"

"Forget Davis and his problems," Renton said. "You get to Bangor."

"I'll leave tomorrow." Trying to sound certain. I said goodbye and hung up the phone, then brushed my hair back off my forehead. The skin was hot and moist. I shouldn't have let Gerry Davis lure me to Denmark. Sure, I was interested in his project, but I shared Renton's aversion to spooks. I wouldn't have agreed to work with any other twenty-year-career-man from the Central Intelligence Agency. Gerry, though, was different.

He and I had a connection that went beyond friendship. We'd met in 1986 during the Warsaw operation. With his help, I'd come through unscathed but he'd concluded I was too innocent to avoid all the bureaucratic land mines hidden in the intelligence field. I'd protested, but he'd insisted that I needed protection from a veteran operative and he'd appointed himself to the job.

The oldest of five children and the only boy in his family, it was natural for him to treat me like another younger sister. He snooped in my life and he bossed me around. He became as dependably nosy, irritating, and *there*, as if he really were my older brother. He bugged me—but his concern touched me, too. By now, he fit me like my favorite old pair of sweats—not flattering, but comfortably warm and certain to cover my backside.

So last spring when he'd asked if I'd help him out, I'd said yes, instantly. I had other motives for returning to Denmark. But my bond with Gerry was the main one and I'd dismissed Renton's warnings about projects run by the CIA. I'd be working with Gerry, after all. But Renton had understood the situation better than I had.

Gerry had come to Denmark to deal with blowback from the CIA's successful—by their standards—operation in Afghanistan. In the mideighties the agency had supplied a thousand state-of-the-art ground-to-air missiles to the mujahideen fighters battling the invading Soviet Army. Six hundred of the Stingers weren't fired in the conflict. Some later turned up in Iranian hands and rumor spread that others had gone to North Korea, Somalia, Libya, and the IRA. In 1993, the CIA began offering cash for unused weapons, buying back missiles for more than a hundred thousand dollars apiece, over three times the original cost. Their motive was simple. Locking up the Stingers in U.S. armories would ensure they weren't used by hostile forces against American targets. The CIA had spent fifty-five million dollars making undercover purchases but sixty missiles still hadn't been accounted for.

Before granting additional funding, Congress forced the CIA to accept State Department and Pentagon oversight on the agency's final effort to track down the remaining missiles. The CIA picked Gerry to run the project. He was an expert on the covert arms trade, and he had one other asset vital to the high-profile project—his reputation for uncompromising honesty. His superiors promised him a free hand and access to whatever resources he needed. The first thing he asked for was a base of operations in Copenhagen. The second was Casey Collins.

I wasn't an obvious choice. My specialty was terrorist attacks on airliners. In my job in the counterterrorism office, I tracked the flows of manpower and materiel in Europe, using a sophisticated form of link analysis to tie people and events together. The bombing of Pan Am 103 in 1988 was my first big case. I painstakingly reconstructed the activities of the suspect terrorist groups, refining my analytical model as I went. Now, when a Western passenger jet exploded, I could pinpoint accurately which foreign terrorists had motive, means, and opportunity to blow it up. I wasn't part of the FBI investigation of the TWA 800 crash, but I'd followed it closely.

I was intrigued by eyewitness claims they'd seen missile tracks in the sky immediately before the explosion. Although experts had an alternate explanation for the flaming trails, I'd kept an eye on the covert traffic in Stingers and their ex-Soviet counterparts. When I needed information from the CIA, I'd gone to Gerry. He gave me everything he had. Generous—and farsighted. He hadn't been forced to waste any time bringing me up to speed.

I glanced at the clock. A full minute had elapsed since I'd said goodbye to Renton and hung up the phone. The office door swung open and Gerry grinned at me from the hallway.

"You were listening," I said, but there was no bite in the accusation. When I'd taken the job with Gerry, I'd known I'd have no privacy. An aging spy, eavesdropping was so automatic with him that he no longer had to count out the sixty seconds he habitually delayed before "happening upon" an unaware person-of-interest. Besides, Gerry insisted, I'd end up in real trouble if he didn't keep his eyes—and ears—on me. I let him get away with that pose. I'd been an only child and Gerry's big-brother act made me feel as if I had more family than I really did.

He sauntered toward me. "See what happens when you try to run off and leave me," he said reprovingly.

Earlier, he'd tried to persuade me to remain in Denmark instead of joining the task force. I'd refused to consider that option. "I bet it was you who left that body in my flat." I gave him a dark look. "Wet work, isn't that what you guys call it?"

"And you say *I'm* paranoid." He shook his head sadly, then put both palms on the desktop and leaned closer. Pink scalp showed where the strands were too sparse to cover the crown of his head. When I'd met Gerry in Warsaw, his hair was so thick and unruly, he used up a bottle of oil weekly keeping it slicked down. He'd mellowed in the years since. Given up the facial stubble and the unstructured jackets with the sleeves pushed up to the elbows. Tonight, he was dressed middle-aged-cool in a Ralph Lauren Polo shirt, knee-length Dockers and sockless Top-Siders. His appearance was more CPA than CIA. He studied me closely and his expression grew as serious as mine. "You're looking pretty grim."

"Feeling it," I said. "Dead biker turns up at my place. A pair of Danish cops give me the third degree. And my boss beats me up because I can't get out of here."

"You knew this dead *rocker?*" He used the Danish word for "biker."

I shook my head. "Unfortunately, he had my initials on the palm of his hand."

"Hunting for you?"

I shrugged. "Damned if I can imagine why."

Gerry looked at me speculatively. "This murder might connect to our project. European motorcycle clubs are well armed."

"But not with shoulder-held missiles."

"The local bikers might have heard what's become of them." He chewed at his lip for a few seconds. "What if they're talking to the criminal organizations in the old East bloc?"

I raised a skeptical eyebrow.

Gerry shrugged. "Only a guess. Bet your buddy Krajewski could fill us in on that. You know what he's working on in Poland?"

"I have no idea." The words tasted bitter, the flavor of unpleasant truth.

Gerry said, "Maybe it's not such a stretch, dead biker to missing Stinger."

"You're dreaming," I said. "This murder has nothing to do with your project. I'm not one of your field agents. Even if a Danish biker did know something about missiles, he wouldn't come looking for me." But as I said the words, I recalled Bella's distress. She'd looked shocked, as if she'd recognized the biker. Could she have sent him to me? But why would she do such a thing?

"Anybody can find out the embassy closes at five." Gerry studied me the way he did when he was trying to read my mind. "Looks like the dead guy was waiting for you to get home from work."

"I thought of that."

He asked, "How'd the cops hear about it so fast?"

"Anonymous phone tip."

"Anonymous?" Gerry's eyes brightened. "So the caller was the killer."

"Almost had to be," I said gloomily. Danes started every telephone conversation by announcing their names. No good citizen acted anonymously.

Gerry jerked his chin down in a crisp nod. "The killer wanted the cops to go to your place immediately."

Why would the killer want that? I didn't have a clue. And I

didn't want to guess. I could tell Gerry was fitting the new facts into the case he was building. He wanted me to stay in Denmark. He'd interpret anything I said as interest in his project. He'd be certain that his pleas were getting through to me. I kept my mouth shut.

"I think we should check it out," he said.

"You'll have to do the checking," I replied firmly.

"Come on, Case. You can't let me down." He kept his gaze on me, beseeching. "You know I need you here to make this project work."

"Somebody like me," I corrected him. "And you'll get that. State will send you a replacement for me."

"You know damn well State hasn't got anybody else like you."

I rolled my eyes toward the ceiling. "You must be desperate, sucking up to me like this."

"See, I've proved it. I need you. You know this stuff. And I'm not counting on State sending anyone else. Not the way things have been going. I struck out with the Pentagon."

"Defense is still refusing to give you Fuentes?" Jaime Fuentes was an analyst who'd done cleanup after a stinging GAO report in 1994 castigated the Department of Defense for their faulty Stinger inventory system. "Last week, you said you'd convinced them he was the best man for the job."

Gerry grunted. "Somebody unconvinced them."

"So they're sending Colonel Markham after all?"

"Which is why you have to stay. Markham has spent his whole career focused on Latin America. Doesn't know diddly about covert weapons transfers in Europe."

"He'll pick it up." There was no painless way to quit Gerry's project, but I didn't have to wallow in guilt. At least I could lighten the bleak picture he was painting. I didn't want to talk about Andy Markham but I forced out his name, my tone as casual as I could make it. "Andy likes to hit the ground running."

"'Andy'?" Gerry's voice was sharp, the same suspicious tone I imagined he'd used with his little sisters when they tried to slip something past him. "Just how well did you know him in Salvador?"

Too well. But Gerry's most endearing trait was the way, grouching and complaining, he always took my side against the world. I couldn't tell him what had happened in San Sal. He would inevitably cast Andy as the villain in that long-ago soap opera. And he'd never be able to work well with a man who'd done me wrong. So I said, "I know he's a quick study."

Gerry's eyes narrowed. "Last week you weren't praising Markham."

"Last week I thought the Pentagon was sending Fuentes. He's the better choice. But Andy can handle it. He's sharp and he's thorough."

"Thorough? You're stretching, Case. He's so thorough, why didn't he figure out the Salvadoran Army was shooting the wrong people?"

I sighed. "He never denied something horrible had happened. He went out to Morazán early in 1982, right after the newspapers started reporting there'd been a massacre of civilians. But he found no proof."

"A decade later, the forensic anthropologists dug up plenty of bones. Maybe Markham didn't look closely enough. They probably were hard to see." Sarcasm tightened Gerry's voice. "Some of them *were* very small."

Baby bones. I shuddered, remembering. "I got to Salvador six months later. I didn't go looking for skeletons. You're not saying *I* wasn't thorough enough."

"You were a vice-consul interviewing visa applicants. Uncovering military atrocities isn't something you can do from inside the embassy. That was Markham's job."

"Not technically. And there *was* a civil war going on—"

"Listen to you. I can't believe you're defending this guy. Only reason you're building him up is to get yourself off the hook. I understand you want to be on that task force. But you're not going to convince me I can do this job without you here. I'm getting a very bad feeling about the whole thing. The support I was promised just isn't there. Markham's not up to the job. *You* are."

"Enough," I said, holding up my hands, palms toward him. "The bullshit's getting way too deep in here."

"That's no bullshit, and you know it. If you'd gone out to the Salvadoran provinces looking for evidence of a massacre, you'd have found it. Neither a war nor technicalities would have stopped *you*. You never give up. That's what I love most about you."

"Don't do that." I shoved at my hair. "This has nothing to do with how you feel about me or how I feel about you. You heard my end of the conversation. I have to join that task force. My career is on the line."

"If we're into careers, let's talk about what's happening to mine."

I pushed myself upright. "You're in a bind. I know that. I wish I could help you out of it. But the first time the task force sends for me, what am I supposed to do, say 'sorry, my old pal Gerry needs me now, call back later?'"

Yes. I could read it on his face.

4   I COULDN'T DENY THAT GERRY HAD COME THROUGH FOR ME BIG-time when I needed his help in Warsaw. Like everything that happened to me in 1986, my problems there began with Stefan Krajewski. Stefan approached me after the American bombing of Libya. In his "official" job as an employee of Polish intelligence, Stefan had learned of reprisals being planned by a radical terrorist group against American targets. He wanted to pass that information to the U.S. government, using me as his conduit. He couldn't risk being found out by his Polish colleagues or the terrorists. To give him a legitimate reason for meeting with me, he wanted me to act as if he'd trapped me into becoming a spy.

I reported Stefan's approach to Bella and she consulted with Washington and the CIA station chief in Warsaw. Gerry was number-two man in the CIA office and he objected to putting an amateur up against someone he believed to be a Communist agent. He feared Stefan would find a way to make me commit treason. But the U.S. was desperate for the information Stefan offered and Gerry was forced to go along with the operation.

Meanwhile, Gerry had discovered that classified documents were being smuggled from our embassy to Moscow. He didn't suspect that the culprit was his well-connected junior colleague, CIA agent Warren Smythe. Smythe used my contacts with Stefan to make it appear that I was the one handing secrets over to the Soviets. Gerry had doubts about me, but they didn't stop him from tracking down the real traitor. He blew the whistle on Smythe and saved me from criminal prosecution. For more than a decade, I'd known I could trust Gerry.

Unfortunately—and perhaps because of what he'd done to Smythe—Gerry acquired a serious enemy inside the agency. He claimed that ever since Warsaw, someone had systematically sabotaged his work. He warned me not to discuss our project with Len Trotter, chief of the CIA station in Copenhagen. Gerry also believed that a sophisticated technician could turn any piece of electronic equipment into a transmitter and he'd banned computers, typewriters, and telephones from the cramped room we shared down the hall. I was worried about his state of mind, afraid he'd succumbed to the paranoia that infected so many long-term spooks.

But in the last two weeks I'd seen evidence that he was right about the sabotage. Funds evaporated, reports disappeared, and field agents suddenly went incommunicado. I'd recognized the merit in Gerry's decision to go low-tech in our private space. If I had to come here to the station chief's office to use a phone, I was less likely to say something I didn't want overheard by Trotter and his minions.

Given his self-imposed isolation and his dwindling resources, Gerry was right. He needed me, someone competent who loved him like a sister.

"Gerry," I said, softening my tone, reminding him—and myself—why I couldn't stay in Denmark. "More than four hundred people are dead. I've got to go."

He said, "You can't be sure yet the Maine crash has anything to do with terrorism. Might be a mechanical failure, like TWA 800."

"This task force exists *because* of problems that surfaced during the TWA 800 investigation." I'd been involved in designing the task force. It was supposed to operate independently of the parent agencies investigating airplane crashes. A select group of highly qualified analysts would study anomalies and make arcane connections, come up with unasked questions, then go outside the standard investigative perimeters to find answers. "I have to be on the scene immediately."

"Your talent is wasted, poking around a crash site."

"Other people do the poking," I said. "They need me to tell them what they've found."

"Sure they do. And so do I, for the same reason. It's your analytical skill, plus that encyclopedia in your brain, that makes you so good." His voice dropped to a conspiratorial level. "And you know my hunch paid off. In Denmark less than a month and we've got more leads than we can handle."

"But not one has gone anywhere," I said. "All dead ends."

"So many rumors, but no missiles to go with them. That fact tells us a lot, in and of itself." He leaned toward me, intent. "I smell funny business. You've got to see this through."

I felt myself weakening. Gerry's hunches often paid off. He'd been right to bring us to Copenhagen. True to its past, Denmark was a hub for covert activity. Maybe I *should* stick around, get to the bottom of this.

Rubber soles scraped on the carpeting beyond the door. A nightstick slapped against a solid thigh. The Marine corporal's head appeared in the doorway. Blond stubble and black framed glasses, hiding a trace of adolescent acne. "You two still working?" He laughed. "Got to be better things to do under the midnight sun."

And more critical things for me to be doing in Maine. I pushed aside my curiosity about Gerry's project. I wished I could help him, but I had to fill State's position on the task force. Renton had made that clear. And I wanted to be part of the Maine investigation. I'd get around the bureaucrat who'd been put in charge. I'd make the task force work the way it had been designed. I had to be on-site to do that. I had to get out of Copenhagen—and soon.

"I can't stay," I said to Gerry. "You know that."

He pressed his lips tightly together and his eyes narrowed like a tailor measuring me for a new coat. A turncoat.

I looked away first and grabbed my carry-on bag.

"Need help with that suitcase?" the guard asked, gesturing toward the Samsonite three-suiter parked beside the door.

I shook my head. "I'll get it on my way out of town tomorrow."

I walked with the guard toward the fourth-floor elevator, listening to his chatter, the skin on my back itchy under Gerry's censuring gaze. I had a compelling, professional reason for leaving, but Gerry mattered to me. I couldn't feel good about abandoning him.

When we got to the ground floor, I said good night to the roving corporal, signed out with the second Marine at Post One, and headed out through the embassy's front door onto Dag Hammarskjölds Allé.

The nighttime glow turned the sky the color of a candled egg. A block away, a commuter train rumbled into Østerport Station. Beyond the sidewalk, a brightly lit bus slid past, leaving behind no visible exhaust. I didn't smell any either, its engine was so finely tuned. A grandmotherly woman in a calf-length skirt and sensible shoes marched by, pulling an elderly golden retriever. For a second

I longed for my German shepherd. I wanted to bury my face in the thick hair on Blondie's neck. But she was three thousand miles away, at a wildly overpriced doggie summer camp in Virginia's hunt country. I was a spendthrift when it came to Blondie.

I strode briskly toward the waterfront. Bella and her son Woody lived in a wharfside warehouse that had been converted to upscale condos. It was fewer than fifteen blocks from the embassy. The sidewalks emptied as I got farther from Østerport. After three blocks, the only other pedestrian was a lone figure a hundred yards behind me traveling in the same direction. I quickened my pace. Looming beside me were the earthworks surrounding *Kastellet*, where some Danish Army cadets slept in ancient lodgings and the intelligence branch conducted its business in a building called *Elefantstok*. I'd spent ten hours in there during the past week, working with Birger and Stig, a pair of crack computer analysts who spoke Danish-accented English and laughed uncontrollably at my mispronunciation of their names. So far they'd uncovered no Stingers changing hands on the black market—a nonresult that puzzled me and offended both of them.

We all knew that the missiles didn't have an indefinite shelf life. The power sources which activated their target-seeking mechanisms and drove their electronics deteriorated over time. The weapons might be useless. Yet the CIA was offering serious money for them. Two smart Danish guys scouring the reams of intelligence reports should have turned up at least one seller eager to unload an unreliable Stinger.

I glanced back. One other walker, still the same distance behind me. Looked like the same person. I was halfway to Bella's. I trotted faster, heading toward the odor of the summer-warmed sea. A pair of gulls called out, wheeling white-on-white above me.

The sky looked like a design of Royal Copenhagen porcelain, the Denmark that I remembered. Back in D.C., sneezing from the cherry blossom pollen, I hadn't listened as Renton listed all the reasons I should refuse to work with Gerry. I was thinking only, *Denmark in the spring*. Thinking back to 1986 when Stefan and I shared a safe house north of Copenhagen. I'd been so passionately certain that we'd be lovers forever.

I'd been wrong. Yet I'd been drawn back to Denmark against all logic, as if by returning in the spring, I'd find something precious that I'd lost. I said yes to the job, not asking who else I'd be working with. I was officially assigned to Gerry's project before I discovered that Andy Markham was slated to join us.

I hadn't expected to find myself working with Andy again— our career paths had gone in such different directions after we'd served together in San Salvador. His assignment to Gerry's project startled me more because I knew it wasn't mere happenstance bringing us together. The job hadn't been filled by pulling a name from a hat. The Pentagon had chosen Andy from a pool of applicants. Why had he applied?

Because I'd been named to the State Department slot?

Absurd. Why, after nearly two decades, would Andy twist his life around to be near me in Copenhagen? I felt silly even thinking that he would. Yet, I couldn't blame his sudden reappearance in my life on coincidence. Andy had made it happen. And I didn't know why. That bothered me.

My mistake, getting involved with Andy in Salvador. I'd worked hard to convince myself I never wanted to see him again. So it disturbed me even more that thinking of him made my pulse race and my chest grow warm. I hated to imagine what would happen when I saw him in the flesh. At least now I'd be able to avoid that.

I'd leave Denmark tomorrow—*if* I could explain away the dead biker found in my flat. Again, I felt a twinge of sorrow.

I walked quickly past *Frederiks Kirke*, the domed Marble Church, and onto the cobblestone plaza encircled by the four mansions of *Amalienborg*. No *Dannebrog* flew from the flagstaff. The queen was not at home. The courtyard was empty, except for me and a pair of guards in blue jackets and beefeater hats. No lights shone behind the windows of the royal residence, the glass a mirror of the white radiance overhead. It was like being watched from a hundred clouded eyes.

I looked back again. The man had entered the plaza at the same point where I had. Ahead of me the shops were shuttered, no friendly convenience stores offering refuge. And no taxis in sight. But Bella's condo was only three blocks away now. I hurried over the cobblestones.

A pair of bicycles rolled by me on the cross street. Both riders were women; neither wore a helmet. The carry-basket mounted on the rear of one bike contained a liter of milk and a loaf of *franskbrød*, the tan crust poking upward like a signpost to heaven. The other bike sported a child's seat in the rear, empty except for a small pink sweater locked into the restraint.

I reached the front door to Bella's building. Thumb pressing the buzzer, I glanced behind me. I saw only an empty street.

"Yes?" Bella's voice came tinnily from the intercom.

"Casey," I answered, my eyes still probing.

Movement flickered in a shadowed doorway, a body shifting position. Someone was waiting and watching.

"Come on up," Bella said, buzzing open the lock.

Bella. She was the key. She'd long ago perfected her Joe Friday-pose as an emotionless cop. Yet her reserve had crumbled when she saw the face of the man who'd died in my flat. And her jitters worsened when she learned he had my initials written on his hand. I had to make her tell me—and the police—what she knew about the victim.

I'd do that. Then I'd be on my way to Bangor. I pushed inside the building and closed the door tight.

5 "TOOK YOU LONG ENOUGH," WOODY SAID. HE OPENED THE DOOR to the apartment wider. "We were starting to wonder if they locked you up." His orange-red hair stuck up in punkish tufts and I heard a rawness under his words, that sore-throated rasp that afflicts boys when their voices begin to deepen.

I tried to hide the goofy expression I felt taking over my face. Woody was embarrassed now by my doting, you-are-the-best-boy-in-the-world look. But when I saw him, I couldn't stop myself from beaming foolishly. I had no nieces or nephews. Woody was the only baby I'd held more than once, the only boy I'd watched grow toward manhood. Maybe other kids were as neat. I didn't know. He was my sole research subject and I was helplessly in love with him.

I stepped past him into the front room, the whitewashed oak floor and white-painted walls backdrop for the multicolored Lego constructions that filled most of the open space. Woody leaned toward me, sketching an embrace so ghostly I caught only a sense of biceps the diameter of two-inch pipe, a memory of a hug. I stopped myself from clutching him. He'd outgrown that and I mourned the loss.

Actually, I'd known Woody since *before* he was born. Bella had gotten pregnant with him while we were in Warsaw. She'd refused to name Woody's father and I assumed she was protecting a married man who'd strayed into her bed. Woody was unplanned, but he was never unwanted. From the moment Bella realized a baby was growing inside her, being a mother became her reason for being.

She was too cagey to let many people see her maternal side. When her male counterparts in security talked about their children, they ruefully compared the size of the support checks they were sending to their ex-wives. None admitted they grieved for their lost kids. Bella aped that flinty-hearted pose, downplaying how hard she'd struggled to keep Woody with her. A single mom, she counted on the salary improvements that came with each promotion. "Motherly" wasn't a career-enhancing adjective in the State Department's Bureau of Diplomatic Security.

Woody was the reason that Bella took emergency leave from her post as regional security officer in Warsaw and fled Poland with Stefan and me in 1986. Stefan and I were running from an assassin sent by the terrorists in retaliation for the covert operation against them. In her second trimester of pregnancy, Bella was trying to get out from under the radioactive cloud blowing our way from Chernobyl.

For the next ten months, she and I were both on leave in Denmark. I'd been her labor coach at the *Rigshospital* and the first of her friends to argue against naming a redheaded boy Woody. I'd even imitated the cartoon woodpecker's hideous laugh. But Bella had been adamant: "Woody"—not Woodrow or Woodward—was what the Danish priest spoke over the christening font.

Since Woody arrived, she'd served most of her career in Foggy Bottom. But last year State had offered her the job in the Copenhagen embassy. That she and Woody were in Denmark was another reason I'd accepted Gerry's invitation.

Woody nudged me toward the counter edging the kitchen. "She said we had to wait for you."

"Don't let him kid you," Bella said. "He refused to eat until you got here." She had her back to us, pulling something from the microwave. I smelled almond paste and cinnamon. She turned and the plate clicked against the tiled countertop. Fresh *wienerbrød*, "Vienna bread" to the Danes, the pastry that everyone else in the world calls "almond Danish."

"He was worried the cops wouldn't feed you," she said, sliding the platter toward me.

I grinned at Woody. "You got that right."

"You know how crabby you get when you're hungry. I didn't want *that*." He lifted a piece of pastry onto my plate, then took a hunk for himself. He added, "Mom says you might not stick around for my birthday. You might have to go back to the States."

Might have to go? I tried to see Bella's face, gauge why she'd given Woody any reason to think I'd still be in Copenhagen on August first to celebrate his thirteenth birthday. But she had her back to me again, fiddling with the coffeemaker this time. I said, "I expect to leave tomorrow. But I've got the list you gave me."

"The list you *asked* for." He didn't look at me, instead brushing at the toasted almond shavings littering the front of his T-shirt. "It's not like I'm a little kid. You don't *have* to give me a present."

"Yes, I do. I don't care how old you get, I will never skip your birthday."

"Well, in that case . . ." He grinned as he pulled notebook paper from the back pocket of his baggy shorts and passed it to me. "I have a different list for you. Since you'll be shopping in the U.S."

As I took the paper from him, I felt a pleasurable warmth in my stomach. Partly from the Danish, partly from the discovery that Woody was still kid enough to anticipate gifts gleefully. I kept my tone light, not wanting my fondness to spook him. "A true international teen, is that it? Expert on compact-disc prices worldwide?"

"Not CDs this year." He downed a twelve-ounce glass of milk, followed it with another piece of pastry. "But don't buy Legos in the States," he mumbled through the food. "I don't want you paying to ship Legos back to Denmark."

Bella set the platter on the stove behind her. "That's your last piece." She turned and squeezed Woody's shoulder, a lingering caress that was at odds with her brisk words. "Casey and I want to talk. You go find something to do in your room."

Woody stepped behind my chair and milky lips brushed damply against my cheek. This time I grabbed him and held on for a hug.

"Let go," he mumbled. But he waited a second before he pulled away."

Looking good," I called after him as he shambled from the room.

I caught Bella's eyes on me. I couldn't tell what she was thinking, the look on her face was so strange. She dumped her coffee cup into the sink. "I'll be back in a minute," she said, heading after Woody.

I slid the last bite of *wienerbrød* into my mouth. Marzipan filling oozed out onto my tongue, rich with almonds and butter, a high-priced delectable from the *bageri* on Amaliegade. Bella's attempt to sweeten me up.

A radio came on in Woody's room, the music too faint to identify. I left the breakfast bar and moved the futon frame around the Legos and in front of the floor-to-ceiling windows. Copenhagen, København in Danish, originally Køpmannæhafn, Merchants' Harbor since 1443, capital of Denmark—the Inner Harbor spread out before me, the sea a gray-green slick.

Woody's door opened long enough for me to hear the Danish announcer kick off an hour of classic rock with a selection from Abba. A minute later, Bella dropped down on the futon and passed me one of the two beer bottles she was holding. The label on mine read PASKEBRYG. Easter brew. Had to be one of the last from Bella's stash of holiday beer. She knew I loved it.

Bella took a long pull straight from her bottle. The moon and stars hadn't yet appeared, the pale sky doming over us as if we were in a translucent bell jar.

I sluiced beer through my teeth, the bitter ale canceling out the soporific effects of the Danish, stiffening my resolve. Bella was so sly, trying to lull me with sugar and alcohol. There could be only one reason. Like Gerry, she had her own agenda. And it didn't include helping me get out of Denmark tomorrow. I'd have to force the truth out of her. Knowing Bella, that might take some time.

I set down my bottle and got right to it. "So what do you know about this dead Bandido?"

"Calls himself Bjørn." She pronounced it the Danish way, Bee-YORN.

In Danish, "bjørn" meant "bear." A good biker name. "You knew him?" I asked, incredulous.

"We'd met." Bella's voice was flat.

"What do you mean, you'd *met*?"

"I ran into him in a biker bar."

"What were you doing in a—"

She cut me off, her voice tired. "I'll get to that. Anyway, I was in this bar and I ended up talking to Bjørn. Soon as he realized I worked at the U.S. embassy, he asked, did I know the woman there who was looking for missing American weapons. I realized he had to mean you."

I couldn't keep my shock out of my voice. "You gave him my name?"

She rolled the beer bottle between her palms. "I tried to put him off. But he said he had something really hot for you. He kept pushing, to a point where I had to give in. I told him to call the embassy, ask for Kathryn Collins."

"You told him where I lived?"

She gave me a hooded look. "You have to ask?"

"No. Sorry."

She shrugged. "These guys seem to have their own intelligence network. No problem getting your address, he wanted to see you at home."

"Back up a little," I said. "You have to tell me why you're talking to *rockers*."

Bella reached down and picked up a tiny figure wearing Lego armor. A piece from the Royal Knights set. I'd given the castle to Woody when he was eight. Looking at the figure brought back the warmth of his smaller body, the little-boy smell of his hair.

Bella took the knight off his horse. She put him on again. "Did you check out that first birthday list Woody gave you?"

She'd get to the *rockers*. She knew I wouldn't drop that issue until she explained. No harm in letting her get there in her own way. All I had to lose was sleep.

"I glanced at the list." It had included only Lego sets, identified by number. "I was surprised he was still adding pieces. Didn't he say he was getting too old for more Legos?"

"The sets he wants are all from different systems," she said. "Only thing they've got in common, each one has a skeleton. He's into bones, Casey."

Bella spoke in normal tones, but I felt as if her pitch had risen an octave, the words reverberating inside my skull. "Bella," I said. "What's going on?"

Bella took a breath. Her lips moved but I couldn't hear over the muffled roar in my head, the sound of Chernobyl, blowing apart. Yet I knew the word she was uttering. My own lips formed the four syllables along with hers. *Leukemia*.

Woody—my Woody—had leukemia.

Awful knowledge swept through me, that swift and pervasive terror you feel as a color-changing medical test strip takes on the undeniable hue of a long-feared diagnosis. It was as if Medusa had come into the room and turned me to stone. I couldn't move my lips. I'd been deafened and made dumb by petrifying dread.

Only my hands moved. I clutched one with the other, trying to still the trembling. But it didn't work. Almost thirteen years ago,

I'd watched Woody come into the world. Then Bella crushed my fingers, as he slid out between her legs. I'd cut the cord linking them together. My heart was so swollen with joy, it felt as big as the precious, slippery body the midwife placed in my bare hands. For all of Woody's life, I'd worked every magic I knew to keep him healthy. I'd knocked on wood and crossed my fingers. I'd prayed for him. Because of Chernobyl, I'd known he was at risk.

As soon as Bella and I reached Denmark in 1986, we'd started researching radiation effects. I'd found books and translated articles from the Danish papers. Childhood leukemia was what I'd feared the most. Last year, I'd told myself the danger was past. Woody had entered puberty. He'd made it through childhood. He was safe. I'd let myself relax.

Too soon! I'd relaxed my vigilance. And now Woody might die.

There was no connection. In my head, I knew that. In my heart, I'd never believe it. I looked away from Woody and cancer scuttled into his blood. I needed a full minute to pull myself together, before I could croak out the question. "Which type?"

"CML," Bella said. "He was diagnosed in January."

CML. The three letters banged into my brain like the latches slamming shut on Woody's coffin lid. My hand covered my mouth, stopping the moan rising from inside me.

CML stood for chronic myelogenous leukemia. Statistically, it was a disease of the elderly. Yet, I'd memorized everything I read about it, not knowing what Chernobyl might do to those statistics. I'd dreaded CML because it was the most difficult to treat. Woody looked so good, he must still be in the chronic phase. The cancer could be managed with medication. Managed—not eradicated. For children who developed CML, only a bone marrow transplant offered any real hope of cure. And the transplant had to be completed before the cancer became acute. The so-called blast crisis could develop in the next two months, or might not come for twenty years. But once malformed and misfunctioning white cells took over, it would be too late to save Woody. He needed a transplant immediately. A matching donor was most likely to be found among his near relations.

Looking at Bella's face, I saw she had more bad news. I said, "Your bone marrow doesn't match."

She shook her head.

Woody's mother couldn't donate. He had no brothers or sisters. That left his father, the unnamed man who'd been in Warsaw with us. Bella would have to be less discreet. I said, "Have you told Woody's dad?"

She made an ugly noise, somewhere between a sob and a scream. "Like that's a simple thing to do."

"Isn't it?" I asked.

"What, you believe he was an adulterous member of the diplomatic corps?"

"You never denied that," I said.

"I couldn't tell the truth." She stood and leaned her forehead against the glass. "He was gone before I knew I was pregnant. I had to hang onto my job."

She was telling me that Woody's father wasn't from the West. During the Cold War, U.S. diplomats were allowed to have only professional relationships with East bloc nationals. As the embassy security officer, Bella was the American officer charged with enforcing the nonfraternization rule in Poland. She'd have been forced to resign her commission if anyone had learned the truth.

Stunned, I said, "You slept with a Pole?"

"What, you think you're the only one who made that mistake?" She turned to face me, her back against the glass, arms folded across her chest.

"But who?"

"Remember those USIS parties with the jazz band?"

To get around the non-frat rule, the U.S. Information Service sometimes hosted "official" functions, inviting local artists and musicians and writers. It had been our chance to mingle with some counterculture types, and pretend no iron curtain was between us.

"I remember," I said slowly.

"He played the drums," she said. "Wanted to be the Polish Art Blakey."

The jazz drummer. I remembered the night I'd heard him play. Thirty Americans crowded into one end of the cultural attaché's living room. The Poles were all chain-smoking Marlboros somebody had brought in from the embassy commissary and the overheated air was hazy with tobacco smoke. I recalled the drum solo. The rhythm was visceral and my heart pumped along with it. I saw the drummer coolly working his drums. Bella standing behind him so close she had to be touching his back, the drumbeats vibrating her body. How had I missed what was going on between them? For a second, I tried to imagine where they'd gone to be alone. I stopped myself. "Wlodek Wojcik," I said. We'd Americanized his unpronounceable name. "Woody Woodchuck."

"So you remember him," Bella said.

"No woman who saw those hands could forget him. But what are you saying? You haven't asked him for a blood sample?"

"I haven't seen him."

"Why not? Nobody cares anymore that Woody's father is a Pole." I pushed hair off my forehead. "So fly to Warsaw and ask him to help. Three flights a day from Kastrup, it would take only—"

She cut me off. "He left Poland in 1986, remember? Never came back, far as I could tell."

I said, "Maybe he's got a brother or sister—"

She stopped me with a weary hand motion. "I hired a private investigator to search for relatives. That didn't go anywhere either. Maybe Wojcik wasn't his birth name. No trace of him or his family in Poland, according to the investigator. He tracked him as far as Marseilles. Wlodek Wojcik disappeared. The investigator didn't have a clue where to look next."

Dead end. A fist squeezed my heart, part of me dying, too. Frantic, I searched my brain for another option. But I found no good ones. I cleared my throat and said, "I'll get tested first thing tomorrow."

"Sure." Her voice was flat. We both knew the odds against finding a matching donor in the general population were twenty thousand to one. Not likely I'd be the one.

"Bella," I said apprehensively, "what's Woody's illness got to do with *rockers*?"

She sighed and then spoke slowly, but I heard a breathy quiver beneath her words. "I went in his room a minute ago, he had his nose back in that Bible the hospital chaplain gave him. Reading *Lamentations* again. You know it?"

I shook my head.

"You read it enough, the words stick in your head." She closed her eyes, the way you do when you're trying to recall a memorized verse. But when she spoke, I could tell the passage was burned unforgettably into her brain. She'd shut her eyes to hold back tears. "'God caused my skin and flesh to waste away,'" Bella recited, "'and he crushed my bones . . . He forced me to sit in the dark like someone long dead.'" She opened her eyes again and turned to stare glassily toward the sea. "Woody says you have to figure that was maybe the first time God gave somebody leukemia."

I stood next to her, my hand on her shoulder. She was too thin, and her skin was powdery-looking. "He's trying to handle it."

"I don't want him to handle it." Her voice was rough with pain. "I want him to get well."

"Of course you do. So do I. But—"

"Before Wlodek Wojcik disappeared from Marseilles, he joined the Bandidos motorcycle club." She looked at me straight on. "That's why I've been talking to *rockers*."

"You were looking for Woody's dad." I sank down on the futon, trying not to show how horrified I was.

"I knew it was a long shot," she said. "But I got lucky."

Disbelieving, I said, "You found him with the Bandidos in Denmark?"

She shook her head. "I wasn't that lucky. No, Bjørn—the guy who's dead? He had the name of someone else, someone who could help me. But Bjørn wouldn't give it to me. He said I had to tell him your name first. Of course I said no. But finally, I had to give in, to get him to talk. I didn't think it would turn out this bad."

"He had a name of someone who could help you? You mean someone in Denmark knows where to find Wlodek?"

"He *might* know. I haven't talked to him yet. He's been away, supposed to get back to Frederikssund day after tomorrow. According to Bjørn, this other Bandido is my best shot." She swallowed. "Was my best shot." She stood at the window, outlined against the dirty cotton of the sky, her gay tunic dulled to the same drab color as the sea. Tendrils of hair broke free from the gel she used, rayed out from her head, reminded me of a rope stretched too tight, the strands snapping, breaking loose.

"You can't contact him because of Bjørn," I said.

"Not because of him."

"Then why?"

Her face was slack, hopeless. "Because of you."

6 "BECAUSE OF ME, YOU HAVE TO STOP SEARCHING FOR WOODY'S father?" I stared at her. "Maybe you better tell me where you think he is."

"Southeast Asia," she said in a dead voice.

Heroin. That was the only link I could imagine between outlaw Danish bikers, Marseilles, and Southeast Asia. Wlodek Wojcik had to be part of the *rocker* drug supply line. The realization flattened me, as though something had been rammed into my gut.

Bella dropped back onto the futon beside me, pulled one of the throw pillows onto her lap. She hugged it against her belly. "Unless you tell the cops I gave your name to Bjørn, the investigation into his murder could go on for a week. You can't afford to be stuck here that long. I'll explain to Jespersen that Bjørn wanted to sell information to you. Someone killed him to prevent that sale. There's nothing you can add to that scenario. You'll be in the clear."

"But *you* won't. The Bandidos will know you've sicced the cops on them. You won't be able to get near this guy in Frederikssund. You'll blow your shot at finding Wlodek."

"Yeah, well, wasn't much of a chance anyway." She shifted to face me, still hugging the pillow. "I can't mess you up with the cops. I might not find Woody's father. And even if I do, he might not be a suitable donor. This whole thing's making me crazy. You know, I was thinking, 'Hell I'm still fertile. If his father doesn't match, maybe a little brother or sister will.'" She shook her head. "Crazy."

"Not that crazy," I said slowly. I'd read about the Korean-born man, adopted as an infant by Americans, who located a sister in Korea who could donate bone marrow. And a middle-aged California couple conceived another child to get a tissue match for their grown daughter. "You couldn't ignore the idea that his father could save him."

Bella sighed. "The baby thing took me over. If I could have another kid, it felt like everything—*everything*—would be all right again."

I heard the rueful undertone. She knew her response wasn't rational. But nobody ever talked about the maternal *intellect*. Instinct was driving Bella. I said, "That's understandable."

Bella interrupted. "You don't need to make excuses for me. I went nuts, that's why I didn't say something to Jespersen at the crime scene." She stood and dropped the pillow back onto the futon. "A half hour ago, you and I and Woody were all eating *wienerbrød*, talking about his birthday, behaving like normal people. And it was like someone was saying to me, 'Bella! Get real. Stop acting insane!'"

"Looking for Woody's father wasn't a crazy idea," I insisted.

"The insane part was going to the Bandidos." She raised her arms and rubbed the heels of her hands along her temples, smoothing her hairdo back into place. "I haven't gotten started and somebody's already dead. No, Casey, you have to pull yourself out of this mess I've made. I know how important the task force is to you. You can't get hung up in Copenhagen."

I said, "And you're okay with telling all this to the cops?"

"Okay? No. God, no." Black smudges circled Bella's eyes, making her expression as haunted as her voice. "I don't want to give up. But I have to face the truth. The odds against me are just too long. I can't manage the miracle it'll take to save Woody." Her throat closed over the last word, choking off his name. She bent down, kissed my cheek. Her lips were soft and her hair gel had the faint scent of strawberries. "I'm going to bed," she said hoarsely. "I'm sorry I dragged you into this. I'll fix that, now. I'll talk to Jespersen first thing in the morning."

I told her good night, watched her disappear into the bedroom. I saw the bent head, the drooping shoulders. I saw Bella defeated. Her door clicked shut.

My face was hot, my mouth dry. I felt like I had a fever, as if I'd been enveloped by infectious agents. All of these people—the dead man, Gerry, Bella—were converging on me like carriers of the virus in a flu outbreak. All so desperately in need of help. And I could help none of them.

I unfolded the futon and spread it out.

I had to leave Denmark and take my position on the task force. I couldn't justify staying. The *rocker* had died in my flat but that didn't make him my problem. Sure, Gerry didn't want to run his project without me, but he'd manage. With all my heart I wanted to rescue Woody. But if Bella had thought my remaining in Denmark would do that, then she'd have asked me to stay. Instead, she'd chosen to break off her search for Woody's father.

A spasm of grief twisted in my stomach. Very likely, Woody would die. Bella was trying to accept that truth so she could help him handle it. I wondered how long it would take her. I wondered how long it would take *me*.

Unzipping my pants, I felt the birthday list in my back pocket. I pulled it out to read the new number one, for gift-givers making their purchases in the U.S.A.

The Visible Man.

When I was thirteen, somebody gave me the Visible Woman. It took me hours to assemble the skeleton. Attaching the clavicle and pelvic girdle to the spinal column. Pinning the humerus to the scapula; attaching the elbow, the radius, the ulna, the hand. Working down below on the femur, the fibula, the tibia, gluing on the patella, pinning on the feet. Painting in the veins and arteries. Assembling the internal organs and fitting them into the central cavity before inserting the front of the rib cage.

I'd had a terrible adolescence. But I'd had one. I'd never been driven to build a Lego boneyard. Search the Bible for a reason for my misery. Build a body from scratch so I could understand how mine was going to self-destruct.

I went into the kitchen and set the empty bottle on the counter. I got Bella's last Easter beer from the refrigerator and wandered with it back to the living room. I sipped from the bottle as I gazed outside. The sky had darkened to navy blue, sprinkled with glimmering stars that mirrored the street lights of Holmen on the far side of the harbor. The brief darkness before the midsummer dawn.

In counterterrorism we sometimes use ideas from the field of epidemiology to help us understand criminal behavior. "Tipping point" is the term describing the moment when a relatively functional situation suddenly becomes wildly dysfunctional.

Woody needed me more than any of the others did. And when

I let myself feel that, my own situation passed the tipping point. I was overwhelmed, caught up in an epidemic of need. My own need most of all. I couldn't do nothing and let Woody die.

In fighting an epidemic, improvement does not correspond directly to effort. Large changes can have small effects. Small changes can have huge effects. It depends on when and how the changes are made.

I'd make one small change in my plans. Delay giving this new information to the cops. Give Bella time to follow up on the one lead that she had. Years ago with Chernobyl smoking behind us, I'd helped Bella get an unborn Woody to a safer place. My life had been entwined with his ever since. From Woody I'd learned your face can get wet, changing the diapers on a baby boy. I'd discovered how a four-year-old fits perfectly under your arm when you read aloud to him, a warm little body whose heart beats faster than your own. That snuggler had grown now into sharp-elbowed adolescence, struggling to keep the world at arm's length.

He'd become a teenager who acted no differently than I had.

I'd tried to convince myself I could leave Denmark tomorrow. Preposterous to even entertain such an idea. Woody had been my boy for thirteen years.

No matter the odds, I couldn't give up on him now.

7 THE WHIRR OF THE REFRIGERATOR MOTOR YANKED ME AWAKE AT quarter to five. My body ached and my eyes were gritty with fatigue.

I gently opened the door to Bella's bedroom. Thursday morning sun pushed through the miniblinds, striping the room with light and shadow. Bella was sitting up in bed, her back against a pair of pillows, her eyes a dark band between alabaster streaks of forehead and cheekbone.

When I sank down beside her on the foam mattress, the slats in the platform bed creaked.

Overnight the bones in her face had grown more prominent, her eyes sunk deeper into their sockets. She looked like a trapped animal, a mother raccoon who'd spent the last few hours trying to chew off her foot, and still hadn't freed herself from the hunter's snare.

"I'll give you till tomorrow night," I said.

She leaned forward, grabbed my hand. Her fingertips were icy. The light hit her eyes, turning the green iridescent. She hugged me fiercely and for a second her cheek was warm against mine. She drew away first, her hand still clutching my fingers. "The guy I'm looking for runs a tattoo parlor in Stenløse," she said. "He's due back at work there tomorrow noon. We can go to Stenløse in the morning and wait for him to show up."

I pulled my hand free and stood. I went to the window and pried apart the miniblinds so I could see the street below. On the far side, a yawning uniformed cop stood where he could watch the entrance to the building. "Probably better you go alone," I said.

The slats creaked again as she swung her legs over the side of the bed. She joined me at the window. "Christ. I don't need cops hanging round me."

I said, "One of them followed me last night."

"You should've told me."

"We had other things to talk about." I took my fingers off the blind. "The one last night wasn't in uniform. But I should've figured he was a cop. Tagged along behind me all the way, like he had nothing to hide."

Bella's voice was sharp. "You've got to get him out of here."

"Relax. You know when I take off, he'll follow."

"You're right." She let out a gusty sigh. "Looks like Blixenstjerne doesn't trust you much. Afraid you'll leave Denmark."

"He's that suspicious? I'll need a good story for him come tomorrow night, how I figured out that Bjørn was looking to sell me information."

Bella blinked. "We can't tell the truth? That I sent Bjørn to you?"

"Not if I wait until tomorrow."

"He'll be more suspicious of you, not less." Her voice got slower, words more reluctant. "If this backfires, you'll be trying to explain why you hindered the investigation."

"Let's take one step at a time. I'll see if I can get something out of Gerry that ties bikers to the missiles. Might give me a way to handle Blixenstjerne. Tomorrow, while you go to Stenløse and make contact with your guy, I'll keep the cops occupied."

"Okay." She stepped over to her dresser. Her back to me, she pulled open a drawer. The motion lifted the oversize T-shirt she was wearing, exposing the backs of her thighs. The skin was threaded with spider veins, as if an artist had drawn on her in fine-tip marker, using deep purple ink. She turned and handed me panties and socks.

I took the clothes from her. "Gerry usually comes in early. I'll grab a quick shower and then go find him."

Her voice more upbeat, she said, "Clean towels are in the cupboard next to the sink."

"Right." I headed for the bathroom.

She called after me, "If you hang around town long enough, you might still get a chance to see your old boyfriend."

I stopped and turned to face her. "The last thing I want is to see Andy Markham again."

Her smile was sly. "Why not check him out, since Stefan's run off?"

"He didn't run off—"

Bella put up a hand to stop me. "Maybe not technically. But you're angry with him, I can tell."

"I was a little ticked off, sure," I said. "But mostly, I'm concerned for him. He's too well known to do covert work. Almost bought the farm, last time. He'll always limp. He knows it's dangerous. He said—" I stopped. I sounded too pathetic.

Bella waited a half-second before she finished my sentence for me. "Said he'd get out of field operations." She sniffed. "So what's he doing in Warsaw?"

"Like he'd breathe a word about it."

She raised an eyebrow. "You didn't ask?"

"A man in his line of work? Secrecy is his favorite vice. He can't give it up."

"Oh, and you're only a little ticked off. You get anything out of the Father-Major?"

She used our old nickname for Holger Sorensen, the Danish Army officer who'd supervised Stefan's work for the Danish Defense Intelligence Service. "Holger's a lieutenant colonel now," I said automatically. "He's still preaching. But he got promoted in his other job."

"Father-Colonel?" She laughed. "Nope, doesn't sing for me. So what'd he tell you about Stefan?"

I shrugged. "I haven't talked to him."

"Afraid he'd tell Stefan you were snooping around?"

No. Holger wouldn't do that. But he knew me too well. No casual question about Stefan would conceal my pain. I didn't want him to see how much Stefan's choice had wounded me. I said, "No point in asking Holger anything. He's as secretive as Stefan."

"You're avoiding your foremost intelligence source in all of Scandinavia." Awareness gleamed in her eyes. "Stefan's got you all turned around. Forget him. I never did think he was right for you."

"You're running your Mother Bella number on me, again." I grimaced in mock horror. "To hear you talk, no man in the world is right for me."

"For sure, you can live without Stefan. You need somebody to take your mind off him. And I know just the man for the job." She looked at me closely. "You can tell me the truth. You've still got feelings for Andy Markham. Warm feelings."

I wasn't admitting *that*, not even to Bella. I turned away to hide my face from her. "I barely remember him. I'm certainly not lusting after him." I pulled the bathroom door firmly shut behind me.

Through the closed door, I heard her say loudly, "Plenty of shirts in the closet, if you want to freshen up your look."

I was washed, dressed and at the front door twenty minutes later. The cop leaned lazily against the far building, his eyelids half shut below his blond forelock. I closed the door noisily behind me, cleared my throat, squatted down to re-tie my shoe. By the time I was standing upright, so was the cop, muttering into a cell phone while he trained an unsmiling stare on me. I started slowly up the street. After a few seconds, I heard the thump of his boots behind me. My shoulders relaxed and I imagined Bella on the other side of her bedroom window, relieved that we'd called this one right.

I paraded along the sidewalk, pulling the policeman away from Bella. I had to get to the embassy, start work on a story that would make it possible for me to leave Denmark on Friday night. Extract what I needed from Gerry without giving Bella away.

I smelled lilacs on the breeze and the silk shirt whispered against my skin. The sun flung long shadows across the pavement, the air cool and fresh in the shade. A perfect morning that begged to be spent sipping fresh-brewed coffee at a sidewalk café. I'd dreamed that Stefan and I might be doing that by this third week in June. It was no accident I knew the air connections between Copenhagen and Warsaw. As soon as I got the assignment to Denmark, I'd checked the flight schedule. The day I'd arrived in Copenhagen, I'd sent Stefan a message suggesting we get together. A friendly note. But he must have feared I was lovesick enough to come to Warsaw in search of him—and he didn't want that. The same day—maybe the same hour—that he'd gotten my message, he'd broken his longstanding rule against phones and called me. He was sorry, he'd told me, but the timing wasn't good. He was terribly busy. He couldn't make it to Copenhagen to see me, not any time soon.

Pride had saved me—I hadn't suggested I go to Warsaw. I was glad for that. When Stefan defected from Poland in 1986, he was thirty years old. He left behind not only his homeland but also an ex-wife. Two days after I'd spoken with Stefan, I read a story about her in *Jyllands-Posten*. Monika Zimny, Stefan's ex-wife, had been an ambitious up-and-coming party member before the Communist government fell in Poland and she'd survived the transition to democracy to win a seat in the *Sejm*, the parliament. The reporter quoted her intelligent remarks about former enemies working together on behalf of Poland. The accompanying photo was grainy and blurred, the kind where you know that the attractive brunette in the picture must be absolutely stunning in person.

Not that I cared. Monika's beauty had nothing to do with Stefan's abandonment of me. In all the years I'd known him, he hadn't said ten words about his ex-wife. No reason to think he had any interest in her.

No reason to think he didn't, either.

A pigeon scolded me for stepping too near a discarded roll. I quickened my pace. Ridiculous to be jealous of Monika Zimny. Or a whole damn country, for that matter. I couldn't waste time yearning after lost love. I had to concentrate on helping Woody. For the next three blocks, I forced myself to focus on how I was going to bluff my way past Gerry.

But Gerry didn't buy my act. He greeted me coldly and he didn't warm up when I told him I'd be stuck in Denmark for another couple of days. If anything, his expression grew more guarded.

Faking casualness, I added that I'd given more thought to his suggestion that the murdered biker was linked to our project. "Maybe we shouldn't be so quick to dismiss that idea."

He folded his hands protectively over the manila folder in front of him. "I didn't dismiss it."

I recognized the file and I recalled it held a reference to the Hells Angels. I waited for Gerry to fill me in. When he didn't continue, I said, "You want to expand on that thought?"

He shook his head and bent over the papers on his desk.

"Gerry," I said, my tone sharp. "One guy's dead. If you're planning to contact anyone, you better tell me who. So we'll know where to search for *your* body."

He gave me a hard look. "Last night you said you were quitting my project. 'So-long-Gerry-it's-been-real.' "

"Not quitting," I said. "Called home."

He went on as though I hadn't spoken. "Today you postpone your departure. Suddenly see a link between my project and this murder. And you don't give me fuck-all for a reason."

"A hunch," I began.

"You want me to tell you stuff, you have to be up front with me. Not this 'hunch' shit." His eyes narrowed. "You and Bella go visit someone else last night?"

Gerry was searching for leads and he suspected I was keeping one from him. I could hear the affront in his voice. He'd trusted me and I was letting him down. I wanted to tell him what Bella had told me. Then he'd know for certain that interest in the missing Stingers had brought the biker to my flat. It was significant information and he'd make good use of it. But as soon as Gerry started investigating the biker-missile connection, he'd spook Bella's source in the Bandidos motorcycle club. I couldn't let him do that.

Of course, I could ask him to delay. But he could calculate the odds as well as Bella could. He'd put our near hopeless attempt to find Woody's father on one side of the scale. Balanced against it would be a breakthrough that could move his project dramatically forward—if he acted swiftly. And on that side, too, would go his overblown desire to protect me. He wouldn't approve my compromising myself with the cops, not even to help my best friend.

Gerry might well plunge forward at Bella's—and Woody's—expense, with a cockeyed idea of saving me from myself. Our mutual affection was a hazard in this situation. Much as I wanted to, I couldn't tell him what I'd learned from Bella. "I'm still working things out," I said. "I'll have a better handle on things by tomorrow night."

"Tomorrow night," he repeated. "And you won't explain that timing, either."

I didn't answer.

He bent back over his papers. His bald spot glistened under the fluorescent light. "I'm leaving in an hour. I'll be out of town most of today. Maybe tomorrow, too. If you're ready to be straight with me by tomorrow night, fine. Meet me here at five o'clock. You talk. So will I."

"Okay," I said.

He glanced up. "If Markham shows up while I'm gone, you brief him in to the project."

"Markham?" I frowned. "He's not due till Monday."

"Hear he's running ahead of schedule." Gerry tapped his pencil on the desktop. "You can do that much for me, can't you?"

"Gerry," I said, "I'm being as straight with you as I can be."

"Yeah, well maybe I am, too." His eyes went back to his papers.

I waited another few seconds in silence, then left his office. As soon as I was through the door, I slumped against the wall.

It wouldn't take Gerry long to deduce that Bella and I had talked only to each other. He'd realize she'd told me something connecting the dead biker to his project. I had to find a way to cover my tracks fast. But the inside of my head felt as though it were filled with soggy cotton batting. I'd slept fewer than twelve hours in the past two days, missed most of my meals. I needed a caffeine transfusion. Immediately. I stumbled toward the elevator.

By the time I reached it, I smelled bitter European coffee over-laid with the mingled odors of chocolate and freshly baked bread. It was the spoor of puff pastry wafting up the shaft from the basement cafeteria. I punched the DOWN button, my eyes on the floor indica-tor. It was early, not yet seven-thirty, and I was so sure the car would be empty, I stepped through the doors before they were fully open.

"Casey," said the man inside. His voice was as rich as the break-fast I'd been anticipating.

Colonel Andrew Markham had arrived.

And I was having trouble breathing.

8 WARMTH SPREAD THROUGH ME. I STEPPED BACK, STOPPING THE doors from closing. Self-preservation. I'd have suffocated if I'd been shut inside. I moved back farther, into the hallway.

Andy followed me off the elevator. The doors closed behind him. "Casey," he said again. He rubbed a hand over his hair. The brown strands were peppered with gray.

I swallowed. "Hi, Andy." My voice sounded pleasant enough. It was huskier than usual, but he wouldn't know that.

He grinned. Then sighed and shook his head. "I had a whole speech ready. What I was going to say when I saw you. Now, I see you. And hell if I can remember one word."

I wanted to look away from him, but I couldn't. He was fifty-one, leaner than he had been in San Sal. Less beer? More authority, certainly. I remembered how he used to redden when he got worked up over something. This time, I was the only one blushing. And my heart was fluttering in my chest as if I were a teenager again. He'd gotten older. I'd zoomed into the adolescentsphere.

He laughed. "Okay, let's start this over." His right arm came toward me, hand extended. "Good to see you again."

My right hand did its job, automatically reaching out to take his. My voice worked too, uttering the words I'd planned. "Glad to have you on board—"

The touch of his fingers closed my throat and set off a charge of feeling that jolted me. I yanked my hand free but I got no relief. My eyes stayed locked to his. They were the seawater color of a polar ocean, the pallid shade made less chill by strong emotion. He said something, too soft for me to hear. Without thinking, I inclined my head toward his.

"Damn," he said. "You look so good."

I couldn't move, I couldn't answer, I couldn't do anything.

The elevator chime broke the spell. The door opened to decant a cheerful Marine. I pushed past him and into the empty car. "Got to go," I said to Andy. I pressed the button for the basement level.

He put a hand on the door to stop it closing. "I was counting on you to fill me in," he said. "I'm in a hurry to get up to speed on this project."

I faked a grin. "Gerry will get you started."

"You won't be joining us?"

"Talk to Gerry first," I croaked. "He's leaving in an hour. I'll take over after that."

He moved his hand and the doors whispered shut. I was alone in a softly lit cubicle strongly scented with lemon wax. The car began to drop down the shaft and I prayed I wouldn't fall into a swoon on the dove-gray carpet.

When I talked about my life as a foreign service officer, I began with Warsaw. Warsaw was where I got started in my professional specialty, counterterrorism. And Warsaw was where I met Stefan Krajewski. Those two events were the story, at least when I was doing the telling.

But before I'd gone to Warsaw, I served in San Salvador. I didn't like talking about Salvador. And Andy Markham was the reason.

I was a vice-consul assigned to the embassy's nonimmigrant visa section. I spent my workdays interviewing Salvadorans desperate for visas to travel to the U.S. All claimed they'd return to El Salvador after a brief visit to America. They told similar stories of their planned vacations, presented identical documents showing they owned real estate and had modest bank accounts. At first, I let some of those questionable cases convince me. But the visas I granted got their holders only as far as an INS officer. The Salvadorans were sent home, minus whatever they'd spent for airfare. INS sent me notices, pointing out my errors and warning me about fraud. My boss advised me to improve my performance.

I got it down to a routine after a while. I politely let them tell me their lies before I recited my speech. *"Lo siento mucho. Si fuera posible, lo haría, pero la ley no me lo permite."* I'm very sorry. If it were possible, I would do it, but the law does not permit me.

I was adrift in the bottomless sea of the past subjunctive tense, powerless to rescue anyone. My turnaround pleased my boss, but I hated doing visas.

Major Andrew Markham worked in the headquarters office for the U.S. military group providing training to the Army of El Salvador. Andy had a knack for working with men. He established rapport effortlessly, as if language and culture weren't barriers between him and the unsavory Salvadoran officers.

He spent his days mingling with the men who made my visa applicants anxious to leave. And, like me, Andy went straight from work to the Marine Bar. Drowning our mutual distaste for our jobs, we slowly became drinking buddies. Nothing romantic in that—not at first. But I found myself liking Andy more than I wanted to. He had family safe-havened in the U.S. A man with a wife and two daughters wasn't a man I'd fool around with—no matter how appealing he was.

I didn't realize he was falling in love with me, too.

I found out.

We both wanted to resist the feelings that were drawing us together. Our romance had a jerky stop-and-go rhythm that might have saved us if only our separate "stops" had been synchronized as well as that final headlong and heedless "go." Being in Salvador was part of it. It's easy to lose yourself in the steamy heat of a tropical war zone.

His tour ended before mine. He returned to the U.S. I thought he'd tell his wife about me. He did, but the conversation went differently than I expected. She forgave him, he wrote in the letter I got seven days after he left. For the sake of their daughters, she was taking him back. For that same reason, he was going. He promised her he'd end it with me. And so he did.

I knew Andy loved me. I learned that he loved his kids more. Why was I so surprised by that? Wasn't that how fathers were supposed to feel? Hadn't my father always put my needs ahead of his own?

I couldn't fault Andy for the choice he made. I blamed him only for knowing his heart so poorly. And for leaving a scar on mine.

Discovering that Andy could walk away from me and never look back—that shocked me. It woke me up, too. What had I been doing, messing around in someone else's family life? When I remembered Salvador, I felt a queasy mix of longing and shame. One of life's nastier tricks, picking that old mistake out of my past and dragging it forward into my present. It wasn't a mistake I'd make twice.

When I'd first realized I could end up working with Andy again, I'd resolved that any encounters between us would be impersonal and cool. Unfortunately, Bella had been right. I still cared for Andy. More than I'd realized. I didn't feel at all cool toward him. And my traitorous body wasn't going to let me fake it.

The chime sounded as the elevator stopped at the main floor. The doors slid open. I blinked. Framed before me was the amazon who served as embassy legal attaché.

I'd had enough aggravation for the day. I didn't need a hovering cop. I punched the CLOSE button.

Dawna Shepherd stuck her hand in the door to keep it open. She was smartly dressed in a navy blazer over a khaki skirt, both made from precisely the right amount of wrinkleproof fabric. No baggy clothing obscured the dazzling physical fitness of this six-foot-three, thirty-year-old FBI special agent assigned to overseas duty. "I was hunting for you," she said. Her West Texas accent turned "hunting" to "huntin'."

She stepped into the car and waved a document in front of me as if she were flashing her shield at a suspect. "The biker homicide's in my jurisdiction. I'll be taking over."

"Takin' over what?" I stabbed the button again. "You want to play murder suspect for a while?"

She smiled affably, unmadeup lips parting to show even teeth. "Blixenstjerne isn't saying you're a suspect. Only that you weren't forthcoming with him. I told him you might be more comfortable talking to me."

Comfortable talking to the FBI? She had to be kidding. "I gave the cops a complete statement last night," I said, skirting the truth. "I've nothing to add."

She studied me. Her collar-length hair was permed and spiraled, kinked blond tresses radiating out in a cloud around her head. The only flaw in her features was an indentation on the end of her nose that made it appear mashed-in. The doors slid open at the basement level. Dawna said, "Let's get some coffee, I'll fill you in on the investigation." She started down the hall toward the cafeteria. She had a masculine stride that moved her torso in unison with her hips.

Of course I went after her. I couldn't resist her offer of more information. I caught up with her at the cafeteria entrance. "What do you mean, this homicide falls into your jurisdiction?" I asked.

"The bureau assists the Danish authorities on biker matters." The tone of her voice was as precisely official as her outfit.

"Run that by me again," I said. "The Danish police called in the FBI because a biker was killed in an American's flat?"

"That you're American is only incidental to FBI involvement," she said. " 'Biker' is the operative word."

"What's the bureau got to do with a local biker gang?" I asked.

"This isn't merely a local gang," she said huffily. "The Bandidos is one of the five biggest One-Percent Clubs in the world."

"One percent?" I repeated, puzzled.

"Not sanctioned by the American Motorcycle Association," she said impatiently. " 'Outlaw' in layman's terms."

"I understand 'big' and 'outlaw,' " I said. "But why's the FBI interested in what the Bandidos do in Denmark?"

She sighed. But her exasperation was overlaid with eagerness. She liked explaining why her job was crucial. "The bureau's been following biker activity for years, worldwide. Hells Angels are the major force—twelve hundred members, eighty-five chapters in seventeen countries. They want international domination. Montreal's been a major battlefield, 'Les Hells' up against Canadian organized crime."

"Who's winning?" I asked.

"In Montreal the syndicate's still hanging on," she said. "But in Europe, biker gangs have taken over a significant segment of criminal activity. They specialize in assaults, assassinations, and of course, narcotics."

Narcotics. She wasn't talking about a bunch of guys getting high together. I said, "What, Bikers control the drug trade?"

"Most of it. The Hells Angels held the biker monopoly in Europe for years. Since 1994, they've been challenged by the Bandidos—violently challenged. We warned the Danish authorities that the conflict was moving in this direction. The National Police agreed with us. But we couldn't convince the local cops." She made a derisive noise. "They had *rockers* all rigged out in Kevlar, packing grenades and antitank weapons, and they were still saying, 'No, won't happen here.' "

I wondered if Bella knew that Danish bikers wore body armor and carried grenades. I said, "I take it the local cops were wrong."

"The Bandidos escalated things more swiftly than the bureau predicted."

"What happened?" I asked.

"The Bandidos' European headquarters were in Marseilles, but France got too hot for them. Their leader was a Dane and he thought they'd be better off here. In August of 1995, two hundred Bandidos showed up in Stenløse to check out their new home."

Stenløse. Where Bella planned to travel tomorrow. "You're saying that the European headquarters for the Bandidos moved to Stenløse?" I asked.

"Officially, a little farther north in Frederikssund. All the leaders of the Bandidos are there. It's a magnet for every violent crazy wanting to move up in the hierarchy. They had a full-scale gang war going with the Hells Angels through most of 1997. The Danes called it *rockerkrig*. There's supposed to be a truce in effect now, but the situation is volatile. It's liable to flare up at any time."

"I've read a few reports of bikers in Scandinavia," I said. "I didn't realize the violence had reached that level. Biker war."

"It didn't get much play in the U.S. media." She leaned toward me. "But the murder in your flat is the lead story today. Every biker killing is front page news."

"You don't get your information from Danish newspapers," I said. She'd made no secret of the fact she could neither read nor speak the language.

"Of course not," she said. "I told you, the bureau is very interested in bikers. We offered our assistance to the Danes. In 1996, the National Police accepted."

I said, "That's why we have two legatts in Copenhagen, you and Charles Townsend?"

"Right. One position for the regular guy. That's Chuck. A second slot for the biker expert. I took over that job the first of this month."

I said, "So you know this stuff?"

"I know it."

"And you and Blixenstjerne think the murder in my flat was renewal of a turf battle, Bandidos against the Hells Angels?"

"That's the obvious explanation." She drew herself up, maximizing her six-inch advantage over me. The color of her eyes changed from sky blue to royal, as though she'd sharpened her focus. "And I agree with Blixenstjerne. *You* know more about this murder than you're saying." She tapped my shoulder with the folded document. "You're going to tell me."

I shivered. I couldn't help it. I was tough. But I'd seen how the arrest-hungry FBI savaged innocent suspects. And I wasn't all that innocent.

9   "Whoa, girl," I said. "Danes won't let you use the rubber hose on me."

She gave me an injured look. "I didn't say I was going to 'make' you talk. I figured if I gave you some background, maybe you'd come up with something helpful. Something you didn't think of when you were talking to Blixenstjerne."

Friendly words in that pleasant accent. But I'd watched her grow taller, seen the gleam come into her eyes. She figured she could get what she wanted from me.

I had to risk it. For Bella's sake, I needed Dawna's expertise on bikers and her inside knowledge of the cops' case. I said, "Guess I'm ready for that coffee."

She waved her arm toward the steam table. "Go ahead. I'm buying."

By the time I got through the line with my coffee, I'd added two pieces of pastry and a bowl of *øllebrød*. I topped the hot porridge with whipped cream.

"You must be hungry." Dawna had a fruit plate and a packet of Ry Krisp.

"Missed a few meals yesterday," I said.

She pointed at the bowl in front of me. "You like that stuff?"

"Love it." It took Vikings to imagine a breakfast treat made from crumbled day-old *rugbrød* and nonalcoholic beer. Danish mothers served it to cranky children for the morning meal. The combination of nutty grain, tangy brew, and sweet cream always improved my mood. I swallowed three heaping spoonfuls before I spoke again.

"You said this biker violence peaked more than two years ago," I said. "Where are we today?"

"In 1996 and '97 the incidents followed the same pattern. Hells Angels assassinated a Bandido. Bandidos attacked a Hells Angel. The Danes kept throwing bad guys into jail. *Rockers* overwhelmed the population in the four maximum-security prisons. The thing to do if you were in jail was join one of the biker gangs for protection. Pressure kept building toward larger-scale violence. The cops managed to get a lid on it in late '97. But I don't count on the imposed truce lasting much longer. Both clubs keep getting bigger, stronger, and more heavily armed. They've got nine-millimeter pistols, revolvers, automatic rifles, submachine guns, plastic explosive, grenade-launchers."

Weapons were the link between me and the dead biker. Had Dawna figured that out? Chary, I asked, "What do you know about the guy they found in my place?"

She looked at the ceiling as if she were reading off a police report. She recited a name that sounded like "ol' banjo molar."

I frowned. Bella had told me the dead biker called himself Bjørn. "What did you say?" I asked Dawna.

She recited the three words slowly and I realized she was sounding out "Ole Bjørn Møller."

"Danes would pronounce that UH-LEE Bee-YORN MUL-ler," I said.

"Ole Bjørn Møller," she repeated impatiently. "Born 1974 in Odense. Educated Vestfyns Gymnasium. Apprenticed as a mechanic. Dropped that to pursue 'artistic interests,' whatever that means. Hooked up with the Bandidos. No rap sheet, he'd never been picked up for anything."

At least he wasn't a notorious arms dealer. My tension eased a notch. I shook my head. "Nothing in his history points to me."

"No." She leaned over, intent. "But his murder has to be connected to the project you're working on."

"I don't see how," I said. "We don't have a shred of evidence linking outlaw bikers to Stinger missiles."

"I saw his hand. No mistaking those letters. Somebody gave him your name. He tracked you down."

She was inches from the truth. "You've got something there," I said, lounging back in my chair. "Somebody gave him my name. But maybe that was a mistake. Ever think maybe it was you he wanted?" Testing her. How seriously did Dawna take herself?

Very. Her blush told it all.

She said, "The idea occurred to me. We're both tall blond American women and we arrived at the same time. Biker leadership wouldn't make that mistake, but the thugs who do the dirty work aren't too bright."

Stretching logic, but not impossible. "Okay," I said. "Suppose this Bjørn was looking for you. Would that be any reason to kill him?"

"If someone wanted to send me a message."

She lost me, logic snapping with a loud twang in my brain. "Someone killed Bjørn to warn you off?"

She smiled broadly. Her teeth were too perfect, I decided. They had to be capped. She said, "It's not impossible. I've got a reputation, back home. Word gets around. I've had a couple of threats already."

A case of mistaken identity. As an explanation, I loved it. A fondness that wasn't shared by the police, or they'd have cut me loose. I said, "You try this one on Blixenstjerne yet?"

"He found the idea plausible." A muscle jumped in her cheek. Hurriedly, she added, "He still has an eye on you."

Blixenstjerne had his eye *only* on me, that was my guess. He was less impressed by Dawna than she implied. Or maybe he gave the biker thugs more credit than she did. I held out my hands palms up. "All I want is to get out of Denmark. If I had anything to tell him that would accomplish that, believe me, I'd pass it on."

"I believe you," she said, but neither her tone nor her expression matched the words. "Why don't you and I go through the whole thing again, see if we can come up with something to get him off your back?"

Dawna wasn't getting anything else out of me. "No point," I said. "I can't help. So what's your next move?"

She shrugged. "Well, I'll go to the funeral tomorrow, see what I can pick up."

All my senses went on alert. "Bjørn's funeral is tomorrow?"

"His mother wants him in the ground fast. Doesn't want his gang to make a spectacle out of the burial like they've done in the past. She's got a mortician picking up the body today. Plans to have the service Friday morning."

Tomorrow morning. Was Bella going to walk into a biker funeral? I pictured her in a tattoo parlor surrounded by a bunch of grieving Bandidos with hot needles. My skin prickled, as though I

were the one being jabbed. "They burying him in Frederikssund?"
I named the town Dawna had identified as Bandido headquarters.

"Not on Sjælland," Dawna said, using the Danish name for the
island where Copenhagen was situated. "Funeral will take place in
some one-horse town on Fyn. They're planting him in the family
plot, right beside his dad."

I let my breath out in a silent sigh. Fyn was the next island
west. A nice distance from where Bella would be.

"Blixenstjerne going to the funeral, too?" I kept my voice casual.

"He'll be there," she said.

Good. Far from Bella. I said, "And he invited you along to help
him check for any suspicious mourners."

She snapped a piece of Ry Krisp in two. "Not specifically."

Not at all. That much was clear from the irritation in her voice.
Maybe the National Police had requested assistance from the FBI,
but the Copenhagen homicide squad wasn't eager for help from
Dawna. I said, "But you're going anyway."

"I figure I need to be there. It's happening so fast, the crowd
will be small. I'll get a real clear idea of who in the gang was close
to the victim." She took a bite of cracker, chewed slowly before she
resumed talking. "Only problem is, not too many people out in the
sticks speak English. I want to talk to any of the family, old friends,
people like that, I'll need a translator." She met my eyes. "You
want to come along, help me out?"

I felt a sudden rush of excitement. I wanted to go. And not only
because Fyn was an ideal destination to draw the cops away from
Bella. My surge of interest was more powerful than that, so strong
I knew I had to hide it. Casually, I shrugged. "I've got nothing
better to do."

"Well, great," she said, an appreciative grin on her face. "I'll
pick you up tomorrow morning at six. You spending the night at
your flat?"

"I don't know if the police have finished—"

"Blixenstjerne told his boys to remove the seal. They're done
with it."

"Done," I repeated. I wondered if they'd found anything inside
the piano. Not a question I could safely ask Dawna. Instead, I said,
"I need to do something about the mess."

"All taken care of," Dawna said. "I told the admin officer to
send over a clean-up crew."

She was being too take-charge for my comfort. Cautiously, I said, "Very considerate of you."

She waved her hand dismissively. "We'll get a security service to install an alarm system."

Dawna was putting new wiring in my flat? Was I supposed to feel more secure surrounded by FBI bugs? "Don't bother," I said. "I'll be gone in another day."

"Maybe not," she said. "And you'll sure sleep better tonight."

I watched her back as she strode away from me. Her walk had more spring in it. She turned the corner and I heard a self-satisfied grunt.

I picked up a piece of Danish. Put it down again. I wasn't hungry anymore. Dawna was too pleased with herself. What mistake had I made?

Bella dropped into the chair across from me. "I was waiting for Dawna to leave. Quite a shock, seeing you making nice with the FeeBees."

"I was getting the lowdown on *rockerkrig*," I said. "Sounds like you'll be walking into international criminal headquarters."

"Bikers are the major threat to civilization as we know it." She laughed. "Dawna talks like that. I can handle it."

I kept my voice low. "They're burying Bjørn on Fyn tomorrow. The Bandidos will probably send a small contingent. Let's hope the guy you're looking for isn't one of them."

"Not likely," she said softly. "Bjørn wasn't tight with this guy."

"I'm going to the funeral with Dawna."

"Good move. All the cops will be looking your way. Nobody'll notice me, slipping into Tattoo Station."

I looked at her. The new lightness in her tone matched her bearing. As if Woody were halfway to a cure.

Were the chances of finding Wlodek Wojcik any better than twenty thousand to one? "I can get that blood test this afternoon," I said hesitantly.

The skin on Bella's face stiffened, making her amiable expression appear pasted-on. In my offer, she'd heard my despair for Woody—an echo of the hopelessness she was fighting. When she spoke, the strain was back in her voice. "I'll set it up." Her eyes were suddenly shiny and she inhaled a ragged breath, visibly struggling for self-control.

I had to help her. I blurted out the first thing I thought of that might divert her. "Colonel Markham's arrived three days ahead of schedule."

"I know." I heard relief in the two words. A safe topic and one she was eager to discuss. "Gerry's been taking him around, doing introductions." She watched me closely.

I kept my voice neutral. "Soon as I get done here, I'm supposed to brief him in to the project."

Bella's chair squeaked as she shifted position, leaning toward me conspiratorially. "I got to admit, I didn't expect your old boy-friend to be *that* type."

"What type?" I asked, surprised.

"A guy who looks and acts like a Boy Scout." She faked a shudder. "I never trust that type."

"I met the last guy you trusted." I imitated her shudder. "A shaved head and a nose ring aren't always indicators of good character."

"He had some nice qualities. Never boring, that's for sure." She managed a laugh. "You can't say that about your pal Andy. You know I hate to criticize your taste in men—"

"Oh, right. Same way you hate drinking beer."

"Be fair. Remember, I said only good things about that Marine security guard you dated in Warsaw."

I hooted. "That was fourteen years ago. Maybe it's time for you to lighten up on me."

She shrugged. "I'd like to. But this Andy—I'm sorry, but look-ing at him puts me to sleep. He's that uninteresting. I can't imagine what you ever saw in him."

I sighed and stared down at my coffee cup. "He could dance."

"Speak up," Bella said. "Sounded like you said 'he could dance.' "

"I did. He could." I looked at her. "Dance. Dancing with Andy . . ." My voice ran down, I couldn't help it.

"You liar," Bella said accusingly. "You claimed you had no warm feelings for him."

"I don't." As soon as the two words left my mouth, I knew I'd spoken them too forcefully.

Bella shook her head mournfully, her perfect rendering of a mother disappointed by a deceitful child. "I hope you handled the Wonder FeeBee better than you're handling me."

I sat straighter in my chair. "You think Dawna needs handling?"

"I've seen her play," Bella said. "Team captain, high scorer, tops in rebounds. Could've turned pro, she was that good."

"She played basketball?"

"You can't tell by looking at that nose? Must have broken it five times. God knows what hit the end of it." She held her fist like a microphone, raised her voice to imitate a sports announcer. "Welcome to the knock-down, drag-out, high-stakes world of iron-fisted college women's basketball." She stood and her voice returned to normal. "I saw Dawna in the NCAA playoffs. When she went for the ball, you'd swear she intended to restructure the other girl's cheekbone with her elbow. Half the opposing team was scared to get on the court with her. I'll say she needs special handling."

I stayed at the table after Bella left, picking up crumbs left from the pastry, pondering what I'd learned about Dawna Shepherd. Her sports background worried me. I knew that Title IX required educational institutions to treat men and women the same. As soon as the 1972 gender-equity law went into effect, college coaches of women players made it their weapon of choice for equalizing athletic programs. They sued for better contracts and facilities. They demanded charter buses and media exposure and prime practice times. And they pushed the women to perform like men. They coached them in aggression.

Their harsh instructions weren't written in any manual but the gist was clear from any close reading of the sports pages. You want to win a national title, you have to knock people around and get over feeling bad about causing pain. Use your elbows cleverly so you don't foul out. Protect yourself, but guard the ball and don't cry if you get hurt. Be just as rough with your teammates as you are with your opponents. Because if you practice timid, you'll play timid. And the team doesn't want timid.

I'd cooperated with FBI agents before. But I'd never worked with one whose history was so foreign to my own. Loyalty—not competition—was my guiding principle. And that made it hard for me to guess what Dawna was really after.

She'd said that she was taking over the biker homicide investigation. To impress the bureau and the Danish cops, she wanted to play a key role in solving the case. So why was she concentrating on me? Her interest in my activities made me uneasy. She'd probed hard, as if she were looking for an intriguing angle that would win her attention back in Washington. I shoved scraps of Danish around my plate as I replayed my conversation with her.

I'd sat and absorbed a lot of information about *rockerkrig*. I hadn't told her a thing.

So what had I done to make her so happy?

I rearranged the salt and pepper shakers.

The question that the police had asked me over and over was why Bjørn had come looking for me. I'd had no answer—until Bella explained that she'd given my name to Bjørn. But I hadn't told Dawna that.

She'd suggested that Bjørn's murderer had been trying to tell *her* to butt out of *rocker* business. She'd been testing me, hoping I'd be unable to resist correcting her. As if I'd blurt out, *He wanted ME, Dawna, not YOU.* I'd avoided that obvious trap only to fall into another one.

I shouldn't have agreed to translate for Dawna. I'd wanted her to believe that I was asking questions about the dead biker only because he was killed in my flat. I'd claimed that no evidence tied his murder to my efforts to recover the missing Stinger missiles. But I'd be in Denmark for only two more days. A truly professional counterterrorist analyst would have spent all that time wrapping up her part in the Stinger missile project. When I grabbed the chance to attend Ole Bjørn Møller's funeral, I'd shown exactly where my professional interest lay.

Dawna had set out her decoy and I'd gone after it. She'd be watching me closely, alert for any clues to the nature and extent of the dead man's connection to the missile recovery project. If I wanted to protect Bella, my best bet was to stay as far from Dawna as I could. Not spend eight hours with her at a funeral.

But I didn't see any better way out of the box I'd gotten myself into. Tomorrow night I planned to tell the police precisely what Dawna had inferred—that Bjørn had sought me out because he knew something about the missiles. The police would be curious to know how I'd arrived at that conclusion. I needed a rock-solid explanation, one that tied up all the loose ends, showed I had nothing further to contribute, and didn't mention Bella. If I spent time near Bjørn's friends and relatives, I'd be able to tailor the perfect cover story. Nobody could argue with me if I said, *I learned it at the funeral.*

I lined up the cream pitcher and the sugar bowl behind the salt and pepper.

No, I had to go with Dawna tomorrow. But I couldn't let my curiosity about this case ruin my concentration. I had to leave the murder investigation to the police, work only on getting myself out of Denmark. Shouldn't be hard to handle Dawna, so long as I played my game, not hers.

I pushed myself away from the table.

Time to go upstairs. Time to play it cool with Andy Markham. *That* was going to be hard.

10 WHEN THE ELEVATOR DOORS OPENED ON THE EMBASSY'S TOP floor, I found myself facing Gerry. As I stepped off the car, he brushed past me into it, his hand already extended toward the panel of buttons.

"What's up?" I asked.

He blinked, as if he'd been too preoccupied to recognize me before he heard my voice. When he spoke it was in the genial-but-harassed tone he often took with me. I heard no hint of our earlier friction. "Markham's waiting for you." He pressed the G button. "Can't talk now. I've got to make some calls. Check my notes, it's all there." The door slid shut.

I was relieved that Gerry was no longer acting as if I'd betrayed him. I wondered who he was rushing to consult. But I wasn't going to linger in our tiny office, studying the files. I didn't want to be trapped in that cramped space with Andy. He'd left me, long ago. I couldn't let him guess that I'd never gotten over him.

I paused in the station chief's office to send a secure E-mail to Renton Funke. I kept my message terse. I'd been delayed again. I'd be unable to leave Copenhagen before Friday night. Then I hurried down the hall to collect Andy. I didn't want to be in the embassy when Renton phoned, as I knew he would. I didn't need him to tell me the price I'd have to pay for this extra day in Denmark.

I tapped in the combination on the pad beside my office door and opened it. Andy looked up from the file he was studying and a grin spread slowly over his face. "So," he said, "you ready to get into this with me?"

Absurdly, I heard romantic promise in the question. Andy and I had gotten into a lot of things, before. I wanted to kick myself for being a sentimental fool. Instead, I held tightly to the door so it wouldn't close and said, "You bet. But not here. I've got some Danes you need to meet at *Kastellet*."

He frowned. "Maybe I should have a little more background first. Go over these files with you. Just the two of us."

The last phrase gave me goosebumps. No, I couldn't risk being alone with Andy. I shook my head. "Best place to start is by talking with Birger and Stig."

He stood reluctantly and I heard a faint undertone of disappointment in his voice. "You lead the way."

Which I did. As we walked along Dag Hammarskjölds Allé, I played tour guide, chattering about the morning of April 9, 1940, when the invading German army surreptitiously disembarked from a coal freighter and blasted through *Kastellet*'s front gate. Not the high point of Danish history but I was scrambling to evade my own.

I was worried about what I'd do with Andy after I exhausted the possibilities for diversion at the Danish Defense Intelligence Service. Andy needed to hear what Birger and Stig had been doing, but I doubted I could stretch things out for thirty minutes. The two analysts were younger than Andy, lower in rank, unsure of their English, more comfortable with computers than with people.

But Andy was as good with other men as I remembered. He made it look easy, as if bonding was always instantaneous between career soldiers from NATO allies. Within fifteen minutes I was standing silently on the fringes while the three men acted like they'd been born into the same wolf pack, chasing identical scents, howling over shared jokes. I'd seen Andy do similar things in Salvador, and not only with soldiers. His magic worked equally well on his sixty-year-old gardener and the brewmaster who led the brewery tour.

The planned one-hour briefing stretched into three. Andy's appetite for knowledge was voracious and he digested new information quickly. He kept a clipboard handy, jotting notes on a yellow pad, the black strokes of his felt-tip pen filling ten pages. His questions became increasingly focused and stimulated Stig and Birger into giving him more detailed and complex answers. They kept on talking right through lunch in the cafeteria. Later, I introduced Andy to five other people I knew and Andy quizzed each one.

At three o'clock, he told me that he had enough background.

He wanted to go through our files and fit all the pieces together. He politely demanded we return to the embassy. I had to take him there. If I stalled longer, he'd realize why: I was afraid to be alone with him. That was a truth I wanted to keep to myself. I kept up a lively patter as we headed back to the embassy.

Andy listened as attentively to me as he had to everyone else and he guffawed at my jokes. I'd forgotten that we both enjoyed our humor sly and dry. As we passed Østerport Station, he suddenly remembered a long story making the rounds in Washington that he was sure I'd love. He was right, of course, and I was the one laughing out loud as we came off the elevator onto the embassy's fourth floor.

My hilarity ended when we reached the open door to the station chief's office. The unsmiling secretary called me in to accept a succinct cable from Renton, sent priority and in the clear for anyone interested to read—his way of putting the screws to me. Sam Baldwin was seriously displeased by my failure to report for task-force duty when summoned. If I wasn't on-site in Bangor by Saturday noon, eastern daylight time, Baldwin would file a complaint with the attorney general. If I still hadn't arrived twenty-four hours later, he'd officially demand my removal from the task force.

Renton had said that Baldwin would cut me no slack. Still, I hadn't expected such a swift and harsh reaction.

My shock must have shown on my face. "Is something wrong?" Andy asked diffidently.

I folded the cable in half and stuffed it in my purse. "A personnel issue," I said. "I'll take care of it."

He hesitated for a second, then said, "If there's anything I can do to help—"

I cut him off with a weary shake of my head. "It's just the usual bureaucratic bullshit."

"I know exactly how to handle that kind of personnel issue." The smile was back in his voice. "Let me buy you a beer after work?"

"No." My negative was abrupt enough to be insulting.

Andy's easy grin only widened. "You're turning down a beer? I never thought I'd live to see this day."

Embarrassed by how rude I'd sounded, I added, "I'm a wreck. I've had no sleep in the past two days. I start drinking now, I'll pass out."

"I think you could risk one beer." The smile had reached his eyes, brightening them like sunshine on the ocean. He was *twinkling* at me, the only man I'd ever met whose eyes actually did that. I knew what he was thinking behind that warm gaze. If I did pass out, it wouldn't be the first time he'd put me to bed.

We'd been friends before we became lovers. Dancing crazily to old rock and roll tunes, drinking too much, laughing too hard. *Enjoying the hell out of each other's company*, that was how the Marine corporal tending bar had once described us. Andy was usually better able to drive than I was. Though not always. I'd tucked him in more than once myself. But all that changed the night we fell into bed together.

Recalling our long-lost lighthearted booziness made me suddenly dizzy. Heat flamed on my cheeks and I picked up the phone, punching in the number for the admin section. Luckily, my flat was miraculously restored and ready for occupancy.

"No beer for me," I told Andy, firmly. "I'm going home to catch up on my sleep."

"The offer's open if you get thirsty later." His tone was friendly but I was sure he'd gauged the situation correctly. He knew I was running away from him.

And I didn't trust him not to chase after me. "Forget about beer," I said. "You'll need the whole night to get through those files." And then I was out of there, my cover blown and my dignity in tatters. I took a taxi to the *Rigshospital*. After I finished giving blood, I picked up a six-pack of *Elefant øl*, elephant beer, went to my flat and tried to knock myself out.

But three extra-strength brews weren't enough. At midnight, I jerked awake to see the red lights glowing in my newly installed security panel. I imagined the FBI microphones cleverly grafted to it. I felt as exposed as I had in Cold War Poland, someone eavesdropping on every noise I made.

The panel lights indicated nothing wrong. Cautious, I checked through the flat. The admin people had taken the piano away and the living room was spookily cavernous. Lurking beneath the scent of Pine-Sol was another odor I refused to identify. Nothing was out of place.

I managed to fall asleep quickly, but at two I woke again, the comforter tossed on the floor, the night air of Scandinavia caressing my skin. Despite its coolness, I was hot all over, still immersed in a dream of Andy and tropical nights and his sweat-slick body sliding over mine. I slept fitfully after that and finally gave up at five.

When Dawna arrived two hours later, I was wired on caffeine, ready to defend myself against the bruising interrogation I anticipated.

But Dawna ignored me and concentrated only on her driving. She raced across Sjælland, exploiting the diplomatic plates on her tomato-red Saab, her average speed thirty kilometers per hour above the limit. I asked a couple of questions about the official investigation, but she was so tight with her information, I stopped. I imagined her as a hard-charging basketball player who hated to turn over the ball. Now she was hoarding facts, trying to control this investigation in the same way she'd once dominated her chosen game. No matter. I didn't need Dawna's cooperation. The Danish police were the key to my future. Sam Baldwin wanted me in Bangor by tomorrow noon. I had to convince the cops to let me leave Denmark tonight. What I wanted from this excursion was a single moment I could point to and say, *Right then I realized why the dead man sought me out.*

The service dragged on and my moment didn't come. We spent a fruitless hour inside the stifling church, then moved outside to the adjacent cemetery. Dawna positioned the two of us against the hedgerow bordering the neat plots. The funeral party clustered near the coffin, twenty feet from me.

Gravel crunched beneath my shoes as I stretched taller to see past the two dozen people between me and the grave. Beyond it, backed by the sun-drenched wall of the church, were Blixenstjerne and Jespersen, so obviously vigilant policemen they might as well have come in uniform. Above me, the Danish flag stirred, its white cross gleaming in the harsh daylight. The faint breeze carried with it the sour odor of the pigs kept in the adjacent *præstegård*, the Lutheran pastor's working farm.

Hemp rasped against flesh and a pallbearer grunted, struggling to slow the casket's descent. The whitewashed lid disappeared into the ground, then the funeral spray of roses and baby's breath slid out of sight. Pine boards touched bottom with a creaking sigh as the box settled in the loose soil.

An answering sigh passed through the small crowd. Ole Bjørn Møller was at rest.

The pallbearers disentangled the two ropes from the coffin and stepped back to make room for the black-robed minister. His face was slick with sweat, the skin flushed to the color of beets above the circle of his white ruff.

69

I heard the click of the shutter on Dawna's .35mm camera. She'd taken at least two pictures of every member of the funeral party. Now she nodded toward the pallbearers and spoke softly to me. "Those six are Møller's running buddies."

I took in the leather pants and ankle boots. The men fit my image of bikers, beefy and bearded. No club emblems visible, but one vest had faded on the back, darker fabric showing where the figure of the man in the sombrero had been removed.

I shifted my weight from my left foot to my right. I had to make something happen in the next ten minutes, before the mourn-ers dispersed. I stretched, trying to work the stiffness out of my neck, my eyes on the activity near the burial plot.

A fleshless woman moved forward to stand at the head of the grave. The wind ruffled her inch-long hair, the silver strands gleam-ing like quartz crystals against the dominant iron-gray. She clutched a bouquet of roses in both hands, her ropy arms pressed against her ribs. I guessed she was in her midfifties. "Probably his mother," I said to Dawna.

"Gitte Møller," she whispered back.

The woman stepped forward and dropped her flowers into the pit. They made no sound. Neither did she. The minister moved closer, his mouth near her ear. She stayed completely still. He placed a tentative hand on her shoulder and she swayed, leaning into him.

Then one of the pallbearers was beside her, a mane of black hair sweeping down to the middle of his back. His gloved hand came up, brushed the bare skin of her elbow. She jerked away from him, as if jabbed by a cattle prod. Her hands dropped to her sides and her shoulders pulled back, though her gaze remained on the ground. She turned her back on the grave and walked toward us. Automatically, people moved aside to make way.

I eased forward, partially blocking the graveled pathway. Not nice, intruding on a mother's grief, but I had to make contact. I searched my mind for a Danish expression of sympathy. Alert, Dawna shifted closer to me, our combined silhouette too large to ignore.

Mrs. Møller slowed as she neared us. She raised her chin and I saw dark eyes glistening. Her glance took in the two of us. Her eyes widened and the blurred misery vanished from them, leaving two black pools, infinitely deep. The muscles in her upper arms tightened.

Her sudden tautness made me tense, too. For one terrible second I was sure she was going to strike me.

But she didn't. Instead she stared at me for a slow count of ten, her look of appraisal so acute I felt stripped, my shabby plan exposed. I stepped back and the pruned branches of the hedge stabbed at my spine. My throat closed over the words of condolence I was going to voice.

She brushed past, her straight back moving away from me. A pair of women fell in behind her, blocking my view.

I turned to ask Dawna if she'd seen the woman's reaction.

But Dawna had her eyes on the grave. "Get ready to translate," she said. "Somebody wants to talk to us."

I looked toward the burial plot again. The same pallbearer who'd approached Bjørn's mother strode toward us, his black mane flaring out behind him. He was in his late thirties, middle-aged for a biker. From the front, I saw that he'd cut his hair to a half-inch buzz on top, shorter on the sides. Neatly trimmed facial hair darkened his jawbone, the growth thickest on his lip and chin. The short-long hairstyle reminded me of Genghis Khan, a resemblance heightened by the man's slit-eyed grimness.

He stopped in front of us. Muscle bulked on his shoulders, the built-up physique of a weight lifter.

I began, "*God morgen—*"

He cut me off. "*Hvem er I?*" Who are you?

I ignored his use of the plural form. "Kathryn Collins," I said. "Here to pay my respects."

My words triggered a change in his expression, from irritation to sudden comprehension. He said, "Bjørn was killed in your flat." His English was without accent, the rootless argot spoken by educated Europeans. The muscles around his eyes relaxed and I saw they were as dark as those of Gitte Møller. He said, "I'm Ulf Møller. Glad you could come to my brother's funeral."

Bjørn's brother—another relative Dawna hadn't identified earlier. And one who was conveniently glad to see me. Before I could seize the opportunity, Dawna said, "I don't advise getting too friendly with this one."

He said, "Who are you?"

Dawna's hand went toward her jacket pocket as if she were reaching for her shield. She stopped herself. "Dawna Shepherd," she replied.

"Here on business?" His voice held a mocking note.

"You bet," Dawna said. "A lot of people expect your *rockerkrig* will get very hairy, very fast."

"*Rockerkrig?*" He mimicked her accent, turning the Danish into gibberish. "I don't follow you. You think some *rocker* killed my brother?"

"Like you don't know what's going on." She glanced over at me. "You believe this guy? Here's Bo Ulf Møller, chief spokesman for the Bandidos. His brother gets murdered and he's surprised we think the Hells Angels were involved."

The man in front of us was not only a relative of the dead man but also an important member of the Bandidos. If I could get him alone, I could claim him as the source of any story I concocted later. I stuck out my hand. "I'm sorry for your loss."

The gold chain on his right wrist jingled as his hand came toward me. His glove was fingerless and I had the odd sensation of soft leather against my palm, callused fingertips rough as an emery board across the back of my hand. He said, "Thank you for your sympathy."

I began, "I'd like to ask you—"

Dawna kept on talking as if neither he nor I had spoken. "Why do you doubt that the Hells Angels did it? He was *your* brother—who had a better motive to kill him?"

My stomach clenched. If Ulf gave an unhelpful answer in front of Dawna, I'd be back to square one, looking for a way to cover myself. My eyes skipped across the landscape, searching for an excuse to sidetrack the conversation. I saw Blixenstjerne and Jespersen huddled against the church wall, listening intently to a uniformed cop. I jerked at Dawna's arm. "Check out the boys from Copenhagen. Local constable is giving them an earful."

But my interruption didn't stop Ulf. "Why'd somebody kill him? Because he knew something. Something so important, an American woman would pay a lot to hear it." His eyes were on my face again. "You, Kathryn Collins. He thought he could sell you information."

I blinked, I was so surprised. His answer was letter-perfect. I'd gotten what I'd come for. I didn't want Bo Ulf Møller to say another syllable. I started talking, intent on shutting him up. "Interesting—"

But Dawna spoke louder. "That explains why he was in her flat. But why'd somebody kill him?"

Her question made my heart pound. Self-interest demanded that I get Dawna away from this man before he spoke one more word.

My feet didn't move.

My head tilted forward a half-inch, as if to close the distance between Ulf and me. Had the dead man been bringing me key evidence about the missing Stingers? Self-interest be damned. I had to hear Ulf's answer. Why had Ole Bjørn Møller been silenced forever?

"*You* know why he was killed," Ulf said to me.

His emphasis on the pronoun dismayed me. What I knew, I knew from Bella. I had to stop him from saying her name.

11

I OPENED MY MOUTH TO INTERRUPT, BUT ULF WAS QUICKER.

"He wasn't murdered for being my brother," he said to me. "No, somebody didn't want him to talk to you."

"Why?" Dawna asked sharply. "What was he going to tell her?"

My muscles tensed as if to ward off a blow. I had to take control of this conversation. "That's not FBI business," I said to Dawna. "Let me handle it."

Dawna's face twisted with outrage. She wasn't going to let me cut her out of any part of the investigation. She said, "Forget it, Collins—"

Ulf silenced her with a curt hand motion. "I'm happy to talk with *you*," he said to me. "But not in front of the police."

Dawna's body was rigid, physically holding her anger in check. She gestured toward the spot where the three Danish cops had been only moments before. "So talk," she said tightly. "The police are gone."

Ulf's eyes flicked to the far side of the cemetery, then back to Dawna. "In front of *any* police.

Dawna began, "I'm not leaving you two alone—"

"Ulf!" The voice of a woman reached us from beyond the churchyard's bordering hedge. "Ulf, *din mor kalder på dig.*" Your mother is calling for you.

Rescued by circumstance. He hadn't yet mentioned Bjørn's encounter with Bella. I should have breathed out a sigh of relief. But I didn't feel relieved. I felt robbed.

Ulf rested his hand on the ornate iron gate, fingertips caressing a finely etched leaf. "I must go."

"Give us another few minutes," Dawna said. "I'd like to hear more."

He gave her a long look, then turned to me. "I must see to my mother, now. If you want to talk, you can find me at my father's old workshop. I'll be there in ten minutes. Look for the Albani sign. And come alone." Pebbles rattled against stone as he turned on his heel and hurried down the steps leading to the street.

"I'll go check him out." I moved in the direction Ulf had gone.

Dawna grabbed my sleeve. "Not without me."

I pulled loose. "I don't think I should pass up this opportunity."

She shook her head. "I know how these guys operate. The Hells Angels killed his brother. The Bandidos are planning how they'll get even. Forget the truce. The whole war's heating up again. Danish *rockers* talk prettier than American bikers. But pretty words don't change anything. He's not going to give you anything useful."

"Maybe." Or maybe Dawna was badmouthing the interview because she'd been excluded. "Easy enough to find out by talking to him."

"You think that's a smart idea?" Dawna asked. "Going alone into some isolated building with a bunch of Bandidos?"

"Not isolated. Right on the main drag. We passed the Albani sign before we turned off to the church parking lot."

Dawna looked blank.

"The poster with the bottle," I said. "Albani's a beer."

Jespersen materialized on the far side of the churchyard. He raised his arm in a sweeping gesture, beckoning to us.

"Typical," Dawna said, straightening her blazer. "We get some points on the board, he wants in the game." I heard the satisfaction in her voice.

I edged toward the gate. "You saw all the cops on the street," I said. "I'll be fine. I'll meet you at your car in fifteen minutes."

"No way, Collins." Dawna reached for my sleeve again. "I'm not letting you run off on your own—"

She was interrupted by a shout from Jespersen. We both turned to see he'd cupped his hands around his mouth, megaphone style. I moved farther out of range, ran my hand along the ivylike design topping the gate. "Go on. See if *they've* picked up anything."

"That bullshit about jurisdiction. You don't fool me for a second." She looked at me hard, then turned her back and strode toward Jespersen.

I hurried down the steps. A uniformed policeman stood at the bottom and he spoke into his shoulder microphone as I passed. I dodged across the highway to the sidewalk on the opposite side. Pigs squealed from the pastor's pen, their odor suffocating. I turned left toward the giant, sweating bottle of Albani beer.

The poster was pasted to a weathered brick building which sat on the corner of the main highway and a narrow side street marked by a signpost reading SMEDESTRÆDE, Smith Lane. Up that street, parked in the shade of the building, were a half-dozen motorcycles, their chrome trim muted in the spreading shadow. A muscular teenager with a walkie-talkie stood guard beside them, his posture identical to that of the policeman I'd passed.

The brick building had a matching chimney, big enough for a forge. Another hint that this "old workshop" had once housed the village blacksmith.

Windows fronted the street, so dirt spattered that all I could see through them were male shapes and motioning arms. I smelled cigarette smoke and when I reached the open area between the smithy and the adjoining buildings, I heard a rumble of masculine voices. The other pallbearers were inside, probably drinking Albani beer provided free by the advertiser. A scruffy man blocked the door. He took one look at me and started muttering into his walkie-talkie, eyes on me as he talked.

I hesitated. I didn't want to walk in on a biker wake. And I had what I needed from Bo Ulf Møller.

Yet he might also have critical information for Gerry. I was no longer part of that project, but the investigative compulsion was too strong to ignore. Stronger than my fear. I wanted to hear more from Ulf. How to get to him?

A woodshed sat twenty feet back from the highway, the open-fronted structure connecting the workshop to a white-stuccoed house on my left. A graceful iron bell was bracketed to the wall beside the thick wooden door. I reached for the rope, but before I pulled it, the door swung open. Ulf stood in the doorway. He waved his walkie-talkie at the guard.

I realized my arrival had been announced.

"I hoped you'd make it," Ulf said. His lips turned up, more a smirk than a smile, and the glimmer of triumph in his eyes matched his tone. He waved a hand toward the workshop. "Let's go there."

"I can't stay," I said hurriedly. "You say your brother had information to sell me. What was it?"

He rubbed his chin. "Well, that would be the location of your missing Stinger missiles, wouldn't it?"

A question, not an answer. Looking to confirm some guesses he'd made. Good guesses, but nothing more. If he had hard information, he'd have put a price tag on it.

"You don't know what he was doing." My voice was as flat as my hopes. "Dawna's right. Your brother was a casualty in your damn war."

"No." He took a step toward me. "She's wrong. Hells Angels didn't do it. They didn't kill Bjørn." His conviction rang in every word.

"How do you know that?" I asked, but a truck roared past on the adjacent highway and drowned out my voice. The engine noise subsided, but it was followed by a rush of Danish from behind Ulf.

He turned and spoke into the dark room. *"Nej! Nej, Mor."* No, Mother.

Her retort was hurried and intense, interspersed with more negatives from Ulf. His voice faded out, leaving only hers. Then she stopped. Ulf turned back to me. "My mother will speak with you."

Hairs rose on my arms. I knew only one thing that she didn't. How her son looked, dead in my flat. "I can't—"

"You must," he said in a voice that allowed no argument. "Come in." He pushed the door open wide and I saw Gitte Møller.

"Alene," she said to Ulf, her voice harsh. Telling him she wanted to be alone with me. He opened his mouth. Shut it. He pushed past me, headed for the workshop.

Her gaze locked to mine. "Talking outdoors, I cannot like it," she said, putting the Danish phrase directly into accented English. "Please, come."

Her eyes defeated me, the pain in them so boundless I could not turn away. Reluctantly, I stepped over the threshold. The heavy door thudded shut. Indoors the air was ten degrees warmer, thick with the smell of potato water boiled over and burned to the stove. I followed Gitte Møller past an iron coatrack. The entry hall opened into an eight-by-eight office filled by a massive desk. A swinging door led from the office into the kitchen, and the two women I'd seen earlier stood at the sink, one washing dishes, the other drying.

Gitte pushed the kitchen door shut and motioned me through the office into the sitting room. I stopped beside an upright piano.

A pair of wooden pocket doors rumbled across the floor, sealing us off from the rest of the house, making the room darker. Nervous,

I glanced around. On top of the piano were a pair of candlesticks, handcrafted from iron to resemble vines twining upward, a miniature version of the design worked on top of the churchyard gate. An artist in iron had lived here, I realized. I reached out to touch a delicate leaf, its web of veins picked out in tiny lines.

Gitte let out a soft gust of air. "Please, sit."

Gingerly, I lowered myself to the piano bench.

My eyes were level with a shelf along the opposite wall. It held a pair of framed photographs. On the left was a family portrait with a younger Gitte, coal-black hair bristling around a serious face. Behind her, a sullen teenage Ulf and a beaming blond husband. All three only background for the baby in a christening gown.

The second picture was of a boy in white shirt and black pants, stiffly posed beside an undersized grand piano. The boy's close-cropped hair was blond and I guessed the picture was of Bjørn, taken at a recital when he was ten or eleven years old.

I shifted in my seat, felt the keyboard against my back. I imagined that younger Bjørn sitting on this same bench, practicing whatever tunes beginners play in Denmark.

Gitte sighed again, the sound unbearably sad. She reached over me to realign the candlestick I'd touched. "My son, he made this," she said.

The room was too small, oxygen too meager. I started to stand.

She put her hand on my shoulder. "You saw him. Please tell me."

I swallowed. "It must have happened very quickly. I'm certain he felt no pain."

Agitated, she shook her head. "*What* happened?"

Trapped. I moved, knocking sheet music to the floor. I bent to pick it up, recognized a jazz piece made famous by Dave Brubeck. "He sat at the piano in my flat," I said.

"Yes. He loves music." She took the sheet of paper from my fingers and replaced it on the holder.

I realized that Bjørn hadn't left anything inside the piano. No, he'd been unable to resist the lure of my landlord's magnificent Steinway. He'd sat on the stool and opened the cover with those deft fingers that turned iron into art. Played a riff with those clever hands. Let himself become engrossed in the sounds he was making, Bjørn dropped his guard and his killer seized the moment.

"Please," Gitte said plaintively.

I cleared my throat. "Someone struck him from behind with a heavy object."

Someone he trusted enough to turn his back on. Someone strong. Someone like his brother?

I saw the terror in Gitte's eyes. Was she asking herself that same question? But why would she fear that Ulf had killed Bjørn? Were the two men at odds?

I probed, gently.

"Do you know why Bjørn came to my flat?"

Awareness flickered across her face, then disappeared. She shook her head, mute.

"What was it?" I asked. "What was Bjørn going to tell me?"

Outside, traffic buzzed along the highway. Inside, a clock ticked. She spoke so softly I barely made out the words. "Americans," she whispered. "He said, 'Americans will pay a lot to know this.' " She paused, inhaled. "Killing your own. The worst thing."

The skin on her face was tinted blue. Blue light washed over the white plastered walls. The traffic noise outside was louder. I heard shouts. A motorcycle engine, kicking into life.

The pocket doors slammed open.

"Get out," Ulf said. "Take all your cop friends with you."

I peered through the lacy scrim over the windows. Parked outside was a local patrol car, blue light flashing. Pulled in behind it was Jespersen's BMW. Last in line and adjacent to the front door was Dawna's Saab.

"Collins." Dawna shouted through the open doorway. "You all right?"

I turned to Gitte. "Sorry," I began.

Dawna pounded into the room. "I see you've got your alibi all set," she said to Ulf. She prodded me toward the door. Outside, Jespersen stood six feet from the door with his back to us as if blocking entry to the half-dozen bikers milling beyond him. She said to me, "I told you the Bandidos were planning to get even."

Alibi. Get even. I stepped gingerly through the doorway. "The Bandidos attacked the Hells Angels?"

"Fifteen minutes ago," Dawna said.

I thought of Bella. I stopped and turned to face Dawna. "Where?"

"Big compound an hour from Copenhagen." She put a hand on each of my shoulders. A perfect circle of flushed skin reddened each of her cheeks and her eyes had a fierce, blue glow. "Got some bad news for you."

My throat closed. I waited, dread enveloping me.

"Your running buddy was killed in the crossfire."

Bella. I put my hand over my face.

Dawna shook me. "I know it's a shock. But you've got to help us, Collins. You've got to tell me: What was he doing down there?"

He?

I sucked in air. "Who are you talking about?"

"I told you. Your partner. Gerry Davis. What was he doing with the Hells Angels in Nakskov?"

12 GERRY WITH THE HELLS ANGELS? NOT LIKELY. ONE OF HIS FIELD agents, maybe. I frowned. "Can't be Gerry. He wouldn't go there."

"We've got positive ID," Dawna said. "It's Davis."

I saw the truth in her face, heard it in her tone. Dawna's certainty rolled into me with the crumpling force I'd felt as a driver when another car came out of my blind spot and collided with mine. My horror rose along with my gorge, as if I were watching again as that first denting impact imploded into a mangled mass of twisted steel.

I was caught, suddenly and unaware, in the middle of an accident. *This is not happening*, I told myself. I remembered Gerry brushing past me into the elevator yesterday. He'd been mentally chasing down a new investigative path, so energized that he barely noticed me. He'd been completely alive, yesterday. *So this cannot be happening.*

My memory of Gerry brightened as if a photographer had snapped a flash picture. And then new images appeared, reaching me like the way action does when it's illuminated by a strobe light. I saw Gerry hit. Gerry fall. Gerry's bloody body on the ground. Each image hit me like a blow. Thinking, *I cannot bear for this to be happening.* Yet it was. It had.

Pain wrenched my midsection and weakened my knees. Only Dawna's firm hands on my shoulders kept me from staggering. Too much to handle. I couldn't take it in all at once. Later, maybe. A piece at a time. But not now. I looked away from Dawna, forcing myself to breathe slowly.

A blue Ford tractor grumbled past on the village's main street. It was three feet from me, so close I could have touched the tedder pulled behind it. Hot air surged over me and I smelled sun-dried timothy. Particles of hay chaff settled onto the damp skin of my forehead. Heat shimmered off the road, blurring the official outlines of Blixenstjerne and Jespersen standing on the far side. Blixenstjerne had his broad back to me, concentrating on whatever was coming through the cell phone flattening his ear. Jespersen watched us somberly, arms folded across his chest, one hand clutching his notepad. He was flanked by a trio of uniformed cops, their eyes on the half-dozen bikers clustered in the courtyard between the Møller house and workshop.

My glance landed on Ulf, then flicked to Dawna. The skin under her eyes was shiny with sweat. Her fingers tightened on my arms as if she were going to shake me again. I backed up sharply, breaking her grip. I stumbled off the uneven cobblestones and onto the gravel strip edging the road. My shoes scuffed the ground, erasing the lines left by a rake. I reached Dawna's Saab and braced myself against the rear bumper, the metal a lump of solid heat against my hip. Dawna had said Gerry was killed in Nakskov. I knew it only as a seaport on Lolland, one of the smaller islands south of Sjælland and connected to it via bridges. Why had Gerry gone in person to a biker clubhouse on Nakskov?

Dawna joined me at the rear of the car, the sun turning her hair to a golden frieze around her face. When she spoke, her voice was impatient. "Why'd Davis go to the Hells Angels?"

My words came out slow and thick. "I don't know."

"That's a lie." She slapped a hand on the trunk lid, the sound as resonant as stone against iron. "You know what he was doing."

"No," I began.

She cut me off. "I heard you try to shut Ulf up. His brother wanted to tell you something about the Stingers. That's why he was killed. Whole thing's turned into a power struggle. Bikers fighting over whether to sell you the missiles or use them against each other."

I was too hot, the sun pitiless on my head, my hair sticky against the back of my neck. "The bikers don't have—"

"Bullshit. That's why Davis went to Nakskov. Trying to buy those weapons. The two of you knew the bikers were armed with Stingers. But you didn't tell the cops. Oh no, you couldn't do that.

The CIA has to protect its sources. Nothing's more important than your goddam sources."

I said, "There's no evidence linking the missiles to the bikers—"

"Stop fucking around." Her breath was coming out hard and perspiration beaded her upper lip. "What'd you plan to do—keep covering this up until they used them?"

"I don't know what Gerry was doing," I said. "*I* haven't seen any connection to bikers."

"Sure you haven't." She had her car key out, the angled serrations gleaming like silver cutlery. The door locks beeped open simultaneously. "You get in the car. We'll follow Jespersen and Blixenstjerne to Nakskov."

I parted the moist strands of hair on the top of my head with my fingers, twisted the ends resting against my neck. "I've got to go to the embassy. Gerry made notes, Dawna. Notes for me. I can't guess what he was doing until I read what he wrote."

"No way." She waved a hand toward the Copenhagen cops. Blixenstjerne had crossed to the BMW parked in front of her Saab. He lowered his heavy body into the passenger seat and the door crunched shut. On the far side of the street, Jespersen broke off his conversation with the uniformed trio. He stuffed his notepad into his jacket pocket and crossed toward us, arriving just as Dawna said, "You're going to the crime scene with us."

"Only you, Dawna." Jespersen's voice was as mournful as his expression. "No civilians."

"She has to come." Dawna's voice had deepened to a growl, the pleasant timbre absent. "She's riding with me."

"Her presence in Nakskov would be inappropriate," Jespersen said.

The cops didn't want me around while they investigated my partner's death? Not a good sign. But it was my opening. I needed to go through Gerry's files—alone. I'd deal with their suspicions later. Quickly, I said to Dawna, "You go with them. We can talk when you get back to the embassy."

Jespersen nodded. "It is best that she return to Copenhagen," he said to Dawna. "If transportation is a problem, you're welcome to join us in my car."

Dawna's hand rose, two fingers brushing the dent at the end of her nose. "Let me make arrangements for her—"

Jespersen shook his head. "No time. We must leave at once if we are to catch the next ferry from Fyn to Lolland." He raised his wrist, double-checking his watch. He shook his head again. "If you prefer to join us later, of course we will give you a full report."

She winced as though he'd threatened to rebreak her nose. Getting to the crime scene apparently mattered as much to her as keeping me on a short leash. I said to her, "I've got a personal stake in finding out who killed Gerry. There's nothing I can do in Nakskov that you can't do better. You go with Jespersen. Let me take your car back to the embassy. Gerry's notes will explain why he went to the Hells Angels."

Dawna hesitated. Her arm came out, the car key in her open palm.

I reached for it.

Her fingers closed over the key before I could take it from her. "As soon as I get finished in Nakskov, I'm coming after you, Collins. You better be waiting for me at the embassy. And you better be able to prove you weren't concealing information vital to a police investigation."

"Of course I wasn't—"

She opened her fingers and jammed the rough edge of the car key against my palm. "We may be on foreign soil, but you can't weasel your way out of this. The bureau's in Denmark by invitation. We have jurisdiction as far as you're concerned. If you've been obstructing justice, then you're looking at a federal indictment. I promise you that."

If she was bluffing, she was damn good at it. She didn't glance back as she strode toward the BMW. Jespersen held the rear door for her. She slid in as though she were accustomed to being chauffeured. The patrol car, first in line, pulled into the traffic lane. The taillights flared red on Jespersen's BMW and he rolled after the patrol car, the convoy accelerating as it hurried south.

A faint puff of chaff settled back onto the road where the two cars had been. The air smelled of asphalt and stone grit. I rubbed at the red mark on my palm, then opened the door to Dawna's Saab. The interior was sweltering, the hot leather pungent as an overheated steer. I bent my head to enter the car.

A finger tapped my shoulder hard. I straightened, my back against the inside of the open door, nothing between me and Ulf Møller. He rested his right hand on the car roof, sunlight glinting from the gold links circling his wrist. The coarse bristles of his beard stood out against his olive skin and when he spoke his words smelled of beer. "You're driving back to Copenhagen alone?"

My eyes went to the far side of the street. The Danish policemen were no longer there. "Move," I said. "I'm leaving."

He lounged against the car. "Whatever happened in Nakskov, no Bandidos were behind it."

"Like Dawna said, you've got the perfect alibi." I stared pointedly at the hand resting on the car roof. Ulf was leering at me like a movie villain. I wondered if that was his habitual behavior around women. Or did he have a more specific reason for intimidating me? My grip tightened on the base of the key. I held the blade between my second and third fingers, poised to use it as a weapon if I had to.

He raised his hand to shade his face from the glare. His eyes were narrowed, dark as gun slots in an armored vehicle. Impossible to read the direction of fire. Our face-off lasted fifteen seconds. He straightened up, no longer touching the car. He dropped his right hand insolently to his side, the gold links jingling softly. His voice was soft too. "Somebody killed *your* partner. Maybe the same person who killed my brother in *your* flat. You might be next on the list."

I remembered Gitte's terrified reaction when I described how her son died. As if she feared that Ulf had murdered his brother. He was *my* prime suspect and now he was threatening me. He knew where I'd be for the next hour: driving alone across a piece of rural Denmark that was mapped on his soul.

I didn't want this bulked-up Bandido to realize how much he scared me. "Get away from the car," I said defiantly, "or you might get hurt."

His laugh came from his belly, full of mockery. "*Your* safety is my concern," he said. He strolled to the middle of the road, raising one hand lazily, as if to stop traffic. I kept my gaze on him as I lowered myself into the driver's seat. He added loudly, "I'll have you escorted home."

"No thanks." I slammed the door, moved the seat forward and adjusted the mirror. The leather burned against the backs of my legs. I turned on the ignition and my headlights came on automatically. Hot air spilled from the vents. I lowered the window for relief.

From the center of the street, Ulf made a show of checking traffic in both directions. He gestured broadly that it was safe for me to make a U-turn, as if he had no doubt I'd be heading in the opposite direction from the crew bound for Nakskov.

Casually, I dried my right hand on my pants legs before I gripped the gearshift. Trying to look unruffled, I cocked my left elbow on the window frame, shifted into reverse and backed with one-handed carelessness into the courtyard. I tossed Ulf a farewell salute as I turned left in front of him. The skin on my face was flaming with heat and my back was soaked with sweat but I hoped my nervousness didn't show.

I glimpsed the gated churchyard and caught a whiff of pigs and then I was beyond the town, the highway curving between gently rolling hills topped by a line of high-tech windmills, their sleek spokes immobile. Warm air kissed my left arm and my tires hummed on the smooth pavement. And Gerry was dead.

The car jerked to the right, responding to the twitch of my hand. I straightened out and eased off the gas pedal.

Years ago, when Gerry and I first met in Warsaw, I'd detested him. He'd been convincingly nasty, calling me "the blond bimbo" and accusing me of plotting to discredit the agency. His every word made me hate him more.

I discovered later that his animosity was an act forced on him by the agency, a bad-cop number to manipulate me into doing the CIA's dirty work. Most people found the real Gerry as abrasive as the bogus one. Not me. I valued loyalty and integrity more than charm. We didn't come from the same gene pool, but somewhere in our DNA there must have been identical cells. I felt as if Gerry were family. And now my family was one less. My vision blurred and I tasted salty tears at the back of my throat.

I pushed at the hair sticking to my forehead. A low-slung white building hugged the roadside, topped with ancient thatch. I slowed for a red hen who'd pecked her way onto the pavement. Her beady-eyed stare was hostile, as if I'd brought *rockerkrig* to her chicken coop.

Remorse swept over me like a wave of nausea. Despite Gerry's objections, I'd resigned from his project. I hadn't told him that the biker killed in my flat had asked Bella for my name.

But Gerry had deduced a connection between bikers and the missing Stingers. And that deduction led him to Nakskov, alone. I'd abandoned him. Stonewalled him. Gotten him killed.

I willed away my grief. No time for that. Mourning wouldn't bring Gerry back. I had to identify his murderer. I would read over any notes he'd left and retrace his path through our files. I straightened my shoulders. I'd find the reason for Gerry's trip to Nakskov. And I'd weed out any speculation of Gerry's that linked the missiles, the bikers, and Bella.

Bella. I felt a twinge of panic, low in my guts. I gripped the wheel tighter and reassured myself. Bella was fine. I'd kept the cops away from her. The crazies had taken their violence to Nakskov, far from Bella and her biker contact in Stenløse. Such a long shot, finding Woody's father via a tattoo artist in Denmark. Not likely she'd succeed, but I had to help her. The anguish I felt for Woody lay like bedrock beneath a new strata of pain for Gerry.

Gerry's death would trigger an official U.S. government inquiry. Washington would send a fully cleared CIA team to pore over Gerry's files and interview everyone named in them. Because of Gerry's cryptic note-taking system, the investigators wouldn't understand every word he'd written. But if he'd scribbled Bella's name on a sticky note, they'd be all over her. They'd watch her so closely, she'd have to abandon her search among the outlaw bikers for Woody's father. To protect Bella, I had to get to those files before the investigative team arrived.

Ten yards in front of me, a red-bordered circular sign announced in black on white that the speed limit had dropped. I downshifted and drove slowly past a line of ocher storefronts, plate glass glimmering in front of displays of clothing and hardware. Ahead of me a traffic light turned red and I braked. Stopped at the intersection, I popped open the glove box, looking for Dawna's fancy map book. I didn't find it. I shrugged. I'd navigated on the way to the funeral; I'd find my way back home.

I glanced up at the light. Still red. An imposing brick building with a red tile roof commanded the opposite corner. Capital letters affixed to the wall announced that it was the local KRO—inn and public house. Next to the entrance perched a statue of a long-eared squirrel peering into a wine glass, a juxtaposition too Old World for my American mind to interpret. I smelled fresh bread and my mouth watered. A long time since I'd eaten. I leaned out the window and sniffed.

From behind me came the snarl of a powerful engine. It dropped to a repetitive growl.

Potato-potato-potato.

The distinctive song of a Harley-Davidson engine firing at low rpm.

I glanced behind me. A bike with a male rider, his eyes hidden by sunglasses. Helmeted, chromed and leathered, a figure as alien to me as a creature from Mars.

My Bandidos escort, courtesy of Bo Ulf Møller.

13

THE TRAFFIC LIGHT CHANGED. ON THE OTHER SIDE OF THE intersection, I followed a red-coated mailman on a bicycle to the end of the next block. The motorcycle matched my snail-like pace. The biker stayed two car lengths behind me through town and maintained that distance when I accelerated onto the open road.

For my protection, according to Ulf. Because someone had killed my partner and his brother. Because I might be next.

A van roared past me going in the opposite direction. It was a beer-delivery truck, painted red, white, and green, and sporting the same Albani logo I'd seen on the Møller's workshop. I remembered sitting in Gitte's parlor, the stuffy room smelling of scorched potatoes, the piano keyboard sharp across my spine. *Killing your own,* she'd whispered to me. *The worst thing.*

Had Gitte been trying to tell me that her son Ulf had murdered his brother? I pictured Bjørn in my flat, stroking the keys of the Steinway. Listening to the sounds he was coaxing from the piano while Ulf raised his arms to strike the fatal blow.

I rubbed the heel of my hand across my forehead. Why would Ulf kill his brother? I wished I'd been able to question Gitte more closely. Still, knowing Ulf's motive was less critical than guessing his next move. No one had named him as the killer. Not yet. But Gerry had been looking in the right place, among the bikers. It was likely he'd stumbled over the truth, just as I had. Now Gerry was dead in a biker assault. And Ulf had sent a biker after me.

I glanced in the rearview mirror. Brilliant sunlight bounced off the chrome backs of the motorcycle's side mirrors, mocking the murky yellow of the headlight. Despite the heat, I shivered. Even in Dawna's Saab I had little chance of outrunning the Harley.

Maybe I should drive to the regional police headquarters in Odense and ask for protection? No, I couldn't afford the delay. I had to protect Bella. And a man alone wouldn't attack me on the open road at Friday midday. Ulf was tracking me so he'd know where to find me.

The motor behind me whined more loudly, rpms hitting the shift point as the Harley increased its speed. I glanced down. I'd pushed the Saab up to one hundred and ten kilometers per hour. I let up on the gas, dropping back to the eighty allowed on secondary roads. I couldn't waste a half hour explaining to a traffic cop why I was leading a Bandido on a race across Fyn.

Every minute counted. I loved Woody. Nothing in my life was more important than saving him. I'd put off my departure for Bangor until tonight so Bella could interview her biker contact. But once she'd done that, I had to leave. Four hundred and eight people dead—the worst airline disaster ever on U.S. soil. My expertise on terrorist groups was specific and essential. The other task-force members needed me with them for the process to work. Sam Baldwin had good reason to be angry with me. I had to meet his deadline. His complaint to the attorney general would automatically put a black mark on my personnel record. One that would be nearly impossible to erase.

The digital clock on the dashboard read one-thirty. I had to stay current, be ready to go straight to work when I arrived in Bangor. I turned on the radio, flicking through a series of quick news breaks on the half hour. But the rapid-fire Danish reports were all of a scandal in the agricultural ministry. I found no international news. I clicked it off. I'd get an update when I reached the embassy. If nobody interfered, I'd be there in two hours.

The Harley engine growled behind me. A reminder that Ulf was watching, waiting to make his move.

Past the built-up area, the road was bordered by electric fencing. It enclosed a cluster of Jersey heifers, their liquid brown eyes circled in darker velvet. I smelled fresh manure, the ammonia scent strong enough to burn my eyes.

Or maybe it was memory that stung like tears. Stefan and I had arrived in Denmark from Warsaw late in the spring of 1986. During our free time we'd explored his adopted country. We'd quickly learned that every dairy man in Denmark spreads a winter's worth of manure on his hay fields during the month of May. I remembered the warmth of the sun on my arm, the weight of Stefan's hand on my thigh, the aroma of cow barn filling the car. Ripe and fecund, the smell of spring and new beginnings.

Lining the road I'd seen hand-lettered signs offering onion sets for sale. The tops of the birch trees had been hazed green by swollen buds and everywhere pastureland had rioted with the mustard-colored blossoms of rape plants, grown for cattle forage.

I pulled my arm inside the car, the midsummer sun threatening to burn my skin. It was June now and the manured fields were past their first cutting of hay, the farm stands were selling new potatoes and strawberries, and the tree branches were hidden by leaves. Nowhere to be seen were those vivid patches of shocking yellow that had delighted my eye years ago.

The landscape had turned from spring to summer and Stefan had taken himself from the center of my life to its margins. I clenched my jaw, swallowed with difficulty. Any more maudlin self-pity and I'd be no good to anyone. I'd been foolish to come to Denmark and force myself to recall that heavenly spring. I had to put my sadness aside. Pull myself together. Get out of this country and on with my life.

Up ahead I spotted a *pølsevogn* parked at the roadside. Food, that was the solution. Without signaling, I pulled my foot from the accelerator and eased off the road and onto the open space in front of the hot dog stand. I braked gently, coasting to a stop.

My follower reacted instantly, yanking his bike into a sharp turn that shot a spray of gravel across the lot. He slid sideways, then smoothly righted the machine, ending up straddling it, the air around him gray with dust. He had his helmet off and a walkie-talkie in his hand before I got my door open. I gave him a long once-over before I turned toward the *pølsevogn*, but I couldn't see much. Sunglasses hid his eyes and the radio covered his mouth. His skimpy hair was the color of a snuff-dipper's teeth and he wore it skinned back into a ponytail so that his wrinkled forehead extended midway across his skull. He looked at least sixty years old.

I carried my lunch to a wooden picnic table shaded by a thick-trunked oak. I'd ordered the Danish equivalent of a foot-long: thirty centimeters of sausage colored a crimson shade never seen in nature. The garish meat was festooned with grilled onions and spotted with catsup and mustard. The casing was so firm that it squeaked when I bit into it. Ecstasy washed over me. The bun tasted as if it had been baked that morning, the *pølse* was spiced to perfection, and the onions blended with the bite of the English mustard for an ambrosial effect. I downed a slug of Jolly cola straight from the bottle, the syrup-sweet flavor like the fountain soft drinks I'd drunk as a child.

The bike engine muttered more loudly. Was he leaving? I watched as he rolled the bike beneath the shade of another tree twenty feet from me. He stopped, his engine idling, his gaze on me. The walkie-talkie had disappeared and he was wearing his helmet again. Ready to move when I did. His grizzled looks disturbed me. Only a nasty biker survives long enough to become an old biker.

Old *and* frail, I insisted to myself. Gramps wasn't going to attack me by himself. And if he did try anything, I could take him.

And I could take Dawna, too. I rubbed my upper arm where she'd gripped so hard she'd left a bruise. She'd shaken me roughly as she informed me of Gerry's death. Was she really so cold? Maybe, like many women in law enforcement, Dawna believed she had to conceal her nurturing side. Or maybe she no longer had one. They'd coached it out of her.

I'd wondered earlier what Dawna was really after. Not Gerry's death—she hadn't wanted that. But there'd been no consolation in her voice and no comfort in her eyes when she told me my partner was dead. Instead, I'd seen hot eagerness. For Dawna, Gerry's murder had changed a local homicide into a major conspiracy. Bigger crime was better, for an ambitious FBI agent.

All along, she'd been looking for a link between the biker murder and Gerry's project. During our conversation at the embassy, I'd denied any connection. Dawna had chosen not to believe me. Instead, she smelled a cover-up and she started sniffing around for evidence. She followed her nose to the usual source of foul odors between the FBI and the CIA: The agency's hackneyed excuse that sharing information with the bureau would endanger their informants. She believed Gerry and I were concealing the truth—that the bikers had acquired the missiles.

She hadn't confronted me with her idea. Instead, she'd watched me closely, hoping I'd give her proof of my collusion with the bikers. She thought she'd heard it in my conversation with Ulf. And the events in Nakskov added credibility to her scenario.

Was that what Dawna was after—the prestige she'd gain if she exposed a major CIA/biker scam? If so, her merciless ambition had clouded her judgment. I'd been through the data a hundred times. The biker gangs didn't have the missiles. Neither Gerry nor I was guilty of wrongdoing. I couldn't allow Dawna to sidetrack the investigation. Trying to prove that I was a State Department rogue wouldn't solve Gerry's murder. Both the FBI and the Danish police had to make finding his killer their number-one priority.

I swallowed my last bite of hot dog and wadded up the wrapper. I had to get to the embassy. I'd make sure that Bella was safe. And I'd go on protecting her. But I'd give Dawna and the police any other clues I uncovered. With that sole exception for Bella, I'd pass on every bit of evidence that might lead them to the murderer. I'd prove to Dawna that her accusations were unfounded. Then I'd catch the next flight to the U.S.

I stood and collected my trash. I was dropping it into the bin when the second bike arrived, coming from the direction in which I was traveling. The third one pulled in seconds later as I was opening my car door.

The new arrivals rumbled slowly past me, so close I smelled sweat and gasoline. The two men wore matching helmets shaped like those used by the German Army in World War II. Their sleeveless vests were unbuttoned to show muscular chests and their tattooed arms were solid as oak limbs. Younger than I was—and stronger.

When I pulled back onto the highway, the two new arrivals fell in ten yards behind me, one positioned in back of each tire. Gramps disappeared in the opposite direction. No need for him to continue, now that the real muscle had arrived.

The motorcycles stayed behind me past the white-steepled parish church at Vindinge and onto the bridge approach at Nyborg. I managed to get some other cars between us before we entered the tunnel but the bikers picked me up again on the other side of Store Bælt, the Great Belt strait. My eyes went constantly to my rearview mirror. The image of the two bikers hung like a surreal shadow hurled behind me by the unrelenting sun.

At Ringsted a second pair of Bandidos joined us, roaring past me in the left lane to take up a position ten meters in front of me, an eerie imitation of a presidential motorcade. As if they were protecting me. But I didn't feel protected. I felt threatened by Ulf's show of force.

My muscles were stretched so tight my arms ached by the time I reached the embassy lot. The biker quartet pulled past the lot entrance and waited on the far side of the street, engines rumbling. I parked the Saab and walked slowly toward the chancery entrance, swiveling my neck to ease the pain. The gate guard was muttering into his cell phone, probably notifying the local police of suspicious characters lurking around the embassy.

Four engines revved to full throttle. The foursome split into pairs and each of the duos roared away in opposing directions. Most likely one pair would set up covert surveillance on the embassy and the other would stake out my house. I checked my watch. 3:45 P.M. I could still make it out of Kastrup tonight. The creepy bikers wouldn't follow me farther than the airport.

I opened the embassy door. I was startled to find Bella standing on the other side. I stopped myself from asking why she wasn't in Stenløse. I knew the answer. The embassy always called the regional security officer when an employee was a crime victim.

She said, "About time you got here." A breathy note of relief took the sting from her tough-guy words.

"You were waiting for me?"

"We have to talk. And according to Dawna Shepherd, I should put you under guard."

"Under guard?" I held on to the door. "What crime am I supposed to have committed?"

"Pissing off the FBI, that's the main thing." She made a disgusted noise and pulled me inside. "Dawna phoned from Nakskov, ordered me to hold you till she gets back at six. Like she can tell me how to run my embassy. What's her problem?"

"You're not going to arrest me?" I asked.

"Arrest *you* because *she* says to? You're no criminal. And that bitch is way out of line. Come on, I've got stuff to tell you before I take off." She herded me past the Marine on duty at Post One and toward the stairs leading to the second floor.

"Take off?" I asked over my shoulder.

"For Nakskov. I have to see the crime scene for myself." Bella followed me up the stairs. "I'll head to Nakskov as soon as you and I finish. Stan Jenkins is waiting for me."

Jenkins was the vice-consul who handled American citizen services, including transportation home for the bodies of those who died in Denmark. I said, "Jenkins will make the arrangements for Gerry?" We both heard the rawness in my voice.

Bella's hand touched my shoulder and her voice softened. "You doing all right?"

"Ah, shit, Bella," I said. Her sympathy triggered a spasm of grief. I felt again that wrenching pain in my abdomen. My lunch churned in my stomach and I thought I might lose it. Lose everything. If I let myself weep for Gerry, my tears would never end.

We'd reached the second floor. Bella tightened her grip, forcing me to stop. With her other hand she smoothed my hair, the way a mother comforts a crying child. "Jenkins will send Gerry home," she said soothingly. "He'll take care of that. I'll find his killer. Everything will be all right." She went on, murmuring similar things in different words.

We stood together like that for sixty seconds, Bella giving me a transfusion of purpose. I reached back to touch the hand resting on my shoulder. "Thanks," I said.

She squeezed my shoulder tenderly and got us moving again down the hall. "We'll handle it," she said briskly, signaling me that she was putting emotion aside, returning to her chillier on-the-job style. She followed me into her office and shut the door. "They started beeping me five minutes after the explosion. Caught me right outside that damn tattoo parlor. I called in, got the word, drove straight to the embassy. When I got here, Len Trotter was already working on it." Bella went behind her desk and sat, waving a hand toward the chair facing her.

I was tired of sitting. I folded my arms and leaned against the door instead. I said, "Trotter notified his people at Langley?"

She nodded. "Three-man CIA team will arrive tomorrow. Coming in under State cover, pretending to be security investigators from my shop. Took us an hour to set that up."

"You got the details of what happened?"

She shook her head. "Cops have the scene cordoned off. Not letting any media in yet. Jespersen claimed he'd pass Dawna everything relevant to Gerry's death. Then he gave Dawna his cell phone and she told me to lock you up. She was on the scene, she said. No need for me to come down." Bella sniffed. "Like *her* report would be enough for Diplomatic Security."

"So you knew I was coming in. But you weren't waiting because Dawna ordered you to. You wanted to talk to me?"

"Right. About Woody's father."

About her aborted mission to Stenløse. "Bad timing, getting called when you did. But at least one positive thing happened today. The cops don't need to learn you talked to Bjørn Møller." I told her about the funeral and what Ulf had said in front of Dawna about his brother wanting to sell me information. "Soon as the investigation into Gerry's death winds down, you can try again to get together with the tattoo-parlor Bandido."

"Don't have to try again." Her words came out fast, her voice light, suppressed excitement bubbling through her all-business attitude. "That's why I needed to talk to you."

I blinked. "You found him before you were paged."

"Better than that." Her eyes blazed, emerald fire. "I found Wlodek Wojcik."

14 STUNNED, I FELL INTO THE CHAIR BESIDE BELLA'S DESK. "YOU talked to Woody's father?"

"Not yet," Bella said. "He left Bangkok two days ago. Due in Copenhagen tomorrow. I'm meeting him at three o'clock, Saturday afternoon."

"You can't meet him tomorrow, not after what's happened."

"I knew you'd say that," she said. "But I have to."

"You can't go near a *rocker* drug supplier. The Danish cops, the FBI, the CIA—three different agencies are investigating Gerry's death. They'll have people all over the biker gangs, trying to find out who's responsible. Somebody spots you with Wlodek, every secret you've got will become common knowledge."

"Calm down. Nobody will spot me—"

"You can't take that chance. They start checking, they'll find out you've been hanging in biker bars. Maybe somebody saw you with Bjørn. Or earlier today, in Stenløse. Imagine how that will look. And when they find out you and Wlodek . . ." I shook my head. "Dawna has less than that on me and she thinks it's enough to build a federal case."

Bella was standing, leaning toward me. "I'm this close, I can't back off."

I was back on my feet, too. "You get snared by this investigation, you won't be around to take care of Woody. And don't forget, Wlodek's an outlaw. You can't go out alone and meet someone like that. No, you have to hold off till things cool down. Maybe you can have Wlodek arrested, later—

"What, get him locked up and then ask him for his bone marrow?" The question came out as a shriek. She inhaled, spoke deliberately. "If I approach him right, I can make this work."

"Your plan's too hazardous. You can get hurt in too many ways."

"I'll take the risk." The "s" hissed between her teeth.

"No." I was so upset I shouted the negative. I lowered my voice and enunciated each word as if she were a new student of the English language. "I'm going upstairs. I'll make sure your name doesn't show up in Gerry's files. You stay clear of this mess. Stay away from Wlodek."

"I can't. He's our only hope. I know I can pull this off. If you do one thing for me."

"What?" I asked, warily.

Bella's words came out in an eager rush. "You told me about Gerry's private code. There's no chance these guys coming out from Langley will be able to decipher it. You're the only one who can interpret his symbols. You can control the information going—"

I stopped her from finishing. "No way. That's what Dawna's accused me of—hindering a police investigation. She finds out I held anything back, she'll nail me."

"You won't be hindering it, not really. Just for the first day, you can steer the investigation team away from Wlodek."

"I can't conceal anything. I owe that to Gerry. I want this investigation to find his murderer."

"I've known Gerry for as long as you have. I want his killers caught, too." She leaned closer and I smelled her gel again, the strawberry scent soured by the nervous sweat on her hairline. "But I can't stop here. I'm too close. Okay, maybe Wlodek's a dead end. I'll know either way by four o'clock tomorrow. Five at the latest. That's all I need. Keep the cops away from him until I've seen him."

"The cops are only half your problem. Wlodek himself is a danger to you. I can't let you go through with this. You have to stay away from that man."

"Case—" Her breath caught on my name, only the first syllable escaping in a puff of air. "We have to do this," she said so softly I had to strain to hear. "For our boy."

Memories of Woody floated toward me. My fingers felt again the slippery skin of the baby I'd caught at birth. I smelled the milky breath of the infant who'd drowsed in my arms. Saw the toddler smeared with a chocolate bunny, the tousled five-year-old who told me endless jokes without punch lines. I remembered the odor of chain grease when I took the training wheels off his bike. That awed moment when he was ten and I first understood the concept of hyperspace because he'd simplified it for me. And two nights ago, when I saw the skull beneath his skin.

Barbed wire tightened around my heart and I ached for a future he wouldn't have and I wouldn't share. Bella's meeting with Wlodek Wojcik had so little chance of saving Woody's life. And the encounter would endanger her. A risky move and she'd known it even before she'd heard my arguments against it. She'd known she'd need my help.

"Till tomorrow night," she said. "That's all I need."

As if a single meeting with the man could resolve everything. I didn't believe that. I feared Bella's plan would create a whole new set of problems for us. She'd need my help more strongly *after* tomorrow. In my heart, I promised her that. But because I knew it was the reply she wanted from me, I said only, "Until tomorrow night."

She leaned closer, her fingertips on the back of my hand, her cheek inches from mine, her breath warm against my ear. "Thanks." A hint of tears clung to her voice. Then she moved past me and opened the door. I followed her into the hall and she pulled the door shut behind us. The lock clicked loudly. She added carefully, "I'll get Stan now."

Bella had a job to do in Nakskov. Just as I had one to do here. I picked words as businesslike as hers. "Tell Dawna I'm working on things at this end."

"I'll tell her," she said over her shoulder as she headed in the direction of the elevator.

With equal purpose, I turned toward the stairwell. I had to find the message that Gerry had left for me. And I had to go through the file he'd been studying on Thursday morning. As I hurried up the stairs, I visualized it, manila striped with a navy blue security warning not to remove it from the embassy. I knew it was in the third drawer of our file cabinet. When I reached the office I shared with Gerry, I punched in the combination on the pad beside the door and shoved it open.

My stomach lurched. Fluorescent light glared from the ceiling fixture. The open padlock lay on top of the file cabinet, the locking bar beside it. The cabinet's third drawer gaped open. I needed only ten seconds to confirm that the file I wanted was missing.

I checked my desk, going through the drawers and searching under the blotter. Nothing new. Gerry's desk held nothing for me, either. Someone had beaten me to the information I wanted.

The door swung toward me and I looked up to see Andy standing in the opening, poised as if to offer me solace. "You doing okay?" he asked.

Something inside me shifted toward him, yearning to be consoled. Until I saw what he had tucked under his left arm—a manila file folder blazoned in blue.

The desire for comfort gave way instantly to horror. Andy had the file. How much harm had he done? "What's going on?" I asked.

Andy released the door and it clicked shut behind him. "I've been trying to discover what Gerry was doing in Nakskov."

The back of my neck stung, panic biting at me like a horsefly. Had Andy found an allusion to Bella? No safe way to ask directly. Instead I said, "You didn't find any note from Gerry to me?"

"No such luck. I've been searching for the past hour. Found only one report that had any reference to Hells Angels."

I knew the report Andy meant. One of Gerry's field men had overheard a barroom discussion of biker firepower that intrigued him. He'd cozied up to a loudmouth Hells Angel named Viggo Skov and proposed recruiting him as an informant. Gerry had instructed his man to start the process while we pursued more promising leads. I'd suspected that it was interest in Viggo Skov that had drawn Gerry back to that particular folder.

"I'm impressed you found the Skov reference so fast," I said.

"I had to be quick. Len was in a hurry for the information."

Len? Was Andy passing information to the CIA station chief? I felt like I was in an elevator, going down too fast. "You've been talking to Len Trotter about this?"

Andy ran his right hand over his hair, his expression puzzled. "He has to brief the spook team coming in. He wanted more background."

"You let him read that file?"

"No, no." Awareness lit Andy's eyes. He snatched up a clipboard and passed it to me. "I gave him a sanitized summary of the project and that's all."

The fiberboard was warm from his hand. I glanced down. His neat printing was stark against the yellow paper, a bare-bones outline of goals and means.

He added, "I'm clear on our status. We don't report to the chief of station. He's not cleared to see our files."

That was the rule Gerry had established. But could I be certain Andy had followed it? I handed the clipboard back and folded my arms. My fingertips were clammy on the backs of my upper arms and the room's stale air had an off odor that made me think of frozen food that had gone through the defrost cycle too many times. "Why were you carrying that folder around?" I asked.

"Looks like Gerry made some new entries yesterday. I was on my way to ask Len if he knew anything about Gerry's code."

My heart pounded as if the fire alarm had shrilled. Andy was too new on the scene to recognize a cryptic reference to Bella, but Len wouldn't miss it. "You didn't—"

"No. Decided to hold off, wait for you to show up." He slid the report from the file, passed it over to me.

I realized I'd been holding my breath. I let it out slowly. No hint of Bella among the pencil and ink additions. Thursday's date written in green ink. That meant Gerry had recontacted his field man on Thursday. The name Viggo Skov circled in green. They'd discussed the informant and Gerry had summarized the conversation by scrawling a green *W* in the margin opposite his name. *W* was the abbreviation for Gerry's nickname for a snitch who wasn't trusted by the organization he was informing on—"a widow-maker." A heart drawn in pencil, an arrow piercing it, the shaft feathered in green. Gerry would love to talk with Viggo Skov. His man was making arrangements. Gerry had thought the interview so critical, he'd chosen to conduct it himself.

I looked up at Andy. "Why'd you change your mind about asking Len?"

"He was on the phone with the police in Nakskov, making a list of the other casualties. Right at the top was that name." He stepped over, touched the name circled in green.

The widow was made. Gerry's informant, Viggo Skov, had died in the assault.

My knees turned to Jell-O and I had to sit down. I braced my elbows on the desk so I could hold my head up with my hands. I clenched my teeth, trying keep my distress inside me.

Gerry and I and our project had become entwined with the latest eruption of *rockerkrig*—a dangerous mingling that demanded thoughtful analysis and extra caution. But Gerry had felt pressured by my impending departure. He wanted more facts so he could force from me the information he knew I was withholding. He'd rashly gone alone to meet Viggo Skov at the Hells Angels compound in Nakskov. He'd walked into a death trap.

And it was my fault.

15 THE STINGY ROOM SHRANK, THE WALLS MOVING CLOSER TO crush me, the light fixture buzzing in accusation. A moan escaped from between my teeth.

Andy's hand was light on my shoulder, a tentative pat of sympathy.

I imagined him only minutes before, standing at Len Trotter's shoulder. The same collegial posture. Far too buddy-buddy with a man Gerry had never trusted.

I'd wondered why Andy had sought this assignment. I'd speculated that it was because I was here. I hadn't guessed that he'd been invited to apply. And that Gerry Davis was the reason.

I shoved myself upright, roughly knocking Andy's hand away. "What the hell are you doing in Denmark?"

He stood straighter as if to increase the distance between my face and his. "I asked for the job. I had seniority. They gave it to me."

"Simple as that? Nobody at CIA requested you—*you personally*—because you get along so well with old hands like Len Trotter?"

"Not so far as I know." His forehead creased. "What are you getting at?"

I lifted my chin, went for his jugular. "Gerry asked the Pentagon to assign Jaime Fuentes. He's been working on your missile accountability problem ever since the Gulf War. The Defense Department's system is pilferproof because of Fuentes. He knows inside-out how Stingers move on the black market. He was ideal for this job. Instead, the Pentagon sent you. Why did they assign a man with no qualifications to the project?" My voice was getting higher. I took a breath of the musty air before I plunged on. "Tell me Andy: Why was everyone working against Gerry?"

He made a huffing noise full of disbelief. "Let me get this straight. You think I was assigned to this project in order to sabotage Gerry?"

"Nothing else makes sense. This job is light-years off your career path. You wouldn't ask for it."

"I would." His eyes darkened to that moss-green shade of seawater at nightfall. "I did."

"Why?"

He stared at me. "I wanted the job," he said evenly. "I'm not part of any conspiracy against Gerry. That's not what brought me to Denmark."

A tingling sensation surged through my veins, as unsettling as a low-voltage shock. I looked away from him and gestured at the office. "I want to go through this stuff, see if I can find anything you missed. I'm expecting Dawna Shepherd to arrive soon with a whole lot of questions for me."

He picked up the report he'd shown me and slipped it back into the file. He held the folder out to me. "You probably want to start with this. I can help you with the rest—"

"I'd rather do it myself." I stood, my face and voice as hard as I could make them. I took the file from him and clutched it like a shield in front of my chest. I was hanging on to control by a single frayed thread. One wrong word from Andy and I'd lose it completely. With exaggerated calm I said, "Alone."

He studied me for a moment before he retrieved his clipboard. He glanced at his wristwatch. "I asked Birger to check into the biker/missile connection. He should have finished. I'll go over to *Kastellet* and see what he turned up."

"Fine." I turned away from him and opened the folder, studying the contents intently. The door clicked shut. I stepped over and flipped the security bolt, then I leaned on the door, the steel improbably soothing against my back. I felt dizzy and I closed my eyes to shut out the fluorescent fixture pulsing above me.

I'd feared that Andy had been planted on the project to funnel information to those people who wanted Gerry to fail. And if Andy had shown Gerry's notes to Len Trotter, he might have harmed

Bella. I'd jumped in immediately to discover the extent of the damage.

But my alarm was groundless. Andy had done everything right. He'd told Len precisely what the CIA station chief needed to know—and not a word beyond that. Andy had answered my other question in the same way. He'd wanted the job, he'd told me. And stopped without admitting more. Only that look in his eyes had given him away.

I felt it again, that tingle of elation.

After all these years, Andy wanted me again.

And that pleased me.

I felt like slapping myself. How stupid could I be? He was still married. Was I going to let him mistreat me a second time?

I shuddered. I would not reopen that wound. I was dealing with too many rough emotions. Dread for Woody. Fear for Bella. Grief for Gerry. I had to focus on those issues. I drew in a shaky breath and opened my eyes.

First of all, I had to confirm that Gerry had left behind no notes referring to Bella. I went to work, searching methodically through each folder. The files were thin, all our reports handwritten on single sheets of paper. Gerry had horror stories of snoopers who'd managed to glean classified information from manual-typewriter ribbons. Not even primitive technology was allowed in our shared space.

We had no telephone extension and Gerry disliked going through the embassy switchboard. I fingered the report Andy had questioned. To contact his field man, Gerry would have gone out to a pay phone. He'd have returned to jot those few cryptic notes. I stared again at the green and pencil markings Gerry had made yesterday.

His last words. I'd found nothing else and neither had Andy.

I'd promised Bella I'd steer the investigation away from Wlodek Wojcik. Helping her wouldn't require me to misdirect anyone. I touched the green circled name, Viggo Skov. The U.S. team of investigators would begin their interviews with the field man who'd recruited Viggo Skov as an informant. For the first critical hours, the investigative focus would be on Skov's organization. The Hells Angels—not the Bandidos.

The cops might have other evidence I didn't know about that implicated the Bandidos. I'd pass along Ulf Møller's assertion that his club wasn't responsible for the assault on Nakskov. Maybe Ulf would keep the cops busy long enough for Bella to meet safely with Wlodek.

I left my office and went downstairs to the bulletin board where the embassy regularly posted updates to breaking news stories in the U.S. Nothing had been added to the reports from Bangor that I'd read on Thursday afternoon. The task force members would have reached some preliminary conclusions by now. But they were holding their information closely while the members planned how to proceed. Something tightened in my chest. My colleagues were making key decisions that would shape the investigation. Making them without me.

Yet I couldn't leave Copenhagen. Two days ago, Bella had stopped herself from asking me to stay. She was crazy, she said, even to think of involving me. The odds against finding Wlodek Wojcik were too long to justify the likely damage to my career. I'd agreed—and then I'd helped her anyway.

Now, those odds had changed. The man was on his way to Denmark. With me covering for her, Bella was going to meet Woody's father. She was gambling her future—and mine. I braced my back against the wall and stared moodily into space.

I wouldn't meet Sam Baldwin's deadline. The task force leader was following the rule book. But Baldwin had assumed that rigid posture before Gerry was killed. If Gerry's death was seen as a mitigating circumstance, the complaint against me would lose its force. The attorney general might even throw it out. After all, the CIA investigative team actually did need my help interpreting Gerry's notes. *The RSO ordered me to stay*, I could say truthfully when I appealed the complaint.

Baldwin was a bureaucrat to the bone. He'd make sure he was on solid ground before he proceeded against me. He'd check with his people in Copenhagen. He'd check with Dawna Shepherd.

Would Dawna tell Baldwin that I'd been detained in Denmark for legitimate investigative reasons?

No. She *liked* the idea that I was a bad guy who'd been covering up agency incompetence, hiding the fact that the bikers were armed with the CIA's aging missiles. Never mind that her idea was wrong. I'd gotten no hint that the bikers had the Stingers. And scrupulous Gerry hadn't discovered any new evidence. If he had, he'd have noted it before he left the embassy. I didn't know why Bjørn had come to my flat, but I was certain it wasn't to tell me that Stingers were part of the *rocker* arsenal. Dawna didn't agree.

Baldwin would love her criminal scenario tying me and the missiles to the bikers. He'd go gleefully forward with his complaint. But worse, Dawna would be breathing down *my* neck. Which would hinder me from protecting Bella. I had to get her to back off.

I knew she wouldn't let go of her idea easily. She had too much to gain from exposing a joint CIA–State Department conspiracy involving Stingers. Somehow, I needed to come up with a theory she'd like even more. But I was exhausted and my brain felt as though it had gone on strike. I needed rest. And perspective. I needed to review everything that had happened with someone knowledgeable. Someone I trusted. Someone I could reach in a hurry.

Only one person matched all three of those requirements. Bella had labeled him my "foremost intelligence source in all of Scandinavia." Lieutenant Colonel Holger Sorensen ran covert counterterrorist actions for the Danish Defense Intelligence Service. Officially he was on leave from the DDIS, serving as pastor of a rural church north of Copenhagen. As if the call of God would keep a man like Holger from working in intelligence.

I pushed myself upright. I couldn't use an embassy line for a long conversation on sensitive matters. I'd have to go to a pay phone to call Holger. I started toward the exit, then stopped myself. Men on bikes might be outside, prepared to dog my footsteps. Before I went through the tedious process of shaking a tail, it made sense to confirm that Holger was at home.

Circumspectly, I reminded myself. In case anyone was listening in at either end.

I glanced down the hallway. The office used by the assistant cultural affairs officer was dark. I turned on the lights and saw a squared-away desktop, padlocked file cabinet, and a book case topped by a gaudy array of *This Week in Copenhagen* brochures, the ones that have art-museum hours in the front, escort-service ads in the back. The room was so tidy, I guessed that its regular occupant had left for the day. I settled into the padded chair and pulled my address book from my purse. A minute later, I was greeting Holger—though not by name.

He didn't say my name, either, but he knew who I was. I could tell by the warmth in his tone after he heard my voice and by the first thing that he said: "I've been concerned for you."

"You heard—" I began.

He interrupted. "Distressing news. We must talk."

"Yes. That's why I called—"

He cut me off again without apology. "This evening is not workable. You must come to me tomorrow morning. Are you free at ten?" He stopped, waiting for me to catch up.

He had something for me. Something so sensitive, he had to tell me face-to-face. My heart beat faster. "I'll be there," I said and hung up.

I glanced at my watch. Five-forty-five. If Dawna kept to her schedule she'd arrive in another fifteen minutes. But I wasn't ready to confront Dawna. I had to talk to Holger first. I couldn't risk her stopping me.

Her car key was in my pocket, resting heavily against my thigh. I grabbed a notepad from the desk and hurried upstairs to Dawna's office. Locked. I ripped a blank page from the pad and scrawled her a note explaining that I was taking her car to northern Sjælland. I'd return tomorrow afternoon with information she needed. I folded the paper once and stuck it in the doorjamb beside the knob.

I imagined Dawna's fury when she read my message. She wouldn't like my high-handed car theft. But I doubted she'd demand that the Danish cops start looking for me. Too embarrassing to ask to have me arrested after Blixenstjerne and Jespersen had seen her give me her keys.

I left another note for Bella telling her I'd return in time to brief the investigative team Saturday afternoon. While they waited for me, they could go through the files. Everything was in order. *You're clean*, in other words. *So stall.*

I was out of the lot by five-fifty-five.

16 I HEADED NORTH ON ØSTERBROGADE AS IF I WERE GOING HOME.
Hot air flavored with exhaust fumes blew in my open window. I
didn't hear the bass notes of a Harley engine and when I scanned
my mirrors, no bike appeared behind me. I cut east on Jagtvej, the
thick foliage of Klosterhaven a green blur on my left. A six-way
intersection loomed at the corner of the garden and I negotiated
my way via Lyngbyvej to the motorway, northbound.

I left the divided highway near Virum and maneuvered through
a series of turns on secondary roads, the back-and-forth I hoped
would keep my destination secret. At eight o'clock I parked my car
in a commuter lot and hiked along the tracks to the local train
station, where I paused long enough to eat a ham roll and reassure
myself that I hadn't picked up a tail. I knew the local KFUM—
Danish acronym for YMCA—offered low-cost lodgings near the
town's main tourist attraction, Frederiksborg Slot. I found the hotel
without difficulty and registered under a Finnish name, gave my
occupation as student and paid cash for a single room, no bath. If
Dawna phoned looking for an American woman driving a red Saab,
the response would, hopefully, be negative.

My Spartan quarters had a single polished window. If I stood
on tiptoe and craned my neck, I could see the green roof of the
castle designed and built by multitalented King Christian IV. The
castle gift shop hawked posters depicting the former monarch in a
1644 sea battle against Sweden. He looked magnificent—a bloodied
sixty-seven years old, blinded in one eye by shrapnel, brandishing
his cutlass. The Danes honored his wish to be remembered as a

soldier-king, though the pictured battle ended in mutual withdrawal and the troops he later commanded in the Thirty Years War were soundly thrashed.

I went to sleep on that thought and woke up Saturday morning to find that my busy subconscious had sorted the few odd facts I had into something like a theory. The scattered pieces fit roughly together.

I found a copy of *Jyllands-Posten* in the hotel common room. It contained an update on the Bangor explosion. Reporters had interviewed a farm couple who thought they'd seen missile tracks in the sky an instant before the plane blew up.

Eyewitnesses had made the same observation when TWA 800 went down off Long Island in 1996. Their claims weren't provable but they were so plausible, I'd been following the black-market trade in missiles ever since. Nobody else on the task force could match my expertise. They needed me in Bangor. That realization grated against my resolve to stay. I ignored the twinge of pain. I wasn't leaving Denmark until I'd done all I could to save Woody's life.

At eight-thirty, I retrieved the Saab. I spent the next forty-five minutes doing evasive maneuvers on the twisting roads of the Gribskov. Literally translated, the name meant, "Vulture Forest," hinting at a dark history unknown to me. I picked up the coast road in Gilleleje and followed it east along Sjælland's north shore to Holger's residence. I was on his doorstep at ten o'clock sharp on Saturday morning.

The rectory was red brick, the front entrance five broad steps above ground level. I pushed the buzzer but heard nothing through the massive wooden door. A thick hedge separated the residence from the church, broken only by the graveled pathway connecting them. In contrast to the modern house, the church was old-style, whitewashed plaster with a square belfry rising high above the shiplike nave. Sunlight gleamed from the exterior. From behind the house came the rasp of a push mower and I smelled cut grass.

I pushed the buzzer again, then pulled back my shoulders, reminding myself to be strong. Holger Sorensen was as dear to me as my own father. And like my father, Holger wasn't reluctant to pressure me into whatever course of action he thought best for me.

I felt a draft of air as the front door swung silently open. Holger took a step forward and clasped my right hand in both of his. His fingers were warm, the skin rough, the grip unexpectedly powerful.

He drew me across the threshold. "Kathryn," he said, making my name sound like an endearment. "I'm sorry if I kept you waiting."

Sunshine poured down from a rooftop skylight, giving a satiny sheen to the lime-washed oak floor, highlighting the silver in Holger's once-dark hair. He released my hands and closed the door. "I was working on my sermon. It took a moment for the sound of the bell to register." He was nine years older and a head taller than me, dressed casually today in a cream-colored three-button Henley shirt over gray cotton slacks faded to one shade lighter than his eyes. He looked like a simple country parson, at this moment bathed in sunlight as if the heavenly father were contemplating his beatification.

I wasn't taken in. Holger Sorensen had never been a simple man and the tactics he employed as an intelligence agent weren't a likely route to sainthood.

"Kathryn," he said again. "I am very glad you came. We have much to discuss."

"I've got only a couple of questions," I said cautiously.

His chuckle was affectionate. "I have more than a couple of questions for you. We haven't spoken since January."

He led me down the hallway that ran from the front to the back of the house. We passed a stairway graced by a polished wooden banister. The scent of lemon wax hovered in the air, giving way to the rich fragrance of fresh coffee as we entered the kitchen. The spacious room stretched twenty feet along the back of the house, the exterior wall filled with multipaned windows and doors. On one sun-drenched sill rested a container of alfalfa seeds, covered by a plastic lid to hasten their sprouting. One corner of the green patch had been clipped low, the tender stems the preferred garnish for Holger's favorite sandwich of hardcooked egg and tomato slices.

A round wooden table was centered in front of the windows and five open books were scattered across it. Outdoors, the sloping lot extended for fifty yards uphill behind the house, the emerald lawn interrupted midway for a pond shaded by a towering oak. A shirtless youth was mowing the section of grass beside the rear hedge. Muscle braided his upper arms and he wore combat boots.

"I'll clear away my mess," Holger said. "We'll have coffee." He closed a King James Version and piled it atop a Danish Bible. The other books were marked with Greek and Hebrew characters.

I sat in one of the four chairs. "You were working on your sermon?"

"Struggling is more accurate." He lifted an armload of books. "Comparing translations of the Twenty-third Psalm."

I raised my eyebrows. "You have a problem with 'the Lord is my shepherd'?"

He laughed again. "No, the final verse is the one giving me difficulty. 'Goodness and mercy shall follow me all the days of my life'—that part." The books thumped loudly against the butcher-block countertop. He pulled two mugs from an open shelf and set one in front of me. "You take your coffee black."

Not a question, but I nodded anyway. He filled my mug and I lifted it with both hands, the steam warm against my face, the scent alone enough to shock my nervous system.

Holger settled into the chair across from me. "How is your father doing?"

Automatically I glanced at my watch, checking the date. Saturday. I phoned my father in Oregon every Saturday. I said, "He has good days." Last Saturday hadn't been one and the bad memory colored my tone, negating my words. Witnessing my father's slow decline was like watching my right arm wither away. A relentless shriveling that didn't hurt physically but made me heartsick and less competent. And alone—so alone. I shivered and raised my eyes to Holger's. I saw the sympathy there. Events had brought my father to Europe the previous winter and despite the damage done to him by Alzheimer's, a warm friendship had developed between him and Holger.

"Difficult for you both," Holger now said.

I broke eye contact, steeling myself to refuse the comfort he was offering. My reasons for coming were secular, not spiritual. I opened my mouth to say that, but Holger spoke before I could.

"Your friend Bella—is she enjoying her tour in Denmark?"

His unexpected mention of Bella startled me. Had Holger divined her role in my current problems? I took a sip of coffee and calmed myself. Holger had met Bella when we arrived in Denmark together in 1986. He'd presided at Woody's christening. Of course he was interested in Bella. And given his connections in the intelligence community, he could help her in ways that I could not. I'd enlist his aid, then move on to my problems.

"Bella's in trouble," I said. "Her son's been diagnosed with leukemia."

"Leukemia? The boy?" He paused and I knew he was recalling the same moment that I was. We'd been in the chapel at *Kastellet*, candlelight gleaming on the polished font, the smell of melting wax blending with ancient dust. I felt again the bittersweet pang of tenderness. I'd held Woody, the lace of his long gown rough against my arms, his tuft of red hair like a beacon in the dimness. Stefan had been with us as a stand-in for Woody's godfather, Bella's favorite uncle.

Holger had asked the ancient questions in Danish and I'd translated them in my head. *Who will protect this child from the Devil?*

I will, I'd promised.

Now Holger said slowly, "I didn't know . . ."

He wasn't faking his distress. His mention of Bella had been guileless. I said, "No one knows. Bella's keeping the bad news to herself." I explained about CML and Bella's search for a matching bone marrow donor. "She thinks she may have located his father."

Holger looked surprised. "The father was missing?"

"The whole story's complicated. Anyway, Bella plans to see the man this afternoon. *If* he shows up." I leaned closer. "That doesn't work out, we'll have to extend the search. You can help us."

Holger said, "You aren't hopeful that the father is the solution."

I shook my head.

He set his mug on the table. "Of course I will help Bella and Woody." He shifted in his chair, spine stiffening, shoulders pulling back. And when he spoke again, the counseling tone was gone. "But first," he said in the voice of a man accustomed to command, "we will deal with *your* situation."

The change disconcerted me. What was behind Holger's unmistakable transformation from minister to soldier? And why did I feel like a trapped mouse waiting for the cat to pounce?

17

"I CALLED YOU," I SAID POINTEDLY. "LET ME TELL YOU WHAT *I* want to deal with." I pushed my coffee cup aside. "I was looking for a link between this outbreak of *rockerkrig* and the project Gerry and I were working on. I think the murder in my flat must be related to Gerry's death. Bikers were involved in both incidents."

Holger rested his shoulders against the chair back as if he were relaxing but his gaze was more, not less, absorbed. "Have you found the connection?"

"I have some ideas. The *rockerkrig* issue may be irrelevant. I think the two biker gangs have no interest in fighting each other because they're going into business together." I leaned toward him, intent. "Maybe the Bandidos and the Hells Angels are going to turn Eastern Europe into a criminal joint venture. If that's true, I think the Hells Angels will control the covert trade in weapons coming out of the former Warsaw Pact countries. The Bandidos will control the supply of illegal drugs going into the same geographical area."

Not a muscle twitched on Holger's face. His neutral voice didn't give away anything, either. "On what do you base this speculation of yours?"

I raised my left index finger, ticked it off with my right. "First, both gangs are headquartered in Denmark. Historically, this country has been a favorite hub for covert activities directed at Eastern Europe. And this time the activity involves weapons. That's what brought the dead man to *my* flat—my interest in weapons. Black-market arms transfers by way of Denmark are an essential element of any deal."

I ticked off my middle finger. "Second, the Bandidos have called their chief drug manager into headquarters for a briefing on the new corporate structure."

Something flickered in Holger's eyes but the reaction was gone before I could label it. He said only, "Clarify that point for me, please."

I grinned. "A lot of guesswork involved in this, I admit. I'm talking about the man Bella says is Woody's father. I know he's been a member of the Bandidos since the mideighties. He's been working for them in Bangkok, probably as their heroin supplier."

I saw Holger's eyes widen, though his face remained blank. He said, "This biker—he has a name?"

"Wlodek Wojcik." I laughed, but with more bitterness than amusement. "Polish, of course. He and Bella met in Warsaw." I took a breath. "Okay, Wlodek Wojcik is traveling from Thailand to Denmark as if he might be coming to participate in negotiations. I think the Bandidos will use him to channel the drugs back to his homeland."

I raised a third finger. "I talked to Bo Ulf Møller, spokesman for the Bandidos. His brother was killed in my flat. In fact, Ulf himself may be the killer. If so, I'd expect him to welcome any police theory diverting attention away from him. Yet, he insists that neither his brother's murder nor the Nakskov incident mean a renewal of *rockerkrig*. Why would he say that so firmly?"

I ticked off my last point, answering my own question. "As one of the higher-ups in the Bandidos, Ulf was surely involved in the negotiations with the Hells Angels. He knows how lucrative the arrangement will be for everyone. While it might help him personally to blame the Hells Angels for his brother's murder, he's not doing that. Nobody—including Ulf—wants to blow this deal. It's far more compelling than the 1997 truce.The era of violence between the two clubs is over."

I stopped. The information had meshed nicely in my mind. But spoken aloud, my arguments sounded flimsy, my logic stretched tight between clues too lightweight and ambiguous to serve as anchors. I said to Holger, "So, what do you think?"

Holger picked up his empty mug, reached across the table and lifted mine. He pushed back his chair, carried both empties to the sink to rinse them. Water splashed against porcelain. He was stalling, I realized. Taking his time, choosing his reaction. Protecting his secrets? Or my feelings?

I cleared my throat and spoke to his back. "Okay, I'm short on facts. But I think I'm onto something—"

" 'Onto something?' " Holger turned, and the opaque expression on his face broke, replaced by a huge smile. "No, Kathryn. Your analysis is perfect. The more impressive because you did it on the basis of limited data." He reached down for my hands, pulled me to my feet. "This is excellent work. You must know that."

Holger had been my teacher once. He hadn't been so generous with his praise then. And I noticed that his benevolent grin today didn't conceal the calculating glint in his eye.

The smile faded and he doled out his next words sparingly. "I have reason to believe the motorcycle gangs based here have expanded their criminal activities to include the covert arms traffic out of the former Warsaw Pact."

Reason to believe. That circumlocution was proof to me that Holger had an operation up and running for DDIS. "Is that what Stefan's doing in Poland—working on this problem for you?" The words came out in a rush, no thought behind them. If I'd paused to think, I'd never have mentioned Stefan.

"I vetoed Stefan's return to fieldwork because of his injury," Holger said. "His business in Poland is on his own initiative."

"Right." I moved away from him to stare out the window. The blue dome of the sky was broken by bands of clouds, a thick gray-white bank massing along the eastern horizon. I caught my lower lip between my teeth. I would not let myself ask again about Stefan.

Holger came to stand beside me at the window. "Your analysis of the biker situation is correct. But it doesn't answer the question you posed originally: Was killing a biker in your flat connected to the killing of Gerry Davis?"

"You're right," I admitted. "The two murders must be linked but I haven't figured out how."

"It is not because the motorcycle gangs have acquired your missing Stingers," Holger said. "No one could have hidden *rocker* possession of such weapons from us." He meant from DDIS.

"Same thing I told the FBI agent, Dawna Shepherd. She thinks I've been concealing evidence from her. Now I can go to her and review the situation in light of what you and I have discussed. This new information gives a broader dimension to the biker problem. She'll like that. And she'll see that I'm not hiding anything. With her off my back, I can work out my next move."

"Your next move," Holger repeated. Outside, a cloud shadow

slid over the lawn and a pair of mallards followed it, splashing onto the pond. Holger plucked a bag of dried corn off the window-sill. "Come. We'll feed my ducks." He opened the French doors leading to the garden.

I followed him across the grass, the cut stems striping my sneaker tops with green. Above us the sky was still blue, but the wind had picked up, carrying with it the salt smell of the ocean. In front of me scudding clouds reflected off the pond water, a shift-ing mosaic in black and green. I couldn't see the mud at its bottom but a stagnant odor clung to the lower air, untouched by the sea breeze blowing over it. Corn rattled into the meter-long metal trough.

"I can't stay much longer," I said. "I've got some business to take care of in Copenhagen." The two ducks swam toward us, the drab female in the lead.

Holger stood and neatly folded the empty bag. The female wad-dled past him to the trough, plunging in beakfirst. The drake pad-dled offshore, complaining noisily. Holger said, "You've been following news of the airliner explosion?"

"I read something about missile tracks," I said. "Any truth to that report?"

"They haven't finished their analysis of the radar." He kept his eyes on me. "But they have found something meriting analysis. That's classified information, of course."

"Things are starting to come together in Bangor," I said. "I could add a lot to the investigation."

"I disagree." Holger held up a hand to cut off my protest. "Not that your contribution wouldn't be valuable. But there's no investi-gative requirement for your presence at the scene of the disaster. Evidence collection and analysis will go on for years. *And—*" He drew out the word to block me more forcefully from interrupting. "I doubt you'd work effectively within the task-force structure."

"What do you mean?" Irritation shortened my words into sharp monosyllables.

His voice remained reasonable. "Your talent is for the swift insight you displayed when speaking of the Danish motorcycle gangs. This task-force business, this crime-solving-by-committee, is a misuse of your skill. You should devote yourself instead to further development of the theory you've discussed with me."

My annoyance turned to hostility. Holger wanted me to do something for him. But he wasn't going to fill me in on the operation he was running for DDIS—that was never his style. I said, "I've got enough on my plate without—"

He interrupted, his voice low, conspiratorial. "I can put you in touch with someone. A man in Dartmouth, England. He's the British expert on the Hells Angels. He could help you put flesh on your skeleton of a theory."

He wasn't backing off. Something I'd said about bikers had increased his interest in me. Standing at his sink rinsing coffee mugs, he'd mapped out a major role for me in whatever he had going. That was the real motive for his effusive praise earlier. Not admiration but manipulation, his old game of turning the unwary into intelligence assets. "Not interested," I said forcefully. "I'm not going to England."

He ignored my combative tone. "If you should change your mind, give me a ring." He enunciated the colloquialism with precise slowness. "I'll be glad to help you." He turned and started back toward the house.

"I have to leave now," I said, trailing him indoors. "I need to get back to the embassy."

He crossed to the left side of the kitchen and pushed through a swinging door. "Let me feed you first."

"I'm not hungry." He wanted more time to pressure me. I followed him into the next room and further protest died in my throat. One end of a twelve-foot-long refectory table was crowded with all the trappings of a celebratory Danish lunch. Paper flags garlanded the centerpiece of cut flowers, the white linen napkins were folded into crowns, and a one-shot stemmed glass sparkled beside each pilsner glass.

The message as clear as if he'd put up a sign: *Welcome home, prodigal daughter.* Telling me that our bond would survive my breach with Stefan.

Holger's place was set at the head of the table. He motioned me into the seat of honor on his right. He set a pottery bowl of silvery fish between our plates. "The *sild* is particularly good."

I spotted a matching dish of curry sauce. My favorite topping for marinated herring. My stomach rumbled so loudly we both heard it. "I should be on my way," I said weakly.

"You have to eat." He pulled out my chair. "Everything is prepared."

I sat. I couldn't rudely rebuff such kindness.

He filled the small glasses from a frosted fifth of *Akvavit Aalborg* and uncapped two bottles of *luxus øl*. The golden liquid foamed to the rim of each beer schooner. He passed me sliced *rugbrød*, informing me it had been made that morning by a woman in his parish. I assembled my sandwich and swallowed the first bite, an exquisite combination of marinated fish, creamy curry and chewy rye.

Holger raised his shot glass. *"Skål."*

I tossed back the aquavit and held the small glass aloft for a second before I put it down and reached for my beer. The flavors blended in my mouth, fish with curry, the caraway bite of the liquor, the flavor of the hops. Holger and Stefan and Bella and I had shared this same ritual after Woody's christening. Even the beer was the same. I focused on an empty bottle, the name PRINS KRISTIAN lettered in black Gothic script over a golden many-sailed Viking ship. *Skatteklasse* two, 5.7 percent alcohol by volume. The tastes and smells unchanged but only the two of us here. And missing also was that sense I'd had of passionate connection to everything in my life.

Holger cleared his throat. When I looked up, he said, "So now will you take charge of the project you were working on with Gerry Davis?"

I finished chewing my last bite of *sild* before I replied. "I came on board only because Gerry asked for me. With him gone, there's no compelling reason for me to continue. An aging Stinger's no greater terrorist threat than a homemade bomb. Once the guidance mechanism deteriorates, the missile is as likely to kill the person launching it as the intended victims. Finding them all isn't that critical."

I studied the stainless steel platter of *smørrebrød*. I passed over the tomato-and-egg and took walnut bread topped by *leverpostej* and garnished with a sliced gherkin. I added, "The team investigating Gerry's death will have questions for me. And I want to do all I can for Bella and her son. I won't waste more of my time on the Stingers. The CIA is obligated to account for the missing weapons, but the project has virtually no real-world value."

Holger looked skeptical. "Not everyone agrees with you. You're aware that one of the CIA's critics claims that a skilled workman using a simple process could restore the Stingers so that they would function perfectly forever?"

I made a scoffing noise. "One critic." I crunched through the

pickle into the smoothness of iron-rich liver paste, my tongue rel-
ishing the change in textures.

Holger rested his silverware on his plate. "Perhaps his judgment
is correct. I understand Gerry Davis thought someone was working
against him. That suggests that someone wanted to make sure the
missing Stingers weren't found. Perhaps the weapons can be made
fully functional and their ultimate use will prove disastrous."

I put my fork down hard, ringing it against the fine porcelain.
I knew Holger too well. He wasn't making idle conversation. He
was methodically trying to back me into a logical corner, one I'd
be unable to argue my way out of. When he had me trapped ver-
bally, he'd move in for the kill. I said, "The sabotage—if you want
to call it that—was directed against Gerry personally. No one would
bother to wreck the project. It's nothing but an accounting exercise."

"You must have reached that conclusion earlier. Surely you can
see such a judgment is no longer valid. It's obvious that someone
is threatened by the work you and Gerry were doing."

"Obvious to you, maybe." My spine stiffened in automatic resistance to Holger's maneuvering. "I told you what I think of the
whole missile-recovery effort. I have no reason to change that
opinion."

Holger leaned toward me and covered my hand with his. His
touch was gentle, as fatherly as the remonstrative tone in his voice.
"Ole Bjørn Møller died trying to give *you* information. Gerry Davis,
your partner, was murdered. You cannot refuse to examine your
connection to those deaths. You owe Gerry more than that. You
owe yourself more."

I jerked my hand away, knocking over a beer bottle. I grabbed
it, jammed it upright between us. "*You've* got a problem with biker
gangs and the covert weapons trade. That's the angle *you're* working. But your situation has nothing to do with me. I'm an innocent bystander."

"No, no, Kathryn." He shook his head slowly. "You are not a
bystander. You stand directly between two violent acts. For reasons
I don't fully understand, you are at the center of what is
happening."

I tossed my napkin on my plate. "You're making a wild hypoth-
esis with nothing to back it up. Murderous reaction to the project
makes no sense."

"Two men are dead. Both of them linked to you and an operation about which you know more than anyone else." His hand was

on my shoulder, heavy. "You have to see where this leads. You know that. You're resisting that truth because it frightens you."

I shrugged out of his grip. "I'm not afraid to investigate Gerry's death."

"Your anger betrays you." He softened his voice. "I've seen you before in a situation like this. I know your pattern. You put anger between yourself and your fears."

"I'm not listening to more of this." Chair legs scraped against the floor as I pushed back from the table. I stood, breathing hard. "I know your pattern, too. You want me to do something for you. But you don't want to tell me what's going on. Well, your tricks won't work, not this time."

"Not tricks. Truth." He stood, napkin crumpled in one hand.

The ivory linen was stained by a yellow smear of curry. "Truth?" I repeated. "Here's my truth. I'm not going to England to see your damn biker expert."

Holger pushed back his chair.

"Don't bother to see me out," I said. "Go work on your sermon. Save your guidance for your flock. I'm not part of it." I cut off anything else he might have said with a tight-lipped farewell.

Outdoors, a chilly breeze raised goose flesh on my bare arms. The sun had disappeared behind cloud cover and the temperature had dropped ten degrees. I fumbled in my pocket for the car key. I'd drunk an ounce of liquor and half the beer in my glass. It would take an hour for my system to absorb that potent combination and reduce my blood-alcohol level below the legal limit. Danish penalties for drunk driving were severe. But I couldn't wait to sober up. I had to get away from Holger and get back to the embassy. I was worried about Bella. Her meeting was at three. I wanted to be there in case anything went wrong. The fastest route back to Copenhagen was via the motorway from Helsingør. But that road was also the most heavily patrolled by the traffic police.

I should stick to back roads—but I didn't know this northeast section of Sjælland well. What had Dawna done with her map book? I tapped my fingers on the Saab trunk. When I popped it, I saw the spiral-bound booklet of maps sitting on top of a navy blue windbreaker with "FBI" printed on the back in electric-yellow ink. Dawna's crime-scene jacket. Might come in handy if I had to talk to any cops. Besides, I was cold. I shrugged into it and rolled up the sleeves. The extra layer felt good. The clouds were charcoal colored, the wind stiffer and more chill.

I got the Saab out of Holger's driveway and onto a two-lane road that cut inland. A longer route, but safer for me. I checked my watch. Two minutes before noon. I'd reach the embassy by two o'clock—if my luck held.

It didn't.

At 12:05, I heard the shriek of a Harley-Davidson engine throttled to maximum speed. And then I heard its echo, a second bike coming on as hard as the first.

18 I SAW THEM IN MY REARVIEW MIRROR, A HUNDRED YARDS BE-
hind me.

Two men on motorcycles, faces hidden by visors as black as the clouds looming in front of me.

No blue lights, no sirens. They weren't cops.

These bikers were completely covered in black leather jackets and pants, a sight as menacing as the Nazi patrols that had terror-ized Denmark during the Occupation. Their demeanor wasn't watchful like the Bandidos who'd tailed me home after the funeral. Each rider in this pair was leaning forward eagerly, like a hunter closing in.

I hunched down in my seat to make myself a smaller target. The speedometer read eighty kilometers per hour, the top recommended speed for this back road.

One bike crossed the center line to the left lane. The other stayed behind me.

I jammed the accelerator to the floor. The needle flew from eighty to a hundred.

The two motorcycles crept closer.

I forced my speed to a hundred and ten. My hands were damp on the wheel, my breath coming through my mouth.

I heard a thud, the sound a bullet would make penetrating the rear of the car. The noise repeated. Something thunked against the rear window. The glass cobwebbed out from the bullet's point of impact on the lower-right side.

I pushed the speedometer needle to one-twenty. The Saab

roared over a bridge and I glimpsed a trickle of stream. Red Danish milk cows grazed in a field on my right and on my left a thin line of beeches signaled the beginning of a forest. I gripped the wheel tightly as the road curved to the right and tunneled into the woods. The road straightened out as I topped a low rise.

Taillights flared red a hundred yards in front of me.

A six-wheeled delivery truck straddled the center line. It was stopped dead, centered between two dense stands of hardwood trees.

The motorcycles screamed behind me.

Trees blocked my way around the truck on both sides, leaving no room to pass. If I jammed my foot on the brake at that instant, I'd skid to a stop with my headlights crushed against the truck's low-hanging safety bar. And the motorcycles would be on top of me.

Ten yards ahead, I thought I saw a meager break in the tree line. Wide enough for a car? I had to risk it. I yanked the wheel to the left and braced myself. The front tires bit into the soft dirt at the shoulder, then flattened a cluster of scraggly firs. A protruding rock ripped off my oil pan, metal screeching as it curled backward. I downshifted and gunned the engine to prod the car forward into the brush. I plowed into a blackberry thicket, canes clawing the side panels. The car crunched to a stop, shuddering, the heavy odor of hot oil blending with the scent of crushed berries.

My seat belt was off, my hands at the door latch. The motorcycles buzzed nearby, angry wasps. Then they whined to a stop.

I threw my weight against the door, forcing it open. I fell out of the car onto the ground on my knees. Lightning cracked, and an echoing bang vibrated the car. I smelled gasoline. I was on my belly, scrabbling away from the car under cover of the canes. A vine whipped across my face, cutting my lip. I tasted blood and my hands were covered by red scratches. I rolled out from under the edge of the blackberry growth and pushed myself upright. I heard the tick of my cooling engine from twenty feet away.

A gun blasted and another bullet smashed into metal. Hunched over, I ran between two beech seedlings and into thicker growth. Blood pounded in my ears and I was breathing hard through my mouth. Branches cracked behind me. The gun fired again, three times. Bark exploded from an oak ten feet to my right. I ran to the left and found myself at the top of an incline studded with granite.

A man yelled something. I couldn't make out the words but the tone was jubilant. Telling his cohort, *I've got her.*

I leapt down the cliff, off balance, jarring my spine, but I stayed on my feet until I reached the bottom. A fallen limb tripped me and I slammed down hard on my knees at the edge of a bare patch of ground, twenty-five-feet wide. Thunder cracked again and a volley of raindrops scattered over the bare earth, sending up puffs of dust. Beyond the clearing, white birch grew thickly and I heard the sound of rushing water. I smelled the ferny odor of a woodland stream. My breath was coming in gasps. Rain pelted my head. I started toward the cover of the trees, running in a crouch. Something whined past my ear, a mosquitolike sound. I dropped lower, to my hands and knees, afraid to go forward.

The skin on my back burned, fear blistering the flesh. At any moment a bullet would sever my spine. The barren space was too wide. I couldn't make it to cover. My fingers closed on a perfect acorn cap. I smelled dirt and leaf mold, and for a second I was a child playing hide-and-seek in the woods. I heard again the mantra I'd whispered to myself.

You can do it, you can do it, you can, you can.

I struggled forward, belly pressed flat against the ground, my eyes on the tree line.

The darkness between the trees moved, began to take shape. Six figures, male, dressed in inky rubber, black circles painted around their eyes and mouths, ghostly white hands cradling assault rifles, battered banana clips curving down. Stone killers, waiting for me.

Panicked, my fingers scratched the ground in search of a rock, a sharp stick, anything I could use to spoil their aim.

One of the men grunted out a phrase in Danish.

Incomprehensible. The voice soft, the tone polite. What was going on?

He said it again, more slowly. *"Er det en filmoptagelse der foregår her, eller hvad?"*

Are you making a film here or what?

A film with real bullets? Was he insane?

"Nej," I gasped. *"Hjælp mig!"*

The same man spat out a command.

My muscles contracted, my body's futile attempt to disappear into the ground. My skin felt too tight, as if the molecules were bunching together to repel bullets. I couldn't breathe.

Automatic weapon fire rattled harmlessly skyward. Warning shots, fired over my pursuers' heads.

My lungs emptied in a rush of air, the sound like a tortured sob. I rocked onto my hands and knees and dragged myself between black-clad legs into the woods. A six-man rubber raft was beached beside the stream. The neoprene was spotted by rain drops and smelled like an old-fashioned inner tube. I sat up, my back braced against the scarred trunk of a white birch, and glanced back at the men. Two had disappeared. Three others were spaced along the tree line. The sixth faced my direction, speaking rapidly into a cell phone. The black fabric lay dully against his body. He was wearing a wet suit. Armed men in wet suits. *Frømandskorpset*, the Danish Navy equivalent of American SEALs. What were a bunch of frogmen doing out in the woods? Were they the ones making the movie?

I heaved myself to my feet, one hand against the rough tree trunk. Rain rattled onto the leaves and a catkin dropped to my shoulder. The sleeves of Dawna's jacket hung in shreds and red welts striped my arms. The cuts stung and I raised my hand to rub my mouth, wondering if my face was stained by blood. I stopped, staring at my fluttering fingers. I jammed my hand into the opposite armpit, trying to stop the shaking.

The man flipped his phone shut. He was my height, broad-shouldered with dirty-blond hair held back from his face by a pair of goggles perched on top of his head. He spoke to me urgently in Danish, an interrogative inflection to words I couldn't understand. I opened my mouth to ask him to repeat his question. I stopped. I couldn't remember a single word of Danish. "Please," I said weakly. "I don't know what you want."

"You're American," he said impatiently. "FBI?"

FBI? I remembered the logo on the back of Dawna's jacket. Gunmen chasing an FBI agent through a Danish woods? Of course this man had assumed my pursuit was made-for-TV.

"Not FBI," I said.

His eyes narrowed and his right hand moved from the top of his weapon to the trigger guard. Suspicious.

Hurriedly I added, "They want to kill me."

"The police are en route. We will stay with you until they arrive." He shifted his weapon, still fingering the trigger guard. Maybe he thought I was making a drug buy and the bikers had turned on me.

I said, "I don't know those men. They must've followed me from the church—"

"What church?" he asked.

I named Holger's parish. "I was visiting the priest."

"The priest," he repeated, studying me. "You mean Colonel Sorensen?"

I nodded. "We had a meeting. I left after lunch."

The frogman's weapon hand relaxed. "The colonel is a friend of yours?"

"And colleague." I put out my hand. "Casey Collins. I'm—"

The rest of my introduction was drowned out by the sound of an explosion, a resonating kaboom that came from the other side of the hill. I saw flames above the treetops, smelled the acrid odor of burning gasoline.

"Your car?" the frogman asked.

"I left it near the road."

He shouted to the three commandos who'd taken up defensive positions in the trees. They formed a square with me in the center and we made our way back toward Dawna's Saab. By the time we topped the rise, my hair was plastered against my scalp and the shoulders of my jacket were soaked through. I saw that the road was empty. The motorcycles and the truck had disappeared. We approached the car cautiously. The pelting rain had kept the fire from spreading, but flames still flickered in the center of the black- berry thicket. The Saab's blackened shell crouched among the charred canes. Sooty smoke rose from the smoldering upholstery.

Through the smudged mist I saw two wet-suited figures half hidden by tall grass on the far side of the car. One man hunched over another who lay on the ground. The crouching man raised his head and shouted. I didn't recognize the long word he used, but from the terror in his voice I knew he was calling for a medic. The commando who'd been beside me was running toward the fallen man. The crouching man shouted again, two short syllables that rhymed and had to mean "hurt bad." He said more, but the only word I understood was "pistol." I stared at the wounded man. His cinnamon-colored hair was impossibly curly, a wiry mat topping his head. His face was dotted with reddish freckles, stark against the too-white skin. Beside me, the blond leader flipped open his cell phone and asked urgently for an ambulance. He snapped it shut, then opened it again and called for a fire truck to join the emergency crew. He took a step toward the victim, then turned back to me. "You wait. The police will have questions for you."

"Your man's been shot?"

His expression was grim. "In the chest."

My own chest ached. "You guys saved my life. But—"

He cut me off. "You say you are a colleague of Colonel Sorensen?"

"Yes, from the American embassy."

"We, too, sometimes work for the colonel." He jerked his chin down in a curt nod of introduction. "*Kaptajn* Flemming Nielsen. I must see to my man. You will wait." He turned and walked away as if he had no doubt my discipline would match his own.

For the next hour, I stood in the woods feeling alternately guilty and useless. The injured man was rushed away with a scream of sirens. A crew of yellow-jacketed firemen dealt with the car and a covey of local police flitted between me and the frogmen, working out the details of what had happened. The rain stopped and the clouds thinned and disappeared. I moved into the sunlight, ghosts of steam rising from the puddles, clouding the air around me. By the time the cops were ready to take us downtown, my hair was dry and my pants and shirt were only damp.

At the police station, I was interviewed by a burly male detective and a pregnant policewoman. She had inch-long sable hair that rayed out from her face, exposing the half-dozen studs decorating each of her ears from the lobes upward. The two of them were thorough and businesslike. We spent an hour going over my statement before they gave me a mug of coffee and left me alone in a boxy room with a gray tile floor and walls to match. The room smelled of disinfectant and ancient tobacco smoke. The only window was in the top of the door and it was fretted by the reinforcing wire sandwiched between two sheets of glass that were probably bulletproof.

I hunched over the coffee cooling in front of me. I didn't trust my shaking hand to lift the mug without spilling the contents. I wasn't cold. I was scared.

Ole Bjørn Møller, brother of a high-ranking Bandido, murdered in my flat.

Gerry Davis, my partner, murdered with the Hells Angels in Nakskov.

And two men on motorcycles had tried to murder me. I gripped the edge of the table with both hands to stop my shudder from becoming convulsive. Someone had figured out I'd go to Holger. Someone had prepared a mobile trap for me. No one could have predicted with certainty which route I'd take when I left Holger's church. Very likely, more than one truck had been standing by north of Copenhagen. Someone had watched me leave and called the best-positioned driver to block the route I'd taken.

Whoever set up the ambush was in command of superb intelligence and formidable resources. I couldn't defend myself against attackers who were so well organized and well financed. I remembered the frogman lying on the ground. A lump like ice formed in my stomach.

I had to get out of Denmark. I checked my watch. Three o'clock. At this minute, Bella might be talking to Woody's father. If, as I expected, he turned out to be a dead end, we'd have to search elsewhere for a bone-marrow donor. Now, I couldn't linger in Denmark and help Bella through that, but Holger would be here for her.

Holger. The police were probably on the phone with him verifying my story. Holger would be concerned for my safety. Concerned enough perhaps to come in person and drive me back to Copenhagen. We could go to the embassy and make sure Bella had returned safely from her meeting.

I heard a rustle of sound from the hallway and glanced at the door. Watching me through the fretted glass was the policewoman who'd taken my statement. She caught my eye, nodded, and moved out of my line of sight. Checking on the prisoner.

Getting to the embassy wasn't likely to be so easy. Two men on motorcycles had attacked me and wounded a Danish soldier. The assault looked like an incident in renewed biker gang war. The local authorities would report to everyone in Danish law enforcement who tracked *rocker* violence. *Kriminalinspektør* Ernst Blixenstjerne would be among the first to hear the news. He was probably on his way to me. He'd see the attack on me as proof that the war had resumed and that I was involved with the bikers. I pressed my hands against my temples, trying to contain the headache beginning there. Once Blixenstjerne started in on me, the interrogation would last until morning.

Bella would have no one to back her up because a Danish cop mistook me for one of the bad guys. The situation infuriated me. I spent the next thirty minutes working up a rage hot enough to dry my clothes.

When *Politiassistent* Niels-Jørgen Jespersen walked in on me at three-thirty, I was on my feet and spoiling for a fight.

I didn't get one.

19

JESPERSEN'S EXPRESSION WAS APOLOGETIC. "VIBEKE IS FINISH-ing with your statement," he said in his mournful voice. "Once you sign it, you're free to go."

"Free to go?" I repeated. "I can leave the country?"

"Your presence in Denmark is no longer required."

I recognized the deliberate phrasing of an official position. Jespersen was acting in his capacity as diplomatic liaison, conveying a decision of Danish law enforcement, made at higher levels. Blixenstjerne had decided to cut me loose.

The policewoman whisked into the room, clipboard in hand. She said in English, "If you find an error, tell me. I will correct it." Her uniform blouse was cut full in front to make room for her pregnant belly and she had to stretch her arms to place the typed sheet in front of me. A grainy fixative glistened on her spiky hair, its sparkle mirrored by the tiny sapphires starring her ears.

I read over my statement, ignoring the hushed conversation between the two cops. I signed the paper and passed it to the policewoman. She said an affectionate goodbye to Jespersen and left the room. He stood up as if our business was concluded. But a Danish soldier had been shot. How could the police possibly be finished interrogating me?

"The statement I gave her is *all* you need?" I asked.

"I'm sure Vibeke covered everything," Jespersen said. "She's an excellent officer. We took advanced training together. The best marksman in the senior ranks."

I pictured the woman in a shoulder holster specially cut for an officer whose breasts were swollen by pregnancy. No doubt the Danish police suppliers had an adjustable model that would also suit the well-armed nursing mother. I wished sharpshooter Vibeke would offer to bodyguard me.

Jespersen added, "Bella advised me that she wants to speak with you."

Her name from his lips set off my internal alarm. I silenced it. I'd been attacked. Of course my security officer wanted a report. "Can I get a ride with you to the embassy?" I asked Jespersen.

"I'm not returning immediately to Copenhagen. But arrangements for your transportation have been made." He grimaced apologetically. "I believe you'll find them satisfactory."

More than satisfactory, I discovered. When I got down to the police station parking lot, I found *Kaptajn* Nielsen and his band of commandos waiting for me in an eight-passenger van. They'd washed off their face paint, showered and shaved and changed into civilian clothes, but they didn't act like off-duty soldiers. They were tense and watchful and the gym bag resting between each pair of booted feet bulged with more than dirty clothes. All of them noted my entrance but not one met my eyes.

"I appreciate the ride," I said as I buckled myself into the middle seat beside Nielsen. "Your idea?"

"The colonel." The harshness in his tone was new.

"The man who was injured," I said slowly. "How's he doing?"

Nielsen looked up, his gaze steady. "His wound proved fatal."

The warning undertone in his voice stopped me from offering sympathy. And what credible condolence could I make when a man died protecting me?

It was my good luck that he'd been nearby when I needed help. Or was it luck? "How did you happen to be out in the woods today?" I asked Nielsen.

"Routine readiness exercise." Nielsen leaned forward and told the driver to get going. The lines from a comb were visible in his hair and he smelled of aloe-scented shave cream. He sat back and said to me, "The defense ministry has a facility in Hellebæk. They run a number of training courses in this area."

I hadn't realized that Holger's parish was only a kilometer from a military training facility. Handy neighbor for a man with a long career in intelligence. I said, "I suppose you planned this exercise months ago."

"Perhaps." Nielsen gave me a long look. "Rapid response is

part of our training. The first *we* knew of this exercise was at midnight last night when we were deployed to Hellebæk."

"Midnight? What pretend emergency were you guys responding to so rapidly?"

When he spoke, his voice was matter-of-fact. "Diplomatic hostage taking."

I was too stunned to say anything in reply. I wondered how many other groups of soldiers had been sent into the woods last night. I recalled the young man I'd seen mowing Holger's lawn. Typically sextons are older, less physically fit, and shod in clogs. That gardener's combat boots had been military issue. So Holger had made sure our meeting was well guarded. But no one had planned on a casualty. Nielsen didn't resume the conversation. His eyes moved constantly, from the road ahead to the traffic beside us, to his men in the van. Their comrade was dead. Nielsen was taking the danger seriously.

I'd been involved in a third homicide. Yet Blixenstjerne had dropped his interest in me. Only Holger could have achieved that. And to get so swift a result, he'd done more than verify that I'd lunched with him. He must have released classified information concerning the Stingers and the biker gangs. He didn't want me enmeshed in a police investigation in Denmark.

And I knew why. I spent the rest of the drive hardening my heart against Holger and his efforts to manipulate me into blindly taking part in his operation.

We reached the embassy at four-forty-five.

At four-forty-six, Dawna reached me. I was signing the after-hours sheet at Post One when she marched up. "A full report," she said. "Now."

I tossed the pen down and faced her. "The only person I'm obligated to report to is my security officer."

"You think so, do you?" She eyed my tattered sleeves. "Trashed my car. Shredded my uniform. You owe me, Collins."

I slipped out of the windbreaker and handed it to her. "Obviously the police investigation into the Nakskov incident confirmed my story. I've got the official word. The cops are through with me. And I've nothing to say to you."

Her jaw jutted out, an FBI agent preparing to subdue a criminal. But she swallowed whatever comment she'd planned to make. She was still treating me like a suspect but she hadn't convinced anyone else I was guilty of wrongdoing. A heavy-handed approach wouldn't work. She had no authority over me. And no leverage without the Danish police behind her.

"You want it by the book, we'll do it by the book." Dawna balled up the jacket and tossed it across the room into a wastebasket. "Try Hinton's pager number again," she said to the on-duty Marine, a gangly twenty-year-old with a downy upper lip.

The Marine nervously punched numbers into his phone, one eye on Dawna.

I said, "Bella's not in her office?"

Dawna made an impatient noise. "Disappeared at two-thirty."

A half-hour before her planned meeting with Wlodek Wojcik. She should have been back by four. The muscles tightened in my stomach.

Dawna stared at the phone, tapping her fingers. She said, "What's the matter with Hinton? Nobody's been able to raise her. She's the RSO, she's not supposed to turn her pager off."

"Probably weak batteries," I said, my voice as offhand as I could make it. No need for me to panic, not yet. Most likely Bella hadn't wanted to be interrupted by beeping while she was with Wojcik. But what was taking her so long?

"I don't want to waste more time," Dawna said. "Hinton doesn't call in the next five minutes, I'll ask those guys upstairs to go out and find her."

"Guys upstairs?" I repeated.

She waved a hand toward the ceiling. "The team in your office. Been reconstructing Gerry's movements for the past ten days. They're hot to talk to you, too. Be glad to help me track down Bella and get the ball rolling."

I couldn't let a bunch of CIA meddlers find Bella with Wlodek Wojcik. "What the hell," I said to Dawna. "I don't have time to waste, either. Might as well go ahead and make my report to you."

"Smart move." She stabbed the elevator UP button. "We'll talk in my office. You start from when you stole my car. I want every detail. Go through it twice, three times if we have to. I don't care if it takes all night."

It wouldn't. I'd make certain of that. If Bella didn't turn up soon, I had to be free to search for her. When the elevator doors slid open, I followed Dawna in. "So tell me," I said to her back, "What'd you find in Nakskov?"

She punched the button for her floor and turned to me. "You want the play-by-play?"

"The highlights will do."

She stared at the wall six inches above my head and recited the facts as though she were giving a scouting report on an opposing basketball team. "Blixenstjerne's people were all over that Hells Angels compound. Found no sign of the missiles. Talked to every sucker they could corner. Not one had a clue what Gerry Davis was doing. Nobody'd heard of you. And not one connected Ole Bjørn Møller to you or Davis. Not a thing to implicate you." She moved her glance to my face. "I pointed out that there was nothing exculpatory, either."

"I'm innocent." I spread my hands in a nothing-to-hide gesture. "Blixenstjerne understands that."

"Somebody leaned on him, that's obvious. Bingo, you're off the hook with the Danish cops. And as far as Blixenstjerne's concerned, you're in the way." She made a disgusted noise. "He wants you to leave Denmark."

"That'd be my choice," I said. The attack had scared me. As soon as I was certain that Bella could manage without my help, I'd go.

The doors opened and we headed for the third floor nook that served as Dawna's office. Over her shoulder, she said, "I wouldn't be eager to work with that idiot Baldwin."

Her words startled me. She had to know Baldwin intended to boot me off the task force. The unclassified cable outlining his intentions had been routinely distributed to the FBI representatives at post. I'd missed his first deadline and triggered an official complaint. "Doesn't look like I'll have the pleasure of working with Baldwin," I said, watching her. "Not much chance I'll reach Bangor by noon tomorrow."

"Noon on Monday," she corrected me. "Jerk extended each of his asshole deadlines by twenty-four hours."

A unexpected reprieve from Baldwin. "Why'd he do that?"

"Because he wanted to show me what a hot shit he is, of course." She got the door open and crossed the room to take the upholstered chair behind a glass-topped wooden desk.

I left the door ajar to make it easy for Bella to interrupt us if she returned. I said to Dawna, "I take it he called you about me?"

"Naturally. Checking on the situation here. He didn't want to put something in writing that'd turn around and bite him later. He had a hissy fit when I told him I wanted you to stay in Denmark."

Puzzled, I said, "You told him I should stay here. And he extended the deadlines so that I could. So why are you so pissed off?"

"He's running a number on me—can't you see that?"

"Spell it out for me."

She grunted impatiently. "He's in counterterrorism. I'm an expert on outlaw bikers. His job is the one that matters. It's not possible that anything *I'm* working on could justify delaying you. I told him he'd be hearing from me again, *through proper channels*." She enunciated the bureaucratese pompously, sounding exactly like Sam Baldwin. Then she laughed. "That scared him."

Instead of passing on her suspicions of me, Dawna had helped my case. Baldwin wasn't going to let her claim an asset he'd designated as *his*. To undercut any protest she might make, he'd given a patronizing nod to her investigation and extended his deadlines. And because she'd be looking over his shoulder, he wouldn't include nasty phrases like "dereliction of duty" in any complaint he made to the attorney general. My dead career had miraculously come back to life. I said, "I agree, Baldwin's useless. But that task force matters to me. If we can finish up here in time, I'll go to Bangor."

"You'll regret it. You know he doesn't want to work with you. He's only eased off this much to cover his backside. And to spite me. Probably already got his complaint written. He's hoping you won't show up by noon on Monday, so he can go forward with your official removal." She eyed me speculatively and her tone grew cajoling. "I do have *some* clout in the bureau. I can convince the director to put a gag on Baldwin. *If* you stay here expressly to help me clean up this mess."

Fat chance, I thought. Dawna's honeyed words didn't fool me. She didn't have my career interests at heart. She wanted me handy while she built her case against me. But I didn't say that. I had to keep Dawna diverted until Bella returned. "Let me try your phone," I said to Dawna. "Maybe Bella's at her condo."

"Her boy's alone there." Dawna pushed the instrument toward me. "I doubt he'll tell *you* anything, either."

I perched on a corner of the desk, picked up the receiver and punched in Bella's home number. Woody answered with a raspy hello.

"It's Casey," I said. "I'm looking for your mom."

"She's not here." After five seconds, he added, "When you see her, tell her to bring egg rolls, okay?"

"She'll be home for dinner?" I asked.

"I don't know." The tone was surly but I heard a note of uneasiness that pulled my own nerves tighter. "She *said* she'd be home by four-thirty. She shoulda called."

Bella *always* called. Even when Woody was in the one-year-old classroom at Kindercare, when her plans changed she'd always phoned his child-care worker immediately. I kept my dismay out of my voice and said, "She'll be there soon, then."

He was silent for a half-second and then his next words came out in a rush. "I beeped her. She didn't call back."

Bella was involved in something truly heavy if she'd ignored a page from Woody. He'd hesitated before revealing that alarming fact. He added, "You're the second person who's phoned looking for her."

Bella had taught him how to respond to callers from the embassy where she served as RSO. He was supposed to be polite, brief, and factual. He wasn't supposed to say his mother had gone missing. And he hadn't given that message to Dawna. Instead, he'd turned to me, the way he used to when a complicated Lego construction went awry. *Help me, Casey. Help me fix it.*

A wave of yearning swept over me, a formless and enveloping need to ease the tightness in his voice, make his world right again. I took a breath and when I spoke I kept my tone light and my body relaxed for Dawna's benefit. "I'm on top of it. Anything else you need?"

He cleared his throat, taking a moment to absorb my meaning. "There's nothing good to eat," he said. "When you see my mom, you tell her I want egg rolls."

Hunger wasn't his problem. Almost thirteen years old, he could go to the store and buy any food he wanted. Except he wouldn't take a chance on missing Bella's call. He was telling me once more: *Find my mom.*

"Pork egg rolls, right?" Letting him know I got the message and I'd act on it.

"Pork," he agreed. The relief in that single syllable zinged through me, a low-voltage charge from comfort given to someone I loved.

I said goodbye and cradled the phone slowly, trying to silence my jangling nerves. I'd reassured Woody but I knew it was too soon to go looking for Bella. Her meeting might have started late and run long. She'd put everything in her life at risk to track down

Woody's father. No matter how much Woody and I feared for her safety, I had to give her enough time to finish the job. I felt Dawna's eyes on me and I said casually, "Her son expects her home soon."

"Then let's you and me get to it," she replied.

I settled into a chair with exaggerated slowness, studying the room. The wall to my left was covered with black-and-white photos of hairy men, long-range shots like the ones Dawna had snapped at the funeral. The three remaining walls were papered with hand-drawn charts containing intricate patterns of circles, lines and squares. The same decor I favored in my own office in Foggy Bottom. We were tracking different sets of bad guys, but we both used link analysis to tie people and events together.

Dawna tapped a pen against the yellow pad centered on her desk. "Your turn," she said.

I put my feet up on the desk to remind her that we were colleagues, not adversaries. She wasn't entitled to give me the third degree. I said, "You want the play-by-play?"

Her smile seemed forced. Her chair squeaked as she tilted it back. She raised her feet to the other side of the desk. I saw the scuffed leather soles of her flat shoes, the amazing length of her khaki-trousered legs. That's where she got her height from, I realized. Her femurs were six inches longer than mine. She clasped her fingers behind her head. "The highlights'll do fine."

She listened without comment as I summarized my conversations with Gitte and Ulf Møller and described the Bandidos who'd followed me to Copenhagen. I mentioned my meeting with Holger Sorensen and detailed the attack that destroyed her car. I ended by briefly outlining what Holger and I had concluded. Avoiding any mention of Bella or Wlodek Wojcik, I explained the *rocker* division of criminal turf.

Dawna pressed on the desk with her palms, rolling her chair back so that her feet dropped to the floor. She picked up her pen and tapped it on the pad. "I can draw in the Xs and Os you've laid out for me, but the plays don't make sense. You say the Bandidos and Hells Angels have divvied things up. One gang's got the drugs, the other weapons. But if they're not at war, how do you account for the attacks on Møller, Davis and you?"

"Maybe those attacks only appear to be the result of gang war." I was looking at Dawna, but what I saw was the haunted face of Bjørn's mother. "Maybe Ulf killed his brother. Faking *rockerkrig*, while at the same time insisting there's no gang war. Good way to muddy the waters so we won't notice he's guilty of murder. Then he staged the attacks on Gerry and me."

"That dog won't hunt," Dawna said flatly.

"It's not so far-fetched. Ulf might have had a personal reason to kill—"

She made an impatient gesture. "Cops always check out family first. Your pal Ulf was devoted to his brother. Loved him too much to kill him."

I heard the mocking tone in her voice. I said, "You buy that?"

"Not hardly. Those scumbags don't let brotherly feelings affect business." She sighed. "I'd have dearly loved to pin this on Ulf. But it wasn't him. At the time his brother was murdered, Ulf was in the visitors' room at *Vestre Fængsel*." She named the maximum security prison at the edge of downtown Copenhagen.

I took a half-second to absorb the news. I'd been so sure Ulf was the murderer. "Someone else killed Ole Bjørn Møller?"

"Couldn't have been Ulf. Cops have him on the security video talking to slime."

"Okay," I said slowly. "Ulf didn't do it. But I still think that incident—and the other two—were sparked by something else. Not *rockerkrig*."

Dawna gestured toward her charts. "I'll run your idea against my analytical model. See how it meshes with what I've got. But I'm betting I'll find all three attacks mean biker gang war's heating up."

"I don't think so," I said.

"We've got three violent incidents involving bikers. Murder in your flat, murder of your partner, attempted murder on you. Through you, all three are linked to the missiles. Very sexy weaponry. The obvious connection is the biker gang war. But you say the truce is more solid than ever."

I lowered my feet to the floor. "It is."

She snickered. "Sound pretty sure of yourself."

"I am sure."

Something glinted in Dawna's eyes. "Maybe you'd like to put your theory to a little test."

20

"A TEST?" I REPEATED. "WHAT DO YOU HAVE IN MIND?"

"Nothing complicated," Dawna said. "You stay here. Keep working on your project. The guilty parties will expose themselves by trying to get to you. We'll know which of us is right."

Disbelief raised the pitch of my voice. "You want me to set myself up for target practice?"

She waggled her hand in a minimizing gesture. "Copenhagen cops have assigned a protective detail to your flat. We can take other precautions." She dropped her voice so I had to lean closer. "You want to find out who offed your partner, you have to do this."

Her scheme might expose Gerry's killer. It might get me killed, too. I said, "You proposed this to Blixenstjerne. And he vetoed the idea."

"He couldn't ask a civilian to take so big a risk. That's what he said." She smiled. "He never said you couldn't volunteer."

I hesitated. I owed Gerry. I wanted to find his killer. Was I doing the right thing, rejecting Dawna's idea?

She picked up on my uncertainty instantly. "We can get these guys." She was as fervent as the captain of a basketball team down ten points at the half. "Stay," she said in that mesmerizing voice. "Finish the project Gerry was working on."

For Gerry. He would have wanted me to do it. But there were too many variables. I rubbed the heel of my hand over my forehead. "I don't know—"

Out of sight in the hallway, something banged against the wall and smashed to the floor. Glass shattered explosively.

I flung myself out of my chair. I dived behind Dawna's desk, pulling her down beside me. She crouched, breathing hard through her mouth, hands scrabbling at her pants cuff, exposing the holster Velcroed to her calf.

"Jesus, I'm sorry," a man said in a voice I knew well.

I rose slowly to see over the desktop.

Andy stood in the doorway, his expression sheepish.

Dawna was upright again, her voice taut with anger. "What the hell were you doing?" she asked him.

"Smacked into some damn picture," he replied. "Wasn't paying attention, I guess."

"Lucky you didn't get hurt." Dawna laid a palm-sized .22 caliber pistol on the desk, the lightweight metal soundless against the glass top.

I stared at it, trying to get my pulse rate down again. Dawna was carrying a concealed weapon, a violation of Danish law, U.S. government regulations, and international agreements. Maybe I could convince her to lend it to me. Of course, if I'd had a gun one minute ago, I'd have shot Andy. I glanced toward him.

He was still in the doorway. "Sorry," he said again. "Didn't mean to startle you." He wore Levi's and a short-sleeved cotton shirt of washed-out Madras plaid. I'd seen the shirt before, a long time ago. The colors had bled and blended to a softer shade of yellow green that set off his eyes. Andy and his shirt, older but wearing well. Both still looking good.

He spoke directly to me. "Post One told me you were in the FBI office. Are you all right?"

"I'm fine," I said. "A little jumpy, that's all."

"So you came up here looking for Casey." Dawna's voice was sharp. "Why were you out there in the hall? Hoping to overhear something good?"

Andy's cheeks grew ruddy. "It's not like you were whispering, you know. I was ten feet from the door when you told Casey she should stay in Denmark. What, somebody attacked her? And you want her to go on like nothing happened?"

"Didn't hit her, did they? Be easier to draw a bead on a jack rabbit." Dawna grinned at me. "Damn, I bet you'd be awesome covering transition defense."

I came around the desk and sat down again. "You reacted pretty fast yourself."

"But *after* you," Dawna corrected me. "Just reflex, covering your play."

Andy leaned toward me and his eyes found mine, the concern in them lapping over me like a gentle tide. His voice was protective. "You have to leave the country."

"She can't," Dawna interjected.

"You don't need Casey," Andy said to her. "I've got a handle on things. I'll run the project."

"You can't get the results I want," Dawna said. She came from behind the desk, closer to Andy. They were the same height. He had more muscle mass but the tensile strength in her willowy body probably made up for that. Of course that only mattered if their argument got physical. Which wasn't impossible. Dawna seemed dead set against letting Andy interfere with her plan.

She locked eyes with him and added. "I don't care how much you've learned in the last few days. That won't cut it with the people who killed Gerry or the guys who attacked her." Her right hand dropped lightly on my shoulder. "They aren't going to be threatened by you. They won't come after you. They'll ignore you."

Andy's face froze into a neutral expression. "That's *your* opinion—"

"That's fact. *She's* the playmaker." Dawna squeezed my shoulder. "We can't win unless Casey stays in the game."

Dawna had abandoned her hunting metaphor. Didn't want to make it too obvious that she planned to set a trap using me for bait. That word didn't sound as attractive as "playmaker." Bait doesn't end up sitting at the Kodak all-American Table at the Final Four.

I wanted to find Gerry's killer but Dawna's scheme was too hazardous. She knew that. So long as she scored, it didn't matter to her who got hurt. And she was suspicious of me. She wanted to have me close enough to arrest when she got the goods on me. No, I wouldn't let Dawna draw me into her scheme. I opened my mouth to make that clear.

But Andy spoke first. "She can't stay," he told Dawna. "Your plan's too dangerous for her."

"You don't make that call," Dawna objected. "Only the RSO can do that." She grabbed the phone again and punched in the number for Post One. "You heard anything from Hinton yet?" She slammed down the receiver. "Where is that woman?"

Dawna was the last person I wanted to go searching for Bella. I spoke quickly. "If I decide to do this, Bella won't be a problem."

Andy stared at me as if I'd dealt him a swift blow to the head. "You aren't seriously considering—"

"I'll sleep on it," I told Dawna, standing. "We'll talk again tomorrow." I started for the door. I wanted out of Dawna's sight so I could start tracking Bella.

"Don't forget the guys upstairs," Dawna said to my back. "They've got some questions for you."

"Sure." I escaped out the door. I walked slowly toward the elevator. I didn't want to answer a CIA investigative team's questions. The scratches striping my forearms began to itch. With my left hand, I rubbed the red welt across the back of my right.

Andy was beside me. "You should put something on that."

I sighed. "I need to clean up. I'm a complete mess."

"Not complete. But close." He plucked a piece of dead leaf from my hair. "I've been upstairs with those guys all day. I gave them plenty to work with. They can wait till tomorrow to talk to you."

"Great. I'll head over to my flat—"

"You're not going anywhere by yourself."

I opened my mouth to protest. I stopped myself. I couldn't go out alone and unarmed looking for Bella. I had to stay in my flat where I had police protection. And I could use Andy's help getting there. I smiled at him. "I'd appreciate a ride home. And I need to pick up something on the way."

We were out of the embassy by six-thirty. Sunlight beamed through rain-washed air and threw rainbowed reflections off the oil-streaked puddles in the parking lot. I followed him to his car, a Volvo station wagon, dark green, the hood spotted with crushed blossoms knocked by the rain from the overhanging wild-rose bush.

I buckled myself into the passenger seat, sitting at an angle to watch traffic beyond the reach of Andy's mirrors. No one followed us when we left the embassy lot. Two blocks up Østerbrogade, I told Andy to park in front of *Silkevejen*, a take-out restaurant run by a family who'd emigrated from Sinkiang a decade ago. Inside, the air was thick with the odors of hot oil and steamed rice. I bought two *Kinafarer* combinations, packed separately.

Andy drove me to the waterfront so I could deliver one bag to Woody. He came downstairs to the building entrance to take it from me. He told me that Bella had phoned five minutes before. Relief made his voice deeper, that of a grown man.

The warm sack in my hand was lighter. "One China Traveler special," I said, passing the bag to him. "I suppose you told your mom to bring egg rolls, too."

His toothy smile erased the impression of maturity I'd had a moment before. He looked an impish nine years old again. "I'll be ready for more by the time she gets home."

"She say what was holding her up?" I asked.

"She's been unpredictable lately. This thing . . ." His voice cracked and the skin on his face flushed. "Since this thing with me, she gets weirded out."

Apologizing for making his mom weird. I felt it again, that sudden eruption of maternal feeling that made me long to wrap my arms around him. But Woody didn't appreciate my hugs now. So, instead, I said, "I'd take you over to my place till she gets home, but I've got company." I didn't want to explain why it wasn't safe for him to hang out with me.

He glanced from me to Andy, waiting in the car. "No problem," Woody reassured me with a knowing grin. "I got stuff to do." He thanked me for the food and I said good night. When I heard the latch click, I left. I didn't want to be near Woody if my enemies reappeared.

When we reached my flat, Andy insisted on coming inside with me. "I heard what you said to the boy. Surely by 'company,' you meant me?"

"I didn't, actually. And you don't need to do this." I led him into the foyer. "The guy in uniform's right outside where anyone can see him. Nobody's breached the security system. Nothing to worry about."

"Nothing?" He moved past me into the kitchen and set the *Silkevejen* sack on the table. "This thing weighs a ton. You'll make yourself sick, if you eat it all."

"Eating half my dinner is your idea of protection?" I opened the refrigerator. All it contained were three bottles of Elephant beer left from the six-pack I'd bought on Thursday night. I set two on the table.

"Got to save you from yourself." He unpacked six egg rolls, a half-liter of fried rice and a couple of fortune cookies. The rich fragrance of steamed pork and cabbage took over the room. "Beats me how you manage to stay so slim."

"Friends like you, that's my secret." I set out plates and glasses and we divided up the food. I chewed my first bite of egg roll slowly, sampling the flavors. I tasted cabbage and green pepper and something unexpected. Had the chef substituted fennel for some ingredient not available in Copenhagen? I took a forkful of rice browned in pork fat. A caraway seed crunched between my teeth. Chinese cooking in Danish translation. I'd have known what country I was in even without reading my fortune. Which began, I discovered, with *"Kungfutse siger."*

"What?" Andy asked. "What does Confucius say to you?"

"Beware of men who steal your food." I stuffed the strip of paper in my pocket. "I'm taking that shower. You want to stick around, I'll make us some coffee after."

"I'm sticking around," he said. "My fortune says 'the night is young.'"

"How do you know it doesn't say 'Yankee go home'?" I asked. "You don't know this language."

"Maybe I took a crash course."

"Sure. Now you speak like a native."

He grinned. *"En hel del bedre end du tror."* A whole lot better than you believe.

His near-perfect Danish stunned me. Andy was too full of surprises. I fled to the bathroom without repeating the phrase in my cookie, a statement I was sure Confucius had never made.

The English version would be *the past is a present to be opened in the future.* I'd read it silently to myself and instantly I'd seen my fingers on Andy's buttons, opening his shirt. Moving down toward the buttons on his jeans. Slowly, until I was looking at Andy's lean, beautiful body. Every bare inch of him.

21

FORGET IT, I TOLD MY TOO-EAGER HORMONES. I'D COME CLOSE to death. My body hungered to feel completely alive. This sudden lust for Andy was biological reaction, nothing more. Well—maybe a little more than that. Maybe a lot more. Now I recalled another sensation I'd forced my mind to forget. How it felt to be cherished. To be loved, the way Andy had made love to me in San Sal.

I wasn't giving in to biological urge *or* romantic impulse. Not with Andy. I wouldn't make that mistake again.

I took a shower—not cold, but plenty long, washing and rinsing my hair twice. It was twenty past eight o'clock by the time I reappeared, my scratches covered by jeans and a long-sleeved sweat shirt. Andy had cleaned up the kitchen and made a pot of coffee. I took the cup he handed me and went into the living room to call my father.

He lived in a residential care facility in Oregon. The familiar climate and geography helped my father retain his orientation, the doctor claimed. He advised against moving him to the D.C. area unless I could make regular and frequent visits. Otherwise the changed surroundings might hasten his mental deterioration.

I agonized over the decision. I loved my father and wanted him near me. But I knew that was a selfish choice. My professional life was too chaotic to allow for "regular and frequent" scheduling. I'd followed the doctor's advice and left my father in Oregon. Four or five times a year, I put Blondie in a kennel and flew west to visit. Not often enough, and never long enough, but my father didn't complain. He'd always understood how important my work was to me and even now it remained important to him, too.

I phoned him weekly. Today, it was eleven-thirty in the morning in Oregon's Willamette Valley before he came on the line. The attendant had tracked him down in the common room watching cartoons on television.

He was chuckling when he picked up the phone. "You remember that, don't you?" His voice was strong, enunciation clear—or as clear as it could be, given that he was quoting a little yellow bird. "I t'ought I t'aw a puddy cat."

We'd perfected the routine when I was six. I responded with my own imitation of Tweety. "I did, I did, I did see a puddy cat." My father's familiar laugh rumbled into my ear. He added, "Come on over, you can watch with me."

He was certain I lived across town in the house where I'd grown up. "Can't make it today." I kept my voice light. "I'm still out of the country."

"Oh, right," he responded quickly. "Slipped my mind."

"That's one thing I wanted to tell you," I said. "I'm not sure I'll make it for July Fourth."

"Too bad," he said. "You love that parade."

"Not as much as you." He'd attended every local Independence Day pageant since 1947 when they resumed again after the World War II hiatus. No matter that he'd seen the same floats fifty times. He'd still cheer for the heavy-equipment dealer who hauled the immense concrete I-beam down the main street with a banner reading YOUR HOMETOWN INDUSTRY AT WORK.

I added, "You know me, the firemen's breakfast is the part I like."

"Fellows make good pancakes," he agreed. "Plus, ham and eggs. Can't miss that."

"I hate to," I said. "But it looks like I'll be tied up with this airline disaster in Bangor."

"Saw that on the news," he said knowledgeably. "So it's not an accident?"

A flash of lucidity. He'd remembered that I worked in counter-terrorism, made the connection. "Doesn't look like it," I said. "I'll know more after I get to the scene."

"Think you'll be on television?" His voice had a hopeful undertone. I'd gotten press coverage during the incident last winter, all of it negative. He'd disregarded the reasons for the coverage, devoted himself to searching the airwaves for the face of his daughter, a fugitive from justice.

"Let's hope not," I said. "Wouldn't want to go through that again."

"Oh, right." He coughed. "You know, I don't always remember things perfectly."

"None of us do," I said.

"Least I'm not crazy." He lowered his voice and I got the impression he was sneaking a glance over his shoulder. "Some of these people. Well, you wouldn't believe."

"I can imagine—"

His voice cut me off, shouting at someone at his end. "You get away from there, you hear me? Soon as this show's over, I'll put headline news on."

"Dad—"

"Casey, I got to go." His words jammed together, he was so rushed. "Fool over there's messing with the TV."

"What, he interferes with your watching United Network News?"

"A troublemaker, that's what he is. Says that anchorwoman gets him all hot and bothered. He makes foul comments so loud I can't hear her." He paused and when he spoke again his voice was anxious and I could imagine the furrows in his brow. "That anchor, that Lura woman. Don't I know her from somewhere?"

Hometown celebrity, Lura Dumont. He'd known her since she was six years old and came over to watch Saturday morning cartoons with us. But before I could remind him, I heard shouting in the background. Sounded like "sit on my face you little fox." My father called out, "Don't touch that channel changer." He said to me, "I've got to go."

I listened to the dial tone for a second before I hung up. I rubbed the back of my hand across my mouth. Forgetting and covering up the lapse. The most difficult phase for Alzheimer's patients, when they understand that they're getting worse, not better. The doctor had told me the next stage would be easier for my father. He wouldn't regret what he couldn't remember.

I picked up the coffee cup. Set it back down again to blow my nose. He'd known who I was, remembered what I did, made that one dazzling connection. Some Saturdays I got far less. Yet my pain was sharper on the good days when I had a clear reminder of the once-whole man I'd adored all my life. On days like this one, the truth was impossible to deny. I was losing my father. Slowly and painfully for us both.

Andy interrupted my sad reverie. "I had this out in my car. I don't know, maybe it's not such a hot idea."

I turned to look at him, standing in the foyer. He held a battered boombox, old enough to be the same one he'd had in San Salvador. "You want to listen to music, you don't need that." I waved a hand toward the foyer closet. "My landlord left behind his CD player and most of his collection."

"This is a custom tape," Andy said, pulling a ninety-minute cassette from his shirt pocket. "Not available on compact disc."

I crossed the room and took the cassette from him. The label read SIXTIES DEATH in my handwriting. "I can't believe you kept this."

He plucked the cassette from my hand. "As if I'd ever part with something you made for me." He slipped it into the machine and pushed PLAY.

"I'm not in the mood for rock—"

The horns cut me off. Followed by the drums and the voices of Jan and Dean drawing us, Stingray and XKE, into the fatal drag race. "Dead Man's Curve" wasn't the first tune on the tape. I recalled that it came somewhere near the end. Andy had planned this. He remembered which songs wouldn't let me sit down.

His hand came toward me. I took it, his fingers firm on mine. My feet moved with the music, the floor cool against my bare soles. The sound set off a chemical reaction in my body, supercharging the protons and electrons. I had to rock with Andy, I had no other way to expend that urgent burst of energy.

I was breathing hard, my forehead damp, my heart pumping as I sang lustily along with Jan and Dean toward the climax. I kept my eyes wide open, though. I didn't want to find myself dancing barefoot across the dark corner of the room where the piano stool had once been.

As the tires squealed Andy gathered me in the classic wraparound embrace, then spiraled me out with such vigor that only the last-minute grip of his fingers kept me from hitting the sliding glass door.

The room was quiet except for the tape hissing through the blank space at the end of the song. I grinned at Andy. I hadn't boogied like that for a dozen years. I hadn't realized how much I missed dancing with a good partner. Andy wiped sweat off his forehead and grinned back at me, my right hand still in his left. The opening chords of "Teen Angel" pealed from the boombox.

Andy tightened his grip on my hand and slipped his right arm behind my back.

My free hand slid over his shoulder until my fingertips rested on the back of his neck. I closed my eyes and pressed my cheek against him. The old shirt was soft and the faint odor of English Leather mingled with the bleachy aroma of detergent. Andy's smell, bittersweet as my memories.

I felt a chill on the soles of my feet, as though we were crossing a colder piece of floor. I lifted my head from Andy's chest, eyes opened wide, fearful I'd see the pristine wall in the back corner, so recently washed clean of blood spatters. We were still at the opposite end of the room, near the sliding glass door. I sighed, a tiny gurgle of satisfaction, and relaxed once more against him, matching my steps to his. So easy to follow Andy's lead.

He made a noise, a stifled sob. His arm tightened against my back. I felt his cheek against my hair. "So damn long," he said softly. "I waited so damn long. To be with you again."

My eyes snapped open. I dropped his hand and pushed him away from me. My words came out strangled, but I got them out. "Your wife, Andy. I can't do this, not again."

He reached for me. "Molly and I are separated."

I backed away. "Right. She's there. You're here. Separated, just like before."

"No, not like that. Molly has a lawyer. She plans to file next month."

"You're getting divorced?"

"Sara finishes at Georgetown this year. Both girls will be on their own." Sara was his younger daughter. She'd started kindergarten while Andy had been in San Sal. He added, "Without them . . ." His voice trailed off.

"I'm sorry." Endings hurt. I didn't wish that kind of pain on anyone.

He shrugged. "I heard you'd joined up with Gerry Davis. On impulse, I put my name in."

My self-centered fantasy had been right. Andy had asked for this assignment because I'd been named to the State Department slot. He wanted to be with me again. Like we were in Salvador.

But I wasn't ready for a new lover. My break with Stefan was too recent. And even without that fresh wound as a reminder, I doubted I could trust Andy to love me enough. I had to stop him from saying more and taking us where I didn't want to go. I made my voice hard. "Am I hearing you right? You told Molly you'd be working with me. And she hired a lawyer, just like that?"

"Not exactly." He rubbed a tired hand over his hair. "I kept my part of the bargain. I broke off with you. And I tried with Molly. But every day, I thought of you. All these years. Every day."

Andy's wife was leaving him because of me? The thought horrified me. My words tumbled out, urgent with the need to make him understand. "You can't let her go through with it. You go home, tell her there's nothing between us. You can still talk her out—"

"Casey." The passion in that single soft-spoken word silenced me. He put his hands lightly on my shoulders. "I asked for the divorce. Before I put in for the job here."

He'd ended their marriage. Because of me? I couldn't let that happen, either. I opened my mouth to tell him so. But the tenderness in his sea-green eyes defeated me. That worshipful gaze— looking at me as if I were more precious than life. I wanted to be loved like that again. I couldn't fight him any longer. I could only follow where he led.

And he knew it. Both his arms went around me and he pulled me against him. "It kills me now to say to you, 'go home.' But you can't stay. I can't let anything happen to you."

His mouth found mine. His kiss was soft, blessedly soft. Warm, wet, drawing me in despite myself. I felt the last of my resistance melting.

His hand slipped under my sweatshirt, his fingertips skimming my back.

Carnal desire rippled through me.

His hand glided over my belly until his fingers caressed my nipple. He cupped my breast, his fingers tongues of flame against my skin.

Ripples of desire surged into a current, a roaring floodtide sweeping me before it, drowning out any wish to say no. I couldn't hear my thoughts anymore. I couldn't hear the song. There was only Andy, his salty taste and his bittersweet smell and his reverent touch.

He'd come back to me. After all these years, he'd left his wife and come back to me. I felt as if I'd drunk a bottle of champagne, intoxicated by the wonder of that return.

Too thick and clumsy, my fingers fumbled at the top button of his shirt, unable to get it through the buttonhole. I pulled my mouth away from Andy's. My breath came out in ragged gasps.

The tape hissed and clunked as it reached the end. I glanced up and saw my reflection in the sliding door. My hair wild, my eyes hot. Beyond the glass was the grassy expanse of the building's central open space, the evening light golden on the wooden frame of the play structure.

I backed away from Andy.

"I do something wrong?" he asked.

"No." I reached for his hand, to tug him to the bedroom with its blessed room-darkening pleated shade.

The door buzzer sounded, an irritating waspish noise.

Who had come calling? Who cared? I held tightly to Andy's hand, pulling him toward the bedroom. He didn't resist. My skin tingled in anticipation. Andy naked. In my bed. In me.

As we crossed the foyer, the buzz came again, loud and unrelenting. Andy slowed. "Cop'll take care of it," I whispered. Beyond the bedroom door, the comforter spread across the bed in a soft, inviting mound.

The buzzer sounded again, droning on for fifteen seconds. An accusing thumb, adamantly demanding entrance. *Open up, I know you're in there.*

I dropped Andy's hand, twisted the bolt, and yanked open the door.

Bella was peering at me through the building's glass entry door. I hurried across the lobby to let her in. Her eyes were bright with excitement. "Girl, have I got news for you," she said, striding past me and into my flat. She stopped when she saw Andy. His shirttail hung out on one side and his mouth had a smeary, just-kissed look.

Bella's gaze went from him to me, lingering on my face. My lips probably were swollen, too. My fingers rose guiltily toward my mouth. I stopped myself, ran my hand over my hair instead.

"Sorry to interrupt," Bella said to Andy. "I need to conference with Casey."

Andy cleared his throat. "I didn't think she should be alone, not after what happened."

Bella's eyes flicked to mine and her voice was full of concern. "You okay?"

"Fine," I said. "A few scratches, that's all."

Bella's gaze went back to Andy, her tone all-business again. "She's got cops hanging around outside. I'll be with her. So no problem if you take off."

Andy's chin moved up and his expression hardened, the way

it had when he and Dawna started debating my future. I didn't want him fighting with Bella. I spoke hurriedly. "I'll be okay, Andy. You go on back to your hotel."

"That's what you want?" he asked.

No. But Bella's situation was sensitive. We couldn't talk freely with him hovering nearby. "I'll see you tomorrow." I put as much promise as I could in the last word.

"Tomorrow," he said reluctantly. His lips brushed my cheek and he was gone.

I bolted the door and leaned my back against it. "Bad timing," I said to Bella.

"Good timing. You don't want to get mixed up with that guy."

"There you go again," I said, "badmouthing my boyfriend. You forgetting that you told me I should check this one out?"

"*Before* I saw him. Now, I'm telling you there's something wrong about him."

"You *always* say that. There's nothing wrong with Andy. Oh, maybe he's a little stiff around women."

Bella snickered. "I could see that."

"You know what I mean. He's more comfortable hanging around guys. You get to know him, he won't bore you." I cast a longing glance toward the bedroom. A red glow caught my eye. I blinked. I'd forgotten my new security system.

"You get to know him. I'm not interested," Bella was saying. "Besides, I had to tell you—"

I put my left hand on her arm, held my right index finger to my lips to silence her. "You were right, I'm perfectly safe," I said loudly. "Dawna Shepherd had an alarm system installed."

Bella made a face to let me know she understood. The walls had ears. I brought the cassette player from the living room and placed it near the security panel. I flipped the tape over. SAD LADIES, I'd written on that side. Prophetic. I pushed PLAY and turned the volume up full blast. Barbara Mandrell lamented loudly that drinking doubles alone didn't make it a party.

I motioned Bella into the bathroom. The air still smelled of shampoo. I sat on the edge of the tub and turned on the cold-water faucet. A thick stream thundered against the enameled cast iron.

Bella sat opposite me on the closed commode. She hugged herself as if trying to contain her excitement. "I found him," she said. "I found Woody's dad."

22 I LEANED CLOSER TO BELLA AND SPOKE IN A HUSHED VOICE. "You were with him a long time."

"Only a half-hour," she said. "Spent five times that long getting to him." She described a stop-and-start drill using pay phones. I realized Wlodek Wojcik must have had someone tracking Bella's movements from point to point, checking to see if she was being followed to their meeting. She'd been sent to the northern edge of Copenhagen via commuter train. She'd followed orders to detrain at Klampenborg and hang around Dyrehave, the park created from the former royal hunting preserve.

She said, "I wandered on the paths for another hour before he decided to talk to me." She turned to grin at the mirror. "Said he still couldn't resist my red hair."

"How'd he react when you told him he had a son?"

She turned away from her reflection. "He was surprised."

"Surprised? He hasn't seen you since 1986 and he took your word for it, that Woody's his kid?"

She waved a hand impatiently. "He doesn't have to take my word for it. I'm not looking for money or a last name or any of that soap-opera shit." Her voice got lower, more intense. "I come to him, an old girlfriend he remembers fondly. I tell him my son is sick and needs a bone-marrow transplant. Would he mind taking a blood test to see if he might be a suitable donor?"

"Right." My voice was sharp. "No big deal, being hospitalized to have your bone marrow removed. To be inserted in a boy who'll call you dad for the rest of his life. Makes perfect sense to me, he'd go along with that idea."

"I'm not stupid. I took it slow. Talked about Woody growing up. Showed him some pictures. Let him get used to the idea, he might like a boy, looks so much like him." She smiled again and her eyes shone green. "It's still there. The spark between us, whatever it was, got us together years ago. That helps."

The man had taken heavy-duty precautions before their meeting. His behavior was what I'd expect from a major drug dealer. Yet Bella was simpering over a compliment from him. I had to snap her out of her daze. "Lust. That was the spark in Warsaw. That was the spark today. You've got no reason to trust Wlodek Wojcik." I was so horrified, I had trouble talking plainly. The Polish name came out garbled.

"Call him 'Pope.' Lot easier to say. His biker name. Pope." The second time she said it, she broke the name into two syllables, blowing little puffs of air out with each "p." Like a smoker savoring a cigarette after good sex.

"Listen to you. You've still got the hots for this guy. No way you can think straight, you give in to those feelings."

She glared at me. "Big surprise, I like the man. I wouldn't have had his baby if I hadn't liked him so much back then. It was more than just sex. And now . . ." She paused and her voice softened. "Now, I look at him, I see my boy. How can I not like him?"

I sighed. "Don't be fooled by him. Having Woody's face and that nickname doesn't mean you can trust him. I don't suppose he told you what he's been doing since 1986?"

"He's been in Thailand mostly."

That fit. "So did he explain why the Danish Bandidos knew how to find him?"

She stared at the running water. "We didn't get into that."

"Did he tell you why he suddenly showed up in Copenhagen?"

She didn't look up. "He came to Denmark on business."

"Business." I was too agitated to sit still. I stood in front of her and forced my voice to stay low. "Heroin. That's Pope's business. He's a drug buyer for the Bandidos gang in Europe."

She raised her chin. "You're guessing. You don't know that."

I didn't *know*. But, I figured that Woody's father had been buying heroin in Bangkok for more than a decade. He'd been sent to Thailand by the Bandidos leadership in Marseilles and he'd done that job for them through the collapse of the Communist government in Poland and the move of Bandidos headquarters from

France to Denmark. With the division of criminal activity between the two gangs, heroin had to be the reason for his return to Europe.

I dropped down to sit on the edge of the tub, the cast iron cold beneath me. I picked up the shampoo bottle, tightened the plastic cap, thinking.

Bella was so desperate that even with all the facts lined up in front of her, she might refuse to believe the truth about Pope. To convince her, I'd have to play my strongest card. I'd have to tell Bella that Holger Sorensen had confirmed my analysis. And even then, I might not succeed. No, I couldn't spell things out for Bella. I couldn't reveal that Holger knew anything about the bikers. Not so long as there was any chance that Bella would see Pope again. If Pope and his cohorts learned of Holger's interest in them, it would compromise the operation he'd tried to recruit me for. I couldn't risk that.

I wiped my hand on my jeans. "Don't act stupid," I said to Bella. "Marseilles. Bangkok. You know drugs have to be involved."

Something flickered in her eyes. Awareness?

I seized on it. "Jazz drummer? Maybe he was into drugs in Warsaw. At some point he had to be a user. It'll surprise me if he shows up for a blood test. You can't seriously think he'll donate bone marrow. You have to forget that fantasy." I leaned toward her. "I gave blood Thursday. When will you get those results?"

She sighed. "Preliminary report on Monday. But you know the odds are lousy for you."

I put a hand lightly on top of hers. "I talked to Holger Sorensen. He'd like to help."

"You asked the priest to help me?" She shook off my hand. "Woody doesn't need last rites."

"Holger will help you look for a donor," I said.

"I've got a donor." She stood, her back against the door, her face shiny from the moisture in the room.

Pinning all her hopes on biker scum. She wasn't thinking straight. I stood, too. "I care for Woody, too. I'm trying to make you understand about Pope."

"First thing Monday, he's going for a blood test," she said forcefully. "That's the only thing I need to understand about Pope." I started to protest but she cut me off, using her brusque, on-the-job manner. "Blixenstjerne wants you out of the country. Says he can't protect you. I agree. You have to go on the next flight out."

I couldn't leave Bella to handle this alone. "I know what you're trying to do. But it won't work. Woody told me this thing has you all weirded out. He's right. I'm staying. Dawna will back me up on that. You can't make me leave."

Her shoulders sagged and she leaned against the door. Her voice sounded as weary as she looked. "I've seen Pope. I've talked to him. Sure, maybe he did drugs in the past. But he's clean, you can tell by looking at him. And he wants to help Woody."

"You're no great judge of character when it comes to men."

"Like your track record is any better than mine?"

My face got hot. "Look at the facts and the conclusion is obvious. You've gone off the deep end. The way you act, I'd think you wanted to play house with this guy."

Her glance skittered away from me. Guilty as charged. Bella was fantasizing about giving Woody his father, full-time. Maybe a baby sister, too. My heart ached to see her torturing herself with wild hopes. I moved closer to her. "Oh, Bella," I said, and my voice was full of my sorrow for her and Woody—and for myself.

"Look," she said tiredly, "if the thing with Pope doesn't work out, I can still go to Sorensen. Either way, I can't have you hanging around. If these guys come after you again, it'll attract attention. I can't have that. And if you get hurt . . ." She pressed her face into my sweatshirt sleeve, one hand clutching my elbow. Her voice came out muffled. "I can't have that, either."

I touched her shoulder, my eyes on the slicked-down strands of her hair. The overhead fixture highlighted the gray strands marbling the red. I smelled the strawberry gel she put on it, overlaid by the odor of meadow grasses from Dyrehave, beneath them both the rank scent of her terror.

"You watch yourself with this guy." I squeezed her shoulder. "I don't want you getting hurt, either."

She straightened up. "I'll be careful." She let go of me and slid her right hand beneath the sweater she wore bagging out over her pants. She added, "I talked to Dawna. She told me what she wanted you to do. I vetoed it, on the spot. Out of the question, using you like that."

She fumbled under her left armpit. The hand came back holding a revolver.

I said, "You took your gun to that meeting?"

"Damn straight." She laughed. "You don't believe Pope's a good guy. But let me tell you, he was such a gentleman he did a poor job patting me down."

"Lucky for you," I said.

She held the weapon out to me. "You keep it tonight."

I shivered. There were cops outside and the house was fully alarmed. Yet, Bella still thought I needed my own gun. So did I. I took it, a .38 caliber Smith & Wesson with five chambers.

"Know how to use it?" she asked.

"Standard embassy issue in San Sal." The weight of it in my hand brought back memories of the pistol range at the Salvadoran military school. The hot sun on my head, the smell of hay from the bales where we mounted the targets, Andy somewhere behind me, protective. I stuck the gun carefully into the top of my jeans. "Thanks."

"You talk to the spook team yet?"

"I was planning to do that tomorrow. But we'd both be better off if I didn't. Ask me no questions, I'll tell you no lies." I turned off the faucet.

"Gotcha." She opened the bathroom door. I heard Lacey J. Dalton singing huskily of the losing kind of love inside of her. Bella stepped over to the boombox and stopped the tape. She looked up at the security panel and spoke directly to it. "You leave Denmark tomorrow. First flight out of Kastrup. That's a direct order from your RSO."

I flipped the dead bolt and opened the front door for her. She stopped in front of me, reached out a hand to pat the lump the S&W made in my waistband. "You take care."

I hugged her. "You take care." She squeezed back. Then she was gone.

I locked the door behind her.

I went to the kitchen and pulled the last beer from the refrigerator. I tore off the white foil covering, pried off the cap and drank straight from the bottle. My last beer in Denmark.

Tomorrow I'd catch that plane. I didn't feel good, leaving Denmark with Gerry's killers still at large. I was experiencing the same sensation his real sisters must be feeling—a visceral need to avenge the attack on family. Dawna had insisted that if I kept Gerry's project going, I'd lure his killers out into the open.

Dawna's plan was tempting, but I knew her primary goal wasn't finding Gerry's murderer. I suspected that she still hoped to prove CIA or State Department wrongdoing. The FBI expanded its turf every time it exposed a traitor in a rival agency. Dawna would be handsomely rewarded if she could nail me for collusion with

Stinger-equipped bikers. She'd rejected my ideas about the *rocker* division of criminal turf. She wanted to keep me close by while she gathered evidence against me.

Bella had vetoed Dawna's scheme because of the risk to me. Reluctantly, I had to admit Bella had made the correct decision. I didn't know how to hunt for a murderer. I couldn't even guess where to start. No, there was nothing more I could do in Denmark for Gerry.

And I'd done all I could for Woody. My staying here longer might make his situation worse.

It was strange how things had worked out. Suddenly, nothing was stopping me from joining the task force in Maine. Sam Baldwin, the Danish police, Andy, Bella—a whole chorus of voices singing the same song: *Go ahead, Casey, go to Bangor.*

Holger, though, had refused to join the choir.

I swallowed more beer. He was concerned about biker gang involvement in the covert trade in weapons and drugs. He'd argued that the deaths of Ole Bjørn Møller and Gerry Davis demonstrated a link between *rocker* criminal activity and the missile recovery project. He'd claimed he didn't understand fully what was going on— a rare admission from Holger. And he'd grimly referred to the potential for "disastrous" consequences. He'd spoken as if he feared international conspirators intended to wreak havoc with the missing Stingers.

He urgently wanted to prevent that outcome. There were expert analysts in the Danish Defense Intelligence Service who could help him. But he'd turned to me—and not because I knew more than his colleagues did. Oh, he'd praised my "swift insights" into the biker situation. And, of course, I'd done my homework on the missiles.

But my real allure for Holger was his conviction that the hypothetical conspirators were interested in me. After today's event, he'd be certain I was the key to solving the mystery. He'd want me to puzzle out the connection between the two murders and the attack on me. If I gave him the chance, he'd try once again to persuade me to go to England and interview his biker expert.

I didn't know why he thought the data available in Dartmouth was so critical. Even if I asked, he wouldn't tell me. He stingily doled out information to his agents on a strict need-to-know basis.

Which meant I knew too little. The three violent acts were all linked to biker gang activity in Denmark. I couldn't imagine how a side trip to England would help identify Gerry's murderer. Maybe Holger had other evidence of a complex international conspiracy involving *rockers* and missiles. I didn't.

I had work to do in Bangor. I hated to leave with Gerry's death unresolved but there was nothing more I could do. For sure, the answer wasn't to close my eyes and jump on board a Holger Sorensen mission.

I tipped the bottle up again, savoring the potent blend of malt and hops. Elephant beer was more precisely classified as ale. The powerful alcoholic content was washing away the crashed-out feeling that comes when ardent foreplay stops cold.

I ran my tongue over my lips, remembering Andy's mouth on mine, the salty taste of his desire. Heady stuff, that he'd sought me out. I'd comforted myself in San Salvador with maudlin fantasies of his contrite return and my icy refusal to take him back. I'd vowed to hang up on his phone calls, return his letters unopened, walk away from chance encounters. He'd avoided those ploys.

As if he'd known that I couldn't refuse to work with him. Cleverly and dramatically, he'd crossed an ocean to reach me. He'd breached my defenses, suddenly appearing in Denmark conveniently single and madly in love with me. I had trouble believing in what was happening. It was too damn perfect. My love life didn't run this smoothly. There had to be a flaw somewhere. But what was it?

Could I be wrong about his feelings? There was no mistaking his hunger for me. His fervor made me so giddy I was no longer certain what I wanted from him. But would that ardor persist, this time?

I couldn't rush so heedlessly into Andy's embrace. Not a bad idea, putting some distance between us. I'd see if he'd find his way to me again. Maybe, I'd be less keen to take him to bed on an ordinary day, when nobody had shot at me first. I emptied the bottle, set it on the counter. Maybe.

The phone rang. My hand went to my waistband, my fingers closing around the butt of the revolver. Nervous, I kept my right hand on it as I walked to the living room. I lifted the phone with my left hand and pressed it to my ear. "Yes."

"Casey?" My name spoken by a man. I'd heard his voice on the phone only once before. But I knew it, with all my heart I knew it.

Stefan. Breaking his long-time rule against phone conversations.

Holger must have alerted him that I was in danger. The line was silent, no static. This could be a local call. In another few minutes he'd be with me. He'd hold me and whisper, *"Moj skarbie."* My treasure, in Polish.

"It's me." I sang the two syllables, the zing in my voice surprising me.

"I heard what happened this afternoon." He spoke distinctly, as if he'd tested each word before he voiced it. "You're all right?"

"I'm fine." And lucky. Good thing I'd sent Andy away. I had to let Stefan understand I'd be in Copenhagen only a few hours longer. "I'm flying to the U.S. tomorrow."

"I'm glad to hear that."

I registered the tone. It matched his words, contained no disappointment. And not a hint of the eagerness I'd expressed. So why had he called? "You're treating this as an emergency—that's why you phoned me?"

"I feared our mutual friend might have persuaded you to a risky course of action."

So that was it. He'd learned that Holger wanted to recruit me. Stefan must have objected to my participation. Keeping me out was important enough to justify breaking his rule against phone conversations. Conveniently important, since he didn't have to leave Warsaw to communicate his objections. I felt the needlelike bite of a wound, reopening. And then rage buried my hurt. Silly me, thinking he'd come to Denmark to save me.

The hell with him. And the hell with any wiretaps on my phone. "Why'd Holger contact you? Does the attack on me connect to what you're working on?"

Dead silence. I counted to fifteen before he spoke. "I was concerned for your safety," he said, his tone as formal as his diction.

"That dog won't hunt." My voice was loud, the sound reverberating off the living room walls.

I waited for another slow count of fifteen. His tone was cool. "I am not familiar with that expression."

"Let me spell it out for you. I don't know why the hell you bothered to call me, you can't say one honest thing to me."

In a stiff voice he said, "I have never lied to you."

"You don't lie to me. You don't say shit to me." I slammed down the phone, breathing hard.

23

I BENT DOWN AND JERKED THE JACK FROM THE WALL. MY hands balled into fists. If Stefan had been in front of me, I'd have struck him. But he wasn't here, that was the point. We had a history together. I'd been in danger before. In Poland in 1986. In Germany last winter. Neither time had I asked him for help. Yet he'd come. Fool that I was, I'd believed that he'd always come when I needed him.

I pounded my right fist into the open palm of my left hand. I was so damn mad at him.

Mad. Yes. Angry.

What had Holger said about my anger? I let my fingers uncurl. The recliner frame squeaked as I sank down onto the leather cushion. Holger had claimed that I used anger to mask my fear. I was angry. And more scared than I wanted to admit.

Somebody wanted me dead. That was frightening, certainly. But underlying that fear for my life was a more haunting dread. I felt it, like ground fog swirling on the dark moors of my subconscious. Stefan had left me. Intellectually, I'd accepted that. I'd convinced myself that I was handling it emotionally, too. But when I heard his voice say my name, I'd reacted like a giddy schoolgirl. Breathlessly eager, sure that he'd come to me.

But he hadn't.

When I looked at my life, its looming emptiness terrified me. My father was dying. Woody's chance of survival was one in two hundred thousand. And Stefan had left me. I was most afraid of that final truth. But not even anger could keep it from me.

162

I stumbled to the slider and opened it wide to let in fresher air. The enclosed courtyard was deserted, the pathways empty of strollers. The late-evening sky arched above me, wan as eggshell, the shadowless light falling softly on the pruned hedges. The stillness was broken by clear and delicate sounds—a jackdaw popping a nightcrawler from the sprinklered lawn, the clunk of the halyard against the wooden flagpole when a breeze ruffled the *Dannebrog*, the jingle of metal tags on a prowling cat.

The air was cool on my arms. The sudden drop in temperature chilled me, proof of how exhausted I was. I smoothed my sweatshirt sleeves down to cover my wrists and pulled the slider shut and locked it. I clicked off the lights in the kitchen and bath and went to the bedroom. It smelled of old dust and tired linens but I left the window closed and locked. I laid Bella's gun on the nightstand beside the bed. Still fully dressed, I crawled under the comforter. I closed my eyes, the security panel a red haze beyond the lids.

At five o'clock in the morning, I came awake all at once. The numbers on the bedside clock glowed green. Beyond the clock was the shade-covered window. The branch of the rhododendron outside scraped against the glass. The fleshy leaves sighed, disturbed by something large.

My fingers closed around the grip of the revolver. I slid out of bed and onto the floor between it and the closet door. Fear tasted coppery on my tongue. I huddled below the level of the bed and as far from the window as I could get. The comforter smelled of goose, and feather chaff tickled my nose.

Something metallic knocked against the glass, the sound like the tap of a heavy ring. Seven taps in all.

Shave-and-a-hair-cut-six-bits.

Whoever was outside meant to attract my attention.

The police, Bella, Dawna—anyone on official business would have rung the doorbell.

But I didn't think my enemies were knocking on my window, either. If the bad guys had gotten inside the courtyard and six inches from where I was sleeping, I'd be dead. Yet I didn't want to expose myself until I knew for sure who was out there.

Maybe I could glimpse my caller through the living room windows. I crawled out of the bedroom, rising to my feet once I'd crossed into the foyer. The bleached-oak floor glowed with sunlight reflected from the white walls of the living room. I extended my head far enough into the open archway to peer across the barren living room.

From the far end, Ulf Møller stared back at me through the glass door. Against the backdrop of dewy grass, his leather-covered shoulders shimmered with the strong morning light, his face a gray shadow between the raven hair capping his head and the sooty fur matting his jaw. His eyes were black gashes in his ashy skin, his expression as unreadable as if I were looking at the empty holes of a mask. Framed and immobile, he made a picture suitable for hanging in Denmark's national gallery of Norse art. Call it *Portrait of a Biker Prince*, imbued with that hallmark juxtaposition of menace and beauty.

More menace than beauty at five o'clock on a Sunday morning. I jerked back out of his line of vision.

He tapped again on the glass in the same rhythm.

Could he teach me Danish doggerel to accompany it? Ridiculous question. More ridiculous still to be lurking in my foyer, gun in hand, when I could shout for help from the policeman out front.

So why hadn't I done that?

Because Ulf had come to talk. If he'd wanted to harm me, he wouldn't have announced himself by tapping on the window. And he wouldn't have stood like a target in front of a sheet of glass. I'd judged Ulf too harshly before. He hadn't killed his brother—Dawna said his alibi was solid. And I knew he hadn't killed Gerry because he'd been with me when that assault occurred.

Of course, he could have ordered Gerry's killing. But he'd denied that the Bandidos were responsible and I was inclined to believe him. The bikers who'd attacked me bore little resemblance to the Bandidos who'd escorted me back to Copenhagen after the funeral. It wasn't likely that Ulf had staged yesterday's elaborate assault either. He knew of it, of course. He'd have been the first person the police hauled in for questioning. Now, he was trying to discover what had really happened.

I'd be gone from Denmark in another three hours. I still didn't understand why Gerry had been killed and I'd been attacked. Here was an opportunity to glean information from Ulf and I couldn't pass it up. I had to risk this encounter and discover what he knew. I'd hold my own secrets tightly while I extracted his.

Nervously, I opened the barrel of the revolver. I had to be careful, in case I was wrong about Ulf. I checked that all five chambers were loaded and snapped the gun shut again. I braced my right wrist with my left hand, and sighted down the barrel. I came into the living room fast, pausing to get Ulf in my sights.

His jaw dropped, teeth flashing white. Then the lips around them curved up. His laugh exploded, audible through the thick glass before his hand rose to muffle the noise.

I kept the gun on him as I unlatched the slider. With my left hand, I motioned for him to move away from the building. A mocking grin twisted his face, but he matched my silence as we walked fifty feet from my flat, the soles of my bare feet quickly wet from dew. The Scandinavian sun warmed my skin through the thick jersey of my sweatshirt and tiny glints came off the polished leather of Ulf's jacket. His mane of hair shone blue black against the back of his neck.

I stepped from wet grass to cold sand and braced my back against the frame of the play structure. We were at the center of the enclosed square made by the four blocks of apartments. "What do you want?" I asked.

"I suggest you lower your weapon." He waved a vague hand in the direction of the surrounding rooftops. "My friends will soon get nervous if they think you're threatening me."

He'd slithered past the cops, along with his gunmen. I let my hand drop, the revolver heavy against my leg, and I toughened my voice to hide my fear. "What, you thought you needed an armed guard while you talked to me?"

"They're not protecting me."

"I don't need them. The police are guarding me."

"And a fine job they're doing. As effective as your boyfriend parked on the street." His laughter was derisive. "The police understand *rockers*, you see. They know our tactics so well, they can take minimum precautions when an American diplomat appears threatened by *rockerkrig*."

Appears threatened? My interest doubled. "You don't think *rockers* attacked me?"

"I didn't say that. We Bandidos didn't chase you down. And the Hells Angels deny any involvement. Somebody's scamming here. We want to know who. If your attackers try again, we'll catch them."

"So you're hanging around waiting to see who shows up. You got me out of bed to tell me that?"

"You'd rather I came into your bed?" He stared at me, deliberately running a pink tongue over plum-colored lips.

165

I let my disgust show in my voice. "Tell me what you want."

"You tell me what happened yesterday." The crude carnality had disappeared from his manner, as if he'd remembered I didn't merit his sexual attentions—our transaction was only business. "Bikers attacking you on the open road—doesn't make any sense. Like somebody's setting us up. You talk, maybe I'll get an idea who's behind it."

"I'll talk." I stared at him. "But you get an idea, you tell me what it is."

He gestured dismissively. "Sure."

I started from when I'd left the embassy on Friday night, so that he'd understand I'd told no one when nor specifically where I was meeting my old friend in the northeast corner of Sjælland. And no one had followed me. "I didn't pick up a tail until I started back to Copenhagen. Two men on motorcycles came after me five minutes later."

"These men—any identifying characteristics?"

Same question the police had asked. I gave the same answer. "Hair and faces completely covered by helmets. Long-sleeve leather jackets covered their arms."

"Long sleeves? On a hot summer day?"

I shrugged. "A storm was coming. But you're right. Your guys showed more skin. All those tattoos."

He rubbed at a blue-inked design on the back of his wrist, a miniature Mexican bandit. The date, 24 JUNI 1980, inscribed above the sombrero.

I moved my gaze from the tattoo to his face. "You think they were hiding gang insignia?"

He grunted noncommittally.

Hiding insignia—or the absence of any, I realized.

He rubbed the heel of his hand over his mouth. "They pursued you?"

I described how they'd overtaken me and started shooting.

His voice rose. "A visored man driving a fast-moving motorcycle one-handed, fired a weapon at you and hit your car?"

"Three times." Mentally, I played back the thunking sounds the first two bullets had made in the car's body. Something fluttered in my stomach. To score so well under near-impossible shooting conditions, my pursuer must have been a marksman in the same class as the Danish policewoman Vibeke. "The third shot shattered the rear window. I thought they had me when I saw the van blocking the road ahead. We've lost a couple of ambassadors that way. I've seen videos of the reenactments. After the chase car closes the box on the limo, the bad guys jump out of the van and blast the ambassador and his bodyguards."

I went on to describe my dash through the woods, but my mind was stuck back on the words I'd spoken. *The chase car.* Terrorists didn't use motorcycle teams to close the box trap. A massive car or truck was a more certain tool, especially against a driver with security training.

"And the frogmen helped you escape from the *rockers.*" Ulf said the last word with such irony, he might as well have prefixed it with "so-called." He added, "Scammers. Got everybody hunting the wrong killer. Fucking cops, they'll never find who did my brother."

He'd jumped from the attack on me to the one on his brother. What had convinced him the same people were behind both? "Why did your brother come looking for me?"

"That's the key isn't it?" He stared at me, hard. "Whoever killed him wanted to stop him from talking to you."

"But what was it he wanted to say?"

Hair whispered over the leather shoulders of Ulf's jacket as he shook his head. "He didn't tell me. Shit, it had been a week since I'd seen him."

"You saw him a week before he died? What did you talk about?"

He gave a sigh of exasperation. "It had nothing to do with this. We were in England, I came back a week before he did. Never saw him again."

"You were in England?" The name of the island nation sent a shiver of anticipation sliding up my spine. The last person who'd mentioned England to me was Holger. "What were you two doing?"

"That's none of your business."

So it was possible that while Bjørn was in England alone, he'd acquired the information that got him killed. When I spoke, I couldn't keep the eagerness out of my voice. "After you left, what did your brother do?"

"I tell you, there's no connection. He had some music gig, nothing to do with the club."

I opened my mouth to demand more details.

He cut me off. "Fucking cops." He wheeled, sending up a spray of sand. "I'll find the bastard who killed my brother before they ever do." He strode away from me toward the far side of the courtyard.

I waited until he'd disappeared. I walked slowly back to my flat, the sun as hot on my scalp as the invisible eyes watching me. Indoors again, I locked the slider and went to the kitchen, flipping on the light. The clock on the stove read five-twenty-five. Opening the silverware drawer, I laid Bella's pistol beside the meat cleaver. I'd phone her later and tell her to retrieve it. I filled the water reservoir of the Braun and spooned in ground coffee from the tin, slowly putting together what I'd learned from Ulf.

I hadn't been attacked by bikers. Professional hit men had come after me. They'd have gotten me, too, if they'd stuck with cars instead of switching to motorcycles. The bike had spoiled the assassin's aim.

The machine hissed and gurgled and the air filled with the scent of coffee. I recalled what Ulf had said. *Got everybody hunting the wrong killer.* Some person or persons unknown was hiding behind a *rockerkrig* smokescreen. Make-believe biker gang war had also been used to conceal the identity of Gerry's murderer. And maintaining the fiction that *rockers* were trying to kill me had been judged as critical as succeeding in the attempt.

It was an expensive strategy and that meant two things. First, Gerry's activities—and mine—were threatening to disrupt a profitable but also shady business. Greed was the underlying motive. There was no reason to think someone had a personal reason for killing me. It was more likely that eliminating me was a simple business decision.

And second, whoever had made that decision was willing to spend big to conceal his role. Which meant that the profits involved had to be big. Idly, I imagined an enormous Daddy Bigbucks lurking behind the scenes, orchestrating events. *Get rid of her,* he'd order the shooters. *I don't care what it costs. Make sure nobody can tie this one back to me.*

I crossed the kitchen to unlatch the casement window. When it was fully open, breeze ruffled the curtain. A distant carillon chimed the half hour, the sound too pure to sully the Sunday morning stillness. I saw the peaked cap and blond hair of the on-duty cop directly below me. Andy's Volvo was parked in the same spot where it had been the night before. No one was visible inside it.

I filled a cup with coffee and inhaled the strong aroma. Holger thought I was at the exact center of a complex grid of conspiracy. He was right. The murder investigations and the missile project intersected at the point where they touched me, as if I stood at a major cloverleaf in a mysterious highway system of international intrigue. If we could discover *why* I'd been targeted for execution, then we could learn *who* had ordered my murder—and the murders of Bjørn and Gerry.

Holger had said, *You cannot refuse to examine your connection to these deaths.*

He was right, again. I had to do it. Other competent professionals were investigating the two homicides. But whoever had ordered those murders had also identified me as a threat. That gave me a unique advantage. I'd already collected the relevant data about my activities. All I needed now was a clearer understanding of the situation. Once I had that, I could quickly pinpoint what it was about me that so alarmed Daddy Bigbucks.

He'd killed my partner. He'd tried to kill me. To avenge Gerry and to save my own life, I had to try to find out what was going on. I heard again Ulf's angry words about cops: *I'll find the bastard who killed my brother before they ever do.* I couldn't rely on the police either. I couldn't forfeit the advantage Daddy Bigbucks had given me.

I had one lead—Holger's biker expert. And one clue—the trip that the Møller brothers had taken last week. Both the lead and the clue pointed to England as the place to start looking for answers. I had to go to England. Holger had been right about that, too.

The buzzer sounded. Through the open window I heard Andy chatting with the cop. They were on a first-name basis, as though they'd had more than one conversation during the night. I opened the door.

"Breakfast," Andy said, holding up a white paper sack. "Hotel up the street let me have some fresh Danish."

I looked him over. His hair was rumpled, he needed a shave, and his clothes were the same ones he'd worn the night before, only more wrinkled. "How'd you know I was up?"

"The light came on in your kitchen, so I figured . . ." His cheeks reddened and he turned to the cupboard. "Let me get a plate for these."

I lifted a pastry from the sack and took a bite. Apricot with a tantalizing hint of crystallized ginger. Sweet taste, sweet as the thought of Andy watching over me. I felt the tug of memory. When we'd spent nights together in Salvador, he'd slept with his body spooned around mine as though to put himself between me and anyone who might try to hurt me. I swallowed and said, "You didn't just happen to drop by and decide to see if I was ready for breakfast?"

He kept his gaze on the plate, filling it from the bag. "I felt better, keeping an eye on you myself. Plus I had all night to think things through. I figured out how to quash this plan of Dawna's."

"So tell me." I poured him a cup of coffee, refilled mine, and helped myself to another pastry. Raspberry, this time.

"She wants you to head up Gerry's project. See who comes out of the woodwork, trying to stop you." He shook his head to show how crazy he thought Dawna's plan was. "Quickest way to get her off your back is to have the project curtailed." He bit into a pastry and chewed thoroughly before he spoke again. "No point in continuing it. We both know it's a useless task. If I make that case to CIA and the oversight agencies, they'll cancel the whole thing."

A useless task. I'd said much the same thing to Holger. But I'd changed my opinion of Gerry's project. Someone had killed him because of those missiles. But I kept that thought to myself. "Curtailing the project is one way to handle it," I said judiciously. "But I'll have to leave the whole mess in your capable hands."

Andy's face smoothed out into an expression of relief. "You're leaving?"

"Bella ordered me to take the first flight out today. Any chance I can get you to give me a ride to Kastrup?"

"I can give you a lift, sure."

"Good." I pushed myself to my feet, reached over to switch off the coffee pot. My gaze went to the clock. "I don't want to call Bella this early. Could you get hold of her for me later? Let her know I left. And tell her I'll phone her in a couple of days, after I've settled in."

"Sure." He stood, draining the last of his coffee. "And I'll give Dawna the word, too."

"Well, then." I'd run out of things to say.

He hadn't. His hand was on my arm. He reached around my waist and behind my back. He held me tightly against him. "You go to Bangor," he whispered. "I'll find you. And I will never let you get away from me again."

His soft breath in my ear started a shiver that reached down inside of me. It would be a long time before Andy found me again.

Especially since he wouldn't know where to look. I pressed myself against him, trying to absorb his heat so I could hoard it for the cold days coming.

No names had been spoken in my phone conversation with Holger on Friday and we'd disconnected after less than a minute. A wiretap at either his end or mine would not have revealed the identity of the other speaker. It would have been difficult for anyone interested in my whereabouts to guess I was talking to Holger. But I'd also left notes for Dawna and Bella indicating that I was headed for northern Sjælland. From that small fact, my enemy had deduced my destination. I had to keep my next move secret from the people I trusted.

I didn't dare tell Andy the truth. I wasn't going to Bangor today. Maybe I never would.

24 IT WAS ONLY SEVEN O'CLOCK ON A SUNDAY MORNING, BUT THE departure hall at Kastrup was crowded with summer travelers. Their voices bounced off the concrete floor, swirled up toward the high ceilings, spun, and stormed down again to mingle with the clatter of luggage carts and the exhortations over the public-address system warning that unattended baggage would be confiscated.

My lips felt swollen and my cheeks burned from the scrape of Andy's stubble against them. We'd parted company outside. It wasn't worth coming into the hall with me, I'd told him. Only ticketed passengers were allowed through the security checkpoint. We'd have to separate after I'd gotten my boarding pass. He parked only long enough to unload my suitcase and kiss me goodbye.

I hiked my carry-on bag higher on my shoulder and rested my hand on the three-suiter. Twenty feet in front of me was a counter that stretched from one end of the block-long hall to the other. The wall behind the counter was dominated by signs for Scandinavian Air Systems but on the far right, I spotted the cluster of U.S. airline companies. Only two passengers waited in front of the lone representative for Global.

The embassy's efficient admin section had notified Global to keep open the ticket I hadn't used on Wednesday. If I'd chosen to take this morning's nonstop flight to Kennedy, I could have presented my unused boarding pass to the agent and gotten a new one allowing me on the plane.

I grabbed the leather strap on my suitcase and rolled it along behind me as I crossed to the pay phones. The number I dialed rang only once before Holger answered.

"Remember yesterday?" I said. "You asked me to give you a ring?"

"Of course," he replied, smoothly confirming that he knew who I was and that he'd heard me repeat back to him the signal he'd outlined for me. He understood I'd be speaking in my version of code. "How may I help you?"

"I'm at Kastrup. I'll be leaving Denmark within the hour." I slowed down and recited the words I'd chosen. I wanted anyone monitoring Holger's phone to believe I was headed for Maine. But I wanted Holger to understand I needed information about a man in England. "Turns out I'm going to end up quite near that expert you mentioned yesterday. I might have a chance to drop by and visit with him. Maybe you could give me his name and phone number?"

"Be glad to. And when you find the fellow, be sure you ask to speak with his good friend as well." He paused, the silence underscoring the importance of what he'd told me. "Hang on a minute while I get that information for you."

His phone clunked as if he'd laid the mouthpiece on his desktop. I heard a metal file drawer rumble open and papers rustled loudly. I studied the second hand on my wristwatch. In thirty-three seconds, Holger was back on the line, apologetic. "I'm afraid it will take me awhile to dig that information out. I'll find it later, send it on to you."

"Maybe I could call back," I said. "I don't know my mailing address yet."

"Certainly," Holger replied. "They make decent coffee at that café in the departure hall. I can probably find what you need in the same time it would take you to drink a cup." He hung up.

Before I got my coffee, I had another call to make. To discover why Ole Bjørn Møller had come to my flat, I had to reconstruct his activities during the week before his death. I needed to know where he'd spent his sojourn in Great Britain. His brother had been no help. But maybe Bjørn had left a contact number with his mother. I knew it was a long shot. If Gitte Møller still had that information, she had no good reason to share it with me. But I had to try.

It took me five minutes to extract a phone number for Gitte from information and another minute to put the call through. When she answered, her voice was weak as though thinned by fatigue.

"This is Kathryn Collins." I put all the friendliness I could muster into my introduction. "We talked briefly after your son's funeral."

"I remember you." She snipped off each word.

Without seeing her face, I couldn't guess what approach might work. Best to start with slightly varnished truth. "I spoke with Ulf this morning. He told me that Bjørn spent time in England recently with a musician friend. Ulf couldn't tell me the man's name. Do you know?"

Silence for five seconds. "Yes."

My breath came out in a gush. I'd been holding it. She knew something—but how to persuade her to reveal it to me? Before I'd settled on a strategy, I heard a wooden clunk. Gitte had dropped the phone. I kept my eyes on my watch. Sixty seconds passed. The second hand swept around to make it ninety. One hundred and twenty. She didn't want to speak with me. If I disconnected and called her back, I'd get a busy signal. I sighed. I'd wait a full five minutes to be certain.

At one hundred and seventy-five seconds, I heard her wispy voice again. "Ole Bjørn went to see Davey. Davey Chaka. C-H-A-K-A." She gave me a phone number, digit by digit. "You will listen to Davey. You and I, we will talk again. Let me also give you Davey's address in Exeter. You may need that." She spelled it out and I wrote it down, my handwriting looping with excitement.

Exeter was in southwestern England—the same area where Holger's expert lived. I'd discover later if the coincidence meant anything. For a microsecond I enjoyed an analyst's high, the familiar rush of delight when two pieces of disparate data fit neatly together.

And then it was gone. When I hung up, my sweaty prints were visible against the gray plastic I'd been clutching. I hadn't expected Gitte to be so helpful. She'd acted as if she'd hired me to investigate her son's murder and she'd known all along where I'd start. I had to be missing something, some fact that would explain why she'd told me so much.

I checked my watch. In five more minutes, I'd call Holger back. But first, I had to do as I'd been told and buy myself a cup of coffee.

The cup turned out to be paper, the coffee lukewarm and weak smelling. I turned away from the vendor and spotted *Kaptajn* Flemming Nielsen in profile, seated at one of the tables, hunched over a Sunday paper as if he'd settled in to wait for a plane. He wore civilian clothes today, faded Levi's that molded his muscular thigh and a green-and-white rugby shirt that didn't hide his shoulders. He didn't look like a mail carrier—but that had to be the job that had brought him to this coffee shop.

I sat at the adjacent table, my back to him. He swallowed noisily, then clunked an empty beer bottle on the table, slapped his newspaper shut, and shoved his chair back. Slowly I turned. "Do you mind?" I asked, reaching for the newspaper he'd abandoned. He acted as if he hadn't heard me, striding away as though he had a plane to meet. I was edgy, but I couldn't avoid noticing how very fine the captain looked from the rear.

I swept the folded newspaper into my carry-on bag and sipped coffee for another minute before pushing the cup aside. I gathered my things and went to the women's rest room. When I emerged, I'd refolded the newspaper after removing the ticket for the 7:50 A.M. flight to Gatwick. That was in my pocket and the Dartmouth phone number for Jack Eden was stowed with that of Davey Chaka inside my bra. My second phone call to Holger was brief. He gave me contact information for a former warden of Maine State Prison— "a man who knows a thing or two about outlaw biker gangs." I wrote down every word. Holger was meticulous. He knew someone might be listening in and he wouldn't risk a fictitious name. The man would be a recognized expert on bikers. If I ever reached Bangor, he'd be a useful resource.

When I hung up, I looked at my watch again. It was seven-thirty. Twenty-seven minutes total since I'd first phoned Holger. He'd responded to my request with high speed and higher security. Someone had granted top priority to whatever operation he was running. I was a small piece in something much larger and I knew I'd be wise not to lose sight of that fact.

I grabbed the leather strap on my suitcase and started across the hall toward the sign for British Airways. The ticket was in my name, Kathryn Collins. Holger hadn't provided a false identity and I'd be traveling on my own U.S. passport, the standard blue one I used when my status wasn't diplomatic. A clever detective could learn I'd flown to Gatwick, but only after a few hours of electronic searching, since the ticket wouldn't show up on my credit card account. Holger hadn't scheduled me for the connecting BA flight to Exeter. He didn't want my final destination to be so easily discovered. He'd given me a head start to Gatwick. I had to disappear into Great Britain before anyone caught up with me. I checked my suitcase and went upstairs and through the security checkpoint to the gate.

During the two-hour and twenty-minute flight, I searched through Flemming Nielsen's *Jyllands-Posten* for news of the Bangor disaster. All I found was a vaguer version of what Holger had told me, that the analysis of the radar reports was not yet completed. I went through the complimentary copy of the London *Sunday Tele-graph* but the sole story repeated the same information. Significantly more space was devoted to a defense of the British sandwich.

Holders of EU passports scurried down the fast lane at Gatwick Passport Control. I inched along in the adjacent queue with other travelers from the former British colonies, wedged between a travel-worn Australian couple and a noisy family of Jamaicans. The un-smiling officials were as surly as their counterparts in the U.S. Their familiar demeanor was what I should have expected to find in the Mother Country, but their suspicious scrutiny annoyed me anyway.

As soon as I was freed by Immigration I found a pay phone. Decency required me to warn Renton Funke that trouble was headed his way.

I'd gained an hour flying east and it was nine-thirty in the morning, Greenwich mean time—only 4:30 A.M. in the Maryland suburbs of D.C. where Renton lived. I heard the sleep in his voice when he mumbled his hello into what was surely his bedside phone.

"Renton," I said, "it's Casey."

"You called this one a little too close," he said reprovingly. "Showing up in Bangor only hours before the deadline."

"I'm not in Bangor," I said. "And I won't be, not for another two or three days."

His tone grew sharp. "What's that mean?"

I held the phone in my right hand, brushed hair off my forehead with my left. "I'm in Europe."

"If you're not in Bangor by noon today, Baldwin will file his complaint. If you don't get there by noon tomorrow, you're through."

"I won't make it. I need more time here." I made my voice hold steady. "Look, you know the circumstances."

"Baldwin extended his deadlines because of those circum-stances. But even I can't justify further delay." Renton hammered out his next words as if he were pounding nails into oak. "The secretary put you on that task force. You don't show up when you're ordered to the site. That's insubordination. Same thing as turning in your resignation."

"I can't leave. I have to finish what Gerry started."

"Your job is that task force," he said, his voice rougher, trying to get through to me. "You don't seriously believe someone used those CIA Stingers to bring down a jet in Maine?"

No. I didn't believe that the aging missiles could be made accurate enough to shoot down a plane of that size and power. "I'm not saying that—"

"If you can't make that specific connection, you don't have a case for staying in Europe. I'm not going down with you on this."

"Wouldn't help me if you did. You save yourself, Renton. This is my choice and I'll live with it. I can't come back yet. I've got to do this for Gerry."

"For Gerry." When Renton spoke again, he sounded beyond tiredness. "Ah, Casey, I can't believe you're doing this. When did you become such a lover of lost causes?"

25

I HUNG UP ON RENTON AND DRAGGED MY SUITCASE OUT OF THE arrivals hall. Gray clouds covered the sky above me, the air so thick with moisture that droplets beaded in my hair. I had to cross two lanes of traffic. Headlamps glowed on the cars and their wipers were busy, squealing and thudding through the mist that quickly coated their windshields. When I reached the boxy Avis office, I used my Visa to rent a navy blue Vauxhall with a four-cylinder engine and a manual transmission. I'd never driven on British roads before, but I'd been told that the adjustment wasn't difficult because the vehicles were right-hand-drive and matched up with the roads. The amazingly resilient human brain reverses old habits. I expected I'd soon be whizzing down the wrong side of the road as if I'd done it all my life.

Shifting gears with my left hand was a problem I hadn't expected. The pedals were where they belonged, clutch on the left, accelerator on the right. And the basic shift pattern was the standard H, with first gear on the upper left, fourth on the lower right. But that arrangement only confused me as I tried to reverse the push-pull of the shifting, and coordinate that with the unchanged dance of my feet. I spent five minutes puttering around the Avis lot, killing the engine repeatedly as I clumsily jerked the lever with my left hand from first gear to fourth. I was afraid to leave the parking lot for the highway, imagining myself stalled at a British Rail crossing, thirty tons of steam-spouting locomotive hurtling toward me. I'd felt the same breathless terror at age fourteen when my father let me try out his Mustang.

But I had to get moving. Gatwick was the first place a tracker would look for me. I soothed my jangled nerves by imagining my father in the seat beside me, instructing me step-by-step again in how to drive a car. I got going, not smoothly and not fast, north-bound toward London. At the first large settlement inside the M25 I found an ATM machine and used my card to get a week's supply of local currency.

It was the last time I planned to use plastic. Electronic snooping had gotten too good. Soon, anyone who wanted to find me would know I'd phoned Renton from Gatwick, rented a Vauxhall, and used an ATM alongside a road that led to London. But if I refrained from further electronic transactions, the only way to track me in Britain would be by reading the license plates on every car that looked like mine. In case my enemy had the manpower to try, I doubled back to the M25 and followed it west and north to connect to the crowded M4 motorway. Under the anvil-gray sky, exits to sites of half-forgotten English history and literature lessons flashed by me as I tried to maintain a safe speed on the rushing six lanes of the divided highway. DUAL CARRIAGEWAY the sign corrected me, one of the few I understood. I didn't have a clue as to the meaning of the one that read NO CATS EYES FOR SIX MILES. The sky stayed the color of iron, the mist turned to drizzle, and I crossed the island of Great Britain. Turned out to be a much larger island than I'd thought.

It was three o'clock when I reached southern Devon, close enough to Dartmouth to contact Holger's British biker expert. I took the next exit, where a sign promised that tourist information was available. Beside the kiosk, I found an old-fashioned red-painted phone booth. I closed myself inside and dialed the number Holger had given me for Jack Eden.

"Constabulary of Devon and Cornwall," a polite male voice responded. "How may I direct your call?"

The county cop shop. I asked for Jack Eden and the connection was completed without another word as if the receptionist had been instructed not to screen this policeman's callers. The phone picked up and Jack Eden identified himself.

"Kathryn Collins," was all I replied.

"Been expecting your call," he said. "I should have something for you by morning."

By morning? Too late. I didn't want to blow the head start that Holger had granted me. "Can't I see you tonight?"

"Got something breaking. I'll be tied up all night. Eight o'clock tomorrow morning is the best I can do."

I couldn't argue, not on an open line. "You want me to come to your office?"

"No. And don't ring me again at this number." I heard a scratching noise as if he'd covered the mouthpiece with his hand. When Eden came back, he spoke hurriedly. "Tomorrow, 8:00 A.M., I'll pick you up at the shipyard in Noss."

"Noss?"

He cleared his throat irritably. "Past the higher ferry in Kingswear."

"How will I know you?"

"Wait on the dock. I'll find you."

"Out in the open? I'd rather not—"

"I don't have time for this. You want to see me or not?"

Brusquely, I repeated his instructions back to him. "The ship-yard dock. Eight o'clock."

He disconnected immediately.

I went to the adjacent kiosk and purchased a Goldeneye map of the area and a Devon guidebook. Around the corner I found a food booth selling take-away meals and bought a tuna sandwich and a bag of "crisps." I alternated bites from each as I sat in my car picking over my conversation with Jack Eden.

Holger had persuaded Eden to see me, but the Brit's distaste for the task was clear in every detail of the arrangements. He'd let me know that my interests took a backseat to his own. Probably secretly hoped that if he made the meeting arrangements inconvenient and unattractive, I'd decide not to see him and leave the area tonight.

Maybe I would. This bucolic backwater was no hotbed of criminal activity. Jack Eden had probably fabricated his law-enforcement emergency. An uncooperative country policeman wasn't going to give me any useful tips about Danish *rockers*. I'd have to look elsewhere.

I chewed diligently on my sandwich. It was precisely as dry and tasteless as the defense in the *Telegraph* had led me to expect. The crisps, though, were high-fat and salty and gave me the strength to ponder my future. Renton had laid out the facts. No State Department job would be waiting for me when I returned to the U.S. By coming to England, I'd acted against my own best interest. Holger had urged me to take this ruinous step, but I hadn't done it to please Holger. I'd been honest with Renton. I was doing this for Gerry.

I spread out the map. I was only ten miles from Exeter, the home of Bjørn's musician friend. I studied the guidebook, charting the best route to the address I wanted.

I discovered it was not in the sections of Exeter touted as the "flourishing commercial centre," "picturesque Cathedral Close," or "historic quayside." When I found my way to Davey Chaka's neighborhood, the only landmark I spotted was the hulk of Devon Prison. An institutional pile of dirty red bricks, it looked as if it had been lifted straight from a novel by Dickens.

I parked on a side street off Howell Road in front of a three-story neo-Tudor townhouse painted white with black timbers, an inexpensive urban re-creation of the English cottage. This begrimed version was cheapened further by conversion from a single-family dwelling to studio apartments. The ground-floor windows were open and I heard music. Not a recording, I realized. Someone inside was playing the piano well. The volume and pace increased as I walked toward the front door and I recognized "Take Five." Sheet music for that same piece had fallen off the piano in Gitte's front room.

I imagined the mysterious Davey Chaka playing piano duets with Ole Bjørn Møller. My mind flashed a picture of an undernourished jazz pianist in Coke-bottle glasses, his body made scrawny by late nights and cigarette smoke, bony fingers pulling music from a deep well of feeling. Never mind that Bjørn had looked nothing like that. He was Danish. A British jazzman would come closer to my Greenwich Village ideal.

I pushed the buzzer beside the front door and the music stopped. I heard footsteps, bare feet on hardwood. A voice growled. "What do you want?"

He didn't sound as British as I'd expected. "I'm looking for Davey Chaka," I said bravely.

The door swung open.

Involuntarily, I took a step backward. That was how startled I was.

My eyes were level with a set of pectoral muscles that rivaled Rambo's. I didn't know the names of all the sinews so well defined before me, but I saw them rippling beneath skin the color of fresh-brewed espresso. The only flaws in the perfect body were wormlike

181

scars inching across his lower abdomen, disappearing into the elastic waistband of his fire-engine red jockey shorts.

I sighed. I couldn't help it, the view was so impressive.

The undershorts were the only clothing he wore. A set of metal dog tags hung from his neck and the chain jingled restlessly as he said, "Your mother didn't tell you, it's not polite to stare?"

He was a good foot taller than me, at least six nine. I raised my gaze and looked into eyes a shade blacker than his skin. *"You're Davey Chaka?"*

"Maybe." He smoothed the palm of his hand across his scarred belly.

The self-comforting gesture from this man was frightening. I thought of a hungry lion, testing the emptiness in his gut before he lunged at his prey. Did I want to be the one to tell Davey Chaka that his piano-playing buddy had been murdered? Murdered in *my* flat?

26

GUARDEDLY, I SAID, "I'M AFRAID I'VE GOT SOME BAD NEWS for you."

"You must be mistaken." His voice had a melodic quality that reminded me of the way South African celebrities speak on television. Only this man was a foot away from me and leering suggestively. He added, "I never get anything *bad* from a woman. You don't want to be the one to change that for me."

His hand went toward the knob. I spoke in a rush to stop him from shutting the door in my face, stating the facts as plainly as possible. "I've come because of Bjørn Møller. His mother told me he was with you earlier this month." I paused, my gaze on Chaka's face. "He died on Wednesday."

The skin tightened around Chaka's eyes and the expression in them hardened into something I couldn't read. "The Bear is dead?"

"He was murdered." I read the inquiry on his face. "Someone smashed his head in. The Danish police think another biker did it, but I'm not so sure."

He lowered his eyelids a fraction, as if to focus his vision. "And who are you?"

I tried to sidestep the question. "My name's Kathryn Collins. I'm following up. Tracking the victim's movements prior to the murder."

Chaka's hand was back on the knob. "You're an American *cop*?" The final word was spoken with a mixture of distaste and disbelief.

"I'm not with the police. More like a friend of the family." My voice came out in a rush. "He was killed in my flat. I want to know why."

Chaka ran his half-lidded gaze down my frame, slowly.

My shoulder muscles twitched. I wanted to lift my arms, fold them protectively across my chest. But I held still, letting those razor-sharp eyes shred my clothes—and my lie along with them.

"You knew the Bear?" His tone was conversational.

Again, I saw Ole Bjørn Møller as I'd found him in my flat, his battered head laid down on the keys of my landlord's piano. Again, I felt that inexplicable rush of pity for someone I'd never met. "Not really," I said.

"Your loss. There cannot be another man with so many gifts." Chaka cleared his throat, a harsh, grating sound that didn't hide the raw emotion beneath it. He stared at me. "Maybe you are a friend of the family. Maybe you are not. What do you think Gitte will say when I ask her?"

My stomach lurched. I didn't want this man to confirm to anyone in Denmark that I'd come to Exeter. But I didn't allow my anxiety to show. He could turn my perilous situation against me.

My laugh sounded genuine. "Call Gitte. She'll tell you to talk to me."

"Perhaps. You come back tomorrow. Maybe I will talk to you." His lips turned up in a taunting grimace. "Or maybe I will beat the shit out of the liar you are."

I backed away from him. The door slammed shut. I spun around and hurried to my car. But before I started the engine, I heard a crashing jumble of chords ring out from inside Chaka's apartment. It sounded as if a very large man had collapsed onto the piano stool, his massive arms and head laid out upon the keyboard in front of him. It sounded like the discordant music of grief.

I struggled through a roundabout—a traffic circle that moved in a brain-shattering clockwise direction—and followed Blackboy Road to the A38. Prudence dictated that I put distance between myself and Davey Chaka. I headed south toward that part of the coast known optimistically as the English Riviera. Clouds covered the sky when I left Exeter, but by the time I reached the resort town of Torquay, the rain had stopped. The grayness above matched the chilly sea below, blurring the horizon. Strollers dotted the beachfront esplanade, their colorful resort clothes as improbable in this climate as the well-tended palm trees and the party lights festooning the downtown pavilion.

I spotted a turreted hostelry of pinkish stone perched on the edge of a cliff and I turned into the parking lot. Quickly stashing my things in my room, I took my parched throat immediately to the hotel lounge. The woman tending bar was no more than eighteen years old, her doughy face still round as a child's above the buttoned collar of her long-sleeved white shirt. When I asked what beers were available, she announced proudly that theirs was "a free house." Not linked to a single provider of alcohol, she explained, but able to offer a full range of ales. I settled for a pint from Ruddles County Brewery, established 1858. The dark beer tasted oddly Christmasy, as if spruce bark might be an ingredient, but it was potent enough to relax my taut muscles.

I carried my mug to a window table. A hundred feet below me, the sea crashed against the jagged cliff. On the far side of the cove, the holiday lights of Torquay struggled to give the impression that viewers were in Cannes. I'd been drawn to this hotel because it sported the blue-and-gold logo of an American chain. Despite that, I figured it was an acceptable hide-out. Not likely anyone tracking me would suspect I'd been made homesick by Britain's impenetrable foreignness.

I'd pushed my luck too far, telling Chaka I was a family friend. Now he'd phone Gitte Møller. My phone card records would reveal that I'd called her, too. Anyone who quizzed her about our conversation would learn she'd given me an Exeter phone number. Now Chaka's call to Denmark would prove that I'd gone directly to him. Hard to guess to whom Gitte might pass that information. It was safer to be nowhere near Exeter.

And I had no reason to return. I doubted Chaka had any useful information about Bjørn Møller. Even if he did, he wasn't likely to reveal it. He was too hostile toward me.

I'd avoid Exeter, but I was stuck in Devon. I had to keep my appointment tomorrow with Jack Eden. He was my only lead. I let my gaze rest on the soothing seascape. It was important now to keep my nerves under control, focus only on the task ahead. Tonight, I had to store up enough energy to get through tomorrow. I had to rest. With effort, I forced thoughts of bikers and missiles from my mind.

What floated into the vacuum was a tingling physical memory of Andy's mouth on mine, his hands on my body, the yearning and the desire he'd reawakened in me. It heated me all over again and that warmth led me to an image of Flemming Nielsen as I'd seen him this morning. I sipped my beer, recalling the view of his sculptured backside as he'd walked away from me. I blinked, surprised at myself, more startled still when my image of Flemming dissolved into the hotter memory of Davey Chaka's slickly muscular chest.

I swallowed more beer to cool the sexual heat rising in me. I hadn't wandered through this particular landscape for so long, I'd forgotten how susceptible I was to the scenery. Since 1986 I'd been passionately in love with Stefan. I hadn't looked—really *looked*—at another man. But Stefan was gone.

I was alone and running for my life, making dangerous inquiries. Yet I was gawking lustily at every hard body that crossed my path. Scared to death and horny as hell. Not the worst investigative mode. At least my senses were on full alert and I was paying attention to everything around me. Well, to the men anyway. I reminded myself that my pursuer could as easily be female. I turned away from the window to eye the barmaid. She misunderstood my interest and brought me another pint.

Despite the double dose of beer, I slept restlessly. I was waiting outside the hotel restaurant when it opened at seven. I asked for the full English breakfast and minutes later the waiter placed a rack of thin toast slices on the table and slid a heated plate in front of me. Centered on it were a fried egg and two fat sausages, encircled by baked beans, a broiled tomato half, and a pile of sliced mushrooms, fresh from the can. I doused the mess with Worcestershire Sauce and used a half-dozen pieces of cold toast and a busy fork to sop up fuel. I was in my car and on the move by seven-twenty.

I followed the highway south to Kingswear at the mouth of the Dart River. Beneath the overcast sky, the river was a smooth expanse of slate blue cupped between sloping banks. The town of Dartmouth was on the opposite shore. I left my car in the public lot near Kingswear's lower ferry and hiked along the quay edging the river. The air was sodden, the clouds hanging low enough to shroud the hilltops marching northward ahead of me. The water had an oily sheen, and the smell of diesel exhaust from the ferry was strong.

My path ended at a rectangular two-story warehouse of faded brick boasting in all-caps and ampersands that the FATHER & SON owners were also SHIPBUILDERS & ENGINEERS. The river in front was jammed with watercraft, their empty masts thick as a forest of winter-stripped trees. From inside the shipyard's largest building came the whine of a power saw but no people were visible. Outside, I felt exposed. I made my way nervously along the gently bobbing sections of the dock. At least there I was partially concealed by the pleasure boats beside me.

I heard the sputter of a gasoline engine and I reached the end of the dock at the same time as a twelve-foot dinghy powered by an outboard motor. The man at the tiller wore a cloth cap and dark glasses. He cut the engine, nosing the boat closer so that the faded orange floats dangling from its side brushed the edge of the dock.

I grabbed the rope holding the floats. "Jack Eden?" I asked.

He grunted an affirmative. "Get in. I want to get this over with quick as I can."

I perched on the wooden bench seat in the center of the boat, facing him. He sat compactly in the stern, right hand on the tiller, left folded across his belly. Beneath the cloth cap, his head was square shaped, the flesh thick on his cheeks, reddened by the wind to a shade the color of uncooked beef. Tendrils of mouse-brown hair curled on the back of his neck and his sideburns were shaggy. He fit my image of a local fishmonger, a man who would cheat you by ounces, not pounds, and wasn't likely to grant you credit. Jack Eden wasn't appealing, but he looked like someone I could do business with.

He revved the engine and aimed us toward the center of the river. The cluster of boats fell away and the weathered buildings onshore faded into the misted green of the hills behind them.

"Is that shipyard still operating?" I asked.

"They do maintenance on trawlers and such. Haven't built a new vessel since 1972. The only boats important to Dartmouth nowadays are those kind." He waved a hand toward a white tour boat that was grinding past us, headed upstream. A minute later, its wake slapped against the sides of our smaller craft. I gripped an empty oarlock and licked spray off my lips. We were a half-mile from the English Channel and the river water tasted of salt.

Another clump of vessels loomed on my left. The largest sported the name ORWELL. It was gunmetal gray with a radar array on top and I guessed at its former military purpose. "Has the river cruise business gotten so competitive they need a minesweeper?"

Eden jerked his head toward the ship. "Belongs to the college. Converted, of course. Students up there spend more time on a simulator than they do out on the water."

Of course. The naval college was located in Dartmouth. "The future officers of the Royal British Navy."

"The royal excuse for a navy," Eden corrected me. We were

passing the center of Dartmouth and Eden kept our boat near the middle of the Dart, as far as possible from anyone watching from either shore. I wondered why this policeman was so uncomfortable being seen with me. He added, "Soon enough, the Hells Angels will have a bigger fleet."

His remark startled me. "The Hells Angels have their own ships?"

"The British gang does," he said. "HA runs a fleet of merchant ships to transport cocaine supplied by the Cali cartel."

"Is cocaine the local gang's main business?" I asked.

"Cocaine's a significant part, but they don't limit themselves to that. Hells Angels here are a major player in the international drug trade. Made themselves rich, they have. Got millions in Swiss banks. Own real estate all over the world. They're big. Very big."

We'd passed the port town and he pulled us out of the mainstream, closer to shore. I spotted a heron at the edge of the water. Beyond him, a stone fortress perched on the rocky hillside. The fort was topped by a crenellated wall, its notches blackened by time and old violence.

Eden eased off on the throttle and the engine rumble softened. He kept his hand on the tiller, adjusting our drift so that the tide carried us downstream. He pointed over my shoulder, and I turned to look behind me. We were at the mouth of the Dart, the sea spreading gray green toward the clouded horizon. "Sixty-five miles that direction, you reach the ship lanes off the coast of France," Eden said. "Closest Coast Guard station is in Brixham, seven miles away. No permanent patrols in this area for more than thirty years."

"So the coast is wide open. What are you saying—the bikers are smuggling drugs in and out of Dartmouth?"

"No, I'm not saying that. They've got their pipelines set up for drugs. Don't have to use old-time methods. But give these fellows some boats, they can move whatever they want, wherever they want. If you catch my drift."

Was he talking about missiles? "Too vague for me," I said. "Could you give me some specifics?"

"No. Like I told your Danish friend, that I can't do. I've put too much time in on this. I'm not going to endanger my operation."

I kept my gaze on him, cataloging the familiar signs. Skittish, paranoid, tight-lipped—the way Gerry Davis often got. Jack Eden was acting like a case officer worried about an agent he'd recruited to work undercover in the enemy camp. I said to him, "You've got somebody inside the local Hells Angels reporting back to you."

"Priest told you that?"

"He didn't have to. I can tell by the way you talk. My partner gets . . ." My throat closed, choking off the words. I swallowed, pushed on. "I know why you're so nervous, talking to me. You're afraid I'll do something that will expose your man inside." I leaned forward. "We have to work together, make sure I don't do that by accident."

He held up a hand. "I decide how far I'll go."

A cormorant wheeled in the air above us, black against the sky. Its haunting cry floated down like a blanket over Eden's silence. "You decide," I agreed reluctantly. "Start with what you think the priest wants me to know."

"All right." He silenced the engine. A gull rose from a rocky outcrop, its spread wings at least five feet wide. Eden pulled off his sunglasses, swiped the back of his hand across his eyes. He squinted at me, his eyes small and dark above the liverish cheeks. "You heard what the comedian said?"

What, he was going to entertain me? "The comedian?" I repeated.

He raised a skeptical eyebrow. "Priest didn't pass on the joke that biker comedian made about you?"

I wouldn't have guessed that a biker in Britain said anything about me. "What are you talking about?"

"You don't know." Eden's eyes widened and a wicked gleam brightened them. "Witty lad. By the time he was done, he had them all laughing like jackals. Described in quite nice detail what *you*"— he paused and stared meaningfully at me—"what you would be willing to do for any brave biker who'd help you get your limber fingers on a Stinger missile."

The cormorant and the gull exchanged insults, black wings beating in counterpoint to large gray ones in the sky above me. And in my brain I heard the jazzy progression I'd been listening for. Bikers, Casey Collins, and Stinger missiles.

"Back up," I said. "I need the when-where-how behind this comedy routine."

"Okay," he said. "You know what the two Danish gangs are planning for Eastern Europe?"

A plainclothes cop in the Devon and Cornwall Constabulary knew the secret plans of Danish bikers? I hid my surprise. "A business deal. Covert traffic in drugs and weapons." I paused, putting that together with what he'd told me of the pivotal role played by the British Hells Angels in the international narcotics trade. "The British gangs had to sign off on that division of turf between the warring Danish *rockers*."

"Right. That's how we picked up on what was happening. Two weeks ago, a biker contingent arrived from Denmark for a marathon session with the local lads."

"Bo Ulf Møller was in Devon on behalf of the Bandidos," I said slowly.

"Right again. His brother was with him but he didn't contribute anything audible to the negotiations. The biggest talker was a spokesman from the Danish Hells Angels." He looked at me slyly. "He was the one, made the joke."

"You're leaving too much out," I said.

Eden's expression shifted from sly to annoyed. "The Danes laid out the plan. There was a lot of jawing back and forth between Brits and Danes, Bandidos and Hells Angels. You don't need all the details. Our lads agreed to go along with the Danish plan."

"This all-powerful British club—they gave up their drug business in Eastern Europe." I let him hear my skepticism. "Granted the Bandidos an exclusive franchise without protest?"

He chewed on the inside of his cheek. "Bandidos had to pay for it, of course."

I could guess the price tag. "The weapons coming out of the former Warsaw Pact. The British Hells Angels got a piece of that action."

Eden shrugged. "Could be."

"Tell me everything they said about the weapons," I demanded.

He slid the sunglasses back over his eyes and said nothing.

I stifled a snort of exasperation and kept my voice at a reasonable level. "I know you're trying to bust these guys working your turf. I'm not going to interfere with you doing that. But I have to know about the weapons. You have to tell me how my name came into it."

He stared at me for ten seconds. When he spoke, his tone was grudging. "Your name, then. They were all of them talking big, the way they do. One of the local fellows said he knew someone in an IRA splinter group. Said the renegade Irish had a big purse to spend on shoulder-launched ground-to-air missiles. The Hells Angel from Denmark found that amusing. Said what the Irish could

190

pay was pocket change compared to what he could get. The U.S. embassy in Copenhagen was paying top dollar for Stinger missiles, no questions asked. That's when he threw in the crude remarks about the American blonde. Had to mean you, of course." He paused, his eyes on me. "I got him on tape, you want to hear."

"I don't have to hear him. What I want to know is if Ulf Møller's brother heard."

Eden shrugged again. "All we've got is a fuzzy audio tape. Only Danish-sounding voice on it is the one telling the story."

"I have to talk to your friend."

Eden responded instantly. "Absolutely not."

"I need every word spoken about Stingers. I must know what Bjørn Møller could have heard."

"You'll have to get it some other way." He yanked on the rope and the motor sputtered and caught. "I'm not letting you near my man."

27 EDEN STEERED THE BOAT BACK TOWARD MIDSTREAM, INCREAS-
ing the fuel until the engine sound was deafening.

The current beat against the bow, jarring my back. The sky
above me was the dirty gray color of sheep on winter pasture, the
cloud cover as impenetrable as the mystery I confronted. I felt as
if I were looking at a muffler with a single piece of yarn hanging
loose. If I could only get a grip on that dangling wool, I could
unravel the tightly knit fabric, expose the truth concealed beneath
it. I raised my voice to make myself heard. "*You* talk to your man.
Find out for me."

"Right," Eden shouted. "If I run across anything more I think
you can use, I'll pass it on to the priest."

I crouched at the edge of the bench seat, bent toward Eden. The
wind at my back blew my hair forward, witchlike, and I tasted
the salty strands flicking across my lips. "I need an answer," I
yelled. "Today."

Eden eased off on the throttle. "I told you, I got something else
going on. I'm not likely to see my man today."

"I'll find him myself."

"You?" His laugh was tart. "Hells Angels are a long way off
the diplomatic social circuit."

"And so am I. I had a partner, name of Gerry Davis. He's dead.
Somebody killed him and they tried to kill me. I'm going to find
out who's behind this. If you won't get me what I need, I'll get
it myself."

I was breathing hard, my fists clenched, my face so hot I knew my cheeks were as red as Eden's. I inhaled, made my words come out low and hard. "If you want to protect your operation, you'll do as I ask."

The same tour boat plowed past us again, this time headed for the channel. Tourists lined the upper deck, bundled into coats and hunching their shoulders. The amplified voice of the guide drifted over us. "On the Dartmouth side of the river, we're coming up on Bayards Cove where the *Mayflower* and *Speedwell* put in before departure for Plymouth in the summer of 1620."

Automatically my glance went shoreward. Set back thirty feet from the edge of the quay was a row of white and black-timbered town houses flanked on one end by a stone fort and on the other by a public house. The guide's voice continued. "This section of Dartmouth was also the site for much of the filming of *The Sailor Who Fell from Grace with the Sea*. This everyday tale of torture, scopophilia, castration, and antique dealing . . ." The sound faded out as the vessel thrummed downstream.

Eden yanked off his sunglasses and gestured with them toward the row of buildings in Bayards Cove. "You be in that pub tonight, between six and seven o'clock. If I find out anything, I'll get it to you."

More delay and another Casey-as-sitting-duck setup. "Why make me wait nine hours for second-hand information? Help me out. Let me talk to the man who was there."

Eden's expression was grim. "Let's get one thing clear. I know you're not going off to chat up the Hells Angels. You didn't scare me with your threat. But the priest told me about your partner. What you said about him—okay, I'll buy that. You have to do something. I'll help you if I can. But my way. Nine hours is what it takes. And I'm the only one to do it. You stay out of it."

I didn't dare push Eden any harder. "I'll be at the bar."

He gave the engine more gas and headed us toward the lower ferry slip in Kingswear. "I'll let you off at this end of town," he said. "Don't want anyone at the shipyard to see us together twice."

I pulled a pen and notepad from my pocket and jotted down Davey Chaka's name and address. When we reached the dock, I held out the paper to Eden. "Bjørn Møller visited this man while he was in England. Can you check, see if this Davey Chaka has a police record?"

Eden brushed aside the paper. "No need to check. We keep an eye on Chaka."

"You're saying he has a record?"

"No. But he *looks* like trouble. Used to be in the South African Defense Force."

So Chaka was a veteran of the combat troops that once propped up the apartheid regime in South Africa. "He's not in the army anymore?" I asked.

"No, but he's doing the same work. Hires out to a private company. One that provides military-type services for selected African governments."

"A mercenary," I said.

"Nineties style. All high-tech and well greased. The pay's good. Chaka disappears to Africa for three, four months at a time. Comes back to Exeter and stays till his money runs out again."

"You think he's up to something in Devon?"

"Can't prove it." Eden sounded disgruntled. "He behaves like all he comes for is the damn organ."

"Organ?"

"First thing he does, soon as he gets into town, is get his name on the list." He must have registered my lack of comprehension. He added, "List of amateurs want to practice on the organ at the cathedral."

"So he is a musician."

"Or he's damn good at maintaining cover. Belongs to some jazz group in Exeter. And he's always hosting what he calls 'jam sessions.'" He snorted. "You're saying this Møller character went to see Chaka. That'd be right around the time the last dirty dozen of 'em showed up, claiming to be visiting musicians. I can check, see if Møller was part of that crew."

"You think Chaka's planning something criminal with them?"

"Of course he is. Chaka's a great keyboard man. But we know he kills people for a living. And these friends who come to 'jam'— every one of them's more accustomed to playing his tunes on a bazooka." He edged the boat up beside a set of stone steps leading to the quay ten feet above us.

"Good to know that." I hoisted myself onto a step shiny with rain and river-splash. "See you at six."

"I'll be there *if* I find anything—"

I cut him off. "Be there. Believe me, my threats are never empty." I turned and climbed to drier ground. I wasn't bluffing. I couldn't stop my search for information. I'd hit the biker bars if I had to, but I hoped my threat would galvanize Jack Eden into helping me. If I was lucky, the prospect of me hanging out with the Hells Angels would terrify him more than it did me.

I walked back along the waterfront toward the public lot. A white Ford Escort with dashing blue trim and matching bubble light on top eased past me. The uniformed cop behind the wheel gave me a cheery wave, a member of the local constabulary more tourist-friendly than Jack Eden. I waved back, then turned to study a store window display while I waited for the squad car to disappear. Reflected in the glass, I saw the line of cars waiting for the upper ferry to Dartmouth. I wouldn't be joining them. I had to go back the way I'd come—to Exeter.

Yesterday, I'd written off Davey Chaka as a dangerous dead end. I could no longer afford to do that. A Hells Angel attempt at humor had linked me to the CIA's Stinger missile buy-back project. While Bjørn Møller was in England, he could have learned that I'd shell out major coin for the aging missiles. A week later in Denmark, he'd asked Bella for my name. But I didn't know why. I knew only that during the week between his meeting with the Hells Angels and before his encounter in Denmark with Bella, Bjørn had spent time with Davey Chaka.

Besides, Eden had told me enough of Chaka's background to increase my interest in the South African. He was a man with paramilitary connections—a man who might well know something about the covert weapons trade. Davey Chaka was the crucial link. I had to try once more to discover what he had talked about with Bjørn Møller.

It was ten-thirty when I reached downtown Exeter. The early-morning mist had thickened to drizzle and I pulled on a forest-green windbreaker that was supposed to be water-repellent, sticking my Devon guidebook in the zipper pocket in front. From a public phone near the post office, I called Chaka's number. He answered by stating his name and I started to give mine in reply.

He interrupted as soon as I spoke the first syllable. "You have a pen?"

"Yes—"

"Write down this number. Dial it in exactly twenty minutes." He recited the digits and broke the connection before I could repeat the number back.

I hung up and glanced around. Adults in raingear and rubber boots were bustling in and out of the post office. No one was interested in me. The smell of hot grease floated out of the closest doorway, a fish and chips take-away doing brisk breakfast business. I checked my watch. Ten-forty. I pulled the hood of my windbreaker up over my hair and began to walk through the steadily falling rain.

Davey Chaka had cut me off before I could say anything revealing. He thought that someone had bugged his phone. Nervous, I studied my reflection in shop windows, alert for anyone following me. I meandered through downtown Exeter that way, ostentatiously admiring the rain-slick stones decorating the pedestrian street. My guidebook advised me that I was looking at "crazed pavement," the design created from the remains of the wall that had encircled Exeter when the town was a distant outpost of the Roman Empire.

The stolid buildings rising above the ancient stones were newer, rebuilt after the Second World War according to the guide. By 1944, the Allied forces preparing for the D-day invasion had secretly massed in southwestern England, but the worst damage was inflicted on Exeter earlier in the war, before the town gained any value as a strategic target. Infuriated by Royal Air Force attacks on the German port cities of Lübeck and Rostock, Hitler had snatched up a tourist guide to the most beautiful places in Great Britain. Named for the guidebook's author, the Baedeker Raids in April and May of 1942 savaged the ancient city. On the worst night—May fourth—forty Junkers flew up the Exe estuary and unloaded ten thousand incendiary bombs and seventy-five tons of high explosive. The nineteen bombing attacks killed two hundred and sixty-five people, injured a thousand more, and leveled fifteen hundred homes.

Six months earlier, I'd been in an area of Germany that had been laid waste by Allied fire bombing. Today I was in England at the site of another civilian massacre. And once again, I was waiting for a man who'd made killing his life's work.

By eleven o'clock the rain had curled the cover of my guidebook and I'd found a pay phone on the back wall of a deserted bar on North Street. The green neon in the window advertised KILKENNY IRISH BEER. The ponytailed bartender was polishing his taps with a once-white dishtowel and the Spice Girls sang from the corner speakers loudly enough to cover phone conversation. I called the number Chaka had given me and when I heard his voice on the line, I said, "Yesterday, you might have warned me that you think someone is listening to your calls."

His retort had a mocking lilt. "Yesterday, you might have warned me that people are trying to find you."

I felt a chill on the back of my neck. "Someone came to you, looking for me?"

"To Gitte. People calling her up, wanting to know what she said to you."

"What people?" I asked.

"Gitte was not clear on that."

She wouldn't have been. She, Chaka, and I spoke such different brands of English, telephone communication was difficult. To find out what I needed to know, I had to talk to Chaka face-to-face. "Can we meet?"

"Anyone following you?" he asked.

"Not unless they're extremely good." I squinted toward the front window to see if anyone was peering back at me. The street outside was empty, the gentle rain a deterrent to strollers. "Anyone following you?"

"He tried, poor chap."

"You think the local police—"

"The locals I know. This man was new. Showed up this morning."

Someone had staked out his house. In all likelihood, Gitte had given Chaka's name to my pursuers. They were using him to get to me. The chill spread downward from my neck, circling around to settle in the pit of my stomach. The hunters were closing in. "I have to see you," I said.

"Indeed you do," he said. "Where are you?"

"Downtown."

"Go to the Rougemont Castle. Follow the Roman Walk. Fifteen minutes, I'll see you there." He disconnected.

I left the bar, heading across North Street and through Guildhall Square to Queen Street and onto the wooded pathways of the Rougemont Gardens. Named for the castle of reddish stone that served as the county courthouse, the park smelled of wet fertilizer. At eleven-fifteen I found Davey Chaka waiting at the tree-lined northeastern border of the garden.

I pushed back my hood so it wouldn't interfere with my peripheral vision and I stayed on the balls of my feet, ready to move fast if anyone came after me.

Chaka was dressed like a pro basketball player, slick black nylon pants and jacket with luminescent white script swooshing down the pant leg, reflecting off the jacket sleeve. The stylized writing read PAX MODERNA. Not a sports insignia, I realized, but the logo of Chaka's employer. A leisure uniform for an enormous muscular man taking time off from his paid job.

Next to him, a break in the greenery framed the grim facade of Devon Prison, sited on high ground north of the gardens.

Chaka registered the direction of my gaze. He gestured toward the penal institution and spoke in the voice of a tour guide. "Unacceptably poor accommodations."

Eden had said Chaka had no record, but the man was talking like a former inmate. I lifted my chin and toughened my voice. "Checked out the rooms down there, have you?"

He gave me a mocking grin. "Report's posted on the Internet. Inspectors deplored the housing provided young prisoners. I am *well* informed."

"Glad to hear you stay up on current events," I said, "because I need to know—"

He interrupted, smoothly finishing the sentence for me. "—what I can tell you about Stingers."

Not the question I'd planned to begin with. I kept my face impassive.

He was watching me and his smile broadened. "Yesterday, I didn't realize who you were. But the Bear mentioned you." His laugh had a smutty undertone. "You're very eager to find your missiles."

I folded my arms. "I *was* looking for Stingers. I left that project. I'm reconstructing Ole Bjørn Møller's last days alive. I want to find out if anything happened to him in England that might help us understand why he was murdered in Denmark."

"Very nicely put." Chaka nodded his head judiciously. Then his face twisted with contempt. "But all bullshit."

"What do you mean?"

"Wasn't something happened to the Bear *here* that got him murdered. Going to see you in Copenhagen is what did that. What you want to discover is why he went to your flat. You think I know."

Chaka's mind was as well tuned as his body. His analysis was perfect. How had he worked it out so quickly? Easy. "You know, don't you? You know what Bjørn wanted to tell me."

"Correction. I know what the Bear had for sale. And it's still for sale."

"I told you. I'm not working with the CIA anymore. I don't have their money to spread around."

"Then, I have nothing to say to you." He turned as if to leave.

A rivulet of rainwater rolled off my hair and under my collar, an icy finger headed for my spine. I grabbed at Chaka's jacket, the wet fabric slippery beneath my fingers. I couldn't let him get away. "Wait."

He turned his head to look down at me. "Oh, you remember you have funds after all?"

"Maybe I can work out a way to pay you later. But I need that information *today*. You talked to Gitte. She told you to help me, you wouldn't have come out otherwise. She wants to know who killed her son. So do I. So do you. You have to tell me what you know."

My fingers clenched his sleeve. I smelled his scent, a blend of fragrances that were at once consolingly familiar and so wildly out of place I couldn't name them. Urgency made my voice throaty. "You have to help me catch Bjørn's killer."

He jerked his arm free. "*I* don't need help to do that." His shiny nylon back was toward me and he glided toward the dripping foliage like the fade-out at the end of an extended lyrical run, the silence reverberating with tension that's never resolved.

28

"YOU NEED *ME* IF YOU WANT TO FIND THE KILLER QUICKLY." I spoke in a rush, a frail lasso of words flung by a lone roper desperate to stop a prize animal from running away.

Chaka's forward motion slowed.

"As for the money," I said hurriedly, "I can call some people. Set something up."

He halted.

"What's your price?" I asked.

He pivoted to face me, his smile haughty. "One million dollars."

I felt as if I'd touched a live wire, the shock of that seven-digit figure as electrifying as one hundred and ten volts pulsing through me. As soon as I'd linked the murders of Bjørn and Gerry to the attack on me, I'd known the underlying motive had to be greed. Now, Chaka was showing me that the stakes were higher than I'd dreamed.

Unless he was bluffing.

I laughed, the sound full of derision. "A million? You better have a half-dozen Stingers in your back pocket, you expect the CIA to hand over that much money."

Beyond the scrim of drizzle, his eyes were as hard, dark, and sharp as polished obsidian. Giving nothing away.

"You know how it works," I added. "You show your good faith first. If I go in empty-handed and ask for a million dollars, nobody will talk to me. Even after they see a sample, they won't give you a payment that large instantly. They'll be analyzing the situation for days."

Days. The word hung in the air between us. Every minute I lingered in Exeter, the danger to me increased. I didn't have days. And Chaka knew that.

He spat on the ground between us. "You want to look at my cards, it will cost you twenty-five thousand."

"For twenty-five grand, I need something up front. You know, like a bar code label that matches one on the CIA missing list."

His voice was harsh. "No free samples. Twenty-five thousand dollars is the final offer."

"I don't have—"

"You can get that amount by tomorrow. Bring cash to the cathedral at six o'clock Tuesday morning. I'll be there."

I closed the distance between us. "I can't get authorization to give you money without some proof I'll get value in return."

"Bring cash tomorrow and you'll get information worth far more."

Frustration made me speak too fast, jamming the words together. "You expect me to take your word for that?"

He glared at me. "If I show you one card, maybe you can guess the rest of my hand on your own. It'll cost you up front, you want me to take that chance."

I realized he wasn't selling hardware. His marketable commodity was information of the type Gerry Davis had termed "pure bullion." Gerry insisted he could calculate the value of the finished intelligence product after microscopic examination of a single particle of so-called bullion. Intelligence that dense was often worth more than a bar of twenty-four-carat gold. Sometimes, it was bullshit.

I looked at Chaka hard. "You say you've got something worth a million dollars. But you'll risk giving it all to me for a down payment of less than 3 percent. What happened?"

He shrugged. "A bad bargain, it's true. But I haven't gone soft in the head. Smart girl like you knows better than to show up tomorrow without the money." He paused and when he continued, his voice was thick with feeling. "For the Bear, I do this much. I won't do more."

He was a streak of shadow among the thick-leaved trees. Where he'd been, a smoky aroma lingered on the breeze. It was the perfume of the Christian religion, the smells of incense, candle wax, and parchment that float in the air of old cathedrals.

I headed back toward the center of Exeter, splashing through shallow puddles, replaying my very unbusinesslike negotiating session with Chaka. He'd proceeded as idiosyncratically as the most famous of jazz pianists, his riff dissonant and unpredictable. He'd demanded an impossible sum and stalked off when I refused to pay. But he'd reversed himself at once, as if he'd suddenly realized that to avenge Bjørn's death, he first had to help me identify the murderer. Maybe Chaka's feelings for the Bear had temporarily won out over his mercenary instincts. To make sure I got the facts I needed, he'd lowered his price to one I might be able to meet in the tight time frame he'd given me. And perhaps he'd chosen that time frame because he knew I was being pursued.

If Chaka had wanted to con me out of money, he would have handled the negotiation differently, doling out tidbits of information, asking for progressively larger payments, building up slowly to the final magic figure.

But he hadn't done that. Because of the Bear. The result was intensely poignant. And very persuasive. Chaka might well have critically important intelligence.

If I'd still been part of Gerry's project, I could have met Chaka's deadline easily. Twenty-five grand was petty cash for the CIA. Unfortunately, I'd lost my slush-fund access. I couldn't get twenty-five *hundred* dollars by tomorrow morning. Paying Chaka wasn't an option. But maybe I could persuade Jack Eden to help me. If I could get the local police to pick Chaka up, I might gain enough leverage to force him to talk without cash in advance.

I glanced at my watch. Eleven-thirty. I'd see Eden in another six-and-a-half hours. Dangerous to dally in Devon, knowing my pursuers were looking for me. I thought of phoning Eden, trying to speed him up. But he'd told me not to call his office. And he'd insisted he couldn't make things happen faster. He had to contact his undercover man, extract the information I needed, and make his way surreptitiously to the pub in Bayards Cove. No, I had to wait until tonight. And in the meantime, I had to be very careful. I shivered, my prospects as chilling as England's miserable summer weather.

I unlocked my car and tossed my soaked windbreaker onto the backseat before climbing into the front. I drove west on the A30 for twenty kilometers before heading south into Dartmoor National Park. Rain lashed against the windscreen, a wuthering day on the Brontës' moors, bleak except for the fifteen tour buses that beetled toward me on the cramped roads. Each time one approached, I had to pull onto the minuscule verge so that the hulking monster could scrape by.

I took tracks at random, driving through wild lands populated with furry ponies and well-kept villages, the shop windows gaudy with souvenirs. No brooding Heathcliff appeared and no heights, either. The guidebook recommended the grand and sweeping views from Hay Tor, but an elevation of 1,491 feet above sea level qualified in my lexicon as a hillock—not high enough to draw me back out in the rain.

By two-thirty, I'd spotted no tail. I was hungry and I left Dartmoor via the park's eastern gateway, stopping a few miles farther on in Totnes. The pub's counterman had the face of a kindly uncle, smooth skin glowing a healthy pink beneath the boyish freckles that dusted his cheeks. He didn't offer me a menu, instead genially recommended the humbly named "ploughman's lunch." I hadn't forgotten my last British sandwich and I asked for a pint of lager to wash this one down. My host insisted that claret was the proper beverage to drink with the lunch and I let him bully me into agreement.

Glumly awaiting another tasteless meal, I wondered again who was orchestrating my pursuit. I'd been careful, but not careful enough. I'd used my phone card to call Gitte. Because of that error, someone had linked me to Chaka and was waiting at his house, expecting me to show up. That I'd been found told me nothing about the identity of the enemy I'd nicknamed Daddy Bigbucks. These days, anyone could buy or hack their way into charge-card records. The FBI did it legally.

I rubbed the back of my hand, the fading welts itchy again. Both Jack Eden and Davey Chaka had referred to a blond woman at the American embassy in Copenhagen. But neither of them had named her. Very likely, few of the bikers knew my name.

I couldn't forget that another tall American blonde worked at the embassy. Dawna's expertise was outlaw motorcycle gangs. She'd been assigned to Denmark to assist the National Police in their handling of *rockerkrig*. But as soon as the first murder involved me—and, through me, the State Department, the CIA and the missiles—she'd been looking for a way to broaden her role.

The counterman served me a glass of the house red and I stared at it gloomily. To advance her own cause, Dawna'd shown that she wouldn't hesitate to endanger me. I'd refused to be part of her scheme. But what if she'd tried to use me anyway? Among the bikers, I'd spoken only to Ulf. Other gang members could easily mistake Dawna for me. Would she pretend a buyer's interest in Stingers in order to get information from the bikers? After all, in the game she was used to playing, breaking the rules was standard practice. She knew how to do that without earning a foul.

I slid the wine glass closer but I stopped before I lifted it to my lips. Maybe Dawna had taken her negotiations even further. Made more suspicious by my departure, she might have used FBI resources to track me to Exeter. If she believed I was a traitor, she'd have no reason to protect me. She could have guiltlessly traded information about my whereabouts for data she hoped would benefit her more.

No, I couldn't forget about Dawna. My best move was to become invisible to her and the FBI.

I sipped the claret. I smelled wild grasses, felt the sun's warmth on my head, heard the sound of a brook chortling over pebbles. *Picnic*, I thought, and the mind-reading counterman set the perfect lunch in front of me: crusty bread, dark brown paté with pickled onion, and tomato and cucumber wedges. He returned with a quartered apple, a chunk of well-aged Stilton, and a dollop of chutney. The repast forced small sounds of pleasure from me as I chewed and drank and swallowed. My avuncular host ostentatiously ignored me, as if he were accustomed to boorish behavior from Americans.

Fortified, I continued south and east, the blue-veined cheese a lingering memory on my tongue, the wine a warming presence in my belly. By the time I reached Dartmouth at four o'clock that afternoon, the rain had stopped. I stashed the Vauxhall on a side street a mile from the river. I hesitated before I locked my pocketbook in the boot. The residential neighborhood was quiet and probably crime-free. But I couldn't risk letting my credit cards fall into the light-fingered hands of a free-spending Devonshire thief who'd advertise my presence in Dartmouth. After I loaded my cash into my front-right jeans pocket, I transferred my passport and plastic into the left.

I walked to the northern end of Dartmouth and made my way around the walled perimeter of the Britannia Royal Naval College and downhill to the waterfront and the town "centre." I noted landmarks and names, committing to memory the layout of the street grid, consulting often with the Goldeneye map-guide I carried. I kept moving, kept watching my back. The gray sky, the cobblestones, the sloping streets—I knew with certainty that I was in a riverside town. And yet my pulse raced as though I were striding across the moors, only steps ahead of the beaters driving me along with the grouse and the pheasant toward watchful men with shotguns.

I saw no suspicious activity. Still, I was edgy, unable to relax. At four-forty-five, I took up position inside the arched entry to the walk-in artillery fort at Bayards Cove. The fort had no roof and above me the sky was the faded gray color of soggy cardboard. The stonework beside me was worn smooth by exposure to four hundred and fifty years of English weather and the cold rocks smelled of the river.

I could see the front of the public house Jack Eden had chosen for our rendezvous. Between five and six o'clock, four men and two women exited. Only one man went in and he was too tall and thin to be Eden. At five minutes after six, I made my own entrance.

The front of the house was taken up by four small tables arranged in front of the fireplace. A fire burned in the grate and the odor of wood smoke mingled with the smell of fried sausage. The bar ran along the left-hand wall, an open staircase rose on the right, and the colored lights of a jukebox beckoned from the rear. The man I'd seen enter had donned an apron and was lugging a beer keg through a wooden door in the back wall. He straightened when he saw me, balancing the keg on his shoulder. He was in his mid-twenties, with the chin-length hair and elegant bone structure I associated with British aristocrats named Colin and Hugh. He used his right hand to lift a lock of hair off his forehead. The gesture wasn't casual. He wanted to be sure I noticed his chiseled features.

No other customers were in the bar but I heard footsteps, someone moving around on the floor above us.

The bartender said, "Chef recommends the smoked mackerel tonight." He broke the name of the fish into three syllables, emphasizing the final one. Mack-a-REL. "Served hot with horseradish."

"Nothing to eat, thanks." I perched on a bar stool. "What do you have on draft?"

An ingratiating smile swept over Colin-Hugh's features, as if my American accent charmed him. "You with the Malpaso scouts?"

"Who?"

His smile dissolved and he brought his free hand up to support the keg on his shoulder. He staggered across the last three feet to the bar and thumped the keg to the floor with a grunted expletive.

His tousled forelock cascaded forward again and this time he didn't bother to brush it off his forehead. Instead, he waved a perfunctory hand toward his taps. "What'll you have?"

I chose a pint of Courage Best bitter because I wanted to say the name out loud. As in, *hang in there girl and give it your courage best*. I carried the huge mug with me as I moved around the room. I spotted an arrow-shaped sign beside the staircase indicating that the kitchen was upstairs. On the wall at the foot of the stairs were photographs of visiting film stars and I paused to study them. I saw Twiggy in her prime, posing for a Honda commercial. Next to her, Kris Kristofferson and Sarah Miles appeared to be having a chugging contest. I glanced at the bartender, morosely connecting his keg to his taps. He'd hoped I was scouting locations for some future movie production. I'd disappointed him by my lack of industry connections. Poor Colin-Hugh, I couldn't promise to make him a star.

A man and a woman came noisily through the door, chattering in a language I thought might be Korean. I smelled strong coffee and heard the hiss and spray of the espresso machine as the bartender filled their order for two cappucinos. A loose-limbed black man strode in next and the bartender greeted him enthusiastically. He ordered Sardinian pizza, hold the anchovies.

Maybe the pizza eater was the Malpaso scout. Maybe Clint Eastwood would show up next to share the pie. That's what I needed, a tough cop like Dirty Harry, not the biker-leery wimp I was waiting for. I checked my watch. Six-twenty. Damn Eden. Where was he?

The dark brew sloshed up the inside of my mug. I willed my hand to stop shaking. I had to know what Eden had learned from his undercover man. And I needed his help to squeeze Chaka. I had to give him the hour he'd asked for. I tried to reassure myself. I wasn't in real danger. Nobody knew I'd come to Dartmouth. Nobody would look for me in this out-of-the-way bar. I had no reason to be so nervous. I should relax, enjoy the ambience. Avoid the local penchant for scopophilia. Or worse, antique dealing.

But I still didn't feel calm. I moved along the wall to read the *Mayflower* passenger list, not surprised to find that none of my ancestors had sneaked on board. By the time I'd read it twice, it was six-thirty and I'd exhausted the wall's entertainment possibilities. I chose a chair near the fire and sat at an angle so I could see through the window to the pavement outside without turning my back to either the front or the rear doors.

I nursed my beer for another twenty minutes, brooding over Eden's cowardice. If he let me down, the remaining options for future action left me a choice between bad and worse.

At six-fifty-five, the front door opened. The man who entered was no taller than Eden. A charcoal fedora hid half of his face. My heart lifted, then sank. The new arrival was too thin to be Eden. Dispirited, I watched him saunter to the bar. His movements were catlike and his leather half-boots stroked the wooden floor rhythmically, in time to music only he could hear. I got an impression of wire-rimmed glasses and a day's growth of peppery beard before his back was to me.

I drained my mug. The last swallow was as bitter as its name, as sour as the taste of loss. I carried the empty glass to the bar. Colin-Hugh jerked his head to toss the hair out of his eyes and gave me an inquiring look.

"No, thanks," I began.

The man in the fedora interrupted me. *"Jeszcze jedno piwo?"*

My scalp tingled, each strand of hair slowly rising to stand on end.

Who was this man who'd invited me to enjoy one more beer?

And why did he speak as though he were certain I'd understand his hospitable Polish?

29 I STARED AT THE MAN IN THE HAT, SAW HIS HAND RISE TOWARD the brim. He touched it with four long, tapering fingers. His nails were blunt-cut and a cushion of nicotine-stained callus ran along the inside of the middle finger. The hat came off, revealing a shapely skull stubbled in black and white, the hair a quarter-inch long as if the man before me had shaved both his face and his head at the same time, at least three days ago.

"Another beer?" He repeated the question in English, his accent unmistakably Slavic.

I saw blue eyes behind the lenses of his glasses, and facial skin made leathery by long exposure to the sun. I looked at the strong nose, the full lips.

I looked at the face that Woody Hinton would have—if he grew up.

My heartbeat doubled its rate. The man before me was Bella's old lover. Woody's father.

I wanted to slap him. Bella had pinned all her hopes on this man. Seeing Wlodek Wojcik again had stirred up Bella's memories and ignited feverish dreams. Dizzied by that potent combination of old passion and new longing, she'd convinced herself that he would help her save Woody. But he wasn't with her in Denmark. Wlodek Wojcik—the man she called Pope—was in England with me. Why had he come after me? And how had he located me? I pressed my fingertips on the bar top to stop them from trembling. The feel of smooth, cool wood steadied me. When I found my voice, it was sharp.

"Why aren't you in Copenhagen," I asked, "getting your blood checked?"

"My blood's there." Pope gestured with an index finger, telling the bartender to refill my glass. It was the economical motion of someone accustomed to instantaneous effects. Military commanders, jazz drummers. They knew how to use their hands. He added, "I left a deciliter at the *Rigshospital* this morning."

My heart thumped wildly, adding to the sense of things gone out of control. I made myself speak slowly. "Why are you in England?"

Pope repositioned the fedora on his head, the motion precise. He lifted both mugs and stepped to the rear of the pub. He placed our drinks on a table beside the rear exit. Then he fed coins into the adjacent jukebox. He punched the buttons as if he'd determined the musical program days in advance.

Bella trusted Pope. I wasn't so foolish. Only Jack Eden had known I'd be in this pub tonight. And no one had followed me here—I'd made certain of that.

I felt cornered. My wisest move was to leave immediately. I hesitated. With Jack Eden a no-show, I'd dead-ended in Devon. My fall-back plan was to carry out my threat. Go looking for Hells Angels and discover what I could from them. I couldn't refuse to talk to the first biker who came calling. No matter how unnerved I was by his sudden appearance. And by the heat he emitted, as though a fire was banked inside him, ready to flame up at any moment.

Reluctantly, I sat at the table. A vigorous sea chantey rolled out of the speakers, the singers loud on the heave-ho's, harmonizing on the dead men's bones.

"Good," Pope said. "More private." He shrugged out of his tweed jacket. Under it he wore a Blue Note T-shirt that hugged his torso. I saw the outline of his ribs but I noticed that his tanned arms were corded with muscle. He was all bone and sinew with no spare flesh, yet the suppleness of his movements told me he was in excellent shape. And if he'd ever been a drug addict, he was at least ten years past recovery.

He looked good—wiry and sexy, with an aura of risk. No surprise Bella was smitten all over again. I knew she had a weakness for unorthodox men. With her fantasies about saving Woody and giving her son his father, she couldn't see past Pope's charm to the real danger lurking beneath it.

I had to be stronger than Bella, protect us both. And Woody. I set my mug down. "I asked, why are you in England?"

"Business for the Bandidos. I took care of that in the forenoon. Then I came looking for you."

"How'd you know to look here?"

"The man you talked to this morning? He told me where to find you."

It wasn't likely that Jack Eden, a British law enforcement expert on biker crime, had voluntarily revealed my whereabouts to a visiting gang member. Yet Pope could have gotten the information only from Eden. Whether by deceit or force, I didn't know. I kept my face devoid of expression. "Why'd you want to see me?"

"I have a message for you."

"A message? Who from?"

"A friend of yours in Denmark. He gave me the name of your contact here." He sipped his lager, watching me. He held his body completely still, but the air around him was charged, as if his energy level was so high he might explode at any moment.

Holger Sorensen was the only man in Denmark who knew I planned to meet with Jack Eden. So Holger had given Pope a message to deliver to me. If Pope was telling the truth. "You'll have to do better than that," I said. "Give me one reason I should believe a word you're saying."

Pope's fingers brushed the back of my hand, his touch on my skin as compelling as a powerful magnet on iron filings, drawing me to him against my will. His voice drew me, too, its timbre vibrating deep inside me as he spoke. "Stefan Krajewski. He was the one who brought me into this."

I flushed at the sound of my ex-lover's name. Was that Pope's intention, to fluster me into revealing information he didn't know? Beside me, the exit door wasn't tightly shut. I felt a cooling draft of night air on my check. "Into *this*," I repeated coldly. "What do you mean by *this*?"

"Two years ago, Stefan came to me in Bangkok. I won't bore you with all the details. He persuaded me I should help him."

I made a scoffing noise. "Why would *you* do anything to help *him*?"

"We knew each other, long ago."

Stefan had never mentoned an old friend named Wlodek. But Stefan had never mentioned a lot of things I needed to know. "Let me guess," I said. "You're another long-lost brother."

Pope laughed. "He had only one brother." He put two fingers on the hat brim, as though he were tipping it to me. "Who now, thankfully, is rotting in hell."

I blinked. Did Pope know that last winter I'd seen Stefan's half-brother die? "Don't thank me," I said. "I didn't kill him."

"I would have. As a boy, if I'd known a way, I would have killed him. What he did to Stefan then . . ." His voice trailed off as if the memory were too painful to voice.

Too convenient a lapse. "You're telling me that your childhood pal showed up decades later and persuaded you to help him," I said. "Let's pretend I believe that. Help him do what?"

Pope's expression was solemn. "Block the distribution of narcotics in Poland."

The song on the jukebox ended, replaced by the grainy stillness between tunes.

I lowered my voice, but not enough to cover the derision in it. "Now I'm supposed to believe you're a nark? Impossible."

"Exactly what I told Stefan. But he never gives up. You probably know that."

A huntsman's horn rang from the speakers, followed by a rollicking drinking song about fair maidens who weren't maidenly anymore.

Two years ago, Stefan was still under contract with the Danish Defense Intelligence Service. He was working for Holger and their brief was counterterrorism. "Stefan was never involved in narcotics interdiction," I said.

Pope shrugged. "Maybe not. But that's what he wanted me for." He raised his beer with taut patience, again letting me puzzle it through.

The scent of baking yeast dough wafted down from above. I smelled tomato sauce and the odor of tinned sardines. The Sardinian pizza was in the oven.

I sipped my beer, forced myself to think.

I recalled what Holger had said about Stefan. *His business in Poland is on his own initiative.* I knew that Stefan had been horrified by the rampant lawlessness in post-Communist Russia. He'd told me he feared that the Polish authorities were too weak to prevent a similar takeover by organized crime. Maybe before Stefan's contract ended with the Danish Defense Intelligence Service, he'd begun assembling a network he could use to bolster Polish law enforcement. If—and it was a very big if—he'd done that, he might have turned to Pope. An expatriate Pole well placed inside the narcotics organization—Pope was the ideal recruit. And if they'd been friends in childhood, Stefan might have hoped he could do that. But could he really have convinced Pope to change sides? Not likely. My voice was steeped in skepticism. "You're saying you're an agent? That you work for Stefan?"

"I said he brought me into it. But six months ago, your Danish friend asked me to work for him." He moved his head closer to mine and lowered his voice to a murmur. "Bikers, arms trade, Warsaw Pact weapons. You made the connection."

Letting me think he'd heard from Holger that I was investigating the link between biker gangs and the covert arms trade in the former Warsaw Pact. Everything he was saying meshed with what I knew. But the best liars always give their stories the veneer of truth. I couldn't rely on Pope. I'd need more convincing proof before I'd accept him as a colleague.

I looked at him steadily. "Maybe you should give me that message now."

"Two messages, actually. The British fellow you talked with this morning had news. He asked me to pass it along."

Jack Eden had given Pope a message for me? I gripped my mug tightly, the glass slippery beneath my fingertips.

Pope let his eyes close and spoke as if reciting from memory. "The Brit said to tell you, both Ulf and Bjørn Møller heard the conversation." His eyes came open. "He said you'd know which conversation he meant."

So Bjørn had heard that the blonde at the American embassy was buying Stinger missiles. I was so focused on showing no reaction, I didn't move an eyelash.

"Okay," Pope continued. "The Brit also said to tell you, during the past two weeks, his good friend has picked up on requests for Stingers from a dozen clients. Colombian drug lords, African rebel leaders, everybody's placing orders."

Behavior that implied the Hells Angels' clients had heard that reliable product was coming on the market. But from where? I leaned closer to Pope. "Have you heard anything about the Hells Angels acquiring a cache of the missiles?"

"No. Not the HA. And the Brit said nothing."

I tapped my fingers on the table top. I needed to talk to Jack Eden. "If the man wanted to give me a message, why didn't he come himself?"

Pope swallowed more lager, ran the back of his hand across his mouth before he answered. "Cops in Oakland, California, advised him they'd picked up some biker he'd flagged as a person of interest. He was flying out tonight to interview him."

Muscles tensed in my chest; I was having trouble breathing. I couldn't verify anything Pope had told me, not with Eden incommunicado. Worse, I couldn't get the additional facts I needed from Eden's inside man. And I had no one to help me bring Davey Chaka to heel.

But I hid my distress and when I spoke my tone was bored. "You say you've got a second message for me?"

"A warning. Ulf Møller has scheduled a big biker party starting at noon on Wednesday."

I glanced at my watch. It was half past seven on a Monday night in England, an hour later in Denmark. "You're warning me about a party in another country that doesn't begin for forty more hours?"

"Right. Ulf has put out the word that the Bandidos have acquired a half-dozen Stinger missiles. He says we're going to sell all six to the CIA."

A million-dollar sale if it were true. But it wasn't. The Danish *rockers* had no missiles. Ulf was lying. Did Pope know that? Or was he waiting to hear if I did? I said, "Have you seen these missiles?"

Pope laughed. "Haven't talked to anyone who's actually touched a missile."

"But Ulf insists he's telling the truth."

Pope moved his chin down, a hint of a nod. "Your Danish friend thinks Ulf is bluffing. That he's trying to draw his brother's killers out into the open. And you need to know that Ulf claims you'll be there Wednesday to accept delivery of the missiles and make the payoff."

I felt as if I'd been sucker punched. I'd been attacked on Saturday. Daddy Bigbucks hadn't succeeded in killing me. But he would have expected caution to force me off Gerry's project and out of Denmark. I'd left the country, hoping that would end the pursuit. But Bigbucks was concerned enough to track me as far as Exeter. He wouldn't call off the chase, not if he'd heard Ulf's wild story. "Ulf's telling people that *I'm* coming to his party?"

"In the flesh."

I was in bigger trouble than I'd realized. My enemy couldn't take the chance that Ulf was bluffing. If Daddy Bigbucks wanted to make certain I didn't return to Denmark to claim those mythical missing Stingers, he'd order his hit team to find me in the next forty hours. Find me—and eliminate me.

The tune playing over the speakers faded out. The silence was complete. Except for the scrabble of gravel on the pavement outside. And from closer by, just on the other side of the wooden door, the faint rustle of one fabric against another, like a nylon sleeve whispering over a flannel shirtfront. They were the muffled sounds of stealth. I strained to listen. I heard only an utter absence of the spoken word.

Across from me Pope was still as a stalking beast, eyes hidden by his hat, head tilted as if to hear better.

Was he also listening to the same furtive noises? Did he fear attack? Or was he part of the assault?

I didn't wait to find out. I shoved my beer mug across the table as I jumped to my feet. Amber liquid sprayed up, splashed noisily onto Pope. My chair crashed over backward, thudding against the floor. I kept my gaze on the entrance as I sprinted the length of the room. Both hands out in front of me, I burst through the front door.

I had the advantage of surprise. And the man covering the entrance was hindered by the caution forced on him by the well-lighted public quay. The shooter had hidden himself and his weapon too well. He couldn't react fast enough to catch me when I was most vulnerable, framed in the yellow wash from the open door. I crouched low, zigged to the right.

I heard a shot and I threw myself toward the archway of the stone fort. Three muffled rounds came from the pub. Had they murdered Pope? Or had he joined with them to kill everyone who'd seen him with me?

Inside the fort, I scurried up the stone steps to Newcomen Road. For a few yards, the street was level with the rooftops of the quayside buildings. To the right it soon veered downhill into Dartmouth's picturesque waterfront.

I heard a thud, a grunt and a curse. A heavy man, tripping on the stones. Followed by a second voice. Two of them, racing after me. In the distance the WAH-wah-WAH-wah of European sirens. Gunfire in Dartmouth, the Devon and Cornwall constabulary coming in loud in their compact squad cars.

I fled uphill, struggling to reach the higher ground far from the river, forcing my path northward, away from Bayards Cove. My rubber soles were silent on the paving stones, my ragged breath the only sound as I struggled across uneven terrain. Rain was falling again and the walkways glistened beneath the streetlamps. Mist haloed the lights and blurred my objective, the wall surrounding the naval college. Earlier I'd spotted a section that was undergoing repairs. Now I'd reached it again.

A pair of footsteps slapped on the pavement behind me. I plunged through the gap in the wall and dodged behind a hedge, wedging myself into an opening at the base of two sturdy laurel bushes. Rainwater slid down glossy leaves, spattered my neck, soaked my shoulders. The drizzle puddled along the curb, gurgled into the storm drain. I pulled the dark hood of my jacket over my head, buried my face in my lap.

The college's hilltop site was dominated by the main building, a monumental construction as inviting as Devon Prison. A driveway curved down to the sentry box at the front gate. I hoped the proximity of the guards would discourage my pursuers.

It hadn't.

The heavy footsteps drew closer.

30

BOOTS THUDDED AGAINST CONCRETE, SO LOUD THE MEN HAD to be fewer than ten feet from me. And then the footsteps paused.

I held my breath.

A dog howled, startling me. I hadn't expected the guard force to have dogs. My two stalkers quickened their footsteps, moving past without speaking. I counted to five and raised my head.

Two stocky men receded into the soup, moving downhill. They walked like professionals, angling their bodies away from each other to give themselves visual coverage over a three hundred-degree scan. In the rainy darkness, they were as anonymous as the helmeted bikers who'd driven me off the road two days before. In all likelihood, the same men.

Anger flamed through me, my rage hot and instantaneous. My life had turned into an infuriating foreign-language film, the kind where I could never figure out what was happening. I felt like *Casey of the Spirits* being chased by *The Avenging Hells Angel*. I'd used every bit of tradecraft I knew to evade the hit team. And yet they'd homed in on me unerringly, as if I wore a beacon. They'd found me as easily as Pope had. He'd learned my whereabouts from Jack Eden. Maybe the shooters had persuaded Eden to talk to them, too. Or maybe they'd put a tail on Pope and that watcher had called for backup when he spotted me.

Wishful thinking. Neither scenario was impossible, yet both were wildly improbable. For Woody's sake, I wanted his father to be one of the good guys. But logic pointed in the opposite direction. It was likely that Pope was working with the men who'd tried to kill me. While I couldn't prove that he'd brought the shooters with him to the pub, caution dictated that I act now as if he had.

An image of Woody flashed in my mind, his face aglow with that heart-melting smile. For a second, my love for him warmed me. Then his face dissolved into Pope's and regret chilled me all over again. Woody's best hope lay in his father's bones. Yet I had to put hope aside and treat the man as an evil villain. I couldn't let my guard down.

I forced myself to imagine the killers waiting outside the pub while I sat inside with Pope. He'd been given a head start so he could beguile me into revealing how much I'd discovered and to whom I'd relayed my findings. When the grace period expired, the shooters had come inside to finish me off. Daddy Bigbucks was so determined to be rid of me, his men had risked a brutal and public attack.

I'd had enough of this nightmarish pursuit. I'd end it. I pushed myself to my feet, intent on joining the cops who'd converged on the pub. They'd protect me.

Or would they? I hesitated. Pope was aware that I'd linked biker gangs to the covert arms trade. How did he know that?

I'd related my theory to Dawna Shepherd and explained that the Danish Defense Intelligence Service had supporting information. But I didn't think that she'd told Pope that I'd made the connection. I could imagine Dawna cutting corners to force events to unfold in accordance with her suspicions. But I couldn't see her repeating intelligence secrets to an outlaw biker.

Pope claimed that Holger told him about me. And that Holger sent him to Jack Eden. Maybe that part of Pope's story was true. Maybe Stefan and Holger *had* recruited him to work for them. Holger had trusted Pope to carry a message to me. Instead, Pope arrived with killers. He could be a double agent, working not for Holger, but for the enemy I'd named Daddy Bigbucks.

And now Jack Eden had gone missing. Maybe Pope hadn't been able to fool Eden. So Pope—or the people he worked with—had forced Eden to reveal our rendezvous. Then they'd gotten rid of him.

That scenario was all too likely. I couldn't turn to the local police for help. Dawna suspected me of criminal wrongdoing. By now, she probably knew that I hadn't gone to Bangor. To the FBI, flight was an admission of guilt. If she'd convinced a judge to issue an international warrant for my arrest, the British cops would execute it. And if Jack Eden had ended up dead . . .

I shuddered. I stood to lose more than I'd gain by hooking up with the cops. Better to lie low, work out a plan that would keep me safe *and* out of jail.

I skulked through the dripping trees, putting ground between myself and the point where my stalkers had lost me. I stepped gingerly, on the lookout for slavering Dobermans.

What I found were beagles. I couldn't imagine what use the Royal Navy had for fifty of Snoopy's brothers and sisters, but here they were, healthy young males and females, housed in separate open pens, immaculately tended. I climbed over the fence on the female side, patting heads and rubbing noses. I let the friendly females crowd around me. The rough scrape of tongues on my hands and face reminded me of Blondie and her slobbery affection. Messy, but comforting. Half of my new girlfriends were in heat. The others were at the opposite end of their reproductive cycles, and the combined odor was ripe. The nearby males were restless and scrappy despite the chill darkness. I strained to hear any distant sounds of pursuit.

The siren noise had stopped but I was sure the police were still busy. They'd be making a sweep through Dartmouth, looking for the shooters. Maybe for a mysterious blonde, too. While the police were actively investigating the gunfight, the hit team would stay out of Dartmouth. But as soon as things cooled off, they'd be back. In daylight I'd be too easy to find. I had to get out of Dartmouth tonight.

I couldn't use my car. My pursuers would know the make and plate number of the vehicle I'd rented from Avis. In their search for me, they'd have found the Vauxhall. They had the technical sophistication to attach a transmitting device where I wouldn't find it. After I reclaimed the vehicle, they'd track me to a good spot for an ambush and close in. Using my car was too dangerous.

I'd have to leave by some other means. As soon as I was out of Dartmouth, I'd dash to the nearest airport and flee to the U.S. I couldn't protect myself in Europe, not from such well-organized pursuit. It was time to give up this lost cause and go home.

Go home. And then what? I'd have to find a new job and start rebuilding my life. With Andy in it? Since I'd left him at Kastrup, I hadn't let myself fantasize about Andy. He'd have to convince me first that he wasn't going to disappear for another seventeen years. I didn't know what proof I'd accept.

I unzipped the front pocket of my windbreaker and removed the Goldeneye map-guide to Devon. In the dim glow from the security lamp, I saw that both Plymouth and Exeter had regional airports. But how to get to one of them? I couldn't return to downtown Dartmouth and search for a taxi. The police might have warned the drivers to watch out for a rain-soaked blonde. I turned back to the map and located the closest large settlement. Totnes was only twelve miles north of Dartmouth. I'd go there and hire a cab to Plymouth. I wasn't foolish enough to go near Exeter. And Plymouth was closer by three miles.

The rain had turned to mist, an enveloping fog that muffled the sound of the Dart. Too bad I didn't have Jack Eden's skill with watercraft. I could have stolen a motorboat and chugged upstream under cover of darkness. Followed the river from Dartmouth to Totnes.

I didn't dare try it. I was afraid of buried snags and tricky currents. I'd have to walk out. I studied the network of roads around Dartmouth. Poking inland from the river, Old Mill Creek lay across my path like a castle moat. I spotted a strand of "B" road that bridged the inlet and joined other country lanes. I plotted a course that zigzagged northward to Totnes. Slow going and extra distance, but with darkness and more luck, I'd evade my pursuers.

At five minutes past midnight, I kissed my new girlfriends goodbye and left their warmth—and the safety afforded by the remnants of the Royal British Navy—to hike in scenic Devon.

On the banks of Old Mill Creek, I found the shipyard that tended the tour boats. The place looked uninhabited, but I moved cautiously past the ghostly structures, trying to remain invisible as I looked for the road out of town. Feeling my way around a maintenance shed, I stumbled over a two-wheeler. Ancient but still usable. It might save my life. I took it. When I got to the U.S., I'd mail repayment to the owner in care of the company that ran daylight cruises up the Dart River to Totnes.

I crossed the inlet and followed the narrow road toward Dittisham. As I pedaled, I recalled what Pope had told me about Ulf's biker party. That part of Pope's tale had rung true. I knew Ulf had reached the same conclusion that I had: Casey Collins and Stinger missiles were tied to his brother's murder. Ulf had used those facts to bait his trap. And then he'd offered his quarry made-to-order cover.

Ulf knew that Bjørn's killer had planned his violent acts so that they appeared to be the result of renewed biker gang warfare. Police spokesmen had blamed *rockers* for the deaths of Bjørn and Gerry. The authorities predicted the Hells Angels would retaliate against the Bandidos for the Nakskov assault. If I was foolish enough to attend a Bandidos party and ended up dead, it seemed likely that the official position would be that I, too, was a casualty of renewed *rockerkrig*.

At least that was the conclusion Ulf hoped the murderer would reach. Ulf had made Casey Collins and the Stingers the centerpiece of a biker gathering because Ulf believed that combination would entice his brother's killer into the open.

The rain had stopped and a three-quarter moon shone weakly through the thinning clouds. The road passed an orchard and the watery breeze in my face smelled of rotting plums. My balloon tires rasped over the gritty pavement and spiderwebs grabbed stickily at my arms. From beyond the line of trees, a farm dog growled. My arms jerked and the front wheel wobbled. I straightened it out as the dog barked an alarm to his masters. Warning me, too. I wasn't the only stranger out tonight in backcountry Devon.

The road rose in front of me. Light glowed in the mist above it, the reflection of headlamps from an oncoming car as it topped the rise. I yanked my front wheel to the left, plowed off the road and into the orchard. The bike sprawled beside me, I pressed myself flat against the ground, my nose filled by the stench of blackened fruit. I counted the seconds as the vehicle crept past my hiding place. By the time the noise of the well-tuned engine had faded to a distant ticking sound, I'd reached twenty-five. Goose flesh rose on my arms. My hunters would move that slowly if they were scouring the countryside in search of me. I crouched beside a plum tree, waiting to see if they'd circle back.

My pursuers were closing in. And it was probably Pope who'd been the instrument of my downfall. I had to warn Bella. But I couldn't call her. Searching out a pay phone and making a late-night long-distance call was too dangerous. I'd reveal my location to anyone monitoring my charge records or tapping Bella's phone.

Metal snapped against metal and an animal shrieked, startling me. Deeper in the orchard, something rustled in the leaves, then was still. I inhaled, trying to calm myself. A small animal had sprung a trap. I'd heard the dying scream of a snared rodent, nothing more.

I listened hard but detected no distant rumble of an approaching car. I stood and lifted the bike. I rolled it to the roadside and searched for any sign of headlamps. Only darkness stretched before me. I forced myself to get on the bike and pedal. I had to get to safety and call Bella. Pope might attempt to use her and Woody against me. Bella had to protect herself—and Woody—from Pope.

I was sweating, the clammy perspiration of fear, not exertion. As the danger to me increased, so did the danger to everyone with whom I'd come in contact. I was a plague carrier, infecting the people who tried to help me.

The narrow road curved past villages named Cornworthy and Tuckenhay and took me over another inlet at Bow Bridge. I knew I'd covered three-quarters of the distance to my destination. Totnes. Yesterday I'd enjoyed the ploughman's lunch in that same town, after my unsuccessful meeting with Bjørn's piano-playing buddy.

Davey Chaka. Yesterday, he'd recognized the danger signs. He'd known that my pursuers were close. He'd lowered his price, settling for what he thought I could raise by Tuesday morning, this morning. He'd calculated that I'd be safe for another twenty-four hours. But he hadn't factored Ulf's crazy scheme into his calculations.

A dark spot materialized in front of me. The flattened corpse of a black cat. A tremor convulsed me and I had to concentrate on keeping the bike upright, steering around the road kill.

I was in peril—and so was Chaka. I wished I could warn Chaka of the danger but I couldn't return to Exeter. My pursuers had staked out his house yesterday. I couldn't safely go there..

The cloud cover had vanished and there was enough moonlight to make out the shapes of the high rounded hills, the light green shade of the fields, the darker red patches of plowed land. I'd lost the cover of darkness—but so had the men chasing me. I could spot a car before its occupants saw me. I was nearly there, nearly home. From Ashprington, the road climbed and I was short of breath. I had to get off the bike and walk the last quarter-mile up hill.

The front wheel squeaked every few seconds. Nagging, like the voice in my head insisting that I go to Davey Chaka. To warn him, sure. But more important, to hear what he had to say. I had to put aside my fears. I had to discover what Chaka knew. He was the key.

I knew that while Bjørn Møller was in England, he'd learned from the Hells Angels that I was buying Stingers. I also knew that Bjørn had talked to Davey Chaka about me and what I'd do in exchange fo a missile. Chaka had added a second critical item of information.

Information, not hardware. I was sure that Bjørn and Chaka didn't have a stash of the missing Stingers. But they'd put a price tag of one million dollars on their combined intelligence.

I'd gleaned enough new data from Pope to guess the nature of their product. There'd been a sudden change in the market for aging Stingers. This competition for missiles was new and it came from groups who'd shown no interest in them before.

So someone must have found a way to make the old Stingers reliable again. As Holger had predicted, some Daddy Bigbucks had gone into the profitable business of selling reconditioned missiles. Somehow, Chaka knew that. After Bjørn told him about me, the two of them realized that the CIA would pay to learn who was retrofitting their Stingers and delivering them to criminals and terrorists.

Davey Chaka must know who was running the operation. But I couldn't meet his price for that information. Was there any hope he'd tell me anyway?

My fingers were cold, the joints cramping on the bare handle grips, my skin faintly blue against the rusted metal. I thought of other hands. Of Pope's, precisely articulating his commands. Of Chaka's massive fists lashing out in pain. Of a third pair of hands I'd never seen in motion.

I hadn't known Ole Bjørn Møller when he was alive. But I'd touched the wrought-iron objects he'd crafted with those hands. I'd imagined the sound of the music he'd played with those clever fingers.

And I'd seen his friend. I'd watched Davey Chaka's internal struggle and the shock of awareness as something moved him to act. Chaka had gone against his nature once. He'd done one thing for the Bear. Maybe he'd do more.

Forget Plymouth. From Totnes, I'd go to Exeter. If I showed up at the cathedral, Davey Chaka might tell me what he knew. I had one opportunity left to learn the truth. I couldn't let it slip away. For Gerry. For Bjørn. For myself.

I had to go to Chaka, one more time.

31 ABOVE ME, THE NIGHTTIME GRAY COLOR HAD BLED FROM THE sky. The fragile morning light was tinted blue, as if it were filtered through robin eggshell. At the top of the hill, I climbed back on the borrowed bicycle. The wind tore at my hair as I swooped down the incline. I felt the same exhilaration I'd known as a child, playing out my fantasies, racing my fat-tired Schwinn down country lanes. Casey to the rescue. Laughing as I sped toward danger. I'd become the reckless hero of my girlhood dreams.

I reached Totnes as a church bell chimed four times. The clouds on the eastern horizon had turned pink. I found the station and called the taxi service number posted beside the pay phone. The answering voice had the cigarette-ravaged rasp of all night-shift dispatchers. He gave the universal lie, promising I'd be picked up in twenty minutes. Sunlight had reached the station's roof by four-forty-five when the cab arrived. It was a dented Peugeot spattered with mud. Beneath the driver's pullover, I saw the piping on the collar of his pajama jacket and a scrap of goose-down was caught in his tousled hair.

I sat tensely on the faded velour covering the rear seat, grateful for the driver's silence. He ran the heater and the defroster and as my clothes dried out, the interior took on the scents I'd brought with me: rained-on beagle and bike-rider sweat. After ten minutes, the driver rolled his window down all the way and left it wide-open for the rest of the twenty-five-mile trip. He dropped me at Exeter's central station, overcharging me for the windblown ride, silently staring at me as I pawed through my dwindling supply of British money. I didn't protest and I didn't tip him, either.

The sleeping prison brooded on high ground to the north. Beyond it lay the townhouse where I'd first met Davey Chaka. I figured my pursuers still had Chaka's apartment under surveillance. I couldn't go there. The cathedral was my only shot. And I didn't like it.

I understood the advantage of using a place of worship for a rendezvous point. Large public churches conferred both safety and anonymity. Still, it was hazardous to meet at one of Chaka's usual haunts. I reminded myself that he was a professional. Plus, he had a strong incentive to minimize the risk to me. I was supposed to have a bundle of cash for him today. He wouldn't want any third parties watching when I made the payment. He'd probably been patrolling the cathedral since midnight, on the lookout for any strangers who might slip in ahead of me.

I had to make certain that none slipped in behind me. The station clock read five-fifteen. I pretended to study the posted schedule while I scanned the area. Overnight, the rains had ended. Puddles between the railroad ties reflected the cloudless blue sky overhead and the steel rails gleamed silver in the daylight. I saw no one. No trains were due into Exeter for another half-hour. As I'd hoped, my pursuers were spread too thin to waste a man watching a dormant railway station.

I set out on my roundabout journey to the meeting. Sun warmed my left side, then my back, as I followed Queen and Northernhay Streets. I went to the site of the old Roman wall and I wandered along the town's perimeter until five-forty. In those twenty-five minutes, I saw no one following me, so I headed for Cathedral Close. I approached from the southwest, following a winding lane from South Street that cut between the deanery and a three-story building of red brick. The Cathedral Church of St. Peter loomed before me, the outlines of the carved figures on the west-facing facade softened by shadow. A broad expanse of open pavement lay between me and the main entrance. Without any cover, I couldn't approach that door directly. Instead, I made a right turn into a rectangular patch of orchard that lay between the church nave and the brick building. A sidewalk ran beside the newer building and as I trotted along it, I passed an open door marked TOILET. A cleaner's cart was a foot inside. Humming drifted toward me, accompanied by the scent of Lysol.

The brick building gave way to a sand-colored edifice that matched the church and connected to it. Looking for a way in, I tested each set of doors I came to. Beyond the chapter house, I found an unlocked side entrance. In fewer than five seconds, I was through the door, up three steps, and inside the cathedral. The dusty air left a taste on my tongue like gravel, the flavor of ancient stones cut nine centuries ago during the Norman conquest.

The unbroken length of the nave ran toward the west door for a hundred and fifty feet. It was lined by shafts of white stone that rose to support vaulting arches. The arches were shaped like titanic musculature, massive marble sinews powering this house of God. I smelled brass polish and old tapestry and all the scents that had clung to Davey Chaka.

I checked my watch. Six o'clock. Where was he?

On my right, the rich brown of the organ case rose from the center of the church, its vertical pipes gleaming silver in the light-filled air space between the nave on the west and the choir on the east. At one side of the altar, I spotted a set of stone steps spiraling upward, presumably toward the organ loft. I put a foot on the bottom step.

"Don't speak." Chaka whispered the words, his breath hot in my ear. His left hand clamped on my right shoulder. "They're waiting for you."

He was wearing a protective vest, the Kevlar a shade lighter than his skin. From his right shoulder hung an Uzi assault rifle. He added, "You got the money?"

I shook my head. No.

His head shake mimicked mine. "Never thought you'd be fool enough to show up without it."

I looked at him, a soldier of fortune ready for combat. And in an instant, I understood my mistake. Chaka hadn't come to sell me information. He hadn't expected me to raise twenty-five thousand dollars by this morning. He'd stressed the money to discourage me from showing up at all. He must have concluded that the men hunting me had also murdered the Bear. I'd been part of his ruse to lure my pursuers to the cathedral. He'd made them believe he was meeting clandestinely with me today. And then he'd set up an ambush. Now, he would exact his revenge.

He whispered, "Let's get you out before the shooting starts." He motioned me toward the door in the south transept by which I'd entered.

I turned, took one step toward it. Something hit the back of my legs, knocking me roughly to my hands and knees. Chaka, forcing me out of his way. Stabbing pain burned upward from my left wrist. I rolled to my right as a gunshot shattered the silence. The report didn't come from behind me. The shooter was in front of me, between me and the exit, blocking my retreat. I scrambled away from him and into the nave. No way I could safely escape down the wide-open center aisle to the west door. I dove behind the altar. Automatic rifle fire rattled, the snare-drum sound echoing and re-echoing in the vaulted vastness. Chaka fired another blast from the Uzi as he inched backward to crouch beside me. His face was streaked with sweat and I smelled his fear. "Fuckers are better than I expected," he said hoarsely. "You know how many of them there are?"

"Three came after me in Denmark. There must be at least one more."

"Shit. I only spotted two last night. Amateur who followed me. Sharper fellow came in later."

Chaka was good but he'd underestimated the hit team chasing me. "Somebody paid big bucks for these guys. He wants me very dead."

"Don't like me much, either," Chaka said. "Sniper set up in the choir had a perfect shot at the organist. Changed my mind about playing him a little tune."

I pushed lank hair off my forehead. "All these guys are shooters. It's not likely one of them bashed Bjørn's brains out."

Chaka grunted. "Their boss is the one I want. He had the Bear done."

For the second time in twelve hours, I heard the raucous sound of a European siren. Somebody had reported the gunfire. The cops were on their way.

Chaka heard it, too. "I'll cover you. Try to make it to the north transept. We can get out that way." He braced the folding stock of the Uzi against his hip and turned so he could fire over the altar.

I positioned my legs like a runner in starting blocks, aiming for the alcove directly in front of me. My left wrist ached, my palm swelling an ugly purple beneath the torn skin. Like a frightened rabbit, I sniffed the air and my eyes searched the nave. My gaze landed on a rectangle of carved wood mounted above the pillars, midway along the north wall. A shaft of errant light bounced off polished metal. "Another one," I shouted at Chaka. "Up in the gallery."

He dropped, trying to regain the cover of the altar. He wasn't fast enough. I heard the single shot, saw Chaka's head whip side-ways, his body fall. I scrabbled toward him and lifted the Uzi from his fingers. Resting the barrel on the altar top, I stitched a line of fire across the nave, trying to hold off the assault.

The muffled sound of an amplified voice penetrated the thick walls. Cops with a bullhorn? My ears were ringing and I couldn't make out the words. I smelled hot oil and heard the sound of footsteps running away. Too much heat. The hit men had missed me once again.

Chaka's massive head rested against my thigh. The denim beneath his skull reddened to crimson. I felt the sticky warmth of his blood on my skin. His naked scalp was slick with it yet he was still alive, his breath rasping harshly through his mouth. "Hang on," I said. "All that gunfire, someone will come soon, give us a hand." Knowing I was lying, that no one would come until they were certain the guns would stay silent.

Chaka must have known it too. "*You*. You do it," he gasped. "For the Bear."

Passing the torch. Now, vengeance was my job. "Tell me what's going on," I pleaded.

Chaka's eyelids drifted down and I thought I'd lost him. But after a few seconds, he spoke again, so softly, I had to put my cheek against his to hear. I listened hard, praying he'd tell me who was reconditioning and selling the missiles.

"What you think, Bear?" he asked as if he were face-to-face with his friend. "What'll she do for us, we bring her new ones?"

He muttered, and I wasn't sure I got it right.

I tried to get him to say it again. But he didn't. He didn't say another word.

32

A LEATHER SOLE SLAPPED THE STONES TO MY RIGHT. I GRABBED the Uzi and twisted around to face the north transept. In the shadow beneath the arch stood a man dressed in black. Pale palms rose like ghostly beacons into the air above his head. "Don't shoot."

A plea. In English, with an American accent. He sounded familiar. The gun barrel wavered. That well-known voice—it belonged to someone who couldn't be here. I steadied the Uzi, centering the barrel on his chest. "Lie face-down on the floor."

"Casey," he said, "are you all right?"

Dizziness washed over me. On Saturday, Andy had asked me that same question. In that same worried tone. Was I hallucinating? I shook my head, trying to clear it. I squinted at the figure before me. "Andy?"

"Yes, yes. It's me, Andy."

I lowered the rifle. "Why are you here?"

He reached me in two strides. "You're hurt."

I laid the Uzi down. "Not me."

Andy crouched and put two fingers at the base of Chaka's neck. "No pulse." He leaned across the body, picked up the Uzi by the strap. He wore black jeans and a matching jacket with a charcoal T-shirt underneath. With a corner of his jacket, he rubbed the Uzi's handgrip and trigger guard. Removing my fingerprints, I realized. "Why are you here?" I asked again.

"Later," he said. "You don't want the police to find you like this."

All my problems had started when I became entangled in a

murder investigation in a foreign country. I didn't want to get caught by another.

I lifted Davey Chaka's head off my thigh and moved him gently to rest on the worn stones. A dead man, sadly I couldn't help him.

Andy dropped the rifle beside Chaka's body, reached for my hand. I let him pull me to my feet. A chill swept over me, blood fleeing from my fingers, the pads as white and wrinkled as if I'd been frostbitten. I cradled my wounded left hand in my right, my touch like an ice pack against my skin.

"Come," Andy said gently. He wrapped an arm over my shoulders, half-carrying me across the south transept. We didn't leave by the side entrance I'd found earlier. Andy took me through the chapter house, down a narrow flight of stairs, and along an underground corridor that smelled of mildew.

An escape route that bypassed the police. How had Andy discovered it? And how had he known he'd need it?

We emerged in a grove of trees at the edge of the close, the fresh air a gentle caress on my face. Andy folded me into a Toyota with an Avis sticker, tucked his jacket around me.

What was going on? I tried again. "Andy, what are you doing here?"

"I was worried about you," he said. "Good thing, too. You needed help."

And he'd helped me. Against all odds, he'd come to my rescue. Warmth flickered inside me, then disappeared. Despite the jacket and Andy's presence, I shivered violently, my self-protective body struggling to slide into the numbness of shock. I couldn't let myself fade out, not with so much still unexplained. Trying to force the memory of Davey Chaka's bloody head from my own brain, I focused on tiny details. Andy dressed like a cat burglar. Rumpled and unshaven as he'd been two mornings ago after a night spent in his car. Yet he didn't act tired, his hands moving with smooth sureness as he guided the car through a roundabout. No sloppy left-hand shifting for Andy. He'd rented a car with automatic transmission. Smart Andy. Plan-ahead Andy. But how could he possibly have planned for this morning?

"I don't understand why you're here. I told you I was flying to Bangor."

"And it was quite a shock when we learned you never got there."

I massaged my aching wrist. "We?"

"Me and Dawna."

Andy was working with Dawna? I hadn't guessed they'd team up. "Dawna? She was that suspicious, she had to check up on me?"

"Not suspicious. Worried. Her sources told her that Ulf Møller was tossing your name around. She wanted to give you a heads-up. Sunday night she contacted the task-force leader, trying to reach you."

Dawna believed I'd defected to her detested FBI colleague in Bangor. She would have expected him to rub her nose in his victory over her. And still she'd made the call. "Dawna phoned Sam Baldwin?"

"He told her you were officially off his team. She hung up, called *me* a liar. I contacted your boss in D.C., learned you were still in Europe. The wrong place for you to be, with Ulf's biker business going on. Dawna agreed. We started searching for you. Dawna called in some favors, got a look at your charge records."

I hadn't envisioned quite the scenario that Andy was describing, but I'd known that if Dawna wanted to find me, that was how she'd do it. "She phoned Gitte Møller."

"Right. The woman didn't want to tell her anything. But Dawna did some fancy talking and got Chaka's name."

Gitte had seen me with Dawna. Giving my friend the same name and address she'd given me—that made sense. But Andy's role didn't. "I still don't understand what you're doing in England."

"You don't? As if I could sit in Copenhagen, knowing you were in danger." His sigh had a fatherly undertone, affection mingled with exasperation. He put his hand on my knee, gave a gentle squeeze. "Dawna asked London to send an agent down. But they were short-handed. So I said I'd do it."

I was surprised Dawna had relied on Andy. He was no field agent, accustomed to chasing down fugitives. "Dawna didn't object?"

"Oh, she objected. But there was no one else she could use. I flew to Exeter Monday morning."

And Monday was when Davey Chaka discovered his house was under surveillance. "You started watching Chaka."

He changed lanes deftly. "Right. He gave me the slip when he went out yesterday afternoon. I was better prepared last night. When he left at midnight, I managed to stay with him."

Only because he let you, I thought. *Only because he assumed he was setting a trap for amateurs.*

Dully, I said, "You followed him to the cathedral."

"Yes. I waited outside in the car in case you showed up. By six, I'd decided you weren't coming. Then I heard shooting. That shook me, let me tell you. If you'd gotten past me somehow . . . If you were in there . . ."

"So you came inside," I said, disbelieving. "All that gunfire and you came inside?"

"Sounds crazy, when you put it like that." He pulled into the lot of a beige-colored two-story motel so pristine it might have been punched out of the standard mold only hours before. He parked the Toyota in front of a ground-floor room. "I'm not suicidal. I didn't rush into the middle of it. But when the shooting stopped, I had to go in. I couldn't stand it, not knowing if you were hurt."

"You're lucky they didn't kill you. What were you thinking?"

"I guess I wasn't thinking."

Not thinking beyond the moment. Years ago in Salvador, he'd been as rash, falling in love with me despite all the reasons not to. This time, he'd risked his life. The realization left me breathless.

I let him usher me into a room that smelled of fresh paint and new carpet. Both double beds were untouched, their tailored, wine-colored spreads stretched smoothly to cover the four identical pillow shapes. A metal suitcase was precisely centered on the luggage rack and Andy's familiar leather shaving kit perched beside the sink at the far end of the room.

I took three steps and stopped. I was still trembling and my skin felt dirty. I didn't want to touch anything. The room's mundane tidiness made me frantic to be clean. Wordlessly, Andy pulled a robe from the suitcase and held it out to me. Clutching the soft terrycloth, I made it into the bathroom. I stripped off my ruined clothes and turned on the shower. The water blasted out in a stabbing needle spray that rattled noisily against the fiberglass liner. The minuscule bar of soap smelled faintly of lavender.

A scent that was better than dogs, better than blood. I kept rubbing it over my skin and my hair until all that remained of the soap was a transparent rectangle. I stayed under the flagellating spray for another five minutes. I should have felt clean. But I only felt beaten.

I wrapped my hair in a towel and my body in Andy's robe and joined him in the anonymous room. I glanced around. "I've got to call Bella."

"No phone in the room," Andy said apologetically.

I started toward the bathroom and my pile of bloody clothes. "I have to find a pay phone—"

His voice stopped me. "You can't go out on the street. You know that. You have to lie low till things cool off."

"I have to warn Bella."

Andy put a hand on my arm. "I'll phone Bella for you."

"You can't," I began. I stopped myself. I didn't have to withhold information from Andy. "Okay," I said. "She has to know that Pope may be dangerous."

"Pope?" Andy turned the name into a question.

I took the sole chair, rubbing my wet hair with the rough towel, thinking. Andy was on my side, but did he really need to know anything about Pope?

The bed springs complained as he sat at one end, facing me. "Who's Pope?"

I didn't want to tell him. Pope was Bella's secret, not mine. I wanted to say to Andy, *That information is classified and you're not cleared for it.* But I knew how infuriating it was, being stonewalled by someone you loved. After what Andy had just done for me, he deserved to know everything. "Pope's a member of the Bandidos gang," I said slowly. Then I explained that he was Bella's ex-lover and the father of her son.

What I was saying was news to Andy. I could tell by the intensity of his concentration and the way he absorbed every word.

"I think that Pope nearly got me killed," I concluded. "I managed to get away, but I'm afraid he may still be plotting."

Andy frowned. "You think Pope arranged the attack at the cathedral?"

"He could have. And the one last night."

"Last night?" Andy's expression was unreadable. "While I was in Exeter?"

"I was in Dartmouth. I had a meet set with a local cop. Pope showed up instead."

Andy sat on the edge of the bed, as if waiting for more details.

My throat was dry, as though I'd been talking for hours. Being silent felt better than talking.

After thirty seconds, Andy said, "You didn't suspect Pope last night?"

"I was suspicious," I said, "but he told a good story."

"Good?" Andy prodded. "Must have been good, if it fooled you."

Had I been fooled? I looked wearily at Andy, letting him be the judge. "Pope claimed to be working with me. Acted like we both knew the same people. Said they'd told him where to find me. But all along, he must have been working with the hit team." I swallowed, my horror threatening to close my throat. "I didn't know they'd go after Chaka."

"But that's not your fault," Andy said consolingly. "He must have known something. They killed him to stop him from talking. Did he tell you anything?"

I saw Chaka's body again, his head wound drenching my leg with blood. His last words had been garbled nonsense. I rubbed my eyes, trying to erase the terrible scene. And the one that lay beneath it, the image of Chaka's friend.

Defeated, I dropped my hands to my lap. "He's dead because of me. I might as well have pulled the trigger."

"The man lived a violent life. Not your fault violence ended it." Andy's arms went around me and he pulled me against him.

I didn't resist his embrace. Andy had learned I was in danger and with Dawna's help, he'd tracked me to Devon. Alarmed, he'd come here himself to search. And despite his lack of operational experience, he'd found me. At my most desperate moment, Andy had appeared. He was no field man, but his dogged determination had prevailed. He'd endangered himself to get me to safety.

I'd loved Andy, once. And I still cared for him—no reason to pretend any longer that I didn't. If I could get over how he'd ended things in Salvador, I might find myself loving him as much as he claimed to love me. Last night, huddling with the beagles, I'd wondered what it would take to convince me I could depend on Andy. Now, he'd put me first, ahead of everything else in his life. What stronger proof could I want?

And soon, he'd warn Bella for me. But not this instant. In his arms, I could shut out my last horrific memory of Davey Chaka. Lifeless, all the magic blasted out of him. My fault. But as guilt twisted inside me, I recalled that Chaka had read the attack differently. By this morning he'd become as much a target as I was. And Andy believed that, too.

For a few more minutes, I wanted Andy to hold me, keep me safe. I pressed my body closer to his and smelled English Leather and the faint residue of Clorox. I inhaled his scent, felt his warmth.

And his love. I could believe in that now. I had proof that wasn't merely "good enough," it was better than good.

Too good, I cautioned myself. *Too good to be true.*

But that was the nagging doubt of a wounded woman. Was I so fearful of being hurt again, I'd back away from Andy now? And I didn't want to back away. Lurking at the edge of consciousness were those unbearable pictures. I wanted Andy to overwhelm me, body and soul, push farther from memory the battered skulls of men who'd died because of me.

Pain and anguish were waiting in icy ambush. But hot and insistent sex would keep the awful chill from freezing my bones. Passion was what I needed, what I had to have.

It wasn't the proper way to mourn. I knew that. But I couldn't escape wasteful nature's plan for me. The cosmic biological urge to replace lives that had been lost. I need feel no shame, if I gave in to that overpowering urge.

And with Andy. We'd make love again, after all these years.

I clasped my hands behind his neck, pressed my mouth to his. His lips were pliant, his kiss tender. But I felt my muscles tensing. Too soft, too reverent. I needed hard and hot. I pulled my face away from his and my hands tore at his shirt buttons, so clumsy I'd have ripped the cloth if he'd let me. He didn't stop me, only helped me. How could he not, this man who swore he'd thought of me every day for so many years? Because of that devotion, he'd crossed time and space to rescue me. "Love me," I breathed as my hands roamed his body. "Oh, Andy, love me."

He opened the robe and pushed it off my shoulders. Naked together on the bone-white sheets, he wrapped himself around me, his mouth on mine. I shifted in the bed, my need so urgent I was trying to slide beneath him, force him inside of me.

When he pulled away, I wanted to shriek.

"One second," he said soothingly as he slid open the drawer of the bedside table.

I heard him rip open a condom wrapper.

My animal heat vanished. And I felt as if I were suspended in the stillness that follows an explosion. Maybe the silence lasted a second. Maybe less. And I was filled with a terrible certainty: Andy's touch would mark slimy trails on my skin.

Had I suddenly gone insane?

The bed jiggled as he turned to face me again. He pressed wet lips against my shoulder.

I forced myself not to jerk away. His chest slid across mine. "Casey," he moaned, moving his body over me.

I couldn't breathe. I was suffocating. I wanted to scream. Teeth clenched, I pushed on his shoulders.

His hips ground against me. "It's okay," he whispered. "It's all right."

"I can't," I said. I struggled out from under him. "God knows I want to, but I can't."

"Don't stop now." He grabbed at me.

I twisted away.

"Ah, Casey, come here, please come here."

I was on my feet beside the bed, my body shaking. Bile was a bitter taste in my mouth. My gaze flicked to Andy, lying in the bed. My stomach recoiled and I had to look away to keep from throwing up.

He swung his legs to the floor, sat on the edge of the bed, the sheet over his lap. "Jesus, what's wrong?"

I snatched up the robe and wrapped it around me, trying to stop my trembling. "I don't know." My voice was weak. "I feel sick."

His voice was compassionate. "I should have known better. After the shock you've had." He stood, moved toward me.

I backed away. "More than I could handle, I guess. I just need to pull myself together."

He looked at me, his face a mask. His hand came toward me.

I held my breath. I'd scream if he touched me again.

He reached down to the floor beside me and picked up his clothes. "I'll get you out of the country. I've nothing left, now. We'll go away together. Find a sunny beach and take our time."

A loving frolic with Andy under a tropical sun. Why did the idea of it make me shiver more? "I was up all night. I'll be better after I sleep awhile."

"You take a nap." He held his clothes in front of him, heading for the bathroom. "I'll get dressed and go make that call."

The bathroom door clicked shut. I huddled in the center of the bed, the robe pulled tightly around me so that only my face showed. The toilet flushed and I imagined the unused rubber disappearing down the drain.

The rubber. When he'd opened the wrapper, my passion had died.

We'd never used rubbers, before. At the time I met Andy in 1982, prophylactics were regarded as an inferior form of birth control, used by monogamous partners only when they had no other way to prevent unwanted pregnancy. Because Andy'd had a vasectomy, it never occurred to me to ask him to wear a rubber in San Salvador.

But AIDS had changed everything. Of course Andy would take precautions with a new partner. I knew that. So why had I reacted so strangely?

Because I wasn't reacting to *what* he did. What had bothered me was *how* he did it. Automatically getting ready for safe sex, moving with the practiced deftness of a man who's reached often for protection. More often than would have been possible during his recent and brief separation.

What had he told me about his marriage? *I kept my part of the bargain. I broke off with you. And I tried with Molly.*

He'd given me up, sure. But he'd had other lovers after me. Infidelity was no part of any bargain he'd made with Molly. He hadn't "tried" with Molly. He'd told her what she wanted to hear.

He'd told me what I wanted to hear, too. *Every day, I thought of you. All these years. Every day.*

The bathroom door opened. Andy held the plastic liner from the wastebasket in one hand. Through the clear film, I saw the dark blue fabric of my blood-stained jeans. the forest green of my windbreaker. In Andy's other hand, he clutched the map of Devon with my passport, cash, and credit cards balanced on it. He set the contents of my emptied pockets on the nightstand and held the bag aloft. "I'll get rid of these, buy you a pair of pants."

The skin under my arms was clammy with nervous sweat. I didn't want Andy to guess at my sudden and intense revulsion for him. "Don't forget to call Bella," I said, trying to sound business-like. I recited her home phone number for him, in case he couldn't reach her at the embassy.

"I'll handle it. You take a nap." He paused, looked at me hard. Then he picked up the keys to the room and the car. "Promise me you won't do anything stupid while I'm gone."

I kept my tone cheerful. "I won't."

He grinned. "That's my girl. When I get back, we can make some plans, where we're going." The keys were in his right hand and they clattered against one another as he opened the door. He blew me a kiss with his left hand.

I waved weakly and he disappeared through the door. A few seconds later, I heard the car engine. I slipped to the window, watched through a crack in the curtains as the Toyota rolled out of the lot.

And then I was at Andy's suitcase, rummaging through it for something to wear.

Maybe I was acting stupid. But I couldn't stop myself. I had to get away before Andy came back.

33

I EXCHANGED THE ROBE FOR A PAIR OF JOGGING SHORTS AND A one-pocket T-shirt, both only slightly baggy. A pair of white athletic socks were a perfect fit. I put on my damp shoes and then found a battered sports cap at the bottom of the suitcase. The faded lettering read LINDA'S TRUCK STOP, PAYNEWAY, ARKANSAS. I remembered Andy wearing it to a poolside party in San Salvador. He'd taken it off to dance with me.

Same song, second verse.

Andy, the liar.

Suddenly I saw deception in his every action.

Originally, he'd been scheduled to begin his assignment in Denmark on June twenty-first. Yesterday. But he'd shown up five days ahead of schedule, arriving in Copenhagen the same evening that Bjørn was murdered. He'd been hovering near every violent incident that had happened since. Excellently positioned to orchestrate events and force an end to the Stinger project. Coincidental, or so I'd thought, until the hit team followed me to England. And so did Andy.

He was no field man, yet he'd volunteered to search for me. Of course, Dawna had objected to sending an amateur. Given his concern for my safety, Andy should have bowed to her judgment. He should have urged her to find a trained agent.

But instead, he'd come himself, as if he'd had some special intuition that would lead him to me. Was it also intuition that had made him study the cathedral floor plan and map out a quick and clandestine exit for me?

And had that same intuition told him he had nothing to fear from the shooters inside the cathedral?

Intuition? Wrong word. The right one had to be "connection." Andy had ties to the men pursuing me.

I rubbed my wrist. I'd gotten as paranoid as Gerry. Did I believe that Andy was one of the bad guys?

Yes.

I had no proof. But Andy's behavior raised too many questions for which I had no answers. And paranoid was safer than dead.

I jammed the cap on my head and tucked my hair inside. I had to get moving. Slipping my passport into the T-shirt's single pocket, the cash and cards into the one on the shorts, I peered out through the curtain. Nobody outside standing guard.

Andy no longer trusted the hit team. He couldn't ask them to watch me. Instead, he'd tried to scare me into remaining indoors. He'd figured that way he could safely leave me alone. So long as I didn't suspect him, I had no reason to go anywhere. He'd promised to call Bella for me. As an added precaution, he'd taken my clothes and the room key. Satisfied I'd still be in the motel room when he got back, he'd left on business he must have deemed urgent.

I put a hand on the doorknob. Did I dare leave the room? If the shooters were looking for me, I'd be far too easy a target as I searched for transportation out of town. I went back to the window. I parted the wine-red fabric and put my face to the narrow crack. The curtains were new and I smelled only the vinyl liner, not a particle of dust.

Outside, a battered taxicab rolled across the parking lot. It stopped at the corner of the building to discharge a slender dark-skinned woman in a housekeeper's rose-colored uniform. Had to be a sign. I yanked open the door and ten seconds later, I claimed the vacant cab. The Pakistani driver got me to the Exeter airport in time to catch the seven-fifty-five flight to Gatwick.

As the plane sailed through the cloudless blue sky, I sipped tepid airline coffee and thought about what I'd done. I'd been on the run for twenty-four hours. I was exhausted, traumatized by the murder in the cathedral. And so distrustful of romance, I doubted most a man who said he'd love me forever. I was making up reasons to suspect Andy. I'd escaped from him so easily that my haste now felt ridiculous.

From Gatwick, I'd phone Bella. If Andy had called her first, I'd know that I'd overreacted. I could imagine her exclamation of disbelief when I told her his use of a condom had set me off. I shifted uncomfortably in my seat. I was embarrassed at the *thought* of confessing that to her.

Bella had disliked Andy on sight. If she told me I was nuts to suspect him, I'd believe her. I would return to safety in the States and I'd contact Andy. I'd apologize and promise to make it up to him. If I was lucky, he'd still want to take that tropical vacation with me. He'd said he had nothing left. Probably meant his job in Europe was over. Mine certainly was. We could go someplace sunny, sit on the beach, figure out what to do next.

I accepted a complimentary newspaper from the steward. The newsprint rattled as I unfolded the front page to study the international news. The seat vibrated beneath me, the steady drone of the engines uninterrupted.

BLOWN FROM THE SKY screamed the paper in boldface, all in caps. Sam Baldwin glared at me accusingly from the three-column photo centered above the fold. Beneath his picture the story summary reported that investigators had found evidence that the airliner was brought down by a shoulder-launched missile. I scanned the text. Baldwin refused to comment further on the missile, but "sources close to the investigation" hinted that the weapon was most likely a Stinger of 1980s vintage, originally intended for use in Afghanistan.

The missing Stingers. Just as I'd feared, one had been made reliable enough to down a commercial jet.

Or had it?

I dropped the paper. My hands clutched the armrests and I closed my eyes. I didn't want to see Davey Chaka's blood-streaked face. But I had to look at him. Had to listen to him. Had to hear what he'd said.

I forced myself to replay our final encounter. Listening again to his dying declaration, I understood. Chaka's information was about *new* missiles. Not, as I'd expected him to say, about missiles that had been made *like* new. Chaka had said new.

Somebody was selling new Stingers. Not replicas, imitations, or ex-Soviet copies. Given the high price Chaka was asking the American government to pay, his information had to be about actual U.S.-manufactured weapons.

New ones.

Chaka hadn't told me the name of the seller.

But I had a good guess. Colonel Andrew Markham had given me the clue.

I didn't know what the investigators had found in Maine but I knew their interpretation was wrong. The plane hadn't been shot down by an Afghan War relic. It was a *new* Stinger missile that had killed four hundred and eight people near Bangor.

And Maine was only the beginning.

Soon, all over the world, Stingers would kill hundreds more.

I knew it.

Andy knew it, too. He was part of it. He had to be. No other explanation fit my facts so perfectly.

The plane started its descent to Gatwick. My spirits plummeted along with it.

My sigh was full of despair. *I* was convinced. But I'd have a hard time convincing anyone else. I wished that Davey Chaka had lived long enough to tell me more. That the Bear's secrets hadn't been buried with him.

Despite the nose-down tilt of the plane, I sat up straighter.

But maybe Bjørn's secrets weren't buried. Maybe he'd told one person.

Gitte Møller had tried to tell me something after the funeral. I had to talk to her. I drummed my fingers on the armrest as the plane touched down on the tarmac. I couldn't telephone her. I had to see her face to know I'd understood her this time.

I wasted only twenty minutes on the ground at Gatwick before I boarded a flight to a regional airport on Denmark's Jutland peninsula. When I arrived in Billund, I went nervously through passport control. I'd gotten a head start away from Andy. I was hoping his shooters hadn't reached Billund ahead of me. When I emerged from customs, I was ready to jump for cover. But the arrivals hall was peaceful. I was relieved to find no one waiting for me. I was also pleased to spot an ATM amid the brightly colored advertisements for Legoland. I needed cash.

When I passed the bank of pay phones, the pain in my chest was so sharp, I had to look away. I ached for Bella. I didn't know if she and Woody were safe and I couldn't contact her to find out. Andy knew I was worried about Bella. He might have people watching her and tapping her phone. A call from me could have terrible consequences for her.

After I extracted three hundred *kroner* from the machine, I found the Avis counter. The rental agent was an expertly made-up twenty-year-old. She wore a blouse of school-bus yellow that blended nicely with the decor. Nervously, I watched as she tapped on her keyboard. I'd had bad luck with cars lately. A Saab torched on Saturday, a Vauxhall abandoned on Monday. Maybe this woman would arrest me. But she was unperturbed when she found my name in her computer as an active customer. She was delighted to rent me another car, or two or three more for that matter. Clearly, she hadn't yet heard what I'd done with the Vauxhall.

I didn't confess and the agent happily turned over the keys to an Opel Vectra and sent me on my way. I sighed. Maybe I could count on another twenty-four hours before Avis came after me, too. Now, I had to get moving. Andy had used Gitte Møller to track me once before. He'd easily guess that from Billund, I'd drive east to her. I had to reach Gitte before he did.

At two-thirty that afternoon I found her in the sunwashed garden behind her house. Dressed in a baby-blue sundress, she stood at the bottom of a trio of shaded steps outside her back door. Her watering can was poised above a clump of red geraniums planted in an earthenware pot. The weight of the water pulled the tendons into tight ridges beneath the browned skin of her bare arms. When she spotted me standing on the other side of her back gate, she lowered the can and her mouth curved into a smile. *"Davs."* Howdy.

A welcoming face and a colloquial greeting. Maybe I *had* become a friend of the family. The gate latch was an artfully twisted rod of black-painted iron. When I lifted it, I felt as if I were touching Bjørn's fingers. I pushed the gate open and the hinge made a plaintive cry.

Gitte studied me. "Did you talk with Davey Chaka?"

"I did." I took a step toward her. "He's dead. Murdered this morning."

My words stole her strength and she sank down to sit on the bottom step. She drew in a deep breath slowly, as if the action hurt her ribcage. Her eyes met mine. "Him, also."

"Him also. And for the same reason. To stop him from talking." I kept my gaze locked to hers as I moved to sit beside her on the cool concrete. "Why, Gitte? Did your son tell you anything that would explain why?"

Her eyes grew larger, the near-black iris blending with the pupil to make pools of impenetrable darkness. A bumblebee cruised between us but Gitte's eyelids didn't move.

Everything depended on her answer. And I needed it now, this minute, before my pursuers caught up with me. I wanted to grab her arm, infect her with my urgency. But doing that might scare her into silence. I forced myself to hold still, silently counting the interminable seconds as they passed.

When I reached seventeen, she leaned off the step and plucked something from the flower pot. She sat upright, staring into space. "I will tell you," she said softly. "All that I know."

34 I'D BEEN HOLDING MY BREATH. IT ESCAPED ME IN A GUSTY SIGH. "Please," I said. "Please begin."

I listened closely, but I was on edge, my senses alert for any sign of the hit team. The story evolved with nerve-wracking slowness, in a jumble of English and Danish. Bjørn hadn't given his mother a coherent explanation. He'd dropped hints, out of context and out of order. They were data fragments rather than solid facts and I had to piece them together. I couldn't risk forcing the conclusion. Instead of looking only for what I expected to find, I had to try different combinations and arrangements. Finally, it made sense.

During Davey Chaka's most recent tour of duty in Africa, he'd found American-made shoulder-held antiaircraft missiles in Pax Moderna's arsenal. Chaka was technically adept and also well informed. He knew he wasn't looking at missiles left over from the Afghan War. He filed his discovery for potential future use.

The future arrived when Bjørn leeringly described what I'd do in exchange for old missiles. Chaka must have responded with the phrase that became his dying words. *What you think, Bear? What'll she do for us, we bring her new ones?*

A lewd question that immediately led to an item for sale. Chaka had no doubt that newly manufactured Stinger missiles were available to discreet buyers. The most likely source of this sudden new supply was a traitor inside the U.S. Department of Defense. The U.S. government was willing to pay handsomely for old missiles. Chaka and Bjørn figured we'd pay more to learn of stolen new ones. They were betting that the American blonde would give them a million dollars in order to stop the weapons from being used against her countrymen.

Gitte had rephrased her son's offhand remarks and turned them into English. I hadn't understood her meaning. *Killing your own,* she'd said. *The worst thing.*

Yes. The worst.

By four o'clock, I knew Gitte was in danger. I asked her if she'd told anyone else what she'd related to me.

She shook her head.

"Not even Ulf?" I asked.

Her smile was tired. "Ulf, he doesn't listen. What can his mother tell him?"

Everything, I could have answered. And precisely where to look for his brother's killer. At every point, what Gitte had told me meshed with my guesswork.

From the highway, came the smooth growl of a luxury automobile, downshifting. A new arrival? I stood quickly, heart thumping, looking for a back way out of the garden. Beyond the mesh fence, I saw a gleaming Mercedes turn onto Smedestræde. The engine noise faded as it disappeared down the road.

Gitte was standing, too. Her gaze went from the side street to me.

I saw the awareness in her eyes. "Do you have a place to go?" I asked.

She raised her right arm, pressed three fingers to her cheekbone, pondering. "I could go—"

"No," I interrupted. "Don't tell me."

She looked at me, absorbing my meaning. *The killers will come for us, now. Don't tell anyone where you've gone to hide.* She moved her chin down in a firm nod. "You will take me to the bus station."

I glanced toward the garden gate. "Immediately."

Her voice was steady. "I will lock my house." The rear door banged shut behind her.

I went through the gate into the central courtyard where I'd parked the Opel. The dirt-smeared windows of the workshop loomed on the far side. Empty, the artist and his mourners gone. I felt as if I'd traveled ten thousand miles in the four days since we'd buried Bjørn.

Fewer than sixty seconds later, Gitte emerged from the house and buckled herself into the passenger seat of the car. She sat silently during the ten-minute drive, her hands resting atop the pocketbook centered on her lap. When we reached the municipal bus station in the next town, the clock on the wall read four-twenty. I put the car in neutral and opened my mouth to thank her for all the cruel work I'd made her do, recalling the last words spoken to her by her son.

Before I could speak, she extended her right hand toward me. I reached to shake it, a formal Danish goodbye. Instead of matching my grip, she pressed something into my palm. I turned my open hand to see what she'd given me. A four-leaf clover, one she must have plucked from the flower pot hours ago, held like a talisman during our long, hurtful conversation. It was limp from the time spent hidden in her fingers.

She got out and stood on the curb, pocketbook dangling from her shoulder. Her bare arms were folded across her chest, an elbow cradled in each hand as if she were holding herself together. Gitte, alone with her pain and her fear. Her dark eyes probed mine and she said softly, *"Held og lykke."* The Danish expression that means good luck.

"I lige måde," I replied. The same to you.

Unsmiling, she turned and headed for the ticket-vending machine, her back straight and her stride sure. As if she were telling me she'd given me all the help that she could. The rest was up to me.

I tucked the clover inside my bra and waited for a break in traffic so I could get back onto the main road. I'd done what I could to get Gitte to safety. Now, I had to get to Dawna and make her understand what was going on.

Despite the Pentagon's new weapons inventory system, skillful conspirators inside the Department of Defense had found a way to steal new Stingers, while concealing the fact that missiles had gone missing. Of course, they'd known that after the first use of a stolen weapon, investigators would swarm over the Pentagon's arsenals and their close scrutiny would expose the scheme. If the conspirators wanted their theft to remain hidden as long as possible, they had to divert investigators away from Defense Department stocks.

I was betting that someone digging through rubble at the Bangor crash site had uncovered planted "proof" that the missile was one the CIA had sent to Afghanistan during that war. And the vocal "expert" on Stinger reconditioning had to be another element in the plan. Very likely, the missiles that Gerry and I were seeking had long ago been collected to make this diversionary tactic credible.

No enormous, shadowy Daddy Bigbucks was involved. The sellers were ordinary Americans. Men like Andy. I could imagine his motive for joining the conspiracy. Planning divorce, burdened with college tuition bills for his daughters—he needed money. When Gerry's project threatened to call attention to the missing Stingers and disrupt the lucrative operation, Andy's past relationship with me made him a logical choice for saboteur.

By the time Andy arrived in Copenhagen, Gerry and I had reached a dead end trying to account for the missing Stingers. But the murder in my flat sent Gerry down a new path that would have brought him to the truth. Gerry's reasoning should have been laid out in the files for me to read after his death. But I'd found nothing. Andy had gotten to Gerry's files ahead of me. I flushed, realizing how successfully Andy had distracted me.

The stream of traffic thinned and I eased back onto the main highway through town.

Andy was involved in a major crime. Apprehending him and his partners was a job for the FBI. A job for Dawna, despite my qualms about her. She was eager to find a traitor and she'd been too willing to suspect me. I was leery of her hard-charging tactics. I'd feared that she had traded away information about me to get equivalent intelligence from her biker contacts. I no longer believed that. Bikers hadn't pursued me to England—the hit team had been sent by Andy's conspirators. They were sharp and computer savvy. They could have pinpointed my destination without Dawna's help. I didn't yet fully understand Pope's involvement. But I was certain the shooters had used him to find me in Dartmouth.

Andy had told me that Dawna was alarmed when Ulf announced he was going to sell me Stinger missiles. I wondered if I'd exaggerated her mistrust of me. Clearly, by the time she'd tracked me to England, she no longer suspected me of wrongdoing. If she had, she'd have asked the British cops to find me and arrest me. Instead, she let Andy claim the job.

No, Andy was the only plotter who'd gotten information from Dawna. And I couldn't blame her for that. He'd used her, too. Once she had the complete picture, she'd be as impatient to find him as I was.

He was our only link to the conspiracy. It wasn't likely he knew where all the black-marketed Stingers had ended up. But he could identify his partners. The FBI could grab the co-conspirators and extract the names of their buyers. The feds would move quickly. They couldn't give the bad guys time to cover their tracks.

A block ahead of me the traffic light blinked from green to amber. When I stopped for the red light, my glance fell on the brick facade of the local inn. A patient long-eared squirrel still waited by its door. At this exact spot, my grizzled Bandido escort had caught up with me. My heartbeat accelerated.

Hit men might be coming at me from both east and west, converging on Gitte's house. I'd make their deadly task far too simple if I drove the shortest route to the embassy.

Yet I had to lay this out for Dawna in person. I couldn't do it in a phone call over a nonsecure line. I had to go to Copenhagen.

But I didn't have to go by car.

The traffic light turned green and I drove straight through the intersection and found the road northeast to Odense. Jumpy, I gripped the wheel with both hands and kept my eyes roving from my mirrors to the oncoming traffic. The back of my shirt was soaked with perspiration by four-fifty-five when I parked near the train station. The next train to Copenhagen was due to leave in twenty minutes. I paid the fare in cash before I found a phone and called the embassy.

When Dawna answered her line, I said, "Have you been to see the Little Mermaid?"

She was silent for a half beat, registering who I was without naming me. So she knew someone was trying to kill me. Still, she was quick. "I hear Legoland is more your style."

Telling me she knew I'd made it to Billund. The airline-ticket charge had shown up on my records. She was trying to help me. Reminding me that others were not. Nervously, I glanced around the platform. I saw only other travelers, waiting for the eastbound train. "Mermaid's better, especially on these midsummer evenings."

"I've tried driving by. Doesn't work." She stressed the last two words so I couldn't miss her message. *Ditch the car.*

"You're in Denmark, you've got to learn to appreciate Hans Christian."

"Andersen," she said. "Of course. Good old Andy."

That fast, she'd figured out who was the culprit. Definitely not a stupid woman. "Yes."

"It'll take some work, but maybe I can get a handle on him," she said. "You better get moving yourself."

"I couldn't agree more." I hung up and joined the waiting crowd. We left on time and I spent the entire trip leaning against the corridor wall outside the rearmost compartment, my face hidden by a newspaper. Dawna had picked up my trail easily. Others would, too. I wanted the solid wall at my back and an exit door in view. I'd come too far to let myself be surrounded.

But how had I managed to get this far, without being caught?

Andy, I realized. Andy had kept me alive.

His co-conspirators must have hired and directed the hit team that murdered Gerry. Andy might have colluded in Gerry's death but his partners hadn't told him that they also planned to eliminate me. When the first attack on me failed, Andy realized what was happening. He reacted by opposing Dawna's plan to keep me in Denmark. He wanted me to return to the U.S. and leave him in charge of shutting down Gerry's project. He figured that would neutralize any threat I posed and his partners would allow me to live.

When I went instead to England, he knew the hit team would follow. He'd rushed after them to cancel their orders. Maybe he thought he'd succeeded. I remembered Andy's shocked reaction when I told him I'd been attacked in Dartmouth. As if he hadn't known that while he was staking out Chaka's house in Exeter, the shooters had come after me. Someone else had countermanded Andy's orders.

The hit team was acting on those lethal instructions when they caught up with me again at the cathedral. But Andy intervened. Right after Chaka was shot, I'd heard an amplified voice. I realized that hadn't been a policeman speaking. Andy had been first on the scene. In Exeter, he was still trying to protect me from his partners. His *former* partners, he'd concluded. He'd said, *I've nothing left, now.* He knew they'd be coming after him. That awareness prompted his offer to take me away to the sunshine. Both of us fugitives from men seeking to protect their ill-gotten, bloodstained profits.

Andy was a liar. But he loved me. He'd proved it over and over again.

Four hundred and eight people were dead in Maine. I was alive in Denmark. And Andy Markham could claim credit for it all.

Being loved like that was more horrible than anything I'd ever imagined.

35 DAWNA WAS EASY TO SPOT AMONG THE SHORTS-CLAD TOURISTS wandering near Langelinie at eight o'clock that evening. Dressed in khaki slacks and a blue blazer, she'd parked herself on a bench beside the arrow pointing to *Den Lille Havfrue*. She sat with her elbows on her thighs, chin cradled between her palms. Above her, the top branches of the birch trees were tipped with gold. The same tawny light gilded the flat surface of the harbor. Offshore, the dainty statue of the mermaid perched on her boulder, sharing Dawna's view of holding tanks and loading cranes on the far side of the open water. Dawna and the mermaid, two benched players waiting to get back in the game.

No one had followed me from the downtown train station. I watched Dawna long enough to make certain that she was alone. At eight-fifteen, I attached myself to a rowdy group of Swedes and strolled past. I trailed my new companions along the waterfront until I reached the Gefion Fountain. At its center, sun-touched spray erupted around the mammoth Norse goddess as she whipped her rampaging ox team, driving the huge beasts who'd once been her sons, forcing them to plow the channel that would divide Sjælland from Sweden. I didn't understand how any woman could prefer the other story about the wimpy mermaid.

Three minutes later, Dawna joined me. "Let's walk." She put an ungentle hand on my elbow. "You talk."

I was safest in this town if I kept moving. And I preferred walking to riding in an embassy vehicle. Yet my back itched, the skin along my spine made rashy by a feeling of exposure. I stared into every shadowy niche along our route.

So did Dawna.

We passed the Resistance Museum, commemorating the underground struggle against the Nazi occupation. As we walked along Amaliegade, I told her what I'd concluded about the stolen Stingers.

She didn't interrupt, but when I reached the end she gave me a scathing look. "Nice work, but you should have told me you were going to England."

"I figured you'd try to stop me. You didn't seem to believe a damn thing I told you about the *rockers* and the missiles."

"I thought you were jerking my chain. I didn't know why you'd do that, unless you had something to hide. Then I tested your biker gang theory against my data. Everything fit. I realized you'd been telling the truth." She paused, then added sourly. "But not all of it."

"Enough so you can be sure who the bad guy is," I said.

"Markham." Dawna turned the name into a curse. "He was so damn eager to go chasing after you. I hated sending him. But London had manpower problems. I didn't have a better way to warn you of Ulf's plans."

"Andy's slick," I said. "He fooled me, too."

"We'll pick him up immediately."

I felt a surge of relief. "You located him?"

"Not yet. I've got somebody working on it." We'd reached the plaza in front of *Amalienborg*. Beside the sentry box, the guard stood at attention, white-gloved hand cupping the butt of his rifle. Dawna slowed, tightening her grip on my elbow, nudging me to turn right, toward the embassy. "You and me, we'll track him down."

I stopped. My words came out fast. "Do you know if Bella Hinton's still in her office?"

"She left at five."

I freed my arm. "You go on ahead to the embassy. I have to talk to Bella first."

Dawna's eyes glowed a deeper blue. "So that's the part you left out. Hinton's involved in this mess. Of course she is. She and the biker with the funny hat. The weirdo they call Pope."

Dawna had seen Bella with Pope?

She laughed. "Don't look so surprised. A dude that wrong comes on the scene, I'm interested. We couldn't keep up with his every move, but I've got excellent photos of him and Hinton together on Saturday. And then look what he did. Went right after you. Too many coincidences to suit me. If you've got an urgent matter to discuss with Hinton, it has to involve Pope, and I need to hear it."

I'd seen the charts and graphs in Dawna's office. She kept good track of her bad guys. Of course when Pope appeared, she'd paid attention to him. I said, "Bella's son has leukemia. Bella's hoping Pope can donate bone marrow for a transplant."

"What are you telling me? Pope is the boy's father?" Dawna put her open palm against her temple as if that would help her process information faster. "Okay, that might explain the Monday morning visit to the *Rigshospital*. But why'd he follow you?"

"You know he went to England yesterday?"

"Right. We lost track of him after he landed at Gatwick. London didn't have a spare man to put on him. I called a cop I know in Devon to see if he could help me out. But before I reached him, he was off to the States."

My hand went to my temple, copying Dawna's move. Too much new stuff, coming too fast. "It's true? Jack Eden went to Oakland?"

"Sure he did," Dawna said. "How'd you hear that?"

I waved away her question. "When you were watching Pope, did you ever see him with Holger Sorensen?"

"Your pal from the Danish Defense Intelligence Service? Get real, Collins. You want me to think that Pope is a snitch for those guys?" Her words came out faster, her urgency audible. "I know Hinton is your friend. But don't let loyalty rob you of common sense. There's a good chance this Pope is running a number on Hinton. You don't want that. And your fairy story won't work on me, anyway. What, you expect me to believe that Danish intelligence sent Pope to England? I suppose that's why he came back today, same as you?"

My heart thudded in my chest. I seized the one critical fact buried in her outburst. Pope had survived the shootout in Bayards Cove and returned to Copenhagen. I started across the plaza. "I've got to talk to Bella."

Dawna was right behind me. "No coaching, Collins. I want to hear Hinton explain her long-time association with an outlaw biker. *Before* she gets an earful of the bullshit you're shoveling."

I stopped. "Fine with me. But I should warn you. I don't know who might be waiting for me at her place."

"You don't get it, do you? The bureau is interested in Hinton. We're watching her. If my man had spotted anyone else doing the same, he'd have let me know." Dawna crouched and slipped a hand up her pants leg. When she stood again, she was holding her pistol tight against her thigh. "If he missed anyone, I'll be ready."

Her voice had a greedy undertone of bloodlust that wasn't reassuring. I hurried her across the cobblestoned plaza. Once we reached the street fronting Bella's condo, we moved more slowly. The two of us huddled in a darkened doorway a half-block away from Bella's building, waiting for a safe opportunity to get inside. At ten minutes before nine, a pair of dog walkers took their time getting their excitable poodle through the entrance. We dashed across the street and crowded into the lobby after them.

I led the way up the fire stairs, Dawna a few steps behind me, covering my back. When we reached the second floor, she guarded the stairwell while I hurried down the corridor to knock at Bella's door.

I heard the distant chanting of Country Joe and the Fish. After a second, the door flew open. The music was louder but still muffled, a radio playing in another room.

Bella grabbed my hand tightly and when she spoke, relief colored her voice. "I was so worried. This biker party that the Bandidos are planning—Pope says it could mean trouble for you. He'll be glad when I tell him—" Dawna crowded up behind me and Bella stopped talking. If she'd been a cat, her back would have arched, her claws come out.

"Dawna knows about you and Pope." I dropped Bella's hand and moved into the center of the room.

Dawna followed me. "Speaking for the bureau, we'd like to know why an embassy security officer is so cozy with a foreign criminal."

Bella shut the door and leaned her back against it, facing us. "The FBI is not going to interfere with this."

She was acting like Dawna couldn't touch her. Pope must have given her the same bogus story that he'd given me. Bella thought he was an undercover agent for Danish intelligence, immune to FBI scrutiny. "I know what Pope told you," I began, "but you have to understand—"

"Not what *he* told me." Her excited voice drowned mine out. "The hospital. Preliminary results are so good, they say it's 99 percent certain Pope will be a match for Woody."

"He matches?" Incredulity left me speechless. But as I studied her joyful expression, disbelief gave way to jubilation. I felt as though the window had cracked and the heavens split open, too.

The distant rumble of the Fish Cheer sounded like angelic exultation. I crossed to Bella and spun her into a fervent hug. "He'll do it?"

Over her shoulder, I saw Dawna, hands at her sides, head inclined toward us. Her gaze was intent, as if she were watching a close game of hoops, trying to guess the opposing team's moves two plays ahead.

Bella freed herself from my embrace, her face triumphant. "I talked to him an hour ago. He was heading off to this biker thing. He'll be tied up with that till Friday. But he wants me to go ahead and schedule the transplant pending final test results." She took a breath, visibly calming herself, and turned to Dawna. "I'm going to help the kid. So don't think I give a damn if the FBI's upset that I've been consorting with criminal elements."

The words came out slower and deeper. And Bella had stopped using Woody's name, as if she didn't want to sound like a mother, begging. Wanting Dawna to hear a fellow pro, doing her job. So why wasn't she announcing to Dawna that Pope only appeared to be an outlaw, that his *rocker* persona was a disguise for cover purposes?

Dawna caught my eye and I saw the gleam there. She thought she'd proven her case. Bella and I weren't singing the same song. I'd been lying about Pope to protect Bella.

The music faded out. After a few seconds, a new tune kicked in, the volume higher. Not so new, I realized when I heard the Doors rhyming "higher" with "pyre."

Dawna said to Bella, "There's no federal law against stealing biker bone marrow. I've got no reason to halt a donation. What I want to know is, what are you giving him in return?"

"You think I'm dirty," Bella said, disbelieving. "What, you're accusing me of trading U.S. government property for bone marrow?"

"Property, information, cash. Or all of the above." Dawna spoke calmly, her voice full of conviction. "Whatever the man wants. Don't pretend he's doing this for nothing. Not when he knows what you can access for him."

Bella forcefully denied the charge. Dawna replied in kind. They went at it, macho words flying like fists, a pair of cops duking it out in the squad room. I followed their exchange, listening most for what Bella wasn't saying. What she hadn't said. What she clearly did not yet know. Like Dawna, Bella believed Pope was a criminal. I didn't, not anymore.

Exhaustion overwhelmed me. Beneath the tiredness though, I was jittery. I jumped when the telephone shrilled. Bella started toward it but the ringing broke off. The music stopped, too. Bella shrugged but the offhand gesture looked unnatural. "For the kid," she said. "He's been talking to all his pals." I heard the fond satisfaction beneath the deliberately chosen words. Woody had good news to share with his friends.

I didn't. I said to Bella, "We've got a big problem with Andy." Briefly, I recounted the Stinger missile scam, explaining why Andy and his partners had tried to derail Gerry's project. "To stop this thing, the cops need to arrest Andy immediately."

"We're working on it." Dawna went to the door, turned to speak to me. "I've heard enough here. I'm going over to the embassy to see how they're doing. You coming with me?"

My jumpiness worsened. For reasons I hadn't fully worked out, I didn't want to leave Bella and Woody. "You go ahead," I said to Dawna. "I've been on the run since four o'clock on Monday morning. I'll get some sleep, join you later."

"I'll be back," Dawna said, looking at me hard. Pointedly letting me know she thought I was colluding with Bella to cover up her security breach. First she'd get Andy. Then she'd come after us.

As soon as Dawna was gone, Bella said, "She's such a shithead."

"Just overzealous. She gets an idea you've broken the law, she goes on the attack. Don't worry, she'll back off when we set her straight." My thoughts were jumbled and I sank down on the futon. "I've had it. I have to get some sleep."

Bella patted my shoulder. "Glad you made it back." She disappeared into her room.

As soon as I was alone, all my jitters returned. The story that Pope had told me in Dartmouth was true. He worked for Holger Sorensen and he'd come to England to warn me. Now that I understood what Andy had been doing, Pope's explanation made better sense. And I had compelling proof that Pope was exactly who he said he was—an intelligence agent. He'd observed the cardinal rule of covert operations. He'd revealed none of his secrets to Bella. He'd told her only what she needed to know.

I was supposed to be a pro, too. But I'd told Andy too much. Still dressed in the clothes I'd stolen from him, I stretched out on the futon. Across the harbor, streetlamps glimmered in Holmen.

Blanched light from the night sky washed through the huge window, reflected off the white walls, bathed the room in a luminous glow. Despite my exhaustion, I slept restlessly, haunted by a panicky sensation that I'd done something beyond repair.

At six o'clock on Wednesday morning, I was jarred fully awake by the telephone ringing next to my ear and the sound of someone pounding on the door.

The phone went silent in mid-ring but the knocking continued. I went to the door and peered through the fish-eye. I saw Dawna, in the same slacks and blazer she'd worn when she'd left me, earlier.

As soon as I opened up, she started talking. "He flew Heathrow to Warsaw yesterday evening. Paid cash for the ticket, that threw us off. But he's still traveling on his own passport. How he got past the Polish authorities is a mystery."

"Probably with more cash," I said. "If he's still in Poland, I know some people who can help you."

"That's why I rushed over—"

The bedroom door burst open, cutting her off. Woody came out dressed in T-shirt and oversize boxer shorts, the cordless phone pushing his hair to a red spike above his ear. He grinned when he saw me. "You are one lucky dude," he said into the phone. "She's still here."

He extended the instrument to me. "That Andy guy you were with the other night. Says he needs to speak with you."

36 Dawna was beside me, whispering into my ear. "Keep him talking long as you can." She pulled a cell phone out of her jacket pocket, punched in a number.

Telling her people to start a trace, I realized. She had a tap on Bella's phone.

Bella appeared in her open doorway, yawning and bare-legged.

"Andy," I said into the phone. My fingertips left wet smears on the white plastic. "Where are you?"

His voice was tired. "I thought you'd go to Bella. Guess you got things figured out. The Stingers, me, everything."

"Pretty much," I said. "You and your friends tried damn hard to prevent that."

"I told them we didn't have to kill you. I said I'd handle you. Nobody liked my idea much, but I talked them into it. I could never hurt you, you know that."

"Somebody ordered that hit team to get rid of me."

Bella moved next to Woody and looped her arm protectively across his back. She was three inches shorter than he was and the gray strands had faded her hair so that it no longer matched his flaming topknot. Their shell-shocked expressions, though, were identical.

"My partners aren't happy that I stopped things at the cathedral," Andy said. "They don't seem inclined to trust me any longer. Looks like I'll have to disappear."

Dawna tilted her head to hold her phone between her shoulder and her ear. Using both hands, she gave me a broadcaster's signal. *Stretch it out.*

Andy added, "Don't suppose you'd like to disappear with me?"

I kept my voice calm. "The smart thing for you to do is turn yourself in. Cooperate with the authorities. If you help them nail the guys you've been working with, you'll get a lighter sentence."

"Best deal I can hope for from the feds is life without parole. *If* my friends let me live long enough to testify. I've got no choice, you know that. I have to run."

"No," I pleaded.

"You'll be okay," he said quickly. "No point any longer in eliminating you. I'm the weak link. I'm the one who can name them. The shooters are after me, not you."

"I wasn't thinking of me—"

"Oh, it's my safety you're worried about." He chuckled, the sound like dry beans rattling into a glass jar. "That's good. You won't mind helping me."

"Helping you?"

"You make sure the police don't interfere with me. If you don't do that; if the cops try to pick me up—I'll tell the world that a Bandido called Pope is a government informant."

"You don't know that."

"I do. From what you told me, I know it for a fact. And the Bandidos will believe me. I know that, too. If anyone tries to arrest me, your friend Pope is a dead man."

He was right. Ulf might interrogate Pope first. But he'd kill him in the end. Potential rats don't get the benefit of the doubt.

"I know you don't want him killed," Andy added. "Give me twenty-four hours. Keep the cops away from me for that long, I won't say a word to harm Pope. Do this for me, I'll do that for you."

He broke the connection.

My gaze went to Dawna. "Sweden," she said. "He's calling from southern Sweden. We're trying to pin it down." Her attention went back to her phone. She made a couple of two-word remarks and disconnected. "Malmö. A pay phone. Couldn't get the exact location."

I realized Andy could have taken the overnight ferry from Poland to the southern tip of Sweden. It was an easy hop from the ferry port to Malmö, the Swedish city directly across the Øresund. "He might be coming to Copenhagen," I said to Dawna.

"Why would he come to you?" Her voice was skeptical. "Doesn't he know you've fingered him?"

"He's on the run. Maybe he left something here he needs for his getaway."

She started tapping new numbers into her cell phone.

"Wait. We have to talk first." I turned to Bella. "Andy's dangerous. Who knows what he might do? You need to take Woody to a safer place."

She tightened her hold on Woody. "Andy threatened him?"

Dawna was watching me intently, trying to figure out what Andy had told me. She folded her cell phone, slipped it back into her pocket.

"Andy's stressed out," I said. "Unstable. I can't predict his next move."

"Get dressed," Bella said to Woody. "I guess we should take a little drive."

"Like I don't know what's happening." He pulled away from her. "Don't forget your extra ammo, Mom." He slammed his bedroom door.

"What did Markham say?" Dawna asked.

I gave her a warning look. "Later."

Bella put her hand on my arm. "Come on, Casey. Woody's not listening. Please—tell me what's going on."

I wanted to explain, but I had to stick to the rules. She didn't need to know the details of Andy's threat. I couldn't tell her. "There's no time," I said hurriedly. "You have to get Woody out of town."

"No time." She dropped her hand suddenly, as if she'd been burned. "You're not going to tell me, are you?"

I shook my head. "We have to get moving—"

"We?" Bella's voice was too high and she looked from me to Dawna. "You don't tell me shit," she said flatly. "Leave me and Woody in the dark while you go off with her. Just get on your white horse and ride away. Because a girl's gotta do what a girl's gotta do."

I started to protest. "Not like that—"

"Just like that." The three syllables were roughened by icy rage. "You're doing it to me," she said in a tight voice. "The same thing he did to you."

"He?" I repeated. "Andy?"

"Not Andy. You know who I mean. Old tall, dark, and lockjawed. Stefan Krajewski. Shit, Casey, you've turned into him. I love you. And you treat me just like he treats you."

Dawna had moved to the open doorway. "Let's go," she said to me.

I glanced at her. My gaze flicked back to Bella. Her green eyes were wide with anger—and something else. Three months ago, if I'd looked in a mirror, I'd have seen that same betrayed expression on my own face. I'd thought then that Stefan didn't trust me with his secrets. And now Bella thought the same of me. I couldn't explain to her, anymore than Stefan could have made me understand, then. I remembered how he'd walked so sadly away. I understood that, too. It hurt too much to see the wounded look on Bella's face. I dropped my eyes and hurried after Dawna.

I stopped when I got to the building's ground-floor entrance. Andy had insisted that I was no longer a target. But the hit men weren't under his control. I stared nervously through the plate-glass window.

"Go on." Dawna's voice was impatient. "I put more men out after we talked last night. From here to the embassy, we're covered."

An off-white Ford from the motor pool was parked in front of the building. I hurried across the sidewalk to it. As soon as we were seated inside, I repeated Andy's threat to Dawna.

"So you weren't putting me on," she said. "This biker really is an informant for Danish intelligence."

"We're only two blocks from their headquarters. We can go to *Kastellet*, and they'll confirm it."

She made a brush-off gesture. "I believe you. But Hinton doesn't know?"

"Pope didn't tell her."

"Smart of you," she said approvingly, "Not repeating Markham's threat. Last thing we need is a hysterical mother getting in the way."

She'd picked up on Bella's passion for Woody. Maybe Dawna wasn't as cold as she pretended to be. "That wasn't why I didn't tell her," I said. "Bella's not the type for hysterics."

Dawna pulled a car key from her blazer pocket. "Maybe not. But I can't have her interfering with the arrest."

"You can't arrest Andy," I said quickly.

"I've got a heart, too, you know." Her face was drawn with fatigue. "I feel for the boy. But we can't allow Markham to escape."

"I'm not saying you should let Andy get away. But when you locate him, you don't have to make your move immediately. You try to arrest him and anything goes wrong . . ." If Andy evaded arrest, he'd burn Pope. I couldn't let that happen. I took a breath. "You can put a tail on him. Keep your people close, but not so close Andy can spot them. After I get Pope to safety, you pick Andy up."

Her voice was firm. "We find him, we pick him up. We're not going to mess up the arrest. What you're suggesting would be rotten police work."

Rotten, indeed. Still, I defended it. "What's the big rush? If you had Andy in custody at this moment and he'd given you the names of his partners, the bureau couldn't make the bust instantly. It's midnight in D.C. Take at least two hours to get people into the office. You've got to arrange the simultaneous arrest of a half-dozen people. Sealing records, setting up independent guards on the arsenals. Your people would need at least eighteen hours to get everything in place."

"No way it would take eighteen hours."

"How long?"

"They could be ready to go by noon, their time," she said grudgingly. "Give or take a couple of hours."

"Noon. It'll be 6:00 P.M. in Denmark. You can give me until six o'clock to find Pope." I was arguing for my benefit as much as for hers. Telling myself that Woody's situation wasn't hopeless. "Come on, Dawna. For the boy. At least let me try."

"Don't make me the bad guy." Angrily, she jammed the key into the ignition. "We get that tricky, we're bound to lose Markham. You're talking lousy strategy and you know it."

I did. And I knew my frontal assault wasn't working. I had to try a different tactic. I held up my hands palm-out, a gesture of surrender. I put all the resignation I could muster into my voice. "You're right, of course. You can't risk letting Andy escape."

"Damn straight." Her voice was full of conviction but she didn't turn the key.

I was getting to her. She didn't want to sacrifice Woody, either. I reminded myself that she'd been trained to compartmentalize her emotions, act on the basis of hard facts. It was time to stop tugging at her heart strings and give her a practical reason to help Woody. "The Danes will understand," I said. "This Stinger mess is more important than anything they're doing. You can disregard the fact that Pope is an asset of Danish intelligence, essential to an ongoing operation."

"I'm not worried about political repercussions." She lost control of her voice so that the last word came out *repercu-UH-shuns*. We both knew how the bureau worked. Lots of people would be glad to share the credit for catching Andy and his pals. But if anyone objected to sacrificing Pope, Dawna would take the heat all alone. "I'm fine so long as I do my job," she said firmly. "And my job now is making that arrest."

"Of course, it is. But you can protect yourself, just in case anything goes wrong. I'd be glad to do liaison for you with the Danes. If you do lose Pope, at least you can say that you kept the locals informed."

She turned on the ignition. "What are you proposing?"

"I'll go to *Kastellet*. Given what happened to me and Pope in England, I'm sure Holger Sorensen is there. He can back me up while I look for Pope. Holger can coordinate that with you."

"That's crazy. Being a liaison doesn't mean going after Pope yourself."

"You heard Bella. Pope's tied up with this biker thing. Somebody has to go to Fyn and bring him out. I know what he looks like. I've talked to him before. I'm the logical person to go."

"You?" She laughed acidly. "What, you think you're a biker expert, too?"

"Come on, Dawna. I need you to give me some time."

"I must be crazy." She muttered angrily as she slammed the car over the uneven pavement. "What the hell," she said when we reached the cross street. "We haven't located Markham. When we do, if I judge the flight risk low enough, I'll postpone the arrest. But that's it, Collins. That's the best deal I'll offer you."

"I'll take it," I said. "I'll call you after I've talked to Holger, let you know what's happening."

"Sure," she growled, not looking at me. Acting tough, but I had her number. She hid her tender side better than Bella did. But sentiment was driving her now. If I was lucky, she wouldn't regain control of her feelings.

I had her drop me at the Gefion Fountain. Behind the scrim of spray loomed the earthworks surrounding *Kastellet*. I hurried into the cool darkness of the tunnel that went through the barricade. The paunchy gate guard recognized me, waving me on without comment. I sped past a red brick building, its lengthy facade broken by stark white doors. Multipaned casement windows were placed in the long wall with geometrical precision, like pieces of translucent graph paper embedded in reddish cork. The third-floor windows stood open, the inhabitants of the attic rooms already desperate for cooler air at six-thirty in the morning.

I went directly to the climate-controlled office shared by Birger and Stig, the two intelligence analysts I'd worked with on Gerry's project.

As I'd expected, Holger was with them. The dark hollows beneath his eyes—and the stack of used coffee cups—told me he'd been in this room all night. He waved me inside and closed the door. Neither Birger nor Stig turned away from their keyboards. I peered over Stig's shoulder. The screen on his monitor was lavender, the color code he used when the file pertained to false documents. He was studying the recent travel of a fictitious Canadian businessman named Fraser.

"They've been at it since you were attacked on Saturday," Holger said. "Yesterday's activity in England narrowed things down a bit. We're clear on at least four of the six men involved in the assaults."

I realized that Birger and Stig were trolling electronically for the men who'd come after me. I studied the screen before me. A man using the Fraser identity had surfaced in the Netherlands yesterday. From Amsterdam, Fraser had flown to Warsaw where he'd paused briefly before going on to Stockholm.

Poland to Sweden. Andy's route. As Andy had foreseen, at least one of the hit men was chasing him.

Holger drew me away from the analysts, motioned me into a chair. "I've been waiting for your report. Another ten minutes, Stig would have phoned to awaken you."

First Andy, now Holger, so sure they'd find me at Bella's. Was my behavior that predictable? I didn't waste time asking.

"We have to contact Pope," I said.

Holger massaged the gray stubble on his chin. "That will be difficult. The Bandidos leadership left Copenhagen last night for Fyn. I have people in the field but Pope is in contact with none of them. His instructions are to stay with Ulf and the other head men. For security reasons, their exact whereabouts is secret."

"We have to find him. Andy's threatened to expose him. The other bikers will kill him if we don't get him out."

Holger held up a hand to stop me. "Your report," he said. "Succinct, complete, and chronological."

I wanted to shake him, get him moving to find Pope. But when his voice became so cold and crisp, only facts moved Holger. I started from when I'd left Kastrup and I kept going until I'd summarized my conversation with Dawna.

He frowned. "I understand the problem with Pope. Your response to your FBI colleague was correct. And not only because you and Pope are acquainted. Because of the recent incidents, *rocker* security is unusually tight for the event on Fyn. None of my people can approach Pope without arousing suspicion. You, however, have the cover Ulf has provided." He stepped to the door, still talking. "You have a role in his melodrama that gives you reason to confront him."

Ulf. I felt a tremor in the pit of my stomach at the thought of facing Ulf again.

Holger opened the door and spoke briefly to a sergeant waiting in the next room. Seconds later, the man had cleared away the night's dirty dishes. Holger resumed speaking to me. "I will make some plans for Pope's safe departure. You and I will go to Odense and work out of our communications center. I will also *coordinate*, as you put it, with your FBI colleague. You must plan to leave for Fyn by 0900."

A firm fist knocked decisively on the door and Holger reached for the knob. "That will be the sergeant with your breakfast."

My mouth watered, I was so famished. I glanced eagerly toward the door, but it wasn't the sergeant knocking.

Dawna stood in the next room, a thick bundle of charts in one hand, a bulging knapsack in the other. "Contrary to what you seem to think," she said, "*I'm* the biker expert."

37

SHE STEPPED THROUGH THE DOORWAY. "ADMIT IT, YOU NEED me."

"I thought you were going after Andy," I said.

"Chuck'll handle that." Charles Townsend was the second FBI agent assigned to the embassy as a legal attaché. "Fugitive apprehension is Chuck's specialty. He liked your idea, that Markham was coming to collect documents he'd left in Denmark. Chuck's working with Blixenstjerne to get authority to search Markham's hotel room. He goes near that place, the cops will have him."

I was on my feet. "You said you wouldn't arrest him."

"Calm down. Chuck and his crew will only watch him. They won't move until I give the word that it's okay to make the bust. That's the other reason I came." She dipped her head toward Holger. "To coordinate the two operations."

Dawna sounded sincere. But arresting Andy was too important to the FBI. We couldn't trust her colleague to hold off. Our only hope was to move faster than they did. And to do that, we needed Dawna's help. "She's got photos of key Bandidos," I explained to Holger. "Records of which ones hang together. If we identify one of the leaders, we can zero in on Pope more quickly."

"We lack such detailed information on the local gang," Holger said. "I agree, her presence will improve coordination. I will make some calls." He stood aside to allow the sergeant into the room with a basket of *rundstykker*, a plate of cheese and a fresh pot of coffee.

The yeasty odor of fresh baking blended with the strong fragrance of the cheese. The round roll was warm and when I split it open steam rose from the interior. I topped half with a paper-thin slice of Esrøm. I allowed myself to savor that first wheaty, sesame-seed topped bite of bread with its tangy morsel of cheese. Then I gave my full attention to Dawna's documents, ingesting the rest of my breakfast as fuel, nothing more.

We spent half an hour mapping out our plan of attack and going over pictures and bio information on the key Bandidos. When we'd finished she collected her photos. Tapping them on the desk, she frowned at my bedraggled clothing. "You can't hang around a bunch of bikers dressed like that." She pulled a pair of black Lycra leggings from her knapsack, along with a stretchy shirt made from a metal-threaded fabric that flashed silver arrows under the artificial light. She added a leather cap and a denim jacket with a stylized number one on the back. "Might be on the large side."

"Yours?"

Dawna shrugged. "I don't always dress like a cop."

I pushed the glittering clothes aside. "But you think like one. And you know what Blixenstjerne's thinking right now. He's got two unsolved homicides. Of course, he'll push for Andy's immediate arrest. With his backing, the FBI can override the interests of Danish intelligence. You don't intend to give me any extra time to find Pope. All of this, it's just a game for you."

"A game. I can tell you never played college ball." She gave me a corrosive look. "You know, right before we went on the floor, me and the other women—we used to slap each other in the face. Hard enough to hurt—we wanted it to hurt. I needed that to get up for what we did to each other out there. That's the kind of *game* I played. It's got nothing to do with my life now."

"What are you saying?"

"You think you know me, because I used to play basketball. But that doesn't tell you anything." She leaned over to straighten the pile of clothes and placed a pair of worn cowhide boots on top. My boots. They hadn't fit into the one suitcase I carried with me when I left on Sunday.

"You searched my flat," I said accusingly.

"You disappeared. Of course I checked out your last abode. Thoroughly." She patted the lumpy instep of the near boot. "Found a little something in your kitchen drawer, thought you might be able to use."

I peered inside. Bella's .38 smiled back at me. I raised an eyebrow at Dawna.

"I want you to find Pope and get him to safety. Any edge I can give you, I want you to have it. See, you're wrong about me. Sure, I talk sports lingo—everybody in the bureau does. Because people understand that talk. But you have to remember, I'm the FBI's number-one expert on motorcycle gangs. I didn't get there by shooting hoops." Her voice took on a defensive tone. "Or maybe you're like Baldwin. Don't give a damn about bikers."

Counterterrorism was my specialty, too. I hadn't understood the reach of vicious criminals like the Hells Angels. "I didn't," I said, "till I saw what they were doing."

"So you get it. I'm not trying to score points. Bikers aren't an opposing team. I'm chasing them for the same reason you chase terrorists. Two sets of seriously bad guys."

Dawna was right. I hadn't understood she was as passionate about her work as I was about mine. I'd rated bikers lower on the criminal hierarchy. And because of that, I'd mistaken her dedication for ambition. I'd inferred too much from her sports metaphors and her basketball experience. And I'd accepted her chilly FBI-agent demeanor at face value. Now, she was proving me wrong. "Sorry," I began, but she cut me off.

"All this stuff you've given me is dynamite. Agreements between Bandidos and Hells Angels, covert deals for control of the former Warsaw Pact. Drugs and weapons. I wrap this all up in a neat little package for the bureau, people will have to take me seriously. Jerks like Baldwin won't be able to grab my resources. I'll be able to do my job the way it should be done."

"If," I said slowly, drawing out the word, "this thing with Andy doesn't blow up in your face."

"Right. We can't let Markham escape. Still, we don't want him to make good on his threat against Pope. When Chuck gets Markham, he'll muzzle him. Okay, there's always a risk that the fugitive will evade arrest. But the apprehension is out of my hands." She grinned. "So you have to concentrate on getting the damn biker to safety. I'll help you every way I can."

I lifted the pile of clothes, balancing the boots in the center. "I'll go change."

I found an unoccupied office and hurried out of my shorts and T-shirt. Beneath the white cotton of my bra, Gitte's crumpled clover lay against my skin like a dark tattoo. I ran my finger over the spot, promising Gitte that ultimately I'd find the man who'd killed her son and bring him to justice. I hoped for more good luck in return. Dawna and the FBI could deal with the Andy problem, save the world from destruction by Stingers. And Holger was focused on rescuing his informant and going forward with his own mission to save Denmark and northern Europe from the criminal designs of outlaw bikers. That left only me to save Woody. Woody's future was in danger—and I'd put it there by exposing Pope's secret to Andy. I had to get Woody's father out of harm's way.

I stuffed my hair under the cap and slipped the revolver into the jacket pocket. When I opened the door, Holger was waiting in the hallway. He eased me back inside. "When we planned the abort signal," Holger explained, "we knew a verbal message was un-workable. Not knowing who would be giving the signal, we couldn't guess what language would be appropriate." Then he took me through the sequence of body movements that would alert Pope that his cover was blown.

"Before you begin," he added, "use the word 'jazz.' Pope will know to withdraw from the operation."

"Withdraw?"

"And depart with you." He spread a map of Fyn on the desk and put his index finger on a smaller island southwest of the larger land mass. "Helnæs," Holger said, naming the tiny island. A cause-way extended from the mainland to the islet, the road ending at a pictograph of a lighthouse.

"Take Pope there," Holger said. "A boat will be waiting. The recognition signal is *dobry wieczór.*" Good evening, in Polish.

I wondered why Holger had chosen a sea route for Pope's escape. Where would he go from Denmark? I stopped myself from asking. This mess was my fault. Time to admit it to Holger. "I thought Pope was lying when he told me he worked for you," I said. "I turned everything around. Took me too long to see the truth."

Holger patted the back of my hand. "You're human. Love blinds us all."

He was as indulgent with me as my own father was, always ready to excuse my mistakes. Holger's words were no comfort. For a little while, I'd been overwhelmed by nostalgia but I knew now that Stefan still owned my heart. "I didn't love Andy," I said. "And still I couldn't see what he was doing."

Holger gave his head a tired shake. "*His* love, Kathryn. His passion for you. He was the last man you would suspect of wrong-doing. He knew that." He pushed me gently toward the door.

I balked. "But—"

"Enough. You have no time—and no reason—to wallow in guilt."

I started for the door. Too slowly to suit Holger. With his open palm, he smacked me between the shoulder blades, propelling me into the hall. "You've done good work so far. But you're not finished. We must leave for Odense at once. You have to move quickly."

What do you do when a pushy Lutheran priest ignores your confession and refuses to impose penance? When he grants absolution that you never asked for? Starts ordering you around?

I felt like punching him. Hugging him, too. I settled for an exaggerated salute and the words that go with it. "*Javel, Herr Oberst. I am yours to command.*"

38 HOLGER MADE US ALL MOVE QUICKLY. BY TEN-THIRTY THAT morning, we'd relocated to the operations center on Odense. Holger had brought in two dozen men he said would help us find Pope. Flemming Nielsen was one of them. He'd buzz-cut his shaggy hair to neo-Nazi stubble and covered his bare forearms with ornate henna designs. He was so changed I didn't recognize him until he turned his back to me. From the rear, he was still unmistakable. Two other *rockers* looked familiar and I realized they were frogmen, too. No last-minute plan had brought these men to the island of Fyn. Three days before, when Ulf announced the biker event, Holger had started preparing to infiltrate it.

Dawna's briefing took forty-five minutes. She focused on Ulf and six other members of the Bandidos leadership, describing the men and their motorcycles. She also had five photos of Pope, but in each one the fedora concealed his face. Holger's people weren't likely to spot Pope in the field. To find him, Dawna would have to chart the movements of Ulf and his cohorts and use that information to pinpoint the locations where Pope was most likely to be.

At eleven-fifteen, Holger issued a cell phone to each of his men and they fanned out across Fyn. Dawna waited in the operations center to take their calls. I reclaimed the rented Opel I'd left in Odense and returned to the ops center to wait with Dawna for reports.

The police had prohibited the bikers from forming a lengthy procession on the highway and the Bandidos were using a church-yard on the east side of the island as a staging area. Starting at eleven, they dispatched twenty-man squads of bikers every quarter hour, consecutive waves in the day-long rally that Ulf had named the *Sankt Hans* Run.

Flemming Nielsen and his two frogmen positioned themselves in Vindinge near the church, but they had trouble picking out any of the individuals we wanted among the assembled bikers. Security-conscious, the Bandidos had swapped bikes and helmets with each other. It was a nail-biting three and a half hours before Flemming's team made positive identification of the club president and his second-in-command.

By two o'clock, I was in Vindinge where I mingled with curious onlookers from the town, watching the bikers for the next hour. None of the other club officers appeared. I realized that the Bandidos had put themselves on a war footing. They feared enemy attack. To avoid a wipeout at the top, the leaders would not congregate in one place until the last possible moment.

I did see five of Ulf's walkie-talkie-carrying soldiers. They were studying faces as closely as I was. I avoided their scrutiny. I didn't want Ulf to start wondering why I was on Fyn. Much safer for me—and Pope—if I could locate him without alerting Ulf to my presence.

Several hundred visiting bikers had skipped the procession and gone directly into party mode, keeping our people in the field busy searching the hundreds of small gatherings. From Vindinge, Dawna directed me west on a zigzag course, following up on sightings of key Bandidos among the flocks of bikers. It was June twenty-third, one day before the religious feast day of St. John the Baptist. In Danish, *Sankt Hans*. And *Sankt Hans Aften*, St. John's Eve, was how the Lutheran Danes referred to their Midsummer Night bacchanal. *Sankt Hans Aften* had given Ulf an excuse for hosting a biker party. But a nationwide festival was a complication I hadn't anticipated.

Half the population of Fyn was out in the streets, rubbing shoulders with *rockers* from the rest of Scandinavia, drawn to the island by the Bandidos' event. I also spotted uniformed police from as far away as Aalborg, emergency reinforcements for local law enforcement.

The day was cloudless, with the temperature eight degrees above normal. I counted a dozen enterprising ten-year-old bicycle riders pedaling feverishly from crowd to crowd, hauling wooden trailers full of long-neck bottles, dealing beer directly to thirsty consumers.

Few of the Bandidos were drinking. One sober *rocker* idled near each major intersection, stonily watching the crowds. Ulf hoped to lure his brother's murderer to Fyn today. Although he wouldn't have divulged that goal to his sentries, he'd have instructed them to watch for violent strangers—men capable of stopping the Bandidos from selling the missiles Ulf claimed to have. Or so I assumed. I'd driven nonchalantly by each watchful *rocker*, avoiding eye contact, checking my rearview mirror to see if I'd triggered a walkie-talkie message. None had shown interest in a woman in a hat, driving an Opel.

Doggedly, I chased Pope's phantom across the island, praying I'd find him before Andy blew his cover. At six o'clock, Dawna phoned me with bad news. Andy had spotted the cops surrounding his Copenhagen hotel before they saw him. He'd fled into the adjacent neighborhood. Given the resources that the FBI had called into the field, he wouldn't remain free for long. He had to know that. I hadn't done as he'd asked. He'd make good on his threat. I was out of time. Yet, exhausted and despairing, I forced myself to continue my search.

At eight o'clock, I parked beside a mom-and-pop grocery store on the west side of the island where I'd been directed by Dawna. The sky gave no hint of twilight, the blueness dimmed only by smoke from the bonfires burning in every village. My throat was raw from inhaling the sooty air and my head ached from the permeating odor of cinders. Yet another fire blazed in the open field facing me. The townspeople celebrating here had dug a trench to contain the flames but the charring grasses inside the fire circle added fine ash to the billowing smoke. The locals stood at the edge of the blackened weeds, their heads bent over what looked like hymn books. The reedy hum of singing voices wove through the crackle of burning twigs.

"No good," I rasped into my cell phone. My throat hurt and my tone was testy with frustration. "No bikers."

Dawna tried to clarify my location. "You're near Gummerup?" She sounded as if she were reading the name of the village off her map, pronouncing it as if she were asking about an equipment malfunction: did something gummer-up the works?

"Gummerup." I echoed her. She'd never understand where I was if I said the name the way the Danes did. "Looks like a family affair. Nobody but folks from the area, having a sing-along."

"Wait five more minutes," Dawna said. "Flemming's watching

the Bandidos' security officer. Something's up. He thinks they plan to rendezvous right in front of you."

At last. I swallowed, trying to soothe my dry throat. "Have the cops picked up Andy?"

"Not yet. Chuck's covered the train station and the airport. He's got people going door-to-door in the ten-block area around the hotel. Markham never had a chance to collect his getaway ID from his hotel room. Man can't move without us knowing it."

"He can get to a phone. He can tell his story to the press."

"And give away his location? That wouldn't be smart."

He'd evaded arrest once. I couldn't let the FBI misjudge him again. "Andy's thorough," I said. "Especially when he's attempting something he's never done before. He always has a well-thought-out plan."

"But he's no field agent. I'm surprised he's eluded Chuck this long. In another hour, we'll have him surrounded. We'll be ready to move in, pick him up."

Sweat beaded on my forehead. Maybe that's what Andy was waiting for, that movie-scene ending. *Come out with your hands up.* I imagined Andy's hand reaching instead for the phone.

A voice rumbled in the background. Dawna added, "Holger says to tell you, Fraser landed at Kastrup an hour ago and rented a car."

I licked my lips, tasted the gritty flavor of ash. The hit man pursuing Andy was closing in, too.

Dawna said, "Flemming's on the other line. Wait right where you are. Anything new, I'll call you back."

I laid the cell phone on the seat beside me. I rubbed my forehead and my palm came away slickly gray. I wiped it on my pant leg. Even with my windows rolled down, I was too hot. But I kept my jacket on, comforted by the weight of Bella's .38 in my right-hand pocket.

I was only ten miles from the cemetery where we'd buried Ole Bjørn Møller. Ulf hoped this Bandido gathering would unmask his brother's killer and he'd scheduled it to climax at midnight not far from his brother's grave. Despite the suffocating heat, I shivered. Andy could tell Ulf who'd killed his brother. But the next time Andy talked, the only name he'd say would be Pope's.

The wind shifted again and another blast of acrid brush smoke burned my eyes. The dense cloud rolled upward from the bonfire, hiding the effigy of the witch impaled on top of the piled wood.

The crowd moved back from the flames but they didn't stop singing. Against the sputter of the fire, their voices reached me faintly like a choir of the damned.

I unfolded the map, tracing with my finger the shortest route from Gummerup south to the lighthouse at Helnæs. My finger jerked across the paper. Andy was cornered—he'd crack soon, spill his guts to the media. The bonfire that the Bandidos planned to light at midnight would become Pope's funeral pyre. I had to find Pope before Andy talked. I didn't want another man dying because of me.

Flames at the fire's center found a new fuel and sparks shot upward with a louder roar. Nearby, gravel crunched and a very pregnant woman in a tie-dyed T-dress danced past me, her protruding belly button encircled by a sunburst on the fabric. Despite her bulk, she was light on her feet, running toward the fire circle. I glimpsed punked-out hair and multiple earrings before she faded into the smudge.

Engines grumbled distantly and grew louder. Motorcycles, more than one. Headed my way. I shook the layer of grit from the map and refolded it before I slid down in my seat and pulled the cap lower on my forehead.

Three bikes thundered into the lot and parked at the far end, twenty yards from me. The riders took off their helmets and positioned themselves watchfully at three points of a triangle. I recognized the Bandidos' blond-bearded security officer and I guessed the other two men were his lieutenants. During the next five minutes, they were joined by the club president and his number two, plus Ulf and three of the four regional trustees. Sixty seconds after Ulf shut down his engine, Pope and the last trustee arrived. I let out my breath. All of the Bandido leaders were in one soot-covered spot.

I pulled off my hat and jacket. The glitter shirt clung to the wet spot on my back. I hated to leave my gun in the car but the biker security officer was too conscientious. I wouldn't get a weapon past him. I was better off dressed only in Dawna's skintight clothes. I imagined Ulf's gaze on me and foreboding ran down my spine like a trickle of cold sweat. Near naked before Ulf—could I pull it off?

I reminded myself what Pope had told me in Dartmouth. Ulf had insisted to his comrades that he had Stingers for sale. None of them would question my presence on Fyn tonight. If I was lucky, I'd get a chance to communicate with Pope. A wind gust blew the thickest smoke in a new direction, giving me a clear view of the cluster of bikers. I climbed out of the car. Ash powdered my bare arms and I smelled hot pine pitch. I slammed my door and the two guards closest to me turned toward the noise. I drew back my shoulders and filled my lungs with the scorched air.

"Bo Ulf Møller," I shouted, "you and I need to talk."

39

THE GROWL OF MALE VOICES CEASED. ELEVEN PAIRS OF EYES were on me as I strode toward the group. The security officer blocked my advance. His leather vest hung open and he wore no shirt. The reddish blond hair on his bare chest curled upward, struggling to join the whiskers straggling down from his chin. Both clumps were dotted with cinders.

I glared at him. "My business is with Ulf."

"Casey Collins," Ulf said. He muttered something to his companions. A wave of lewd laughter rippled through the group and I knew I'd missed another telling of the Casey-loves-missiles joke.

The security officer motioned me to raise my hands. He held his own out, palms open as if he were going to pat me down.

"Forget it," I said. "You can see everything I've got under this Lycra."

Ulf guffawed and barked out another command. The blond looked at me hard, taking seriously the need to eye-frisk me. After twenty seconds, he stepped aside.

The other bikers had formed a semicircle with Ulf in the center. Pope stood at one end of the arc, the crumpled fedora back on his head, a lighted cigarette between two fingers. The hand rose smoothly to his mouth and the tobacco glowed red as he inhaled.

Ulf swaggered forward two steps. "You're ahead of schedule."

Acting like we'd made a deal. He was playing this one as I'd hoped he would. He'd expect me to deny that I was there to buy Stingers. He probably planned to call me a liar, have his buddies punish me.

"Your schedule," I said, "not mine. I'm ready to do business."

"Oh?" He drew out the word and I imagined him thinking fast. Maybe I was making an honest effort to recover the missiles. And maybe not. By playing along with me he'd learn if I was legitimate. And he'd postpone that moment when his buddies discovered he'd been lying to them. He grinned savagely. "Let's see your money."

"Don't be ridiculous. Tell me where those missiles are, you'll get the money."

"I said I'd give you the missiles at midnight. I'm sticking to that." He had to suspect I was running a number on him, but I detected no doubt in his voice. He made another succinct remark to his friends. Their laughter had a brutal edge that sent a chill down my spine. "I trust you'll meet our price." His tone was oily with skepticism.

"We're close enough for jazz." I put my hands on my hips, raised my chin aggressively. "But your security arrangements are much better than mine," I said, raising my right hand to smooth my hair. I folded my arms on my chest. I'd given the signal. Now, I had to give Pope a reason for leaving with me. I said to Ulf, "I need some protection. Me and my money will both feel much safer if you're looking after us."

I stopped. Ulf narrowed his near black eyes and studied me.

He wouldn't let me get him alone. The risk of ambush was too great. So why hadn't he instantly refused to go with me? I hid my dismay, waiting.

He ran his ugly tongue lasciviously over his lips. "Maybe I can spare you a few minutes, you're that eager for my company."

Panic surged up from my gut. If he followed me to my car, I'd have to take him hostage. Could I get to my gun before he did? I locked my eyes to his and willed away my terror. "A few minutes won't cut it. I need your guarantee that I won't be ripped off en route to the exchange. You ride with me."

Behind Ulf, a man snickered. He muttered something in Danish. The biker next to him laughed slyly. They were probably mocking Ulf's seduction technique.

The grin left Ulf's face. "You have to look after yourself."

"Forget it. The deal's off."

Ulf grunted irritably. He turned to the security officer, asking him in Danish if he could spare a man with a walkie-talkie to ride with me to the bonfire. "He'll have a radio *and* a weapon," he warned me in English.

The man who'd snickered earlier made another mumbled comment in Danish. From the jeering reaction, I guessed he'd offered himself for the job. I didn't look at Pope. I couldn't risk blowing his cover. But what was he doing? He had to act soon or we'd both be in trouble.

The thick-bodied president elbowed Ulf aside, his face twisted with annoyance. With his bald head and black-framed glasses, he looked more like an irate mathematician than a biker honcho. "I need every man here. We've got things to do. You get yourself to the meeting."

I let a whine creep into my voice. "I don't know where this place is, I'm supposed to be at midnight."

"I will do it." Pope tossed his cigarette to the dirt, ground it beneath his boot heel. "The rest of you have business to discuss. You don't need me for that. She can start with me, do the rest of you later."

Another burst of smutty laughter. I spoke loudly to be heard over it. I couldn't appear too eager to accept Pope. "That man won't do. Listen to his accent. I need somebody who knows his way around this island. I need you, Ulf."

"I've had enough of your bullshit," the president said to me. To Pope, he added, "You want to go with her, fine. But I want her out of here, now."

I felt my tension ease. My ploy was going to work. Then I saw Ulf's slit-eyed grimace and my stomach knotted. I wasn't home free yet.

"Wait a minute," Ulf said. "We don't know what she's planning."

"That's Pope's problem," said the president, "not ours." In Danish, he ordered the security officer to give Pope a walkie-talkie and a pistol.

I wheeled and headed for the Opel. I heard Pope's footsteps behind me. Felt Ulf's eyes on my back. I wanted to break and run but I made myself stride normally, an angry woman who'd been bested in an argument, forced to take the consequences. I squeezed the car key, heard the comforting beep as the Opel's doors unlocked.

As soon as I got into the driver's seat, I grabbed my jacket, yanked out the .38, and slid the barrel under my thigh. I left the grip sticking out so I could grab it in a hurry. As Pope slammed his door, I turned on the ignition. I drove sedately around the back of the grocery and out onto the highway. I wove through the pedestrians, talking fast, telling Pope of Andy's threat. "Holger's got a boat waiting for you on the south coast."

Pope braced himself in the seat, positioned to watch the road behind us. "I appreciate your help," he said formally.

"I owed you one. It's my fault you were in danger." I corrected myself. "Are in danger. Ulf suspects I'm trying to get away with something."

"Yes." He flicked on the walkie-talkie and held it to his ear, monitoring the biker's net. We'd reached the edge of the village. I turned onto a cramped country road that cut between rolling fields. Smoke hung over the hay stubble and blurred the horizon, turning the sun to a dirty white ball. We soon left the evening strollers behind and I flipped open the cell phone and punched the redial to call Dawna. When she answered, I said, "I've got Pope." I couldn't keep the triumphant note out of my voice.

"You're en route to Helnæs?" She asked the question flatly, no jubilation in her tone.

"Your guys can pick up Andy, no problem."

She snorted. "He got away from them. Turns out he had a car stashed. Crummy little Ford he bought a week ago. One of those trolls at *Kastellet* turned up the make and model. But Markham was too quick for us. He made it past the cops and over the bridge before seven-thirty."

"The bridge? You mean he's driving west?"

"He must have guessed that we've got Sjælland bottled up. Only weak spot was the bridge over Store Bælt. He was smart enough to see that. We figure he had another set of documents with the car. Cash, credit cards, passport. He's trying to make it to Jutland."

"Shit." Once he reached the peninsula, Andy would have a choice of twenty different points where he could catch a train, plane, or ferry out of Denmark. "You have to stop him before he reaches the bridge. You can't let him cross from Fyn to Jutland."

"We don't have the manpower. The police have an emergency in Odense. Some bar brawl turned into a riot. Second-generation immigrants from the Middle East up against the local street toughs."

A rumble in the town where Hans Christian Andersen was born. Could this near longest day of the year get more violently surreal? "So the cops are tied up in Odense?"

"And we don't have enough cars out on the highway to find Markham. He'll be expecting trouble at the bridge. He's bound to take evasive action."

"We can't let him get away."

"No kidding. And you have to figure that Fraser character is headed in the same direction as Markham. Holger's got his people on the lookout. Soon as you've made your delivery, he wants you and me to team up, cover the southwest quadrant."

She disconnected. I stuffed the phone in my left pocket, slowed to make a left onto another narrow lane.

"Single headlamp, a kilometer behind us," Pope said.

My eyes flicked to the mirror and I saw it, too. "Ulf?"

"He found an excuse to leave the others and came after us." Pope waved the walkie-talkie at me and named the town we were approaching "Ulf knows our direction. He's been trying to raise one of his men who's on guard up ahead."

If a Bandido sentry intercepted us at the next intersection, Ulf would overtake us. There'd be two bikers against the two of us. Too evenly matched to suit me.

The walkie-talkie crackled out a call sign. I heard the name of the upcoming settlement.

I swerved to avoid a chicken, forced myself to slow down as we rolled into the outskirts of the town. The lone headlamp glared in my mirror.

Pope mashed his thumb on the push-to-talk button, scratched his fingernails up and down on the walkie-talkie's face and growled into the instrument. I realized he was trying to jam Ulf's transmission.

Ahead of me, I saw a stop sign. Beyond it, a marked police car guarded the intersection. The noise of Ulf's bike thundered in my ears. We couldn't outrun Ulf. But I couldn't stop to ask for help from the patrolmen parked across the way. It would take too long to make them understand the gravity of Pope's situation. Before they could summon reinforcements, Ulf would have called more Bandidos to the scene. A pair of Danish cops couldn't protect Pope from a mob of angry bikers. No, we couldn't stop.

I fluffed my hair, widened my eyes and pressed the gas pedal to the floor. "You're a good but frightened citizen," I yelled at Pope. He yanked off his hat, dropped the fedora in his lap, and slid his metal-rimmed glasses to the end of his nose.

I was going eighty-five kilometers per hour when we reached

the intersection. We slammed straight across without slowing. The light rack on top of the patrol car blazed blue. In my rearview mirror, I watched Ulf hurtle through the intersection, directly in front of the cops. The siren screamed in protest. My eyes were back on the road, searching for the turn to Helnæs.

Pope grunted. "Cops forced him off the road."

I yanked the wheel left. "They'll give him a ticket, let him go." And he had enough men watching the roads to eliminate the ones we hadn't taken. He'd quickly narrow down to the correct choice. I hunched over the wheel. I had to get to the rendezvous point before Ulf caught up with us.

But after only ten minutes, I was forced to slow to a crawl. A Skoda had smashed into a massive oak so recently the driver was still trapped inside. Two husky men were trying to free the victim while a dazed female passenger sat on the berm, her face streaked crimson with blood.

Automatically, my foot lifted from the accelerator. I forced it back down. I told myself that the two men already there would care for the injured woman, and I averted my eyes and inched around the wreckage without stopping. Once past, I upped my speed. Pope braced himself in the seat beside me but he said nothing to slow me down. For ten more minutes, I drove with single-minded intensity, flying down the causeway as if pursued by demons. When we reached the island, cars crowded the public lot and the overflow had parked along the access road. I jammed the Opel into a muddy opening at the end of the line and turned off the ignition. When I threw open the door, I heard surf crashing against nearby rocks. Pope and I ran down the road, passing a bonfire so huge, it could have served as a beacon for a returning band of Viking raiders. The salt-soaked driftwood burned with a blue flame and a raucous roar. Beneath the harsh scent of seared seawood, I smelled rotting kelp. The sky was light, glowing with the eerie whiteness of midsummer, but the fire threw shadows like stripes of early nightfall across the strand.

The sandy path brought us to the base of the dormant light-house. Offshore, I saw the dark shape of a fishing trawler. A dinghy bobbed at the water's edge and a tall figure materialized beside it. My fingers found the .38 in my pocket. I opened my mouth, ready to voice the recognition signal Holger had given me.

Gunpowder exploded behind me, that artificial boom I knew

from childhood. I turned to watch as fireworks shot from the witch's blasted head. Above me, vivid green streaked the pallid sky.

"*Dobry wieczór.*" Pope spoke before I could, his voice eager. Instead of waiting for a reply from the man, Pope stepped forward and embraced him.

My fingers tightened on the revolver. Why was Pope breaking the rules? And how had he learned the correct signal? And why didn't the man respond?

The man let go of Pope and moved toward me. "*Dobry wieczór,*" he said. The sound of his voice resonated in my soul. Stefan Krajewski.

A wave of yearning surged over me, so strong and so sudden I couldn't speak. I inhaled, tried again. Succeeded this time. "*Now you show up. After I've done all the hard work.*"

40 THEN, PURE EMOTION CARRIED ME INTO HIS ARMS. I SMELLED the sea on his skin, the bitter fragrance of French tobacco, the musk of his sweat. The familiar scents that I'd struggled so hard to forget. Stefan had allowed his work to draw him away from me and I'd doubted his love. But Andy had shown me the downside in becoming a man's only passion.

Stefan's cheek was rough against mine. *"Moj skarbie,"* he murmured. In Polish, my treasure.

I was home, my heart knew it.

Stefan said softly, "Wlodek needed my assistance, so I came. Holger assured me that *you* were doing perfectly well without me."

"Not perfectly." My reply was muffled because my face was buried in his neck.

His chuckle vibrated my chest. "Always, we run that risk when we allow Holger to take advantage of us."

"You warned me. But I had to do this."

"We make it too easy for Holger, you and I. Always, we find ourselves doing as he wishes."

I pulled away from him so I could see his face, the long bone of his nose, the angular curve of his jaw. "You, too?"

A smile played across his lips. They didn't move, though. He never answered questions like that. Lockjawed, Bella had called him—before she accused me of becoming his twin. I'd treated her just as he treated me. Now I understood why he acted as he did.

I broke the silence. "I'm thinking, I might give you one more chance with me."

"I would take it, of course."

"Only, you have to tell me more. You can't go on, keeping me totally ignorant of what you're doing."

He looked over the top of my head, as if staring into a future I couldn't see. When he spoke, his voice was husky, weighted with sadness. "Nothing's changed for me."

"I know that." I rephrased the accusation Bella had hurled at me. But I was proposing a truce. "I know that a man's got to do what a man's got to do. But a little more, Stefan. You have to tell me a little more."

His eyes met mine. Maybe there was a new softness there, a yielding I hadn't seen before. I thought I heard it in his voice, too. He said, "I cannot bear my life without you in it." His mouth was on mine, stopping my words.

Pope interrupted us. "I hear a motorcycle."

I broke away from Stefan. "Time for you to get going."

He motioned Pope into the dinghy. Stefan grabbed the painter, splashing into the water, shoving the boat farther out. Pope took the center seat and the oars rattled in their locks as he prepared to row. Stefan hoisted himself over the side. "*Dziekuje bardzo,*" Pope called to me. Thank you very much.

"I love Woody," I said. "You can thank him."

"I will," Pope said. "Holger is arranging everything." He bent into the oars.

I strained to see Stefan in the dimming light. "We can talk," I said urgently to him.

"Soon." I heard the splash and dip of the oars as the dinghy moved away from the shore. My shoulders dropped. I'd done it. Pope was safe.

Three quick explosions shattered my moment's peace. Fireworks? The sound was more like gunfire. I turned toward land and heard the thrumming of approaching engines. Bikers. Arriving too late to catch Pope.

I hurried up the path to the lighthouse. Gunpowder thumped again and a red and blue starburst filled the sky. Beside the lighthouse, two motorcycles buzzed like furious insects. The aerial display turned their chromed fenders to glistening purple mirrors. The two helmeted riders were a contrast in body types.

The beefy man yanked off his helmet. Ulf.

The slender woman bared her head. Dawna.

She waved angrily at Ulf. "Fucker spotted me down the road, followed me. Shot out the tires on your Opel for the hell of it."

Ulf swore. "I don't know what you bitches are up to—"

Dawna cut him off. "Go on back to your party. We're working."

Ulf revved his engine, but he didn't leave.

Dawna turned to me. "Cops spotted Andy on the motorway. They lost him. He must have turned off before he reached the bridge. Probably headed this way."

"You think Andy's trying to make it to a ferry?" I asked.

"Plenty of them depart from Fyn," Dawna said. "We should check out the closest ones. We're advising everyone to approach him with extreme caution."

"We don't have to be that cautious," I said. "Andy's not violent."

"With extreme caution," Dawna repeated forcefully. "Chuck found a pair of shoes in Markham's room with blood traces on the soles. We're betting that sample will match up with the body in your flat."

"My brother's blood on his shoes?" Ulf's bellow rose above the grumble of his engine. "The man who killed my brother—*he's* looking for a way off this island tonight?" He clapped the helmet back on his head. His engine shrieked, and without another word he tore out of the lot, spraying a rooster tail of stones toward me.

"Get on," Dawna shouted. "I think Ulf's guessed where Andy will go."

Hurriedly, I swung my leg over the rear saddle and wrapped my arms around her waist. Gravel shot out behind us as she turned the bike.

Farther along the causeway, Ulf's taillight flared red. Dawna went after it. At the mainland Ulf turned right and followed the curve of Helnæs Bay. Dawna roared after him, laying us flat on the turn, racing along the shoreline like a madwoman. The wind stung my eyes, forcing out tears, and my hair streamed behind me. I held more tightly to Dawna and smelled the tropical-fruit scent of her shampoo, beneath it the sweaty odor of the hunter, closing in. Open fields spread out to our left, dotted with smoldering fires, shadowy figures moving in and out of the flickering light. Except for the strange white sky, it was so like a nighttime crash scene, I caught myself straining to see the shattered fuselage of a downed jet. I shuddered. We had to find Andy. We had to recover the missiles he and his partners had stolen. Before another plane went down.

For the next twenty minutes, we chased Ulf down the main highway toward Faaborg. Congestion forced him to slow when he entered the medieval port city. Dawna shortened the gap between us to a hundred yards. We saw Ulf zoom along a narrow cobblestone street, cut around a white-painted church topped by a bell tower, and bounce down a set of steps into a broad pedestrian arcade. The public area was deserted, the residents drawn to another part of town by the celebration.

The plaza was bordered by long ocher-colored buildings with red-tiled roofs. The open space ended at a cross street. On the other side of the road was the harbor. Masts sprouted from hidden watercraft, the poles extending above street level like a dead and leafless thicket. Ulf skidded to a stop at the water's edge. He jumped off his bike and ran nimbly along the docks toward a squat brick building. The embarkation point for the ferry to Germany had to be nearby.

Dawna slid to a stop beside Ulf's bike, tossed off her helmet, yanked her gun from the ankle holster and gestured with it toward a baby-blue Ford parked illegally in a bus stop. "Markham's car. Call it in. I'll follow Ulf."

I pulled out my cell phone and tapped in Holger's number at the op center. When he answered, I told him I was at the ferry slip in Faaborg, standing beside Andy's car. "Dawna's following Ulf," I added. "He thinks Andy murdered Bjørn. Ulf will kill Andy if he finds him before we do."

"I'll send the others," Holger said. "Stay alert. The man who calls himself Fraser was last seen headed in your direction."

Fraser also wanted Andy dead. Dawna and I might be the only people in Faaborg with a stake in keeping Andy alive. I held the .38 loosely in my right hand, six inches away from my thigh. The plaza was empty, a vast expanse of sand-colored paving stones interrupted only by a meager rectangle of green lawn at its center. Along the edge sat the hull of a Viking longboat artfully arranged on a bed of whitened stones. I crossed in front of it to reach Andy's Ford. My left hand was sore from my fall yesterday in the Exeter cathedral. Gingerly, I put my battered palm on the hood. Still warm. "Andy," I said softly. "Speak to me."

From behind me came a sound so faint, I sensed the words rather than hearing them. It was as if a hoarse man had whispered "over here." I spun around, peering through the sooty twilight at the carved head of a sea serpent gracing the longboat's bow.

A rifle cracked. At the same instant something thunked into the metal where my hand had rested a moment before. The bullet bit through the hood and rang against the engine. Pain flamed across the skin on my left arm. I looked down. The bullet had sliced through my sleeve.

41

I DOVE ACROSS THE HOOD OF THE CAR, SLIDING TO THE GROUND on the other side. My left wrist couldn't take the weight. I toppled, landing hard on my right elbow. The impact sent my revolver skittering over the cobblestones.

The glass of the windshield shattered, simultaneous with the report from the gun. The shooter must be Fraser, the hit man who had chased Andy to this spot. Had Fraser also killed Davey Chaka? Probably. He wanted to finish the job he'd started in Exeter. Finish me, finish Andy. Half under the car, I flattened myself against the pavement, my nose filled with the tarry odor of blood-hot macadam. Another bullet hit the car on the driver's side. I shivered, wondering if Fraser was skilled enough to ignite the gas tank.

I braced myself, waiting for the next bullet. But seconds later, a shot exploded from a different direction. Somebody firing from the water's edge. And the bullet didn't come near me.

Andy did. He shot up out of the center of the longboat and leapt toward the car. He paused only to scoop up my revolver before he stopped beside me, crouching with the gun in his hand. He pressed the barrel into my side. He slid his left arm around my waist so that my body was tight against his. "You all right?" he asked.

"Strange thing to ask when you've got a gun stuck in my ribs."

He rose to his feet, pulling me upright with him. "You're okay?"

"Get down, he'll blow us both away." I tried to slide to the ground again.

Andy gripped me harder and gestured with the gun. "He's not the problem."

I looked where he'd pointed. The massive apartment block loomed on the far side of the plaza. A body was draped over the railing of the third-floor balcony, head hanging down. Someone had shot the shooter.

"Must be one of your friends, did you that favor," Andy said. "I need you to persuade them to do a favor for me."

My eyes roved the waterfront, trying to spot the helpful sniper.

Andy prodded me in the ribs. "Tell your friend we're going for a ride. That you'll be fine so long as no one bothers us."

I wouldn't be fine alone with Andy. We wouldn't get far before he realized the hopelessness of his plan.

I forced out a laugh. "You're taking me hostage? For that to work, people have to believe you'd kill me."

"Open the car door." His voice was grim. "You'll drive."

I didn't move.

"Dammit, Casey. I'm not going to jail. Don't make me hurt you."

"You won't. That's been your big problem all along. Making sure nobody hurt me."

He yanked his left arm back, used it to jam me against the car. The barrel of the pistol left my ribs. Returned as a point of coldness pressed into the base of my skull. "Come on," he muttered through clenched teeth. The cold metal moved a millimeter toward my spine as if his hand had twitched.

I closed my eyes.

Holger's sharpshooter couldn't help me. At this range, any bullet that struck Andy would go through him, get me, too.

I prayed.

Andy sobbed. "Oh, Christ, Casey. You could have helped me a little."

The pressure on my neck eased. Andy staggered back until he was an arm's length away from me. I braced myself against the car, using it to keep myself from collapsing as I turned to face him.

The gun was still in his hand. The barrel was in his mouth. His finger was inside the trigger guard. He exhaled, the way experienced shooters do before they pull the trigger. He was giving up, getting out. But we needed Andy alive.

I reacted without thinking.

I put the heel of my right boot against the side of the car and launched myself at him. I caught his right wrist in both my hands, forcing his arm to my right, away from his body. The impact carried us both to the ground.

The gun exploded.

I was out of the line of fire, but I cried out like a woman mortally wounded. I didn't want Andy to fire again. Unlikely as it was, I hoped he'd believe that he'd shot me.

He didn't resist when I pulled the gun from his hand.

He pushed himself heavily to a sitting position. Then he was on his feet, moving toward the car.

I was standing, too, gripping the revolver with both hands.

Andy had his hand on the car door.

"Stop," I said.

His laugh was bitter. "I got to warn you, I rigged this car myself. Anyone comes near me, I'll blow us both up."

"I can't let you drive away, Andy. You try to get in that car, I'll have to shoot you."

He looked at me, his eyes full of pain. "You stopped me a minute ago. You don't want me to die. You won't kill me." He waved a hand toward the waterfront. "And they won't, either. You've all got your orders, haven't you? Bring Andy back alive. Nobody's going to stop me."

I stared at him. An ordinary man capable of such monstrous evil. He'd stained my life with his terrible love. He deserved to die. But I couldn't be his executioner.

"You're right," I said. "I have my orders."

I shot him in the left knee.

His scream was real. It started low, rose through the scale to a pitch so high it pierced my eardrums. The awful sound resounded with the agony of loss and betrayal. It tore a hole through my soul.

Like a magnet, the sound drew people from the shadows. The frogman medic ran to Andy. Flemming appeared, accompanied by a pregnant woman in a tie-dyed T-dress. Vibeke. She carried a rifle with a laser scope.

Dawna was beside me. "Sorry I left you in this mess. Ulf, that dumbass. He ran the wrong way. Cops have him."

She put an arm across my shoulders, and together we stared at the crew working on Andy's leg.

Dawna said, "Well, *his* dancing days are over."

Such a cruelly flip remark. I should have told her to watch her mouth. But I stopped myself. Dawna didn't understand me and Andy, our history together.

Hurting him so deliberately—it was the hardest thing I'd ever done. For a second, I heard the last plaintive chords of an old song from the sixties, the death music we'd listened to in San Sal.

The sound died out, as if a door to the past had slammed tightly shut.

42

DAWNA SNIFFED SUSPICIOUSLY AT THE CRUMBLED DANABLU topping her roll. "How does a girl get a toasted cheese sandwich around here?"

"She doesn't." I relieved her of the offending blue cheese. "Soon as I get to Washington, I'll ship you a case of American cheese so you can grill your own."

"Throw in a few cans of tomato soup while you're at it."

I made a face. "Wonder Bread, too?"

"You don't fool me, pretending to be a food snob." She shook a remonstrative finger at me. "You'll eat anything. And right this minute, you'd sell your soul for a big ol' American hamburger."

I popped the last cheesy bite into my mouth and licked my lips happily. "I admit, my appetite is coming back."

"I never noticed that you lost it." She snickered. "I got to tell you though, winning a close game whets *all* my appetites."

She and I faced each other across a table in the cafeteria of the Danish Air Force Base at Skrydstrup. A military helicopter had collected Dawna, Holger, and me in Faaborg and brought us due west to the Jutland peninsula. Andy had made the same trip in a medevac chopper, attended by Flemming and his crew.

Dawna twisted around to survey the room. "What became of Flemming? He's got the buns that interest me."

"Won't you be traveling back to Copenhagen with him?" I asked.

"Don't imagine he'll be a lot of fun with the colonel looking over his shoulder."

"Holger's okay," I said.

"Right. A colonel *and* a priest." She picked up another cheese-topped roll and sniffed it suspiciously. "And there's the prisoner."

Andy. The Copenhagen homicide team wanted him for the murder of Ole Bjørn Møller. I realized now that he must have sought me minutes after he arrived in Denmark. That Wednesday a week and a day ago, he'd come to my flat and found Bjørn in it, waiting for me. Given Andy's talent with other men, I could believe he'd convinced Bjørn that he was working with me on Gerry's project. Once he'd persuaded the biker to reveal his secret, he started looking for a way to eliminate him. While Bjørn was absorbed by my piano, Andy had bashed the biker's head in.

When I'd danced with Andy, I'd been glad that he hadn't led me over the piece of floor where Bjørn had bled to death. I hadn't known that he'd been in my flat before. That he'd stepped in the dead man's blood.

Dawna lifted her coffee cup as if she were toasting me. "Safe journey," she said, before taking a sip.

I reached under the table to touch the case resting between my feet. Holger had already interrogated Andy about selling the Pentagon's missiles and Andy's signed statement was inside. I was only the courier for the official document. I hadn't taken part in the questioning, but Dawna had told me of Andy's cave-in. "Turned like a snake in the grass," was her description. "Gave 'em up, every one of his partners." She'd used Skrydstrup's secure communication facilities to transmit the names of Andy's co-conspirators to the FBI in D.C. The feds had made their first arrest two hours ago.

Now it was six o'clock on Thursday morning, June twenty-fourth, the feast day of St. John the Baptist. In the planter beyond the window, St. John's Wort was in full yellow bloom. And across the Atlantic, the authorities would soon have their platter full of the heads of traitors.

In fifteen minutes, I'd leave Skrydstrup and fly south in one of the Danish Air Force Gulfstreams to connect to a U.S.A.F. flight from Wiesbaden to Andrews Air Force Base. By the time I turned my official document over to the FBI, they'd be able to tell me who'd bought the stolen missiles. I'd go straight to my desk in the State Department's counterterrorism office and put what they'd told me in with the data I'd accumulated over the years. I'd start by tracking those Stingers that had been shipped to the terrorist groups I followed routinely. After I found those, I'd go after the rest.

My opposite numbers at CIA, DIA, and FBI would be doing the same. The president's national security advisor had a crisis response team standing by. They'd coordinate police and military actions globally.

Dawna put down her empty coffee cup. "Wish I could see Baldwin's face when he learns you've been called up to the major leagues."

"Only half the story is at the Bangor crash site," I said. "What Baldwin is doing is important, but I have to work on the other half." I leaned toward her. "One thing bothers me. Who called the cops last Wednesday and told them there was a dead man in my flat?"

"Andy. He spoke only the word for 'murder' and gave your address. Muffled his voice to hide the accent. Amazing no one suspected him sooner." She shook her head. "Fool thing to do."

A fool for love. On the day he arrived in Denmark, Andy hadn't known I'd been summoned to the States to take part in the Bangor investigation. He thought I was still working on Gerry's project. He'd expected me to come home from the embassy at any moment. He hadn't wanted me to be the one to find Bjørn's body.

I shivered, remembering Bjørn. And Gerry. And Davey Chaka. Each death hurt, the loss personal. I saw the bombing victims in Bangor differently now. Together, they were a horrible statistic, the worst airline disaster in U.S. history. But they were more than a number to me. They were four hundred and eight people that *I* had lost. I would not rest until we located every missile that Andy had stolen.

Holger crossed the room to our table. "Your plane is ready," he said to me. "I'll walk you out."

I stood, picked up the courier case in my left hand and extended my right toward Dawna. "I'll pack up your clothes, send them along with the CARE package."

"You keep the shirt and jacket." She stood and her grip was firm, her skin warm and supple. "That look is *you*, trust me. When I get to D.C., I'll take you out on my bike, we can raise a little hell together."

I had a sudden vision of Dawna and me, chromed and glittering, flying along the Skyline Drive. The picture gave me a zing of pleasure. "You have a Harley?" I asked her.

"Of course not." Her expression was as affronted as her tone. "BMW, R1200. The Cruiser. Now *that's* a bike."

I laughed. "So who's the snob?"

"Two snobs, that's us. Makes us good together." She swatted me on the ass. "Teamwork. The key to a winning season."

Then Holger got me moving out the door and down the hallway.

"I need you to contact Gitte for me," I said hurriedly. "Explain everything in Danish so she understands about Andy."

"Of course." He steered me around a corner and through a set of glass doors. "Do you want me also to phone Bella for you?"

"I'll call her." I had to try to make Bella understand why I'd kept her in the dark. She loved me. She'd forgive me. I hoped she would. I loved her, too.

Holger's stride was a foot longer than mine. I was trotting to keep up with him, panting from the effort. I added, "You'll make the arrangements for Woody?"

"Yes. I will keep you informed."

I grabbed his arm to slow him down. "I talked to Stefan."

"Yes?" He kept moving forward, his expression noncommittal.

I planted my feet, forced him to stop, too. "You arranged that, didn't you? Ordered Stefan to pick up Pope?"

"Don't be ridiculous. I would not ask Stefan to make a dangerous nighttime rescue by sea. That's a job for a younger, fitter man."

"You wouldn't ask. So why'd he come? He has that strong a commitment to Pope?"

"Don't be absurd. He came only because of you. No one could have stopped him. You know that better than anyone."

I smiled. I did. But I wanted to hear Holger say it, too. "You don't fool me. You set it up. Made sure he knew the danger to me."

His voice grew gentler. "As his friend, I could not do otherwise."

Such a matchmaker. As if he'd known I'd grow less critical of Stefan after I'd been in the field myself. More willing to come second, if the work that came first mattered to me, too. More willing to accept secrecy. *Some* secrecy. But I wasn't going to admit to Holger that I was softening toward Stefan. My old Father-Major didn't need to know that his manipulation worked.

He cleared his throat. "I must tell you, I resolved the problem I was having with my sermon."

"Good." I nudged him. Now I was the one in a hurry to get moving. I didn't want him preaching to me.

He wouldn't budge. "I've compared the various texts. There's no question, the final verse of the Twenty-third Psalm is usually rendered incorrectly. The verb isn't 'follow.'" He watched my face. "Properly translated, the psalm ends 'Goodness and mercy shall *pursue* me all the days of my life and—'"

I cut him off. "I got to tell you," I said, "when I looked behind me this week, I didn't see goodness and mercy back there."

"Perhaps you didn't look far enough. Everything has worked out quite well for you."

So he did know about me and Stefan. He'd figured me out, as usual.

Goodness and mercy.

If Holger had his way, I'd never outrun them, no matter how hard I tried.

And really—how could I complain about that?